The Fireballer

"Fleet and fun, *The Fireballer* will appeal to fans of *The Natural* and Robert Coover's *The Universal Baseball Association.* Frank Ryder is a classic American hero—the phenom who has to overcome his own terrible past. Mark Stevens has done the impossible: He actually had me rooting for the Orioles."

—Stewart O'Nan, coauthor of *Faithful* and author of *Ocean State*

"Seldom do I read a book that knocks my socks off the way *The Fireballer* did. This is a feel-good baseball story with a hold on the vernacular, the heart, the soul, the big picture, and the subtleties of America's favorite summer pastime. The characters are beautifully etched, and pitcher Frank Ryder may be the most likable hero since Gary Cooper gave life to Lou Gehrig on the big screen. I guarantee that you don't have to be a baseball fan to be swept up by this moving tale. With a full heart, I recommend—no, insist—that you read *The Fireballer.*"

—William Kent Krueger, author of *Fox Creek* and *This Tender Land*

"Mark Stevens's *The Fireballer* is a timeless baseball story told with a love of the game and fast-moving prose that will leave you cheering and crying at the same time. Frank Ryder is the most appealing of heroes, taciturn and loyal, talented and haunted—truly haunted—and with a fastball that will change the game. With its authentic baseball scenes and its rich heart, *The Fireballer* is a novel that rests comfortably with other classics of the game."

—William Lashner, author of *The Barkeep*

"*The Fireballer* is not just a great baseball yarn that any fan of the game will enjoy—it is also a richly layered exploration of character, regret, and redemption."

—Lou Berney, author of *November Road* and *The Long and Faraway Gone*

"The old game of baseball keeps coming up with new stories about the next twist or turn in the sport. In *The Fireballer*, Mark Stevens has invented a startling 'What if?' that stretches the limits of the game. More than a baseball book, the novel is a journey through the mind and heart of a gifted, but tragic, athlete who finds a road to redemption."

—Stephen Singular, *New York Times* bestselling author

"*The Fireballer* is a compelling story that I found hard to put down, rich with authentic baseball details and full of heart. Mark Stevens hits it out of the park with this intricate and moving tale of redemption."

—Robert Bailey, *Wall Street Journal* bestselling author of *The Golfer's Carol*

"Mark Stevens has crafted a powerful, heartfelt story—with a memorable baseball backdrop—that carves out a place alongside classics like *The Art of Fielding* and *The Natural*. Stevens knows the game—but it's his deft narrative and characters that help this book truly sing. I couldn't put it down."

—Alex Segura, bestselling author of *Secret Identity*

"You don't have to know baseball to love *The Fireballer*. At the center of this bighearted book is Frank Ryder, a star pitcher tormented by a mistake in his past. Readers root for Frank not for his fastball, but because his redemption delivers us all."

—Stephanie Kane, award-winning mystery writer and author of *True Crime Redux*

PRAISE FOR MARK STEVENS

No Lie Lasts Forever

"An original, memorable, and deftly scripted psychological thriller of a read from start to finish, *No Lie Lasts Forever* showcases author Mark Stevens's impressive mastery of the genre and a narrative-driven storytelling style that makes for a fun and compulsive page-turner of a novel."

—Midwest Book Review

"A first-class thriller."

—*The Denver Post*

"Mark Stevens is a master storyteller. *No Lie Lasts Forever* brims with unforgettable characters who move like quicksilver through the light and shadows of human transgression and deadly obsession. In prose that is at once fluid and gripping, Stevens summons the haunted voices that whisper inside all of us. A stunning book."

—Jeffrey Fleishman, author of *Good Night, Forever*

"An appetizing blend of a terrifying glimpse into the mind of a serial killer, tragic secrets, and surprising twists in Stevens's latest nail-biter."

—Sandra Brannan, author of the Liv Bergen series

"A compelling chase by one monster for another. Provocative, surprising, and rapid-paced."

—Reed Farrel Coleman, *New York Times* bestselling author of *Blind to Midnight*

"Rarely in a thriller am I compelled to reread passages, but Mark Stevens's sharp writing had me doing just that. Visceral, cerebral, and spellbinding, *No Lie Lasts Forever* will grab you and force you to hold on tight until the last page."

—Christine Carbo, bestselling author of the Glacier Mystery series

"Author Mark Stevens has a gift for combining intriguing characters with propulsive plots. In *No Lie Lasts Forever*, Stevens brings us an irresistible premise—a serial killer sets out to prove he didn't commit a murder—and rounded, complex characters: the killer, the disgraced journalist he teams up with, and a cast of police, politicians, and journalists with their own agendas. I turned pages late into the night, jumping at every squeak and bump along with reporter Flynn Martin, who knows that being in cahoots with a killer could be the best story of her career. If it doesn't get her killed."

—Barbara Nickless, *Wall Street Journal* and Amazon Charts bestselling author of *The Drowning Game*

"I never thought I'd be so invested in a serial killer. The PDQ murderer is a character for the ages—complex, calculating, at times sympathetic—and he makes the pages shudder and howl. His relationship with a disgraced reporter is the stuff of classic crime fiction. In *No Lie Lasts Forever*, Stevens breaks free of all the old tropes, crafting a tense, surprising, and gritty tale about our darkest impulses, our quest for truth and redemption, and the lengths we go to for the people we love. I adored this book."

—I. S. Berry, author of *The Peacock and the Sparrow*

TWO TRUTHS AND A LIE

OTHER TITLES BY MARK STEVENS

Flynn Martin Thrillers

No Lie Lasts Forever

Stand-Alone Fiction

The Fireballer

Allison Coil Mysteries

Antler Dust

Buried by the Roan

Trapline

Lake of Fire

The Melancholy Howl

TWO TRUTHS AND A LIE

A THRILLER

MARK STEVENS

This is a work of fiction. Names, characters, organizations, places, events, and incidents are either products of the author's imagination or are used fictitiously. Otherwise, any resemblance to actual persons, living or dead, is purely coincidental.

Published by Thomas & Mercer, Seattle

www.apub.com

Amazon, the Amazon logo, and Thomas & Mercer are trademarks of Amazon.com, Inc., or its affiliates.

EU product safety contact:
Amazon Media EU S. à r.l.
38, avenue John F. Kennedy, L-1855 Luxembourg
amazonpublishing-gpsr@amazon.com

ISBN-13: 9781662529627 (paperback)
ISBN-13: 9781662529610 (digital)

Cover design by Damon Freeman
Cover image: © Dave Wall / ArcAngel Images; © Natalya Erofeeva, © SoomO2020, © Atria Borealis / Shutterstock

Printed in the United States of America

For Jody, who is always one step ahead

CHAPTER 1

She should have known better.

When she thought about it later, she realized she'd let herself get lulled into complacency.

Into routine or by routine.

Take your pick.

Into thinking he had changed.

◆ ◆ ◆

For four weeks of trial, Harry Kugel walked the ten steps from the side door to the defense table with his head slumped forward.

For four weeks of trial, he sat upright. He might whisper in his lawyer's ear. He might put his hand to his mouth and issue a soft cough. But he was a poised model of courtroom behavior.

For four weeks of trial, Flynn Martin sat in the front-row pew directly behind Harry Kugel. She didn't need to reserve it. Her fellow reporters understood.

On day one, when Harry first walked those steps from side door to defense table, Flynn was surprised at his clueless bearing. He stared straight ahead from his chair at his counsel's table, where he would sit for hours. He didn't look around. He didn't hang his head. He could have been a businessman striding to a table to close a deal, one last check of the numbers before the handshakes and champagne.

Harry Kugel's attire took full advantage of his right to appear to the jury as an innocent state bureaucrat mistakenly identified as PDQ, the serial killer. *Who, me?* He walked into the courtroom as if the side door were a special portal to his mansion of carefree privilege, never mind the pair of beefy Denver cops who stared at Harry as the trial proceeded at its methodical pace toward its inevitable conclusion.

Thirteen months after the arrest, Harry Kugel had lost weight. He hadn't had much to lose from the get-go, but on his first trip through that side door, he looked smaller than she remembered. Gaunt.

He wore the same black suit every day, but the shirts switched from gray to blue, and the ties rotated among four.

Flynn kept a running tab for amusement.

Day 1: Black suit, gray shirt, yellow paisley tie.

Day 2: Black suit, blue shirt, gray striped tie.

Day 3: Black suit, gray shirt, solid maroon tie.

And so on.

Noting his apparel was silly, but during the trial, Flynn liked to keep busy. Her notes were jotted down with all the other swirling doodles and her lame attempts, each day, to play courtroom sketch artist and generate a reasonable rendering of the ice-cool Black judge or the slender and tall assistant DA who interrogated witnesses with an easy aplomb.

The judge was no fool. Flynn kept a running tab of scratch marks under two headers. A scratch went under H. L. ("Harry Lives") for each time the judge sided with the defense. A scratch went under H. D. ("Harry Dies") for each time the judge agreed with the prosecution. Even though Colorado had outlawed the death penalty, a life sentence was the same thing to Flynn. Bye fucking bye.

Harry's case, if the judge's daily decisions were any indication of a trend line, was circling the drain.

Given her prominent position near the front of the room, Flynn vowed that her attention would never wane. Whenever she felt a tug of weariness, she'd focus on Harry Kugel's three victims and the brutal ways the three women had died. The effect was like mainlining four shots of espresso.

The puzzle was Harry's weird demeanor, in the face of so much evidence, during his entrances.

Harry's lawyer knew. All the reporters knew. The assistant DA's smooth delivery carried a touch more confidence with each passing day. Harry's parents, who had declined all interview requests from Flynn or any other reporters, knew it too. The jury, despite each of their personal claims that they had the ability to keep an open mind, watched evidence grow like an animated time-lapse movie of plate tectonics showing how mountains are made.

The big problem for Harry was everything Harry was carrying in his bag the night he was arrested. Syringe. Fentanyl. Mask. And all the theatrical tidbits that went with the instruments of murder. And then there were the needles and the supply of fentanyl in his condo. And his DNA at Mary Belson's townhome and Mary Belson's spine-tingling testimony of how she'd fended off his attack.

On and on.

To her relief, the prosecution saw no need to call Flynn Martin to the stand. There was plenty of evidence to show that Harry Kugel had been in regular contact with Flynn Martin for weeks leading up to his arrest and that he had invaded her home in an over-the-top attempt to prove his credibility. But the prosecution focused its case squarely on PDQ's long-unsolved trio of murders, the detailed patterns of the scenes he'd left behind, and the direct link to his attempt to kill Mary Belson.

The defense, such as it was, attempted to discredit expert witnesses and raise questions about how evidence had been obtained or processed. The defense team was left spinning in place, bald tires looking for traction in mud.

The only doubters in town were a band of freaks who showed up outside to rally support for Harry Kugel. Mostly women, but not all. Flynn interviewed the three delusional souls together while standing in Civic Center Park over the lunch recess. She did her best to maintain a straight face and show respect.

Betty Kerr worked as a receptionist for a chiropractor in Lakewood. Wendy Kazanski, a hefty bruiser with a cross tattoo by her left eye, worked at a Jiffy Lube in Thornton. The third, by comparison, came across as level-headed. Ellie Stuffel said she was a student of the American judicial system, and she'd come armed with facts about prison conditions and recidivism rates and knew how other countries ensured convicts were provided dignity through humane living conditions.

Kerr knew Harry Kugel could not be a serial killer because he loved classical music too much and knew so much about composers. "He's not put together like a killer," she said. Kazanski pointed out that the state did diddly and squat when it came to actual rehabilitation, and, well, Harry had healed himself "and squelched every desire to murder for over fifteen years." As a result, she said, he should be allowed to walk free.

"But don't you think he should pay a price for the three murders if he's convicted?" Flynn had asked.

"What good does that really do if he's no longer a threat?" said Kazanski, perplexed.

"Don't you think the families of the victims will feel better knowing his freedoms will be taken away, given that he ended three lives?"

"This trial isn't about serving the needs of the families' *feelings*," she said. "It's about Harry, and he didn't do it."

Stuffel wore a small white button on her red paisley top: I ♥ HARRY. She stood erect like a proud athlete. Medium-length dark hair pulled back from her face in a ponytail so tight it could've been a cheap work-around for a facelift. She wasn't unattractive, but there was something off kilter about her face.

"What do you mean by the button?" Flynn said. "Have you met him?"

"I don't need to," she said.

"Have you communicated with him?"

"He hasn't replied," said Stuffel. "But I've sent him encouragement. He needs to know he's not alone."

Flynn bit the inside of her cheek so hard she worried about drawing blood. But asked, "This is someone you'd like to get to know?"

"I feel like I already know him," said Stuffel. "Now he needs to get to know me."

Flynn's story exploded. X lit up. The station's Facebook page spilled comments like Niagara Falls. Talk radio jumped in the fray. The network aired her piece a day later and Flynn was debriefed, standing in the spot where she'd conducted the interviews, for three minutes by the morning show anchor in New York. *The Denver Post* waited a day and then dispatched a reporter to create their own version of her interviews in an obvious attempt to catch up with the buzz.

The in-the-flesh crowd was supported by plenty of online chatter, Reddit threads, TikTok proclamations, and random YouTube discussions claiming that Harry had been railroaded.

One woman claimed she would marry the killer, even if it meant the only contact would be during visiting hours sitting on chairs while Harry Kugel was shackled to the floor.

◆ ◆ ◆

To put on a good show, the jury pretended to mull things over for a full day and now, four weeks later, the sentencing of Harry Kugel.

Also predictable.

Also a done deal.

Except Flynn feels a strange sensation, an unexpected queasiness, as she realizes the Harry Kugel saga is reaching the finish line.

She realizes how much mental space he's occupied in her thoughts and how much she's been worrying that he might slither off the hook and find a way to avoid prison. She assumes she's not alone. The whole city likely feels some equivalent sense of relief, of a return to level ground.

Of reassurance that justice comes around.

Of course, any veteran reporter knows dozens or hundreds of stories where victims never taste anything close to that messy emotional business of closure, let alone sense that the legal system is really watching out for their needs.

But big noisy cases like PDQ? The system knows how to put on a show. *We got our man. We will afford him every courtesy the legal process allows, but we will give the city the satisfaction it craves.*

The station wouldn't let her cover the trial. She was too integrated into the fabric of Harry's capture. The city knew Flynn's role in exposing a clique of corrupt cops, including a few top dogs, at the Denver Police Department. The massive shake-up began on the first day after Harry's capture. The station granted her leave to attend the trial and bear witness to how one arrogant, self-absorbed narcissist was being held accountable for his ugly crimes.

But today, the station has agreed to let Flynn Martin cover Harry's fate.

Which isn't a question.

Which is only a formality.

In fact, Flynn Martin has written the script for her live shot and rehearsed it in her head.

Harry Kugel is fucking going away forever and forever and a day, and when he's done with that he'll be breaking rocks in hell for all of eternity.

One can dream of saying what the whole city is thinking!

But instead she'll play it with the appropriate control and serious demeanor that the moment requires.

This morning, Judge Imani Washington sentenced former state bureaucrat Harry Kugel to life in prison following his recent conviction on three counts of first-degree murder and one account of attempted murder of a fellow state employee, who served as a key witness for the prosecution. The sentencing draws the curtain on a case that left the city wary and on edge for more than fifteen years.

She will fill in a line or two about Harry's reaction as the sentence is read and she'll mention any gasps or cheers from the room as a whole, from Harry's parents, and from the friends and relatives of Harry's victims.

◆ ◆ ◆

The room, as it was for trial, is elbow to elbow. Court TV waits. The podcast people from *Dateline: True Crime Weekly* wait. The assistant DA waits. The defense table waits. A cough. Low chatter.

Flynn keeps her eyes on the side door. She might need help with a transition to her Harry-free world. And the best people she can think of to help her process the approaching transition are the two men in her life—her father, Michael, and her son, Wyatt. Between them, they'll have good suggestions. Ex-husband Max would simply advise that she stop thinking about Harry Kugel. But ex-husband Max is the kind of guy who thinks you tell an overweight person, *Start putting less food in your mouth. Simple, case closed, you'll be skinnier tomorrow and skinnier next week. What's the issue?*

As tender and sympathetic as Max was during the days and weeks after Harry's arrest, Flynn has realized that she is never going back to his black-and-white view of the world. Max told her once that he saw his role as a cop as no different from that of a garbageman, "Except there's no set route and some days it's ordinary trash and other days you're dealing with toxic waste."

And here comes Harry in through the side door.

Same clueless bearing.

Black suit, black shirt, red tie.

The first splash of red. Flynn doesn't need to check back in her notes to know that fact.

Red . . . *danger.*

Red . . . *passion.*

Ugh, thinks Flynn, *you are seriously paying way too much attention to this evil creep. Stop it.*

Harry sits.

The judge enters.

Everybody rises, everybody sits.

It's kind of like church, but Flynn's only experience there has been as a reporter covering funerals and memorial services. Raised by two agnostics, who rubbed off beautifully.

The judge gives Harry one last chance to speak. The moment is theater. The judge is obliged to give Harry his time. It's in the script, even if the whole room knows Harry's heels remain on the plank and even if he is looking straight past his toes and the water is churning with starving, short-tempered sharks.

"I rehabilitated *myself,*" says Harry. Voice calm. Clinical. Flynn heard the same bullshit drivel the night he was arrested. "I was an upstanding, hardworking, taxpaying citizen. I killed my monsters. I left the old me way behind. I'm reborn. There was then and there is now. The state can save itself a lot of money by keeping another cell empty and letting me go. My track record at work is exemplary. I am a good neighbor. I care about fine and refined music. I ask the court to see me as who I am today and let me walk out the front door of this courthouse a free man."

The judge replies as if Harry Kugel never said a word, emphasizing that Harry Kugel was convicted by a jury of his peers and that he has not once demonstrated an ounce of remorse or once uttered any words to indicate he is willing to take responsibility for his actions.

"And as a result, I sentence you today to three consecutive life terms," says Judge Washington. "Plus another twenty-four years for the conviction on the charge of attempted murder."

Harry's body doesn't flinch. Soldier erect, statue still. He's got his back to Flynn.

Two cops move to the defense table, handcuffs ready.

He turns. He leans over the oak rail that separates the well of the courtroom from the pews. Harry Kugel's lawyer utters something like "Whoa," and Flynn hears a quick collective gasp flash through the room as if the tiger has discovered that the zookeeper's failed to lock the cage.

Harry's eyes switch from bouncy to dull. He delivers his message in a voice intended so only Flynn can hear.

But barely.

A voice of wrath.

"This is not over. No way. No how."

CHAPTER 2

"So, why do cults form around convicted killers such as Harry Kugel? Why do these superfans develop fixations on supporting someone when all the evidence leads to a clear conviction of seriously dark crimes?"

Dr. Hayden Thompson oozes authority. "PsyD" in her title. All the board certifications. Years of practice. And she looks great and sounds great—lively, articulate, poised. She's done these expert interviews dozens of times on the four o'clock show, the chattier and more relaxed versions of the tighter formats at five, six, and ten.

"'Superfan' is an interesting term." Thompson wears a sleeveless black dress with a V-neck. Short, serious, dark hair. "Don't forget that the 'fan' part of 'superfan' is from the word 'fanatic,' and that means 'marked by intense uncritical devotion.' A dangerous combination."

The live interview on set was Flynn's idea, to follow up on the story about the nutjobs who kept vigil during Harry Kugel's trial.

"But what we're talking about often with celebrity stalkers and people who join cults is some form of delusion. A delusional disorder. And what is a delusion? It's an unshakable belief that something is real, even when there's overwhelming evidence to the contrary. Paranoid delusions. Or delusions of grandeur. Delusions that someone is planting thoughts in your head or that others can read your mind. 'Psychosis' is simply an umbrella term for somebody who has lost touch with reality. And one small belief can become, almost, a crusade."

"Are these delusions then—an illness?"

"Definitely," says Thompson. "A mental illness that impacts your ability to function in daily life. Some delusions come and go. Others consume a life. And there are layers. Mild paranoia might be a good thing—you always check the locks in your house before leaving home. Severe paranoia might mean you're unable to leave the house because you think the world is after you."

"So it's not a matter of logic?" says Flynn.

"In fact, logic can seem threatening to your identity and your group's identity. Once you believe something, everything becomes evidence to support your view of the world. If you're worried that people are always watching you and the repairman comes to fix your dishwasher, you might think he's taking too long because he's also installing a spy camera to connect to the great control room in the sky."

"Are these delusions treatable?"

"Most of the time. There are antipsychotic medications like risperidone and olanzapine." The words roll off her tongue as easily as *milk and cookies*. "And there's cognitive behavioral therapy too."

"But some people don't want to get treated."

"They don't know they're delusional, of course."

"So it's not a matter of trying to convince them," says Flynn. "Through logic?"

"No. Even the arguments you bring to them become further evidence of their beliefs."

"So what's the best way to communicate with someone who is experiencing a delusion?"

The conversation is lightly rehearsed, with the rough talking points reviewed earlier in the day on the phone.

"You reach them emotionally," says Thompson. "You can ask them how their beliefs make them feel about the world or their lives. And then it's fine to share that your emotions are different, that you're experiencing the world in a different way."

"And how is it possible for these individuals to get in the corner of a guy like Harry Kugel when they haven't even met him? Can't possibly know him?"

Thompson thinks, but not too long. They're live. And she can't appear to *not know*.

"Because they think they know him—through the stories they're told by reporters. And others who will come around down the road to revisit him in books or whatever. They buy the story. They buy the myth that he got better on his own—and then, I suppose, got railroaded by the system."

"Well, thank you, Dr. Thompson. Anything else to add?"

"I think the news media plays a big role—more and more today."

"How so?"

"It's a big responsibility—broadcasting irresponsible, false, or harmful information. The news media's role is to inform, not mislead. Elevating a voice that leads others to believe that it's okay to think the world is flat, for instance, is completely irresponsible."

This take is not rehearsed. And comes out of left field.

"So I shouldn't have interviewed the people who thought Harry Kugel was innocent?"

"I'm a psychologist, not a news director," says Thompson. "Interview anybody you want, but your decision on what to put on the broadcast is a whole different question. Are you doing it to inform your viewers, or entertain them? It's a choice. Every day."

FOUR MONTHS LATER

CHAPTER 3

Flynn Martin is getting the runaround.

She hates being manipulated. And she really dislikes when a government agency or a private corporation declines her request for an interview with the people in charge and foists her off on the public relations slickos with their rehearsed talking points and their practiced polish.

Her station? Her upper ups? They don't care as much about *who* makes the points as long as they get made.

"I don't know why Mr. Atkins can't do the interview," says Flynn. "It's his hotel, it's his hotel's reputation. I appreciate your willingness to give me a few comments, but I think the community would like to hear from the owner. Are you on staff?"

"As I explained, I am with a private firm hired by Mr. Atkins to handle communications."

Maybe it's the sunglasses. Or maybe it's the shirt and tie, but no jacket. Must be Casual Crisis Friday. Or maybe it's the way he says "traumatic incident" and "we deeply regret this traumatic incident" like he's a waiter describing the lunch special. Even the word "incident" sounds minor, inconsequential.

"What does that mean? Deeply regret?" says Flynn. "What are you doing for the victims?"

"Miss Martin—"

James Paterson. One more consonant and he could be a mega-selling author. Day-old whiskers. A giant gold class ring with a garnet stone on his pinkie. Weak chin. Hair like an oil slick.

"Yes?"

"That's not a question I'm prepared to answer."

"Why not?"

Because you literally did not prepare an answer back there in your public relations war room, when you should be able to cough up a basic question like we're two regular human beings exchanging information.

"I can get back to you."

"Is the plumbing company that was hired to put in the HVAC system for the hotel's pool area also the plumbing contractor for the rest of the hotel complex?"

"Again, I can find out for you and get back to you."

"Do you think, even though the pool area is now closed because the HVAC system is sitting in the lazy river and because there's an investigation going because you have two people being treated for critical injuries at the hospital, even a week after the 'incident,' and you have major repairs to make, that people should feel confident about booking rooms at the Mayflower?"

"You have taken an enormous leap in the conversation, Miss Martin—"

"Call me Flynn."

"—and I'm not going to go there with you on that particular question."

"Is the building safe?"

The hotel in question sits in the distance over his left shoulder. They are set up in a corner of the empty asphalt parking lot, giving an extra oven effect to a hot August day, which she is battling with light gray linen slacks and a loose sleeveless marigold button-up shirt.

"We have hundreds of wonderful guests every single night, given our convenient location here by the airport."

"Six hundred rooms in all, yes?"

"Correct."

"And are you inspecting all the plumbing throughout the hotel? Throughout the whole convention center too?"

"This was an isolated incident involving heating and cooling for the pool area."

"And we showed the cell phone footage of the broken pipes—the sections that did not fall in the water—and our experts said they could see rust and corrosion inside the ductwork. They said for a hotel that is only two years old, there must have been a failure to inspect. Does that sound accurate? To make sure there wasn't water building up inside and, of course, creating additional weight?"

Behind Flynn, photographer Tamica Jones clears her throat. It's a subtle sound. It's so soft it's possible Mr. Paterson doesn't hear it. But Flynn gets Tamica's message. *Nicely done.*

"Very premature," says Paterson. "It's only been a week."

"Can you tell me how much money this hotel has received in tax incentives from the City of Denver?"

"Actually, we're in Aurora."

"Yes, I knew that." *Wanting to see if you did.* "From Aurora?"

"I'm not prepared to talk about that today."

"Sixty-seven million dollars in incentives," says Flynn. "State and city sales. Incremental property tax from the county. Lodgers' tax. Occupational privilege tax. It's all public record."

Flynn has her own personal reporter war room and sits with two other generals to think through how the conversation will flow. One is her father, Michael, who remains razor sharp at seventy-one. Number two is her photojournalist, Tamica, who has a bullshit detector better than a bomb-sniffing bloodhound. She also has a keen sense of justice and equally despises corporate PR hacks. And if the issue involves the environment, the third is her twelve-year-old son, Wyatt. In this case, it was Tamica who dug up the tax incentive tidbit.

"I don't see how that's relevant," says Paterson.

"You don't think there is an implied obligation to the public, given these tax breaks?"

"The hotel is privately owned."

"And publicly subsidized."

"And?"

"And again, can you tell me if you reached out to the families? There is a grandfather from Oklahoma who has had two brain surgeries in the past week and a six-year-old girl from Idaho with a shattered pelvis. She flew to Denver for a beauty pageant. Both remain in the hospital. And eight others who have been treated and released."

"We are quite aware of the injuries," says Paterson. "I will get back to you. Our thoughts and prayers are with all those who were in the pool area that day."

CHAPTER 4

"No notes," says Goodman.

"No notes?" says Flynn. "How will I know it's really you?"

"It happens. Once a decade I feel this urge to leave well enough alone. I mean, how hard did you press to ask for someone other than the hired PR gun?"

"Plenty hard."

"That's all I need to hear," says Goodman.

"There should be a law that bozos like this one are banned from wearing sunglasses," says Tamica. She's at the controls in the edit room, next to Flynn. News director Rick Goodman sits on the raised platform behind them. "We need to see his eyes twitch."

"Mr. Paterson will watch this later and think he could have handled a few things better," says Goodman. "I still can't imagine what it was like to be there when this giant ductwork comes falling from the ceiling. Shit is supposed to stay put in a new building."

"Two years old," says Flynn.

"Is that in the piece?" says Goodman.

"It's in my lead-in."

"Which you'll do where?"

"I was thinking that I would be on set in the nice, air-conditioned environment that is our studio."

"That's funny," says Goodman. "I was thinking it would be from the parking lot at the Mayflower, but this time get close enough so it's not an out-of-focus dot on the distant horizon but make it clear this is a massive hotel complex."

"I don't suppose you're willing to negotiate?" says Flynn. "I could say I've got a date, maybe, and the extra hour round trip out to the hotel and setting up and all, you know, cuts into my primp time and reduces my chances for a wonderful Friday night out with a potential new beau, and my future happiness and sex life and overall mental health depend very much on my being able to stay downtown tonight, to not get dehydrated out there in the dusty gross heat, and, well—do you get the picture?"

"Loud and clear," says Goodman. "Request denied."

"Every mile we don't drive is another win for the planet. Does that cause you a lick of pain? Can you find the spot inside where you sense an ounce of guilt?"

"I'll bike to work for a week as penance," says Goodman.

"You live in Castle Rock," says Tamica. "Thirty miles each way."

"In that case, I'll be late for work and late getting home. Please don't nag me. Speaking of Castle Rock, you heard about Franktown?"

"They're fifteen miles apart," says Flynn.

"Just generally," says Goodman. "It's how you city folk view anything out in suburbia, all lumped together."

"Okay," says Flynn. "There's a big fat generalization. What about *Franktown*?"

"Double murder."

"Murder-suicide?"

"Definitely not," says Goodman. "And the bodies have been there for a few days."

"Ew," says Tamica.

"Neighbor found them," says Goodman. "Might have been a week."

"Double ew," says Tamica.

◆ ◆ ◆

"Are we going to ask for permission?" says Tamica.

"Permission for what?" says Flynn.

"To be back on the property."

"It's a hotel parking lot," says Flynn. "It's ninety percent empty. You could build a movie set out there, for crying out loud. We were there this morning. We'll pretend we never left. Since when were you a rulemonger?"

Tamica drives. Flynn rides shotgun in the station's SUV with the bright blue matching logos on each door. Flynn has long learned to keep her gaze ahead, to not see what kind of reactions they draw from fellow drivers. Trolls are everywhere. The last decade or so of elected politicians dismissing the work of credible reporting has taken an ugly toll.

But giving up is not an option. *Not* reporting is not an option. *Not* reporting lets the fascists win. The uncaring hotel owners who don't recognize that their moral and public obligations are no different from those of bank robbers and scam artists.

"Monger?" says Tamica. "Me."

"Yes."

"Meaning?"

"You know, like cheesemonger, fishmonger, gossipmonger."

"A dealer?"

"Yes. Do you deal in rules?"

"I don't like getting my ass chewed out."

Tamica's baseball cap, featuring the station logo, is pulled down low. Dark sunglasses. Ebony skin. Her hair is an even quarter-inch buzz cut all around. Tamica Porter looks more like someone who plays drums in an edgy riot grrrl punk band or performs raunchy stand-up comedy. That is, until you watch her remarkable eye for B-roll, how she lights a room for an interview, or how she edits stories with a snappy signature style.

"Nobody likes that," says Flynn.

"Just call Mr. Paterson and let him know we're darkening his door again. What do you think?"

"I think if he tries to tell us to shoot from across the street or something, that we'll make that part of the story, and the callous treatment will add to the defensive mode they find themselves in, especially for someone, by definition, who is in the business of fucking hospitality."

Flynn grabs her phone, finds James Paterson in recents, hits the call button, puts it on speaker.

"Knock yourself out," says Paterson. "I'll alert security. You guys need a cold water sent out or anything? Would you rather shoot inside where it's not so hot?"

"Holy smokes," says Flynn after she hangs up. "What got into him?"

"He's scared," says Tamica. "And that's a good thing."

CHAPTER 5

"I detected a certain edge."

"Was it that obvious?"

"I think the average viewer would conclude that the ownership is a bunch of coldhearted galoots, if that's the point you were trying to make."

Her father, Michael, sits on his concrete balcony eight floors above Cheesman Park. Remnants of chicken tacos are sprinkled on two plates. One last nacho chip waits in the white paper bag between them. There's nothing left of the orange gooey cheesy dip but the smears on the side of the plastic tub. The night is hot.

"Well," says Flynn.

"Well what?"

Her father has never cut her an inch of slack. She loves the dynamic. This porch and these chats are her reality checks.

"Well, it's not like I had to try that hard. He kind of shot himself in the foot, don't you think?"

"Your story got aired," says Michael. "It's really not my call."

"Except."

"Except if I were running the show, I would lean more toward fact upon fact and less of the business where you're telling viewers *how* to think about what they're seeing and hearing. The point isn't about the quality of the public relations talent."

"But sometimes that is the story," says Flynn. "The culture of the organization behind the crisis. Do they care?"

"It's not that big a deal," says Michael. "I'm happy I get to catch my daughter's work."

"You know you don't have to watch the show live."

"It's habit. It's the highlight of my day."

"Not hardly."

"Okay, looking through new lawsuits and analyzing government budgets is the highlight of my day, but still. I like to see what you're up to. By the way, where's Wyatt?"

"Sleepover."

"Away or home?"

"He's at home. They're working on a science project."

"It's August."

"School starts in August," says Flynn. "Where have you been?"

"Seems like a crime," says Michael. "All this heat."

"And it's what STEM kids do, though now it's STEAM of course. Gotta have the arts. They're building a solar oven, and they want to bake s'mores tomorrow out on the sidewalk."

"That kid is going places," says Michael. "Some Friday night for a twelve-year-old. And your weekend plans?"

"Staying cool. Laying low."

"No dates?"

The question isn't judgmental. It's information gathering.

"Movie tomorrow night with a guy named Axel."

"Like Rose?"

"Oh, very good, Dad—that was quick. No, with an *e*. A-x-e-l. And he's not a rocker. He's an analyst."

"First date?"

"And probably last."

"Then why did you say yes?"

"Because."

"Because it's what you do?"

"Because stability. Appearances. No kids."

"Or so he claims."

"Now that's cynical."

"Keeping it real. What does he analyze?"

Axel Sheen reached out for the first time the day after Harry Kugel was sent to prison. He wanted to compliment her on the coverage. Said that he hoped she knew that "the whole city" appreciated what she'd done. And then asked her out. He knew it was a lark. Acknowledged his chances were low. Said all the right things about how she shouldn't trust a stranger but then claimed to be a "boring accountant" who preferred "harmless hobbies" like board games and only asked her to not close the door to the possibility. Flynn thought he was a bit naive to think it would take her more than a day to decompress, but she heard something charming and self-effacing in his baritone voice.

"I assume he analyzes numbers," says Flynn. "Is that enough for you?"

"Every number has a story behind it."

"Says the man who turns long-ass budgets into scintillating prose."

"Whatever," says Michael. "He sounds perfectly boring and might be just the ticket."

"I might give dull a whirl."

The implication needs no explanation after being married to action hero wannabe Max, the cop. Wyatt's father. The arrest of PDQ and the end of that saga led to a few weeks of tender words with Max and one weekend away in a mountain cabin where they tried to negotiate a new playing field. But in the end, Flynn couldn't pull the trigger and go back around on the same track.

"How dull can he be with a name like that?" says Michael.

"Axel Sheen," says Flynn. "Doesn't it sound, I don't know, a bit fussy?"

"Ever heard a saying about books and their covers?"

CHAPTER 6

Flynn parks her Kia EV9 in her assigned spot on the second floor of the parking garage. At Wyatt's urging and on behalf of the climate, and also timed with the move downtown, Flynn made the switch from leasing cars with internal combustion engines to buying an electric one. The vehicle's stealthy quiet, in fact, still unnerves her.

Flynn plugs it in, stands for a moment, and waits.

It's habit. She hates parking garages. She doesn't trust them. The crashing HVAC duct over the hotel pool only adds to her general distrust and paranoia about the ability of concrete to hold up the weight of all these cars, never mind the building that rises above it.

She stands and waits.

She's grown an extra radar.

She inventories footsteps. Listens for incoming and outbound cars.

And then walks down the ramp, waves her fob at the control pad that releases a door that gives her access to the garage elevators. When she told Max she was selling the Congress Park house that PDQ had invaded and ruined forever, he warned her to not consider anything above the seventh floor because "ninety-nine percent of fire trucks in the world" don't reach any higher. Still, Flynn didn't want to be that close to the ground, so she opted for a unit on the twenty-eighth floor, buying the property through an irrevocable trust that kept her identity off the property deed and identified Wyatt as the beneficiary. It felt good to do something for Wyatt's future and it felt good to keep her name off public records. Her role in PDQ's capture and the whole way it had played out, beginning with the disaster on live TV and all the online yammering about her choices, left her feeling like an open book printed with transparent pages.

Flynn misses her old house with its creaky floors, drafty windows, and century-old quirks. The new place is sleek. Floor-to-ceiling glass wraps the living area. A medium-size balcony means you can go outside to listen to the sirens and garbage trucks. Two beds, two bathrooms, an office, a kitchen, and enough closets for a champion of the minimalist lifestyle.

But she sleeps better with the doormen, the security system in the lobby, and the separate keys needed for the dead bolt and keyed lock. Even with PDQ locked away for life, the residue of paranoia he left behind lingers like the stench of bad fish.

Wyatt and his pal Jeremy Banks sit on the living room couch playing a video game, headphones on. Wyatt gives her a smile. Jeremy barely looks up. Wyatt is spaghetti slender and undersized for his age. Max wants him to hit the weight room and get into a home exercise routine, too, but when he's with Flynn she lets him do what he wants. He likes his hair on the longer side, and he's become fascinated with British postpunk bands like Wet Leg and Dry Cleaning. Jeremy is the athlete. He talks about whether to attend East High School, when he's old enough, for lacrosse and basketball. He's two inches taller than Wyatt with short blond hair, a dusting of freckles, and an easy smile. They bonded over learning. Wyatt spotted Jeremy reading a fat nonfiction book about James Cook, and that was that.

The solar oven they've built takes up one corner of the kitchen counter, mere steps from the living room couch because the main living area is all one big room. The solar oven is a small pizza box with the inside lid and interior wrapped, à la Christo, in aluminum foil. A wooden shish kebab skewer has been repurposed to hold the top open like a lid prop on a grand piano. Adjacent are the mirepoix ingredients for tomorrow's s'mores experience. Chocolate bars. Graham crackers. Marshmallows.

The condo is spotless. Pristine. Wyatt is a centered kid with an innate curiosity about the world. He firmly believes in the calm that comes with organization. Flynn watches Wyatt as closely as she monitors her own post-PDQ fears. There were more than a few weeks when he seemed withdrawn and incommunicative, though of course the onset of puberty could also be blamed for the sudden sullenness. It was a passing phase. Wyatt resented the move downtown. There was pleading. There was begging. There was deep, deep grief. Wyatt's logic matched her own rational moments.

Chance of a repeat? Zero.

PDQ in prison? Check.

Could she banish the ghosts in the old house with new paint and fresh room configurations? Sure, on paper. It made sense.

Staying meant she didn't let the bastard win.

But Flynn knew. Deep down, she knew.

Moving on required new surroundings, new patterns, new undercurrents. Wyatt's petulance lasted a few weeks, and then came the switch to a new school focused on STEM and STEAM and project-based learning with a heavy environmental focus. Wyatt found his tribe of hardworking kids who ran at the speed limit of learning, on cruise control, and were all bound for college. Clearly, the baton of journalism would only pass from Michael to Flynn. Wyatt asked plenty of questions about the news, but he didn't show a lick of interest in telling the stories himself.

Flynn changes into her navy shorts and loose sleeveless pullover top. She pours herself a glass of wine, closes the drapes with the press of a button, and takes the drink out to the balcony. The night air remains hot and, by Denver standards, sticky. She spots a hotel room across the street and, like a twisted voyeur, watches a man sitting on the end of his bed watching television. He stands, wearing only a light T-shirt and dark underwear. He is fit. It's not easy to tell, but he looks young. He walks away. Flynn stares at the window, willing him to return, and realizes that she owes it to herself and her lame sex life to give Axel Sheen a chance. She needs to be open to a surprise. She needs to shake up her rut.

Her father's gentle admonishment about the tone and substance of her story echoes in her head. She has often wondered about the "gotcha" aspect of her business. Is it journalism or an effort to shame? Is it reporting or pointing fingers? How much time each day does she spend searching for fresh information compared to all the time put into the production of the news itself—driving, setup, shooting stand-ups, editing?

TV reporting is an effort in reductionism. In finding each story's essence. Blood and mayhem are good. Crying is better. So many stories start with something printed in *The Denver Post* or one of the online news sites like *The Gazette* or *Colorado Pinnacle*. As a result, a feeling of rehash pervades her work. So does the feeling that it's all inconsequential, even if she does get recognized as *that reporter* who caused one of the biggest reshuffles in the DPD's history and whose work, albeit unconventional, helped put PDQ behind bars.

Now she's back to one-offs. Occasionally, crime. For the most part, she gets meaty topics. Some stories last a few days. Some stories hang in there for weeks. But more often than not, she parachutes in for a day, looks and sounds like she knows what she's doing, and heads back to the assignment desk control tower in the morning for her next news mission. She's great at feigning interest. In fact, she's often interested. She meets cool people and she's on a first-name basis with the governor, the mayor, and a host of other leaders in politics, arts, nonprofits, and school district superintendents up and down the Front Range. Lawyers. And cops. She knows, unfortunately, too many cops.

The crime stories are weird. She wonders at her ability to stand in front of a playground where a child was killed by a stray bullet and—live on your home TV screen—calmly report the tragedy. She wonders about her shameless ability to ask for interviews with a murder victim's parents. Or a murder victim's children. Or a murder victim's next-door neighbor.

Or a murder victim's best friend. She wonders about her ability to report on random death. A lightning bolt on the golf course. A rockslide on the road to Black Hawk. A brakeless semi roaring down a steep pitch of I-70. A bicyclist hit by a drunk driver. A fire lit by kids seeking revenge, only they get the wrong house and three children perish.

Or PDQ's three random victims.

Where does she park the emotions?

What does she do with them? She knows that if she thinks too hard about any of the stories, she will lose it. She is fully capable of losing it, of feeling the jolt from the electric third rail if she touches it or gets too close.

There are days and weeks when she wonders at her ability to dump the pain as if she's the owner of a powerful vacuum toilet that turns it all to inconsequential dust.

Flynn believes in each day's story. But she wonders if she hasn't simply improved her ability to frog-hop from one lily pad to the next. There's a brief belief that you're getting the story right, that the essentials are there, but you don't dare wiggle around too much because you might find yourself, with no warning, all soaking wet.

The question is, What to do about it? And does it really matter? Why not leave well enough alone?

Steady is good.

Steady *income* is good.

She needs stability for Wyatt through high school and for another four years after that.

She gets to think. She gets to talk with people who are driving change. Or who think they can make things better.

Flynn finishes her wine, rinses her glass, and puts it in the drain rack to be a good sport along with her neatnik son. She might pour another glass after the kids settle down and watch the late news, see how her hotel HVAC duct story will get treated on the ten o'clock show.

See if she thinks she's being fair.

See if her father is right.

See if she can watch the piece as a random observer.

Maybe.

Or maybe she needs to stop analyzing everything. Maybe she needs to be herself.

Do her work.

Keep her head down.

And be thankful.

◆ ◆ ◆

Wyatt asks for permission so he and Jeremy can stay up and play games on their phones.

"For how long?" says Flynn.

"Half an hour," says Wyatt. "I mean, we're both pretty tired."

"It's Friday night," she says. A good mother would have planned something for the weekend. Or had the ingredients on hand for morning pancakes. Something. "Knock yourselves out."

Flynn flips over to her station. The ten o'clock is coming up, though of course she can stream the HVAC hotel clip anytime too. No—a movie might be better. Something light. A romance or a period piece. Kings and queens and trickery. A trip to another time. Some distracting gratuitous nudity wouldn't be a bad thing, especially if it sparks her to make more of an effort around Axel Sheen or, if he doesn't work out, someone.

She flips through her streaming options, numbed.

Jeremy thanks her "for everything," and Flynn realizes she's done precisely nothing. Wyatt comes in for a warm hug and says good night.

"Oh, and I brought home a permission form to go on that field trip next week—we're going out to Dinosaur Ridge," says Wyatt. "Dinosaur tracks, Mom."

"Pretty cool."

"There's an envelope for you too."

"Okay," says Flynn.

"I put them on the table in the front hall."

"I must have missed them."

"I figure that's a good spot to leave things for each other," says Wyatt.

"Absolutely fine."

"Good night then."

"One more hug, sweetie."

The start of the school year, the start of school communications and newsletters, and she really should be doing something more than making sure Wyatt gets there each day. With Wyatt's school much closer to Flynn's new downtown condo, the new arrangement is that Wyatt will stay with her when there is school and spend all three-day weekends, fall break, and spring break with Max in the far southwest corner of Denver. There are enough teacher planning days to ensure plenty of three-day weekends. Special holidays are TBN. To be negotiated. She and Max have an easy postdivorce relationship, and more than once Flynn has stopped herself to realize she's lucky to have three guys in her life who are decent, calm humans. Michael. Wyatt. Max. Seriously, what did she do to deserve them? Why doesn't she sit on a school committee or help with fundraising? What does she do to give back? So many opportunities to feel like she's not doing her share.

Flynn retrieves the form from the front hall table, finds a pen in a cup by the stove, signs where it says Parent Signature, and wonders who wouldn't approve of their offspring seeing dinosaur tracks. Maybe the evolution-doesn't-exist crowd? Or protective parents who think that exposing your kids to the fact that dinosaurs once roamed the land might be too traumatic, give them nightmares? Flynn puts the form back on the table for Wyatt to find.

She's sure the envelope is a personal entreaty to connect with school committees or volunteering, but the small, neat typing on the front makes her stop.

One word.

FLYNN

Tiny font, bold face, underlined.

Gray envelope.

Tightly sealed.

Well, she's been fooled by plenty of texts that begin with heartfelt openings, only to realize they are mass political spam. This is likely some such trick.

She finds her letter opener in the same cup as the pen, slits the seal with more than the usual effort.

Inside, a white sheet of paper.

> Miss Flynn,
>
> Nice condo.
>
> Of course, you don't know me.
>
> But I know you.
>
> I know what you're afraid of.
>
> I mean, why the move? Right?
>
> You thought it was over, right?
>
> Think again.
>
> I will be in touch.
>
> You will do nothing.
>
> Because you will have no choice but to do nothing.
>
> Soon—very soon—you will realize why you will do nothing.
>
> This time, no patterns.
>
> The pattern is no pattern.
>
> This time, I won't and don't need your help.
>
> You?
>
> You get to sit back and observe.
>
> This time, The Prototype Rules.
>
> Oh and PS—it's already started.
>
> The killing.
>
> Might be killings.
>
> Who knows?

CHAPTER 7

Flynn goes cold.

Top-to-bottom cold.

Her hands shake. She stares at the words, stares at the words, stares in sheer utter disbelief at the words. Her mind races to the sight of Harry Kugel being put in handcuffs, right there in court.

She witnessed that, did she not?

Should she call Cañon City, make sure the state penitentiary didn't accidentally let him walk?

Is it a joke? A warped wackadoodle practical joke? Everyone in her life knows she walks on eggshells.

No.

She stares at the door to Wyatt's bedroom, wondering when or how or where the envelope was handed to him. And if the person who wrote the fucked-up note knows about Wyatt and his school, then that means Wyatt is already in jeopardy and she should have moved to Australia and changed her name, got a makeover, and taken up landscaping. Or accounting.

Flynn puts the letter on the kitchen counter. Stares at the envelope.

FLYNN

No markings on the back. Nothing else inside. And now her hands have been all over the envelope, and of course Wyatt handled it and someone at school.

Someone at school.

There is going to be a record. Security cameras. All the comings and goings. Nobody is ever as slick and unseen and invisible as they think they are. We're all being watched. We're all being monitored. The envelope didn't flutter like a rogue leaf out of the sky. There must have been a directive. A request. But on what basis? Schools aren't mail services. Why would they comply? Someone will remember something. A teacher. Someone in the office will recall the peculiar plain gray envelope with the tiny fucking font.

Flynn's mind races. The queasy yucky gross feelings all come rushing back, only this time Wyatt is right here right now and probably awake playing games on his phone and she wants to call Max, needs to call Max, but Wyatt will hear if she's agitated. He's sensitive.

She can't freak out.

The balcony.

She takes the letter, closes the sliding glass door behind her, and sits.

Her phone shakes. She shakes.

Presses Max on speed dial.

Listens to the phone ring. And ring.

She knows the number of rings before she'll hear Max's leave-a-message voicemail greeting. It's a timing thing. Flynn gets that sinking feeling.

"Must be important," says Max.

"Yes."

"You outside somewhere?"

"On my balcony. You alone?"

"Maybe." Which means no. "You okay?"

"There's a—"

Words come hard.

"You broke up there."

A tear threatens to burst from its banks. She pushes it back, her whole hand pressed against her cheek. Shudders on autopilot.

"Can you come down here?"

What if Wyatt wakes, sees Max?

"Right now? It's ten thirty. I'm—"

"With somebody?"

"As a matter of fact."

Max McKenna, a six-foot-tall physical fitness nut with warm blue eyes and cheekbones that turn heads, is never long without. Unlike her.

"I'm sorry, but—"

"Can you tell me what's going on?"

"I got a message. A letter. Another one of those letters."

"A letter. In the mail?"

"Wyatt brought it home. Brought it home from school. My name on it."

"What does it say?"

"It's like he wrote it."

"Who *he*?"

"Harry. Him."

"He's behind double razor wire. And stun–lethal fencing. A hundred miles away. And he's never tasting freedom again."

"I know," says Flynn. "At least, I think. Can we check?"

"There's nothing to check. What does the letter say?"

Flynn finds the button for her phone's flashlight, unfolds the letter. "I'm going to put you on speaker," she says.

Reads it, listening to her own worried wavering voice.

"Jesus," says Max.

She takes him off speaker. "How is it possible?"

Plenty came out during the prosecution and trial about Flynn's relationship with PDQ in the weeks leading up to his capture. But many of the text exchanges were sent via apps that burned the words and left no permanent trace.

The first letter was a different story.

The first letter arrived with the creepy American Girl doll the night Harry Kugel invaded her home. It was Harry Kugel's sick means of proving to her that he was the genuine PDQ. The letter and the doll were turned over to police, but the gold mine of evidence against Harry

Kugel was Fort Knox voluminous. So the letter never got introduced to the public record. The district attorney kept the case focused on the attempted murder of Mary Belson, all the evidence found in Harry's bag the night he was captured, and the fentanyl and needles in his condo.

"It's got that same tone," says Flynn. "It's like the writer knows Harry's style."

"And it came through school?"

"Wyatt brought it home with a field trip form."

"So we start with the school and figure out how the letter got there and who brought it in. If it came today, someone is going to remember."

"I was thinking the same thing," says Flynn. "Who's *we*?"

"Us, of course."

"No," says Flynn. "No police. Whoever wrote it knows Wyatt. It's a message."

"So you're going to let this build and escalate like last time."

Accusation and conviction all said with casual aplomb.

"I can ask," she says. "But the place to start is with Wyatt, and I don't want to alarm him. You know?"

"If you don't make a big deal out of it, you won't."

"I'm not so sure about that."

"Stop handling the letter. Put it somewhere. You won't believe what the cops can do. Might seem like nothing, but there are so many details. Possible leads."

"Remember. *You will do nothing.*"

"It's a fake. It's bullshit. It could be a joke."

"Doesn't feel like a joke."

"You can't sit back and wonder. You have to attack. Right back. And Wyatt is my kid too."

"That's why I'm calling."

"Maybe there's an easy explanation at school."

"Easy?" says Flynn. "Even if this is someone's idea of perverted humor, it's not easy."

"So you're going to be in mental knots all weekend while you wait? It's Friday night, and unless you have the entire school staff's personal cell phone numbers, you got three sleeps until you can talk to anyone."

"Actually, I think I got his teacher's number. The portal for parents to monitor attendance and grades. I logged in when school opened last week. There was a message from the teacher with contact information."

"So call her."

"Him," says Flynn. "And he looked so young."

But she can't remember his name.

"I'm going to Cañon City."

"He didn't do it."

"Maybe he had it delivered. He mailed it to someone who dropped it off."

"All outbound mail is checked," says Max. "Incoming too. This isn't Harry."

"He's gotta know something."

"And he's going to tell you."

Not a question. Said with no extra emphasis to draw out the sarcasm.

"Well," says Flynn.

It would be extremely weird to look Harry Kugel in the eyes. Weird but not difficult. Flynn has done her share of stories about prison reform, prison conditions, and prison guard pay. She's familiar with most of Cañon City's facilities, including the federal supermax. She has long wondered if incarceration really works, but there is no question when it comes to the idea that the Harry Kugels of the world are not candidates for rehab.

"Well what?" says Max. "What are you going to do with Wyatt? Have him wait in the car in the prison parking lot while you get that monster to crack? I can have top-notch investigators there by the time you're done with your morning orange juice. Let them see if it's worth fretting about."

"You don't think it is?"

"I don't know until I know," says Max. "Bring in the pros. If I wanted a reporter, I wouldn't call some kid who's just walked out of J-school. I'd call you. You know what you're doing."

"Nicest thing I've heard all day," says Flynn.

"It's true."

"You watch tonight?"

"You know me better than that."

"Some things never change."

"You need the cops," says Max. "First thing. Attack. Go after it. You'll feel better. I'll feel better."

"I feel like he'll know immediately. He knows Wyatt's school; he probably knows where we live."

"Some of these detectives dress like car salesmen."

"And look every bit like cops."

"One advantage of living in a building with thirty-five stories—he can't possibly know who is going in and out of your door."

"True."

"Call me first thing."

Flynn says goodbye and hangs up.

"Mom?"

Flynn spins around like her chair is on fire. Wyatt's face is smooshed in the gap of the open sliding glass door.

"Honey."

She gasps.

"Who was that?" he says. "Are you okay?"

CHAPTER 8

"I don't know why you won't tell me what's in the letter."

"Because it was mean and threatening and, really, you don't need to worry," says Flynn. "Someone is trying to scare me. That's all."

Some version of this conversation with Wyatt took place on Saturday and Sunday too. Flynn managed to find enough distractions to get her through the weekend. The days were hard. The nights were harder.

"Why can't you ignore it?"

There are two dozen different cross-city routes between downtown Denver and Wyatt's school. All her choices today say *Nice try pick again.* KBCO on the radio. Tom Petty. Fleetwood Mac. Wyatt turns up Hozier's "Too Sweet."

Most days, Wyatt takes the school bus. Flynn's condo sits a quarter mile outside the school's 2.5-mile walk zone, but Flynn is already wondering if she can figure out a way, without alarming him, to announce that she will be his daily chauffeur going forward. The mornings work with her schedule. The afternoons do not. How much does a bodyguard cost? Should she quit the news business, figure out one of those jobs reviewing products online that claim to earn you thousands of dollars a day? And homeschool Wyatt? Never leave home again?

"I could ignore it," says Flynn.

"You told me you get trolled all the time."

"Every day."

"So what's the difference?"

"This was personal."

"And you're going to make a big scene?"

"Is that what I do, make big scenes?"

"Sometimes."

When Wyatt gets in a worried funk, his brow drops so far it feels like it must take concentration to hold it there. He stares out the window on his side, not looking at her.

"I'm going to ask questions," says Flynn.

"Like you asked me."

Under gentle questioning on Saturday, Wyatt revealed that he'd seen the letter in his backpack when he'd pulled out the field trip form at home. He remembered being handed the form and figured the envelope must have been with it, but for some reason hadn't noticed. He didn't think much of it. She asked him if he remembered anything unusual at school. She asked him about his bus ride home, if he remembered leaving his backpack anywhere for a long minute or two. The delicate quizzing proved fruitless.

Wyatt's school is a gleaming two-year-old steel-and-glass structure near the interstate, north of City Park. Flynn parts with Wyatt after clearing the metal detector security system and screening vestibule. She's directed to a reception desk, signs in as a visitor, and receives an orange round sticker that proclaims her status as GUEST.

She arrived thirty minutes before the school day's first bell with the idea that she will need to catch Wyatt's teacher before classes get rolling, but Flynn knows permission is vital.

And that means the principal.

Audrey Ballard bounds out of her office when notified by her friendly secretary and apologizes for not returning Flynn's weekend calls. She'd been camping in the Red Feather Lakes and hiking to a place called Molly Lake with no coverage and then her phone ran out of juice.

"Not much I could do until this morning, anyway," says Ballard. She is trim and attractive. Shoulder-length straight dark hair. Forest green blouse. Black slacks. A creamy summer tan glows on her white cheeks, reminding Flynn she needs to get outside more often.

"What was in the letter?" she says.

"I'm afraid that's between me and the writer. And, as I said, there was no name. However."

Flynn pulls a large ziplock from her handbag. The envelope sits at the bottom. The letter is at home, hidden in one of the *Vanity Fair* magazines she never has time to read.

"I brought this in case someone at the front desk remembers it being dropped off. This dark gray envelope? Not very common, right? Or maybe Wyatt's teacher remembers how it got to his classroom."

Ballard leads the charge. The school serves eight hundred students in grades six through eight, and managing the front reception desk is a rotating responsibility of three different women—one Black, one Hispanic, one White. A layered Neapolitan of staff.

Shrugs. Headshakes. Nothing. "Sorry, no."

The walk to Wyatt's classroom takes them down gleaming wide corridors. There is nothing like a spiffy new school, thinks Flynn, to give you a feeling of confidence in the future.

Ballard reminds Flynn that she was a teacher at an elementary school nearly a decade earlier when Flynn covered a school bus accident. The driver had had a heart attack, lost control of the bus, and bounced up an embankment into the living room of an old brick bungalow across the street from the school.

Flynn recalls the chaos and mayhem and screaming kids. She had been quick to the scene because she'd been interviewing one of the school's teachers about brewing unrest among the teachers' union. And, months later, won an award for breaking news because her station had cut into afternoon programming and Flynn was covering the scene before ambulances arrived.

"Could not believe all the kids survived," says Flynn. "I mean, when I first saw that bus half disappeared into the house."

"I know," says Ballard. "But still—a horrible day. Do you ever try to process accidents? You know, how unfair they can be? Random? I mean, in your line of work?"

Flynn can't think too hard about it, in fact, or she might go crazy. Had a certain anchorwoman named Sara Cornette not taken a vacation on a certain week, Flynn might not have become tangled up in the hostage-taking situation that had led Harry Kugel, quite literally, to her door. And had that certain anchorwoman not been on vacation, Flynn might not be back in the awful mental squeeze she's felt ever since Friday night, and she might not be walking these halls at this very moment.

"Life can be strange and unpredictable," says Flynn. "Funny you bring it up."

Bernie Levine is short, with tight curly red hair, silver glasses, and an upbeat demeanor. He wears tan slacks, a white shirt that needs ironing, and an extra-long blue tie. He's not Wyatt's full-time teacher, but Wyatt's first teacher each day for science. He knows nothing about the envelope in the ziplock. But he did pass out the permission forms for the dinosaur tracks field trip. "There was nothing extra that I gave Wyatt—and by the way, really enjoying his contributions in class. Wyatt is going places."

"So someone slipped the envelope in his backpack when he wasn't looking?"

"Lunch," says Ballard. "Or during gym. There are times the hallways look like the scramble, you know, Shibuya Crossing in Japan?"

"Your visitor log," says Flynn.

"What about it?" says Ballard.

"May I see it?" says Flynn.

Maybe Harry Kugel forgot that he shouldn't jot down his name during his one-day magical escape from maximum security?

What is she looking for?

"I'm not sure I've ever been asked that question," says Ballard.

"You do keep the sign-in sheets?"

"Yes, but I might have to check with the district's legal team."

"Do you have to take it to that level?"

"I mean, it's sort of a privacy issue. I think. You know, this day and age. I better check with downtown."

"But let's say I was the last visitor of the day on Friday and I signed in, I could see all those names on the list above me, right? Name and organization. Time, et cetera?"

Ballard ponders it for a moment. "I see what you're saying."

"So we go back in time. I'm just glancing at the names ahead of me."

Back in the office, Flynn scans the list. Twenty-four official visitors on Friday, from Lucia Puente at 8:37 a.m. to Tom Watterson at 3:49 p.m. The names mean nothing, but when Ballard takes a call on her walkie-talkie, Flynn takes a moment to snap a photo of the list.

"Any subs last Friday?" says Flynn.

"We have subs every day. And Fridays more than usual."

"Even the first week of school?"

"Even the first week," says Ballard.

"Is that something you keep track of—names and such?"

"Now you're getting into personnel territory that we better get cleared," says Ballard. "You know the communication office at DPS?"

"Of course," says Flynn. "I assume you have delivery people too?"

"Naturally."

"And any contractors working on the building?"

"They've been working on a plumbing issue in the kitchen," says Ballard. "I mean, people come and go all day for a variety of reasons."

"Video surveillance?"

"All over the place, except not in classrooms or gym locker rooms."

How long would it take to stitch together Wyatt's Friday routes and interactions in the school's corridors and lunchroom? Would it reveal the necessary detail?

"And?" says Flynn. "You know what I'm thinking."

"And you know what I'm thinking."

"Check downtown?"

"I'm afraid so," says Ballard. "I know it's a public record. But the request would take staff time to pull it all together. Assuming you want every camera."

"How many are there?"

"I don't know the number off the top of my head," says Ballard. "Maybe twenty."

"Then yes, every camera."

"All day?"

"All day."

"Eight hours times twenty cameras?"

"Whatever it takes."

"One hundred and sixty hours of material?"

"Yes, please," says Flynn.

"Because of an envelope."

Because of the word "killing."

Because the letter read like it was written by Harry Kugel's dark fucking doppelgänger soul.

"Yes." Flynn smiles. "Don't worry. I'll get this cleared with, how you say, *downtown.*"

CHAPTER 9

All the reporters.

All the clamor.

All the steely, careful replies from Arapahoe County law enforcement.

Flynn needs to wrap her head around what's being said about the quadruple murder. Quadruple something. She needs to join the fray of shotgun questions. Hell, she often leads the charge. Everyone must know something's wrong. Or up. Or both.

But her head is in Wyatt's school last Friday, imagining a dozen bizarre dark scenarios of how the envelope was squirreled into his backpack.

She didn't have one minute to go to the station to muddle and muck around. Or stew, brood, or kick something.

The order to scamper to this cul-de-sac of faux mansions came as she was walking to her car, and now she finds herself standing in the way-too-intense morning heat in the huddle of reporters who are all trying not to stand too close.

Flynn replays her chat with Nancy Lang, the ex-reporter comms team honcho at the school district headquarters. Just as some ex-hippies make for the most ardent capitalists, Nancy Lang has turned into the queen of corporate protectiveness. She wanted to know why Flynn Martin needed all the videotape and a list of all the substitutes who'd been called in to work at Wyatt's school the previous Friday.

And Flynn hears the echoes of her own snark, telling Nancy Lang she doesn't need a reason, that public records are public records, and she wonders if she should have been more *transparent,* as the buzzword goes, to explain that it's a personal request and not an official journalistic reporter fourth estate keeping-your-asses-in-check kind of request.

Fourth estate? Why did the phrase even pop into her head? The fourth estate means the other three are relevant.

Nobility.

There isn't a noble leader left on the planet.

The clergy.

Religion has found a big old hole to hide in. And where are the peace-minded, love-oriented church leaders of today, calling for an end to wars or fighting for racial justice?

Commoners.

Try getting that word into your newspaper story or TV script.

Should she have said that her request involved making sure PDQ isn't back or that PDQ doesn't have a shadow puppet?

How would she walk the straitlaced, buttoned-down Lang through that one?

Focus, Flynn.

Fucking focus.

Hears herself say:

"Is there any similarity to that recent case in Franktown, when the bodies went undiscovered for many days? A week?"

Sheriff Gates Moore is tall, rail thin, clean shaven, and dark. Taupe Stetson. Buttoned-up black shirt defying the heat. Black tie. A tight mouth that chooses words carefully.

"We're aware of that case in Douglas County. We will, of course, look at everything."

"Can you provide a bit more detail as to why you think foul play is involved?"

Newspaper reporter Samuel T. Tucker. Never Sam, always the middle initial. Bald. Deep voice, stiff neck, fearless spotter of sanctimony and bullshit.

And Samuel T. Tucker just asked the very question that will help me snap back to now. Thank you.

"The investigation is early days," says Sheriff Moore.

"Any signs of struggle inside?" says Flynn.

"The scene is still being processed," says Moore. "In general, however, no. The main thing is their whereabouts, which are unknown at this time."

"When were they last seen?" says Tucker.

"A neighbor's doorbell camera captured their car backing up from the garage at four a.m. one week ago," says Moore. "From what we know now about piecing together their plans, this is right on time with their plans to fly to Orlando for a vacation. But they never boarded the flight. They didn't park at any of the airport lots, on- or off-site. The vehicle we're looking for is a white 2013 Ford Expedition. License plate KQL-756. We will release the video to you all later today. It doesn't show much, of course, at four a.m. Pair of headlights, a rough outline."

"Did you see the vehicle on any other neighborhood cameras?" says Flynn. "Or on the highway?"

"We continue to look," says Sheriff Moore. "We need the public's help on this. Even though it's been a week, we ask everyone to think back—if they recall seeing anything unusual on the road involving a white Ford Expedition."

The news conference is being staged a block from the house in question, where Shannon Way begins its short journey to a giant dead-end circular apron of asphalt that simmers in the morning heat like an enormous burnt pie. Crime scene trucks are parked at the house of doom in the distance, but the view is otherwise lifeless. Flynn counts seventeen houses down Shannon Way, around the asphalt dead end, and back. The houses are white, a sure sign of a strong HOA and a likely match for the vast majority of occupants. The houses are monstrous and sit so close together and equidistant from each other that they could be teeth in a giant zipper.

"What tipped deputies off to the disappearance—if that's what it is?" says Flynn.

"They had boarded their dog for the week, and when they failed to pick him up on the appointed day, someone from the kennel drove to the house. They chatted with a neighbor who was there, someone who had also expected them back. The newspaper delivery had restarted yesterday morning, too, but it was still on the porch."

Someone still reads a printed newspaper? And has it delivered?

"And when officers responded, the house was locked. No sign of forced entry?"

This is fellow TV reporter Andrea Beamon. Chief competitor. Poised, tall, Black, and wicked smart. Makes delivering live stand-up during a rolling earthquake look about as challenging as folding the laundry.

"Yes," says Sheriff Moore. "Normal from the outside."

"But you decided to enter the house."

"Yes, after using other means to contact the parents, home and work. We are looking for Patrick and Victoria Kline. Patrick Kline is a senior warden of the vestry at New Hope Church. Victoria is a teacher at Willow Creek Country Day. And children Zachary and Adina."

Moore takes a moment, a bit choked up.

"Ages?" says Flynn.

"Patrick is forty-seven, Victoria is forty-four, Zachary is eleven, and Adina is nine," says Moore.

Zachary. *Eleven.* Only a bit younger than Wyatt. Adina, if she's gone, an even shorter life than that.

But—whole families don't vanish.

One of them, thinks Flynn, had a secret.

One of them knew trouble was on the way.

Maybe it's Flynn's way of punishing the parents, piling guilt on the victims—if that's what they are.

Maybe it's easier if Flynn can conjure a storyline and imagine that moment when one of them took a risk. Then she can chalk it up to something. Pride. Greed. Lust. Or maybe one of them went for the trifecta. A business deal gone bitter. Maybe Victoria Kline had a fling and found out too late her new beau was a jealous psycho.

Follow the money. Or follow the fucking.

"We need everyone on Shannon Way and the surrounding neighborhood to take a minute and recall what they were doing Monday morning, predawn. Or even later. Or anything overnight the night before. Talk among your families and friends and think back. It hasn't been that long. We need to get a solid picture of all the comings and goings."

Not unlike my own desperate analysis at Wyatt's school, thinks Flynn.

"Does it appear targeted?" says Beamon.

"Early stage of the investigation," says Sheriff Moore. "But it never hurts to remind everyone to know who they are greeting at the door."

"So there is a possibility it's random?" says Flynn.

"It's early," says Sheriff Moore.

Whole family disappeared? Definitely news. Without question. Every single murder deserves attention, but a whole family in one fell swoop? Likely national news too.

The Kline family story will overshadow all the news for days or a week until there's an explanation. At least, an explanation that allows the city to steer its attention to the next emotional or actual crisis. There is always a "next."

Flynn has long wondered about the overlooked murders. The cheapies. The ones among those with less means.

There were 337 murders in the state the year prior. Nearly one every day. And more than a hundred of those went unsolved. Which means that over the past decade, assuming another hundred murders each year are pending resolution, a thousand killers are out there starting to think they will march all the way to their graves having taken another human life and never paying the price, other than to carry the burden around in their sad, grim souls.

A thousand.

Going about their lives.

The sensational cases like the Klines will suck energy and attention from the lesser-than murders. In a perfect world, every life taken by another human being would draw around-the-clock attention and detailed murder scene analysis à la JonBenét, at least under the working theory that close parsing of the facts and media cheerleading for the detectives would lead to every case being resolved.

But, again, the math. Newspaper staffs, a quarter their size from a decade ago. Television news, maybe not quite the same professional bloodbath, but shrinking. And fewer eyeballs on TV watching the news while they devour scraps, delivered complete with instant opinions from TikTok and X. Would the country be in better emotional shape, and not tiptoe dancing on eggshells, if the fairness doctrine hadn't been gutted by Reagan? If news channels were required to deliver thoughtful discourse and not allowed to tie their saddles to one political horse?

"What are you thinking?"

Tamica pops the bubble of Flynn's musings. The news conference has broken up. Reporters scatter like fallen leaves in a stiff wind.

"Do we really need neighborhood reaction?" says Flynn. "I mean—don't we know what they're going to say?"

"It's over on Parker Road. Seven point five miles." Tamica holds up her phone, a solid blue line showing the way.

"Or the school?" says Flynn.

"Private school kids," says Tamica.

"They are?"

"The sheriff mentioned it. Willow Creek Country Day School."

"Maybe it's the heat," says Flynn. "Burning my brain cells."

"Roger that."

Still, Tamica looks as cool as a chilled pickle. She is five ten. Her once spindly frame has sprouted muscle thanks to a new female partner who is a gym rat, boxer, and pole dancer of the artistic variety. Tamica's expression defaults to earnest. Focused. And kind. Her eyes engage when they look at you, no flitting about. Her fingernails are neon orange, glow-in-the-daylight accents against her long-fingered brown hands.

"I guess back to neighbors?" says Flynn.

"Fine with me. You look—I don't know, distracted?"

"Maybe."

"Something with Wyatt?"

"You know me that well?"

"Either Wyatt, or is your dad okay? Boyfriend stuff?"

"Dad's fine. And you know there's no boyfriend. You'd be the first to hear."

"Ever think of trying option L?"

This is a running joke. Flynn grants her a grimace.

"Expand your horizon. Double the size of your sea, which means double the number of fish."

"Too set in my ways," says Flynn. "Emphasis on *way* too."

"Just saying."

"You're thinking about sex after hearing about all this misery?"

"Why not?" says Tamica. "And it's not about the sex so much as it is the comfort. You know? Closeness. Reassurance. It's like reading the obituaries."

"Excuse me?"

"Reading the obits. It's always the best side of people, reading about all they accomplished. What they stood for. How they left their mark and their offspring too."

"Yeah, but they're dead. That's the sad part."

"But the obits let you see a life in full. You think of all the things they set in motion by the fact that they existed. Reading them is a reliable source of calm. Life goes on."

CHAPTER 10

The horror doesn't exist until somebody says, "I never thought it would happen here."

Tamica stays on the street while Flynn knocks on doors. Three "Not going to get involved." Two firm declines with "Did not know them" claims. One clueless house cleaner. Finally a woman in purple yoga pants and a white tube top, four houses from the Kline abode, agrees to step outside.

"Can you give me your full name and spelling?" says Flynn.

"Liz L-i-z Walden."

"How long have you lived here?"

"Six months."

"Where did you move from?"

"Dallas," says Walden. "Husband's job. Plus, it's way too hot in Texas."

"Hard to imagine hotter than this."

"Plus humidity and thunderstorms like nobody's business."

"Do you have children?"

"A boy and a girl. Eight and six."

"Do you know the Kline family?"

Liz Walden is five four, tops. Ultra fit. Chiseled triceps as she folds her arms. Thick brunette hair. Wide eyes that look around as if she realizes this might have been a bad idea, that the neighbors might be watching.

"Seen them around, sure. What are they saying happened?"

Flynn recaps the high points.

"*Disappeared?*" says Walden. "How is that possible?"

"Did you know him?"

"He's churchy. He stopped over when we moved in and wondered if we'd found a place of worship. That's the way he put it. I mean, it's devastating to think something like that could happen here. Right here. I don't know what to tell my kids."

Thinking, *With you there*. What will she tell Wyatt? When? How?

"Did you know them well?"

"Can't say we did. We had kind of a block party barbecue thing on Memorial Day right here in the cul-de-sac, and Patrick rolled his big grill to the sidewalk. I mean, the size of that thing. Anyway, he spent most of his time on the hot dogs and hamburgers and didn't really mingle."

"Okay." Flynn knows they have the money bite already. The "devastating to think" one.

They are set, but she asks Tamica if she's got any questions. Tamica steps away from her camera. "No, not really. But is your husband home?"

"Yes," says Walden. She brightens as if the mere thought of hubby gives her a glow. "They let him work from home two days a week, but they insist he come to the office the other days."

Walden scampers back up the brick walkway to her front door, disappears inside, and emerges one minute later with a guy who could be George Costanza's twin brother and whose shorts and wrinkled polo shirt are the casual incongruity to his wife's spiffy vibe. Barefoot. Balding. A touch pudgy. Wire-rim glasses.

"No camera," says Roger. "Not my thing. Nothing personal. I've watched you since we moved here, Ms. Martin. In fact, my brother is a newspaper reporter in San Antonio. So no disrespect."

"That's fine," says Flynn. For random interviews like this, it's never a winner to push or beg.

"Yes," says Roger. "And?"

"The sheriff is wondering if anybody saw anything unusual last Sunday night or Monday morning."

"No," says Roger. "I mean, I'll give it some thought because those poor people, you know? But nothing abnormal. You come home on a dark street, hit the garage door remote, and park inside your garage. Not like you stare down the block and see if you can spot an unfamiliar car. Or even could."

"Or maybe someone on foot?" says Flynn.

"From a week ago? Unless they walked right past your house at that time of night and you didn't recognize them. And you know all the yards are fenced, but we back up to a greenway with a bike and walking path. At least on this side of the block. So that would be the better route in and out, if you can figure out how to get over the fence."

Flynn looks at Tamica. No nod is needed. They'll head around to the greenway next.

"Is there anything else you can tell us?" says Flynn.

General jump ball questions don't work very often.

Liz shrugs a question at her husband. Roger's lips clasp like he's daubed them with superglue.

Flynn waits.

"We have to keep this, what do you call it?" says Liz.

"Off the record," says Roger. "Unattributed to us."

"Fine," says Flynn. "Not a problem."

"The neighbors? The ones who live closer? Always talked about their fights."

There it is. The first crack. *See?* Something was wrong. They should have figured it out. They could have figured it out. One of them was hiding something.

"Shouting?"

"All of that," says Liz. "You could hear stuff in the backyard. Kids crying, too, to get them to stop."

"It's really none of our business," says Roger. "But it was not a smooth relationship. Still. The kids? And of course it could have been something else altogether. We're already speculating, and that's not the healthiest activity on earth."

◆ ◆ ◆

Flynn wanders along the wide greenway at Tamica's side as she shoots B-roll that will help viewers visualize the scene. That is, if the violence came from outside. If it was murder-suicide, nobody will forgive the dead dad for including the kids. Or the dead mom, if it was her. It does happen. But it's rare. If it's murder-suicide, it's going to be the dad. Women rarely initiate that means of ending whatever misery is tanking the marriage.

The greenway isn't green. It's brown and crispy. Water restrictions, no doubt, have limited the HOA's ability to maintain the pretense of a shared meadow.

The fences are tall. All the houses have back gates to access the path. Crime scene tape marks the rear of the Klines' residence and temporarily blocks traffic for dog walkers and bicyclists. Two men and a woman stare into the grass between the walkway and the Klines' fence, moving methodically on their hands and knees.

A cluster of adults watch from the house opposite the Klines'. Fences, fences, fences. Flynn wonders, Who was the first to define their pasture? Mark it *mine*? And lord over their land? A caveman, maybe, with the need to divide, separate, hide. Flynn spots a woman watching from a second-story window next to the Klines' residence. Maybe she saw the fights, since she had an angle looking down into their backyard. Maybe she has the inside scoop.

Flynn's phone trills. The number is one of her favorites.

"In the middle of something?"

It's her father.

"Only trying not to think how a whole family disappears."

Also trying not to think about the envelope and Wyatt and how she's going to examine all that video footage the school district is going to cough up. And what are the odds that the moment she needs is on camera?

"I've been watching the news conference, thanks to one of your competitors who broadcast it live," says Michael. "Heard you asking questions."

"Lucky me." A gaggle of neighbors have gathered on the street where she and Tamica entered the greenway. "A neighbor told us the Klines had issues. Fights."

"I did a quick search," says Michael.

"And?"

"And nothing. I thought there might be something because those two in Franktown weren't found for days, but I couldn't find a connection. Not on the surface, at least. The husband in the Franktown case was involved in a cryptocurrency exchange, but that means nothing."

"And Patrick Kline?"

"CPA at one of the big firms downtown," says Michael. "Chief solutions officer."

"That's his title?"

"They have a chief transformation officer too."

"Maybe the crypto joint used the CPA firm for their services?"

"Not a bad idea," says Michael. "I'll check the public filings."

"And let me know when you have an hour to explain how crypto works?" says Flynn. "Or a day."

"Blockchains? Oh sure, well, blockchains are the decentralized ledger of transactions that's shared across a peer-to-peer network of computers—"

"Dad?"

"What?"

"Not right now, okay?"

"If you say so."

Michael, retired after a long and stellar career as a star reporter at *The Denver Post*, the kind of reporter who took complicated government transactions and broke them down into plain English, always with an eye out for whose nest was being feathered, is a citizen journalist who continues to derive great pleasure out of digging into public records and public spending. He writes a mix of news and well-researched columns for a twice-weekly Substack feed with seven hundred subscribers. He's also Flynn's not-so-secret journalistic wingman, a guy who knows his way around databases and public records and doesn't mind helping her.

"You okay?" says Michael.

"This one is really hard," says Flynn. "Those poor kids. I mean, I'm assuming the worst."

"You have to," says Michael. "Whole families don't just disappear."

CHAPTER 11

"Live at noon," says Goodman. "I'm sure you figured as much. You're the lead. Ninety seconds. If you can get the sheriff to come on with you, that would be great."

It's 11:25 a.m. Flynn is walking back to the station SUV that Tamica drove to the scene. They need to stitch together a few of the sheriff's sound bites and some of the B-roll. She doesn't want to spend time cajoling the sheriff into more on-camera time. Besides, he's not going to say anything different. Or differently.

"I can ask," says Flynn. "We've got a neighbor too."

A UPS truck makes its rounds along Shannon Way. A young, fit man in a tank top, pecs out to here with one colorful sleeve of tattoos, leans against the frame of his bicycle, staring down the street. From his sweaty brow, it looks like it was a long trip. Near him, two women chat. Arms folded. They are there to watch what little is happening. Lightweight tops, shorts, sandals, sunglasses. Mid-thirties. One puffs a cigarette.

"What's the neighbor say?"

Flynn has Goodman on speaker for Tamica's benefit.

"It's off-camera, but the Klines had noisy fights."

"We'd need someone to confirm," says Goodman. "Cops ever called?"

"Checking that right now," says Flynn.

"Can't use that unless we get corroboration."

"Sure," says Flynn.

"We'll need you there for the four and the five," says Goodman.

"I've got calls I can make," says Flynn. She might be referencing a nonstory about the video footage at Wyatt's school, but it's not untrue. "And we can try the church or the school or both to see if we can get comments."

"See you in thirty-two," says Goodman.

"Yep," says Flynn.

There was a time when she would start to feel tense and rushed as the clock ticked down to a live shot, but her head and body have both learned to keep an even keel. Flynn writes her live lead-in so the package begins with the neighbor, and the script sets the scene and weaves in the sheriff's best bites too. She wraps the script by highlighting what isn't yet known.

Her phone chimes as Tamica edits.

Twelve minutes to go.

Axel Sheen.

"Hi there," says Flynn.

"Catch you at a bad time?"

"No," says Flynn. "I have a full sixty seconds to talk. Live shot coming at noon. And I am sorry about the last-minute cancellation."

There was no way she could have entertained anyone or considered leaving Wyatt's side for a second over the weekend.

"It's okay," says Axel.

She hears the disappointment. "It can't be helped."

"Is this a stall? I'm a big boy. You can tell me."

"No," says Flynn. "Really."

"Sure?"

Is she? "Yes."

"In that case, a friend here at work handed me two tickets to a concert at the Botanic Gardens. Tomorrow night. He's a hot trombone player from New Orleans."

Before moving from the house PDQ forever ruined, at least for her, she could walk to the Botanic Gardens to take in a show. Wine, picnic, blanket, music, sunset, bliss.

"Sounds good," says Flynn. Dare she leave Wyatt at home in the condo, or lean again on Michael's good graces for a couple of hours?

Axel says he'll text about final arrangements and who will bring what. He jumps off. Even if Axel isn't the one, Flynn thinks, she needs to put more time into looking.

It's been a long time since she's had anything going on a regular basis and, well, nothing at all, regular or irregular, since those cold dark weeks of the scary dance she played with PDQ.

Too long.

She owes it to herself. But she can't for a second imagine bringing someone home to her condo unless Wyatt was on an overnight with a friend. She also can't imagine taking the time to swing by Axel's place after the show and, say, getting right down to business so she isn't out too late. And is it sex she wants, or does she want a guy friend for a few months who turns into something romantic? And how exactly do you go about this? Have the rules changed? The signals? From everything she's gathered, people are much more to the point about what they want and how they want it, and the whole long process of really getting to know someone scares the daylights out of her, but so does the idea of fucking for fucking's sake and skipping along like emotions don't matter.

"Date, huh?" says Tamica.

"Midweek date," says Flynn. "No expectations."

"Oh, I am one hundred percent sure he thinks that."

"It's the rule," says Flynn. "If it's a Monday, you don't even have to shake his hand. Tuesday means a peck on the cheek. His lips. Or *her* lips in your case. Your cheek. Wednesdays, he gets a hug and a two-way kiss, but like a saying-hello-in-France kind of kiss, and that's it."

"Thursdays?"

"You can let the kiss linger and maybe not slap his hand away if he gets frisky."

"You live in a strange world, Flynn Martin."

"Thank you." Flynn pulls out a pocket mirror to see if her face looks melted off.

"You might want to check these rules with him. Text him a list. Because you're revealing you aren't aware that times have changed."

"No, he knows," says Flynn. "And if he doesn't, he better learn to read my mind."

CHAPTER 12

"So much yet to learn about what happened in this sad story developing today in Arapahoe County." Longtime anchor Sara Cornette in her IFB. "Did the sheriff say when he would release more details?"

"No," says Flynn. Neutral face. Unexcitable face. Dead eyes. "But we will of course keep everyone up to date as information becomes available."

"Thank you, Flynn Martin—live at the scene today. On Wall Street at this hour, analysts are watching the Federal Reserve—"

"Clear," says Tamica. "Have you done this before?"

"Once or twice."

"Well, it shows. Now what?"

"You need lunch?"

"All I need is a bottle of water so cold it's a minute away from freezing through. Are we going to hang around here?"

Twenty years ago, Flynn might have headed back to the newsroom to make calls. Twenty years ago, it was twenty minutes to anywhere in Denver. Now, with traffic jams worthy of any big city, the round trip will eat ninety unproductive minutes at a minimum, and she needs to be back for another live shot for the four o'clock show. She could make calls from the front seat of the station's SUV that Tamica drove out or from her own car, but it's too hot. And uncomfortable. She can follow the other stations and make the rounds to the Klines' school and church, but those comments fall into a category Flynn calls "fluffy yakkers." People who are willing to talk but who say nothing of substance. The odds of coming away with anything meaty, and that will move the story forward, are low.

Options? Knock on a house and ask if they're willing to take in an overheated news crew? Head to a local library and hope that one of the air-conditioned conference rooms is open? Coffee shops work if they aren't overrun. *Maybe.*

Flynn has this nagging hunch that the Franktown double murder and this one in Centennial are connected. Flynn isn't opposed to listening to her gut, even if there were bodies in the Franktown case and, so far, none in the Kline case. Her father will call if he finds a nugget, but she should be poking around too.

Occasionally she has called her ex, Max, to see if the cop scuttlebutt grapevine has settled on a motive. She wouldn't use it, necessarily, but it could give her an angle to pursue.

But Max is Denver and this is Arapahoe County, and the two law enforcement ecosystems may as well be Mars and a passing asteroid.

"Decisions," says Tamica. "But keep in mind that I could use a bite. We all gotta eat. Well, maybe not you, but the rest of us do."

Tamica mentions a taco place one mile west. Flynn decides she'll follow in her car. She'll mentally list calls to make on the drive over and actually call to the school district to check on her videotape request. It won't hurt to find out if there's been progress. And it won't hurt to remind them that she isn't joking.

Lookie-loos are dispersing. News trucks too. Flynn remembers where she parked her Kia, around the corner on a street parallel to Shannon Way.

She gets a text from the Arapahoe County Sheriff announcing a news conference that will provide updates at 4:00 p.m. Location: Sheriff's HQ. Cleverly timed to give the sheriff some live screen time. And a text from Goodman right behind the first, forwarding along the sheriff's.

You got the 4 p.m. with the sheriff?

Texts back: On it.

◆ ◆ ◆

Flynn's Kia roasts like a baked potato in the hot sun. She'd squeezed into the spot upon arrival, but now the car sits alone. She's glad she cracked the windows but still takes a moment with both doors open to let the scorching air inside escape to the torrid air outside. She kicks herself for not using the app on her phone to get the AC going earlier. She doesn't deserve newfangled things. The steering wheel is like touching a metal spoon seared by a welding torch.

Flynn reaches for the envelope tucked in where the dashboard and windshield come together. She thinks for a moment it's a flyer from somebody in the neighborhood trying to get the media's attention, or maybe it's been there for a while and she failed to notice, and then she sees the color.

Impossible.

Inconceivable.

Or maybe she's too jacked up. Have all her nerves decided to move outside her body and take up residence on her skin?

She stares at it. Stares at it to go away.

The station's SUV with the bright logo and *News You Can Trust* splashed across the side crosses in front of her at the end of the street. Tamica glances her way, twirls a sideways finger out her open window. *Let's roll.* And goes out of view behind one of the neighborhood mansions.

Blood drains from Flynn's head. She's memorized the color. She's memorized the shade. She could match it on a Pantone wheel within seconds, no problem.

This envelope is the same.

The fucking same.

Reaches for it.

Tight seal.

Opens it.

A small square of paper flutters to her lap. It's as big as a postage stamp. It's a photo of Wyatt. A school photo. Posed and stiff.

Miss Flynn,

My crime scene?

Maybe.

Maybe not.

You can decide.

Well, you can guess.

You might never know.

The Front Range of Colorado is home to 5 million people.

Plus or minus every day, yes?

This time, no patterns.

This time, I won't and don't need your help.

You?

You get to sit back and observe.

You will do nothing.

The pattern is no pattern.

The Prototype Rules.

CHAPTER 13

From a block away, dressed like any suburbanite and yakking casually on the phone like any red-blooded American, it feels good to watch Flynn Martin panic.

Also so good and reaffirming and so satisfying to know that Flynn Martin would show up where she was supposed to be, at the epicenter of the juiciest story around.

So predictable.

Moth to flame, dog to bone, vampire to vein.

Inevitable.

Delusional, you say?

Misinformed?

Enamored with Harry Kugel?

Ha. Ha.

And another ha.

Flynn and her expert—and all the experts—can go fuck themselves.

Complete bullshit.

Flynn Martin and her expert shrink have zero clue.

Yet.

And delusion isn't even in the picture.

But the entertainment factor? Almost off the charts.

CHAPTER 14

Flynn climbs out of the car. Looks around. Up the street, down the street. To the sides.

Around.

Around.

There are a few folks, but it all looks so benign. Conventional. The world going about its business.

Her mouth as dry and taut as snakeskin.

Rereads the note.

Holds the photo of Wyatt in her palm, feels this yearning ache to walk off the job and call it Take Your Mother to School Day all the way through high school, college, and postgrad work too.

Calls Goodman, puts in her request.

"Yes, tomorrow," she says.

"Short notice," says Goodman.

"Something came up. And I have a kajillion vacation days in the bank."

"Thought you'd want to stay on the Kline story."

"Wish I could," says Flynn.

"One day?"

"That's all."

And nobody can know what she's doing. Or where she's going. If something happens along the way and it has to come out, she'll deal with it then. She should be interviewing bodyguards for Wyatt, but there's an even more compelling need.

"The Kline case is going national," says Goodman. "Orlando news stations are trying to find the hotel they'd booked, to prove they never showed."

"Sorry," says Flynn. "I need the day."

"And I need a reason."

"No, as a matter of fact," says Flynn. "You don't. Check my contract. One day. I'll be right back in the mix, and do you think it's worth recapping that double murder in Franktown today?"

"You're changing the subject."

"Yes."

As Flynn talks, she scans. All the humans have scattered back to their air-conditioned comfort zones, but she spots a video doorbell on the house directly across the street. And one on the house next to her car too. And one next to that.

All she needs is one image, which is also what she needs from the footage the school district is going to cough up. As soon as she gets a match, she'll take it to the authorities and they can pull all the surveillance footage from around Shannon Way and around Wyatt's school and there will be a triangulation of lightning-fast detective work involving seamless interagency cooperation and they will find the fucking creep prankster asshole and she can resume routine levels of everyday paranoia and not the kind of jacked-up dread gnawing at her marrow.

But . . . *sit back and observe?*

Never.

"Got to mention Franktown," says Flynn. "Especially since the sheriff said they're looking at it."

"Seems like a stretch," says Goodman. "We've got bodies in Franktown and nothing in Centennial."

"Agreed," says Flynn. "But we should ask Douglas County detectives now if they're checking with Arapahoe County about the Kline case, to see if there are any similarities with what they're looking into out there."

"But how do you plan murders or disappearances, knowing your crime won't be discovered for days?"

"In densely populated neighborhoods," says Flynn.

"You'll check on the Franktown case?"

"Got it," says Flynn.

Was Mr. Envelope watching the news conference? How the hell did he track her all the way here?

Or did he anticipate?

Roll the dice?

The Kline news had broken Sunday evening, though details had been sketchy, which always occurred to Flynn as a bizarre thing to say because if they're sketchy, they aren't, in fact, details. She's also personally vowed to never hear the phrase "foul play" come out of her own mouth because it's meaningless and sounds so playground childlike, when it's always referring to someone's murder. *Authorities suspect foul play.* Where the hell is the play?

So did Mr. Envelope make a wild-ass guess that Flynn would show up in the neighborhood when the sheriff called the news conference?

Flynn texts Tamica: Something came up. I'm hanging here. Snag me a couple barbacoas?

Nobody is home at the house directly behind where Flynn parked her Kia. At least, nobody answers the door. Isn't that why video doorbells were invented? Keep the riffraff at bay? Discourage porch pirates? Further isolate yourself in a cold, lonely, fucked-up world?

Tamica replies: I can turn around if you need me.

Flynn: Unrelated. Get food.

◆ ◆ ◆

A young man answers the door across the street. He offers his name with the innocence of the 1950s, invites her in. Noah Gifford looks like he could have walked off a college graduation stage that morning. His hair is boot camp stubble. He wears a green tie-dye T-shirt over tan shorts. He's barefoot.

He looks far too young to be the owner of a thirty-five-hundred-square-foot house, but inside where there would normally be couches and a giant television screen is a desk big enough for a corner suite on a top-floor office in Chicago or New York. Flynn counts five computer monitors. Four are crammed with numbers and what look like spreadsheets. The fifth, the largest, is streaming stock market updates narrated by a disembodied voice who is as excited as if announcing a winning touchdown in OT.

"Options and derivatives," says Gifford, muting the announcer.

Flynn explains what she's after, but not why.

"Somebody who approached your car?" says Gifford.

"Yes."

"And you're a reporter?"

"Yes."

"Here for that awful thing on the next block?"

"Yes."

"What a tragedy. You never expect something like that to happen in your own neighborhood."

"Yes," says Flynn. "I am sure."

"My Ring cam saves me all kinds of hassles. And I always hoped it would come in handy for something like this."

Gifford sits at one of the computers, clicks keys.

"That's your car, the electric Kia?"

"Right."

"Nice rig."

"Thanks."

"I've got the best video doorbell, with color and night vision," says Gifford.

The image of her car is as sharp as if she were looking out the window.

"Okay, this is the live shot, let's go back—how far?"

"An hour?"

Gifford switches to an archive tab on his desktop app. "You can record up to a hundred and eighty days," he says. "That is an absolute ton of data, so I set it at a week and it's motion activated, so the dead times don't take up storage."

Gifford keystrokes the reverse command. The video runs, but for the first few seconds it looks like a still shot until a dog walker passes on Gifford's side of the street. He's moving backward with a miniature dachshund in Charlie Chaplin double time.

"It should be obvious," says Flynn. Anger and desperate curiosity intertwine in a tight braid. What will she do with the image? Who does she trust? *You will do nothing.* Wyatt's tiny photo a clear message.

She knows who she needs to look in the eye.

It will be a two-hour drive south. An unknown number of hours there with the security rigmarole, and two hours back if she doesn't hit traffic.

Wyatt will never know.

Max will never know.

Should she tell her father? Tell—or consult with him?

And is tomorrow even a visiting day? She knows squat about visiting days or procedures. He's not a run-of-the-mill inmate and might have his own personalized visitor plan. And what if he declines? The ball will be in his court, but she has a hunch his curiosity and ego and arrogance will draw him out.

And then Flynn realizes her name will be recorded. What bureaucrat or warden will review the log of visitor hours and share the information among colleagues or cohorts?

Flynn's warped relationship, the fact that she trusted PDQ for days and days, is well known.

And her image will be recorded too.

Not unlike the video she's watching now.

A kid backpedals on his bicycle to the side of the Kia. Stops. For a second Flynn thinks it's coincidence that a kid would stop at her car. Maybe he was peering in to see if there was something of value to snatch.

"Play it forward?" says Flynn.

"Him?" says Gifford. "The kid?"

"Know him?"

"There's tons of kids on bicycles around here, but he should be in school."

Gifford rewinds the video until the kid is out of frame, ushers him in at normal speed. The bicycle is a BMX. Purple tires, tall handlebars. The kid is a young teen. Long blond hair, with a tan Greta Van Fleet T-shirt.

"Love those guys," says Gifford.

So does Wyatt. "Too loud for me," says Flynn.

The kid clutches the envelope in his right hand. He reaches his skinny arm into the Kia, pulls it back, pedals away.

"Fuck," says Flynn. "Sorry."

"Not who you expected?"

"No," says Flynn. "Delivery boy."

"Delivery boy?"

"Hired help," says Flynn. "Have you seen that kid around?"

Gifford sweeps a hand at his stock-watching war room. "Can't say I pay attention out there, but what you need is video of the kid being hired by the message-delivering stranger. Right?"

Flynn notes the time stamp on the video—11:42 a.m., while she was editing with Tamica.

"Which could have happened anywhere for miles around," says Flynn.

"True."

"Or the kid himself," says Flynn. "Can you text me a screenshot of him? One without my car in the background?"

CHAPTER 15

"Is this where I say something clever about fava beans?"

Her guts feel like she's swallowed a rock.

"I want nothing clever."

"What can I possibly do for you?"

"Tell me how."

"Tell me how—*what?*"

Private, windowless room. A heavy odor like a sweaty locker room with a top note of bleach. A table big enough for World War III peace talks.

Maybe all she needed was a phone call to the warden to double-check that PDQ didn't stow away in a sack of dirty sheets and exit via laundry truck? Or that he wasn't scooped off the prison yard in a daring helicopter rescue worthy of *Mission: Impossible.*

"How I'm getting notes that sound like you," says Flynn.

"Sound?"

"Okay, they *read* like you wrote them."

"I haven't the foggiest."

Harry Kugel is shackled, wrists to the table and ankles to the floor. Compared to when she last saw him, in court, he looks like he was sentenced to life at 24 Hour Fitness, not the state penitentiary in Cañon City. He looks younger, tighter, though his overall weak pallor makes it clear he doesn't get much vitamin D. He is pink pale. His dull eyes lock on her like a tractor beam. Looking at him makes her realize how much he has haunted her nightmares and her awake time too. Will anyone mind if she presses his eyeballs into his skull with her thumbs?

"The notes are in your style," says Flynn.

"As in?"

"As in style. And tone."

"I was unaware I had a style."

"They are threatening. And nasty."

"I'm sorry."

"No you're not," says Flynn. "And they remind me what you said."

"What I said when?"

"In court. To me."

Harry shakes his head. "Don't recall."

He's fucking with her.

"That this wasn't over."

"I said that? If so, what was I thinking? Look at me. I'm as powerless as a baby getting her first thought. Probably something like 'Nipple good.'"

"You warned me about this," says Flynn.

"These notes were delivered to you?" says Harry.

"Hand delivered."

"Recently, I take it."

As in yesterday. The second one is in her car, locked in the glove compartment. She hasn't discussed it with one soul.

"Yes."

"How many?"

"Two so far."

"We did have some good conversations."

"Nothing about it was good."

"Except all the rats you exposed in the police department."

"Maybe."

"And the adrenaline felt good."

"But it didn't end well for you."

"End? I hate that word. Do you think there will be more?"

"More?"

"Letters."

Flynn ignores him. This was always the issue. She rehearsed it a zillion times during the sleepless night since Letter #2 appeared yesterday and she rehearsed it another zillion times during the long drive from Denver. Cañon City sits along the Arkansas River where the water exits from Royal Gorge. Due to thick traffic at all the popular bottlenecks, the drive took two hours. Flynn hates pulling favors, but a friend in the DOC comms office helped her book the visit on short notice and outside normal visiting hours, an effort that ate into the time yesterday afternoon when she should have been working on the bizarre story on Shannon Way. If there was a Journalist Fitbit that measured ability to focus and produce, her wrist device would be blaring alerts every ten seconds.

To Flynn, there are two possibilities.

Whacko Theory *Numero Uno* surmises that PDQ was grooming someone before his downfall and capture. This does not seem likely, since PDQ wanted to go down in history as one of the infamous serial killers who never got caught. The period of time when the walls closed in on him only lasted about a week, and really, in the end, there were only one or two screwups. So it's unlikely that he could have found someone, and established trust, while he was sweating out whether the pincers would close all the way.

Whacko Theory *Numero Dos* ponders the idea that someone has come to visit Harry Kugel, earned his confidence, and asked him for Serial Killer Survival Tips, like there's some sort of handy guide to random killing that would sit in the bookstore next to the bomb-making instructions found in *The Anarchist Cookbook*. But the problem with that theory is, *who?* She can't access the visitor logs without a lawyer and a compelling reason, a trip to court, and likely a whole public splash about what she's digging into. Certainly Kugel's legal defense team would fight her every step of the way, and the public would scream, *Give it a rest.*

The other problem with Theory Two is it's only been five months since Harry was sentenced, although she can't discount that he had visitors while he was being held in Denver before and during the trial.

Still, who saunters into prison, requests visiting time with a notorious killer, and calmly inquires about their secrets to success? Or, in Harry's case, where he thinks he blew it?

"You have visitors?"

Harry looks around at the dull gray box. A guard sits on a chair behind Harry.

"That's my business."

"People trying to help?"

"Religious types, you mean?"

"Or anyone," says Flynn, thinking of his band of supporters who held vigil during his trial.

"Nobody trying to save my soul, if that's what you mean. Franz Liszt called it the 'light of wholeness.'"

Flynn flashes on one of Harry's signature moves from his murders, setting the victims up to suggest the dead women were listening to Holst's "Jupiter" on an iPod Nano. She never pondered the idea that she'd be subjected again to Harry Kugel's deep thoughts about classical music. *Fuck.*

"Wholeness and holiness are the same thing," says Kugel. "Do you know that?"

Flynn says nothing.

"It's about putting the two sides of yourself back together as one whole. Liszt and his affairs, the way he cheated on women? Not for the faint of heart, yet he composed the *Transcendental Études.*"

Harry pauses. Listens to the air. Moves his hand like a bird in flight.

"Exquisite explorations of mysticism," says Harry. "I mean, a practicing Catholic, but he had a long and intense affair with a married woman. Carolyne. With a *y-n-e.* He lived a complicated life and yet he was so popular, women fought over his cigar stubs and coffee dregs. His *stubs.* His fucking *dregs.* Check me on all of this. You'll see."

"So you have music," she says.

Making conversation.

"They give us tablets," says Harry. "They charge us for the streaming. Comes out of our account. But I'm not saving for life after I get out because we all know."

"Know?"

"Know that isn't happening."

"And you can listen on the tablet?"

"And headphones. Well, cheap earbuds, and I can tell you the quality is abysmal. I'd gladly let them slice off one of my pinkie fingers for a decent pair of Sennheisers."

"Did you have visitors in Denver?" says Flynn.

"Yes, they were after my cigar stubs. They all want their lips where my saliva has soaked through the cap of a fine Cohiba. And I don't smoke. *Yeccch*, if you know what I mean. Maybe I should offer my fingernail and toenail clippings instead. I could keep them in an envelope and sell them by the dozen. And, no, I'm not telling you about my visitors."

"But you've had some."

Harry heaves a heavy, impatient sigh.

"The world sees opportunity in unusual places."

"Meaning."

"One man's effluent is another's incentive. You know, used chewing gum getting turned into skateboard wheels. Used coffee grounds as rich bedding for growing mushrooms. I am trash, therefore."

"What?"

"Harry Kugel gets all sorts of weird come-ons. They all think they know me."

Flynn hates it when anyone talks about themselves in the third person.

"Give me a sample."

"No," says Harry.

"Anyone after your story?"

"Like?"

"A writer. A podcaster. I don't know—a brain researcher."

"I may have had some inquiries," says Harry. "But I consider that my private business. What did these letters say?"

She's contemplated this one. She's rehearsed the way she'll keep the description general and smooth. The one thing she won't mention is Wyatt. She won't give him the pleasure of hearing her son's name after he snuck into Wyatt's bedroom, after he later befriended Wyatt in disguise, after he swiped Wyatt's phone, after he scared the ever-living crap out of her.

"They promise another round of murders. Which may have already started. And they threaten me with various ways I'll be harmed if I enlist the authorities."

It's faint. Ever so faint. It's only one side of his mouth, the left. But there's a distinct crack.

A smile.

"Does ring a bell," says Harry.

"There's only one reason to target me," says Flynn.

"Do tell."

"You. Of course. Like you have unfinished business."

"Your reputation, though," says Harry. "I mean, your efforts. Your *involvement* with me was well known. Not exactly hush-hush, you know?"

"It feels personal."

With Wyatt, way more fucking personal. Flynn suddenly feels so far from her son she could be tapping rocks with a pick on the dark side of the moon.

"I urge you not to focus on feelings."

"There are many other reporters someone could taunt. And threaten."

"But you have experience," says Harry. "If I was starting a new, shall we call it a 'campaign,' I'd want the best. Someone with experience."

"Do you want someone following in your footsteps?"

Harry stares. It's not at her. It's through.

"Guard," he says. He pulls his hands straight up so the chains are taut, waiting for his escort back to hell.

CHAPTER 16

Again, the predictability factor.

Off the chart.

So easily provoked to race down to have a chat with your old pal.

You thought Harry fucking Kugel had something to do with it?

What?

How?

The fucker is in prison.

Did Harry Kugel model premiere levels of execution, back in his day? Does Harry Kugel know a thing or two about high standards of skill and performance? Without question. I have my own questions.

I need to learn.

But what a waste of time—driving all the way down here. For what? For exactly what?

And then you walked right by me.

Frazzled, frustrated, ragged.

I could smell the worry.

But it wasn't Harry.

It was me.

CHAPTER 17

Traffic over Monument Hill north of Colorado Springs stretches ahead like a ribbon of shimmering tinsel. Her Kia clocks seventeen miles per hour.

She calls Michael, tries to sound unalarmed.

"I'm stuck in traffic," says Flynn. "Any chance you can pick up Wyatt?"

"Sure," says Michael. "You want him with me at my place, or shall I deliver him to yours?"

"I'll pick him up later," says Flynn.

"How much later?"

"After my date. Botanic Gardens."

"With Axel Rose?"

"Yes, Dad, that Axel. You going to run the joke into the ground?"

"Dads are good at that. Where are you now?"

"North side of Monument Hill, watching the sun beat down on approximately all the cars in the western United States."

"Something in Colorado Springs?" says Michael.

"I'll fill you in later," says Flynn.

Will she? She's not sure. All she knows is how refreshing it felt to emerge from the caves and confines of the penitentiary and back into the blazing sunlight. How the hell can Harry Kugel be connected to the two envelopes?

How can he *not* be?

"I better get going," says Michael.

"Sorry I didn't give you much warning."

It's a three-mile shot from Michael's condo in Cheesman Park north to Wyatt's school.

"That's okay."

"Where would I be without you, Dad?"

"Same question back to you," says Michael.

"I have *another* question."

"Now?"

"It'll only take a second," says Flynn.

"Fire away."

"Is there one central place where all the Colorado murders are tracked? Around the state but particularly across the Front Range?"

"You do know you're talking to a guy who spent the day exploring new models of the state's school finance formula with a statistician from CU Boulder? Did you know schools could have fully funded the arts for the past decade if the state made one small tweak in the—"

"Dad."

"Yes."

"I do care, but."

"Is this the Klines? The Shannon Way stuff?"

"Maybe," says Flynn.

"I don't think there's a central statewide database all in one spot. The CBI has a website with all the statewide cold cases."

"I need the hot ones."

"Across how many jurisdictions?"

"Not sure."

"Fort Collins to Colorado Springs?" says her dad.

"I guess."

"All the murders in all those jurisdictions?"

"Something like that."

"How far back?"

"Two weeks? Three?"

"So can't you google 'recent murders in Colorado'?"

"I don't know what I'm looking for."

Or should she wait for PDQ II to drop her a hint?

No.

The pattern is no pattern.

"You want all the bar fight murders? The drunk party killings? The cheapies?"

"Are there any cheapies, Dad? That seems, I don't know, awfully judgmental."

"You know what I mean. Not in my book, but the ones that are quickly solved and belong to a certain class of citizen. Look, I better get going. Like five minutes ago. But Colorado has two hundred and forty separate law enforcement agencies, and a third of those, maybe half, are here on the Front Range. That would be a whole lot of digging. Legwork. Calling. Especially if you don't know what you're looking for."

CHAPTER 18

It comes out of, well, nowhere. There is no single anatomical spot connected to the feeling. No mysterious mythological G-spot. No undiscovered lobe of the brain. No switch that flips and says, *Try him on for size.*

It's a sense of opening up to the possibility.

Axel Sheen is funny. He's an easy talker. He's not overly pushy with the questions. She gets no sense she's playing fifty questions and keeping a mental checklist of the compatibility factors. It's as if the date is a slice-of-life chat about whatever the night gives them, and it's okay to listen to the music, watch the gathering of the White People of Denver as they sip wine and nibble on cheese, and be in the moment.

Flynn puts on a good show that her mind isn't busy with the envelopes or replaying the conversation with the creepozoid in Cañon City. Or wondering how hard she'll press to get access to those videos at Wyatt's school.

Axel Sheen's beautiful eyes offer a place to lose herself. The eyes are deep set. They're parked under a prominent brow, and they are so blue they could have been transplanted from a health-nut California surfer, but Axel's thick head of curly dark hair reads more bookish and introspective.

He's from Chicago. Well, Wheaton. But he talks about Chicago with enthusiasm, especially the music scene and all the bands he was into in college and how he once played bass in a punk group and opened for a band Flynn thinks she knows. Wishes she did. He's never been married, no kids. Flynn scolds herself for not squelching the *So he claims* Greek chorus in her head. He owns a condo in hipster, artsy RiNo and plays lunchtime pickup basketball at the downtown Y.

They're both wearing gray shorts. Her sleeveless pullover is coral. His short-sleeved shirt is lime. She thinks they look refreshing together, like two slabs of sherbet. They're both wearing sandals, and if he's judging her by her feet, well, there's your whole window to the soul right there. Clean, sure, but nothing girly. Pedicure twice a year whether she needs one or not and, anyway, she barely thinks about doing anything with her fingernails beyond biting them down, so the toes don't deserve special treatment. Or love.

What's catching her off guard, and maybe she's channeling her inner Tamica, is the fact that she's counting and pondering and considering and wondering how many dates until she takes this delicious-looking man to bed, and yet she hates herself the whole time for thinking that way. But also would it really be the end of the world if Wyatt was introduced to Axel Sheen over his morning Cheerios?

If she asks for what she wants, can she get it? And how bad could it be? What are the true downside consequences? And why did she make him work so hard to get to this moment?

In this corner, A Good Time.

In that corner, Patience and Dull Routines.

Touch gloves, and then to your corners, protect yourselves at all costs, and come out fighting, prompts the imaginary referee. Does Good Times own a decent uppercut? Patience, by definition, has to know the rope-a-dope.

Wyatt must know how the world works. Once kids are on the internet behind closed doors, you may as well kiss innocence goodbye and skip the teenage years of slow awakening. Coming of age takes approximately a minute and a half, and Wyatt is probably worried his mother isn't getting enough. Of anything. Does she really want him to grow up thinking his mother is chaste and virtuous?

"Jazz?" says Sheen.

"What about it?"

"Do anything for you?"

"I mean, it's expressive and energizing and all that good stuff," says Flynn. "But I can't say I know what's good or bad."

They sit at the top on an old blanket. He's leaning back on one propped-up arm. The fingers on his other hand cradle a glass of cold prosecco. An empty plate sits between them—cheese, crackers, slices of apple. Flynn wonders what Harry Kugel is eating tonight, then immediately scolds herself for wasting idle thoughts on him. Her next glass of bubbly will be a secret toast to his rot-in-hell status.

The amphitheater at the Botanic Garden surrounds the stage on all four sides. The air smells of sunscreen and fresh lawn. She doesn't dislike being in public or large crowds, but she ran into five people she knew during a trip to the bathroom, turning five minutes away into fifteen. Flynn scans the vast sea of humanity and, of course, can't help wondering if she's being watched.

"It must be cool," says Sheen, "to know that you're never going to play the same song twice, that you can shake it up every time."

"Haven't given it much thought."

"I feel sorry for all the dinosaur rock acts tromping around and, you know, if they don't play 'Come Sail Away' or 'Listen to the Music' the same way it was recorded fifty years ago, they'll get booed off the stage," says Sheen. "Must get boring."

"Boredom sucks." Flynn says it idly. "Except if you're a rock star. At some point, don't you get addicted to the attention?"

"Like a junkie," says Sheen. "And you know which songs pay the bills."

"I'm not going to lose any sleep over their so-called struggles," says Flynn.

"What *does* keep you awake?"

Flynn studies Axel Sheen's pale legs. Slightly more dark hair above the knee than below. His hips are trim, and his shirt is untucked and pulled up, giving her a wedge of flat stomach to admire.

"How long have you got?" she says.

"Don't reporters find a way to turn it all off at the end of the day?"

"Can't speak for anyone else."

"I mean, that stuff with the serial killer was probably next level."

"Truly not my favorite topic, if you must know."

"Got it," says Axel. "But from a really cold, almost clinical angle, wasn't his planning impressive? And then to disappear, hiding in plain sight all those years?"

"Like I said," says Flynn. "Finding one scrap of anything good in that monster's work seems, I don't know, reprehensible and un-American. To even look for something good, I mean—"

"Sorry. That's probably a third rail you don't want to touch for another century or so."

She puts a hand on his bicep, gives a little squeeze. "You didn't know—it's okay." Smiles. "Now you do."

The date ends in the parking lot across the street. No offer for one final drink in a dark booth at a special bar.

"Can we do this again?" he says.

"Of course."

"Even with my conversational faux pas."

"No more apologies."

"Didn't want to assume," he says.

He comes in for a harmless friend hug. She goes up on her toes to make it more even. He's a shade over six feet by her keen sense of algebra.

"I'll text you a few openings," says Sheen. "See if we can come up with a plan."

"Deal," says Flynn.

Thinking, if she didn't have to pick up Wyatt, that date number two could commence right now.

If he wanted.

CHAPTER 19

Unannounced visitors aren't rare, but they are rarely this persistent.

"Who is she again?" says Flynn.

Marge Olson, the station's receptionist, is a loyal palace guard who could manage the Wall of Westeros all on her own. "Her name is Annie Baker. A writer."

"And?" says Flynn.

"I told her you were busy. And I told her the best thing is to email you, but she says it's important and she'll keep it to five minutes."

"Why do these people not take a hint?" says Flynn.

"I don't know."

"How long has she been waiting?"

"About forty-five minutes."

"Small conference room," says Flynn. "I'll be there in two. Don't offer her water or coffee."

"Are they getting anywhere with the Klines?" says Olson.

"Not that we can tell."

Flynn spent most of the morning pestering Denver Public Schools for the school video footage and trying to find coworkers or neighbors who will talk about Patrick and Victoria Kline.

"So scary," says Olson. "Those poor children."

"Heartbreaking," says Flynn.

◆ ◆ ◆

Flynn googles "Annie Baker writer."

Her site is clean, bright, simple.

Connect goes to a simple form and offers a LinkedIn icon. No X. No TikTok. The About bio is brief. It shows a bachelor's degree in journalism and a master's degree in clinical psychology, both from CU Boulder. Annie Baker likes reading time and "potent, spicy" chai tea too.

The Books page is empty. "TBA" are the only three letters. Articles shows a lengthy list of credits including stories for the respectable Chalkbeat website, an article about incarceration and recidivism rates for *The Colorado Sun*, and a piece about a controversial new state park for *High Country News*.

◆ ◆ ◆

In person, Annie Baker barely resembles her photo.

"I really need to update that website," says Baker. Two chairs have been pulled back to make room for her wheelchair, a sleek model that looks built for racing. "That's sort of an internet billboard, you know? But, yeah, darker hair back then, and I bet you hate it as much as I do, but don't you find it silly how looks open doors? But you can't fight male-dominated City Hall or the way the world works."

Annie Baker could be forty. At the oldest. She has straight dirty-blond hair to her shoulders. Her eyes are dark and intense behind black-framed cat's-eye glasses. Modest silver-and-turquoise teardrop earrings. She is trim, but it's impossible to judge her height. Plain beige top with short sleeves. She doesn't say a word about having to wait, pulls out a notebook binder, and opens the recording app on her phone, shoves it across the table so it's halfway between them.

Flynn gets the feeling she's the one who has been summoned to a meeting.

"I'll make it quick," says Baker. She cocks her head as if she knows her face has a good side.

"Rail Yard Ale," says Flynn.

"What?"

"The sticker on the back of your binder."

Flynn hates herself for making small talk.

"I know," says Baker. "I collect cool logos. Love the drawing of the two locomotives. Early days of the Wynkoop, from what I'm told. Hard to believe a sitting US senator once owned a joint that slung beer."

"He was mayor first, then governor," says Flynn.

"I guess you never know," says Baker.

"Yeah," says Flynn. "But if you're thinking you'll be taking notes—"

"Look," says Baker. "I know you have your hands full."

"More than."

"I was told five minutes."

"Right."

"I'm proposing a true crime book—blow by blow, minute by minute, of the entire takedown of PDQ. With accompanying podcast. I have a friend who might make an offer on the movie rights—we'll split it fifty-fifty. All you have to do is answer my questions. I'll write everything. I'm thinking the tone leans a touch academic and takes this all seriously, but we will go in-depth on each of his three killings, and we won't flinch when it gets into the details of the murders. In other words, I think highly readable but smart enough that we get invited on the lecture circuit too. As good as *American Predator* or *I'll Be Gone in the Dark*. I get access to all your notes and materials and complete access to all the exchanges with Harry Kugel. We show the importance of the media—that's the thread running through the whole book. A not-so-subtle celebration of reporters."

"I am sorry to rain on your parade," says Flynn. "But no thanks."

"Because you already have something in the works."

"No."

"Have you declined other proposals?"

"I talked to reporters immediately after he got caught," says Flynn. And turned down a dozen true crime podcasts. "But I really don't see the value in committing so much of my time to writing it all up and putting it in a new package."

"You know that people gobble this fodder up like mashed potatoes at Thanksgiving dinner? If this goes well, maybe you've got a career as an author. Or coauthor."

"And we don't really know each other. This would take a lot of work to pull together and do it well."

"We can try one chapter," says Baker. "One chapter. See if we *connect*. Writing style, workflow, the way we organize a story. Give me two hours a week and I'll handle the rest. I know how it starts—with you coming home not knowing that Harry Kugel is sitting in Wyatt's bedroom closet. And then we back up, and I can see at least one chapter where we do a thorough psychological evaluation of Harry Kugel too. You know, kind of re-creating the official court analysis that found him capable of standing trial. I've got the book outlined if you'd like to see it. And believe me, I'm a collaborator to my core."

"Again. No. And no thank you. I'm trying to put this all behind me."

And so far unsuccessfully.

It's impossible to imagine adding any additional load to her current burden.

"I'm sure. And now you've got this creepy murder of a rich White family, and those always suck up all the oxygen, don't they?"

"Unfortunately, one hundred percent of the time."

"Doesn't seem fair, does it?"

Baker takes off her glasses and sets them on the table with a gentle touch.

"What?" says Flynn.

"I mean, there are other murders going on—most likely, anyway, right?"

"No single newspaper or television news-gathering outfit can cover it all," says Flynn. It occurs to her to be mindful that Annie Baker might have come here with a ruse to get in to see her and is recording on a hidden device for some crazy reason. "But I've long thought about the fact that, if every murder was treated with the same journalistic resources and journalistic pressure, the world would be a different place."

"*That's* what I was trying to say," says Baker. "Exactly. You get it."

"I do," says Flynn. "A whole book, in fact, could be written about the disparate treatment by the media of crime stories based on the income class of the victim. No newspapers jump off the rack with a headline that screams 'Low-Society Murder.'"

"Right?" says Baker. Her eyes are green, a color Flynn isn't sure she's ever seen up close, but her right iris is half brown. "Maybe we add a chapter that attempts to capture all the other murders that happened while PDQ was doing his thing."

"This isn't something that I'm interested in pursuing," says Flynn. "I mean, there's plenty of material out there."

"I want to put the readers right in *your* shoes, though. Blow by blow. Thought by thought. And I want it to read like it's all going down *right now*. We'll ping-pong back and forth with Harry Kugel's movements. And that means getting your perspective on every day and every big decision. For instance, your disbelief at first that it was really him."

"So you would need in-depth interviews with Harry too?"

"Believe me, I started with you because that's the bigger mountain to climb. I know, not likely."

"No," says Flynn.

"Have you seen him since the trial?" says Baker.

Flynn shakes her head.

"I never want to see him again."

CHAPTER 20

The room's not buying it.

The general consensus is *Where the heck exactly would this budget-strapped station get the resources?*

"It would be a statement to the community," says Flynn. "I mean, isn't the vast majority of our job to get our viewers to care? Doesn't it start right there?"

"I don't see how you stop all these other reporters from covering their beats for, what, a month? Two?" says Goodman. "How long?"

Flynn has been joined by Tamica Porter, who is on board with Flynn. The station's crime reporter, Chris Casey, won't commit until he knows which way the wind is blowing. He's twelve years younger than her and yet to show any true journalistic enterprise, in Flynn's humble but evidence-based opinion. The station's assistant news manager, clearly being groomed for the top job in a decade or so when Goodman retires, is Gabriella Vasquez. She's a product of South High School and CU Boulder and always leans into unusual ideas and offbeat ways of thinking about doing stories.

Casey's opinion means squat, but Flynn felt compelled to have him in the room because he's nurtured relationships with cops up and down the Front Range.

Goodman isn't a fan of disruptions. He squeezes a tight fist when it comes to spending extra money, but he's mindful of the station's middling ratings too.

Vasquez, in Flynn's view, holds the key.

"I'm not sure how long the project lasts," says Flynn. "But I want to go back to the beginning of the month, capture all the murders that we can identify, and document each one."

"Why go back?" says Vasquez. "Why not begin, say, on September first?"

"We've got to make these initial calls anyway," says Flynn, "to explain what we're looking to do, and I assume all open murder investigations will be readily available, so why not? In fact, we could launch the project on September first. Announce it then too. But start with a snapshot of August."

"Five full minutes every day?" says Goodman. "How are we going to cover other news?"

"I think I need four reporters," says Flynn. "Five would be great, but four will do. They don't have to be the same ones every day, but it would be good for some consistency. And for maybe a whole month, we don't do weather segments every twelve minutes and, for a few short weeks, maybe we don't treat the Denver Broncos like our city's collective mental health depended on their ability to move a football with head-bashing brute force while trying to avoid CTE."

"Maybe we roll it out next spring," says Goodman. "Take a few months and plan it out."

"No," says Flynn. "We've got the perfect reason right now. The Klines. They are sucking up serious media oxygen. You know it. I know it. The Klines are White. And wealthy. So now is the time to ask ourselves as an organization how we go about deciding which murders count, which murders get this kind of attention."

"Do we know it's murder?" says Goodman.

"You think they'll, what, *turn up*?"

"I'm open to miracles."

"It's a murder," says Vasquez. "And I'd like to think we would be in full alert mode if the same thing happened to any family of four, but I do think Flynn is onto some creative, out-of-the-box thinking here."

Vasquez is tall and slender with a cascade of bushy dark hair. She is fit and curvy with an unfussy style. Slacks and solid tops. She presents as straight-up straight, but she's in a relationship with a left-wing city councilwoman from Aurora. Vasquez is known in the newsroom for her ardent feminism, matched only by her belief that all reporters need to develop better sources in overlooked communities.

Her comment settles the room. And Goodman must weigh the political pros and cons of taking her on.

"I think it's bold," says Vasquez. "I think, in a way, we're holding a mirror to ourselves and asking about the whole process of what gets covered. And how. We're the ones holding the flashlight, and we can shine it where we want to. It might be a useful project to look at the bigger numbers in Denver. How many murders were there last year, and which cases drew the most attention. We probably know the answer, but we can't be afraid of a little accountability. And then own it."

"I mean, the Front Range is a helluva lot of jurisdictions," says Casey. "And a helluva lot of people."

"And we spend a lot of time here jumping at PR pitches and putting a helicopter in the sky when there's a long line of cars at a drive-through for a new hamburger franchise from California, and all we're doing is helping advertise a big national chain that will help maintain our high cholesterol."

Flynn glances around. Nobody looks to jump in.

"If we cover the opening of a new IKEA or Krispy Kreme, we should be covering the efforts of a husband and wife who struggle and save to put their first food truck out on the road, you know? What's the difference? We decide what the news is, and in this case we can decide to put more of an effort into the business when one person takes another person's *life*. It's a pretty big fucking deal, and the question is whether we've grown numb to the issue because we downplay it too. We announce the murder, or maybe it's a suspicious death, and move right on down the road to *next*. You know it. I know it."

"We could create a mini war room of sorts," says Vasquez. "We have a weather desk—why not a murder desk?"

"Sounds grim," says Goodman. "So what about all the open unsolved cases? There are cold cases going back decades."

"And the state's got a website that tracks all of those," says Flynn. "Again, I'm thinking we go back to August first or July first and take an inventory of all the homicides. Maybe we feature one or two of the overlooked and under-covered murders every day, and there's the possibility that the increased attention draws out valuable information."

Isn't it okay to harness the resources of her television station in a way that will help ease all the sleeplessness and unease from the two envelopes? Should she bring those in and pass them around? The idea that she should bring them to the cops gnaws at her hard, but the counter-thought is always one word.

Wyatt.

"Social media campaign too," says Tamica. "Some snazzy graphics. And you know it's not the end of the world if it doesn't catch on. We're saying we're not comfortable with how we deploy our resources."

"And what about the Klines?" says Goodman.

"What about them?" says Flynn. "And the murders in Franktown too."

"What have we got to move the needle?" says Goodman.

"I think that's precisely what Flynn means," says Vasquez. "We should be asking that question about all the unsolved cases."

"Exactly," says Flynn. "Right now, we're all one snarling pack of reporters putting a groove in the pavement to Shannon Way. It's a rut. And ruts dull the brain."

Twenty minutes later, Flynn is back in Goodman's office, steps from the reporters' cubicle farm.

"Oh, the irony," he says.

"I know," says Flynn. "Try not to hate me."

"How about if you stand on a desk out there and confess your sins?"

"It's a solid tip," says Flynn.

But it's not a tip about the Klines.

Unless, in fact, it is.

"So solid that you want to break your oh-so-fresh vows?"

Goodman is a good loser. He doesn't hold grudges. He reminds Flynn more than a bit of her father, who saw all the changes coming in journalism, particularly the insidious requirements to fuel the social media beast, and quietly stepped away.

"It's something I've been waiting for."

"But not something you can share with your news director?"

"It's an eyewitness. A *potential* eyewitness. Could be flaky."

Not an eyewitness to the Kline family misery.

Is she lying?

Yes.

"You'll take Tamica?"

"The deal is no camera at this stage. I'm going to see what they're willing to say."

"And the only way to get this information is in person."

"Afraid so."

"To Shannon Way."

"Yes."

"And why not bring Tamica and come up with another angle while you're out there?"

"I suppose," says Flynn.

She'll hate misleading Tamica more than she does deceiving Goodman. But that's not the only reason she wouldn't mind going alone. There are days when she feels as if the television news business is so bigfoot-heavy and cumbersome. All the gear. All the setup. For so little airtime. She envies the nimble tools of the quaint print tribe.

Digital recorder (maybe) weighing in at six ounces. Notepad. Laptop. And the end result is a long article with depth and nuance. It must be nirvana to flit from story to story with all the burden of a hummingbird.

"Make it so," says Goodman. "And Flynn?"

"Yes?"

"I was only playing devil's advocate, you know? About your idea."

"I get it," says Flynn. "I do."

CHAPTER 21

"I need to know what this is about."

"Can we start with your name?" says Flynn.

"No."

"How about where you live?"

"Not a chance."

"This is your son in the photograph?"

"Definitely."

"His bicycle?"

"Of course."

"And you live nearby?"

"A reasonable deduction."

"And you called me and had me drive all the way out here, but you won't let me talk to him?"

Flynn puts her at forty or forty-five. Chalky pallor. Yellow shorts. Loose white shirt. Spiky chestnut hair, frantic dark eyes behind black oversize square glasses with a heavy prescription. And a physique and round face with a chubby chin that reminds Flynn of Roseanne Barr circa *Roseanne*.

"I want to know what my son's photograph is doing on Facebook."

"I asked one of your neighbors to post it. He said there was a Facebook group for the neighborhood. That's who you contacted, right? Noah Gifford?"

"And then he told me it was for the *news*." She says it like a slur. "For Flynn Martin."

"And here I am."

The metal bench where they're sitting bakes in the sun. Two useless saplings on either side of the bench will offer a nick of shade in about twenty years. Four tennis courts are adjacent, but only the one closest to them is in use, given the temperatures. A teenager whacks neon-green projectiles spit out by an automatic launcher. The court is littered with balls, evenly split on both sides of the net.

"Why did you think you had a right to post my son's photograph. On social media?"

"I'm sorry," says Flynn. Why hadn't she asked for the woman's name before heading out? Flynn feels like a sucker. "It's about a simple question."

"Then ask me."

"Did you ask him why I might want to chat with him? If anything unusual happened the day they had the big news conference down here?"

"See that?" she says. "*Down* here. You think Denver is the center of the universe."

"No, ma'am, I don't. It's an expression."

"Don't you have murderers and gangs keeping you busy? Why do you need to talk to a kid on a bicycle?"

Flynn looks around. Tamica stands outside their news truck across the street, watching. Given the wide swath of asphalt in these side streets, she's too far away to hear the conversation but can no doubt read body language.

"Who is that?" says the woman.

"My photojournalist."

The woman says nothing, stares.

"She's quite talented," says Flynn.

"Is she the one who wants to talk to my son?"

"No, that's me. Tamica doesn't even know about this. Could we start over? Could I apologize but also tell you it's important?"

"She's a dark one."

"She's African American," says Flynn.

"You recording this?" says the woman.

"I am not."

"I know you got all these tricks. Your friend recording?"

"No," says Flynn. "She's not. We're not."

"Maybe my voice?"

"No."

"You got a hidden microphone?"

"Absolutely not."

"Why did you put my son's photograph on Facebook? You think he saw something that has to do with what happened to that poor family?"

"No," says Flynn. "Somebody asked him to deliver something to me, and I need to see if your son can describe the person who asked him to do the favor. And I don't need your son's name; I only need to know what he saw. Who he talked to."

"So you can put it in your story and tell a lie about it. Twist it around."

"You told me on the phone that you could help."

"I am. I am *helping* myself. To the opportunity to tell you to your face to never post a photo of someone you don't know. Especially *my* child."

"He looks fourteen. Fifteen?"

"Don't you people get it? *Jesus.*"

CHAPTER 22

"What the heck was that even all about?" says Tamica.

Flynn is back in the truck. Tamica is behind the wheel, but they haven't decided on what's next.

"A long shot."

"A long shot that didn't pay, if I'm not mistaken."

"Correct."

"And never going to?"

"That's my assumption, based on her hatred and distrust of the media."

"What's the angle on the Klines?"

"It's not related to them," says Flynn. "Well, maybe it is. Maybe it isn't."

Even PDQ didn't take two at once, let alone four.

The pattern is no pattern.

"'It's not related' doesn't make a lot of sense. We're three blocks from the scene."

"I know," says Flynn. "There's some weird shit going on, and I hope I can tell you about it soon."

"Gee, I've never heard those words before."

"I'm not happy about this either."

"Does Goodman know?"

"No," says Flynn. "And now that my main reason for coming here fizzled the fuck out, we need to find something else."

"And so she wouldn't agree to an interview?"

"I needed to talk to her son, but she wouldn't let me near him."

"Now what?" says Tamica.

"Let's let her watch us go," says Flynn. "Then we'll park and think."

Tamica makes a right, a left, and pulls into a solid patch of shade a block from Shannon Way. The truck's windows are up, the air-conditioning on noisy full throttle.

"What about coming up with an angle on the Klines?" says Tamica. "While we're here?"

"Sure," says Flynn. "I'm feeling so welcome and embraced."

"You have to keep an open spirit, an open heart."

Tamica is kidding. She's one of the least woo-woo people Flynn knows.

"Oh please," says Flynn. "Neighborhoods like these are designed to maximize the feeling that you live all alone and don't need to rely on anyone for squat. All these porches and not one person outside."

"It's a hundred and one flipping degrees."

"Still. And the more we sit inside our houses and cars and crank the AC, the hotter it gets outside because we're burning up the planet. Anyone see a losing cause here?"

"You sound like Wyatt."

Which makes Flynn think she should be sifting through school video footage for the spawn of PDQ or the spawn's puppet. *Wholeness and holiness are the same thing.* Who the hell is whole? Who the hell is only one thing?

"Neighborhood charm is why you moved to a condo way up in the sky in a guarded tower downtown?"

"I know I'm not a role model for community cordiality, and I don't need you or anyone spotlighting my failures as a human being. We'd be here all day."

In fact, the fewer elevator chitchats and awkward hallway encounters in her condo building, the better. Does she really want to get to know her neighbors? Would Axel Sheen provide additional protection or distract her so badly she wouldn't see the next envelope coming, though there better not be another fucking next envelope, and by the way, doesn't Axel Sheen sound like some kind of exotic, borderline poisonous drink? The name sounds so fussy and pretentious, but she really can't shake the idea of him. His lightness and humor.

"Maybe we should bring a lemonade stand with us for situations like this," says Tamica. "You know? 'Ice-cold lemonade, five cents! Oh, by the way, do you know who would have wanted to make the Klines disappear along with both their children?' You know, our own little effort to humanize the media. Remind them we're real people."

"Speaking of which," says Flynn. "Who is this?"

The man is coming for them. He crosses the wide empty street of hot-coal asphalt on an angle. Worn forest green baseball hat, a white Colorado Rockies T-shirt, yellow running shoes, no socks. Full beard, long oval face with deep-set eyes. Skinny.

He approaches on the driver's side. Tamica's window slides open.

"Hi," says Tamica.

"Hi," he says. "I'm sorry, I don't know your name."

"Tamica Porter."

He offers a handshake. Tamica takes it. "A pleasure," he says. "And you're Flynn Martin."

"That's right," says Flynn.

"I've been following you since, well, since."

Since the day I fucked up at a hostage situation that went horribly wrong. A day that is capable of turning me into a puddle of worthlessness if I spend more than a nanosecond thinking about the random nature of death or the fine young lady who was Debbie Ernst from Apple Valley, Minnesota, before the big fuckup. The alleged fuckup that led me to PDQ. Or PDQ to me.

"I thought you would like to know something."

"Sure," says Flynn. "Your name?"

"Peter Wright. I thought you should know—" He pulls out his phone. "You are the hot topic of conversation."

"What?" says Tamica.

"Scroll up," says Wright, handing over his device. "You're all over Nextdoor."

Martha Fleming: She's talking to this lady by Creekside Tennis Courts.

Holly Day: Off-camera.

Erin Nagy: It's gotta be the Kline business. I'll go out there and tell her to get lost.

Martha Fleming: By the looks of it, she's not making any headway.

Holly Day: Wrapping up now and heading south. Driving slow. By the way, I need a pet sitter for this coming weekend. Two cats. Our regular sitter is in Lisbon. Thanks.

Alan Kimble: Flynn Martin has parked over here near Shannon Way. She's waiting in her car for something, I guess. My daughter would love to take care of your cats, Holly, DM me.

"Jesus," says Tamica. "Thanks."

"I thought you'd like to know," says Wright. "It's a tight neighborhood," he adds. "Never a burglary, nothing."

"I can see why," says Flynn. Never a burglary, but only the occasional family that goes *poof* in the night. "So we're probably inspiring new posts as we speak. I mean, the fact that you're here talking to us. You're now part of the chatter?"

"Without question. Give it about thirty seconds," says Wright, "and I'll hit refresh if you want. But I'm the scourge at the HOA meetings who wants us all to do a better job at recycling, and I actually think we're morally obligated as a community to work with the town and build affordable housing, you know, give up an acre on one of our parks or something and get some diversity in here. Economic diversity, genuine diversity. It's suffocating, you know? The same-sameness."

Flynn opens her door, comes around in front of their truck, shakes Peter Wright's hand for the whole damn Shannon Way *Truman Show* world to see. And discuss.

"What do you do?" says Flynn.

"Software engineer."

"Family?" says Flynn.

"It's the law," says Wright. He's got an easy smile. "Two point four kids, et cetera. My wife teaches school."

"Where?"

A flash of concern crosses Wright's face. "I guess I didn't think this through."

"What do you mean?"

"Well, I wanted to come out and make you aware of the neighborhood chatter, but I guess I didn't think this would cross-pollinate, you know?"

"No," says Flynn. "I don't."

They are in a huddle by Tamica, who remains seated behind the wheel of their truck. Flynn glances around at the houses, wondering which curtains are being parted for a peek out from the dark, cool interiors.

"Shit," says Wright. "I'm a big believer in the news."

"And?" says Tamica.

"We'd be nowhere without you all, and I think we need to do more in schools to give our kids critical thinking skills, so they can tell when something's crap."

"But," says Flynn. "Where does your wife teach?"

"Willow Creek." He says it sheepishly. "I know, here I am Mr. Contradiction because I'm all about diversity but then my wife teaches at a private school that looks like it belongs in a remote village in Norway."

"We all have our reasons," says Flynn.

"And my wife's is safety," says Wright. "School shootings, you know? Plus we get a healthy discount on tuition."

"I understand," says Flynn. Should she consider private school for Wyatt? "No need to apologize."

"Well, thanks," says Wright. "And now I think I know what you're going to ask next."

"You probably do," says Flynn.

"Yes, I knew the Klines."

"And?"

"It's unfathomable," says Wright. "As everyone has already said."

"What does the chatter on Nextdoor say? Is there any working theory floating around that's bubbled to the top as the leading contender?"

"There are theories," says Wright. "All speculation."

"Stray question," says Tamica. "But has anyone said anything about a connection between the terrible thing that happened here with that double murder in Franktown?"

"It's all thin gruel," says Wright. "But, sure. You can find all sorts of trash trying to make a link. But there's one detail on the situation here that the cops haven't released."

"What's that?" says Flynn. "What are the cops not telling us?"

"There's another son."

"Excuse me?" says Flynn.

"Older. Adopted. Twenty-one or twenty-two. Jed."

"Jed?"

"Jedidiah, and I think his parents wanted him to use the full name."

"Jesus," says Tamica. "So Old Testament. Jedidiah. Zachary. Adina."

"Wait," says Flynn. "Is Willow Creek religious?"

"Not officially," says Wright.

"Jedidiah went there too?"

"Yes."

"Graduated?"

"I'm not sure. He moved to Colorado Springs or Pueblo, but again that's rumor mill fodder. He wanted to get out of there."

"Your wife's name?"

"You'll leave her out of this?"

"Of course."

"Kim."

"Teaches high school?"

"Middle school. But she remembers him."

"What was Jedidiah like?"

Wright takes a moment. "Let's say he was not a happy camper."

"Okay," says Tamica. "Where was Jedidiah when the rest of the family was allegedly driving to the airport or, at least, supposed to be heading there?"

"That's the question," says Wright. "That's exactly the question."

CHAPTER 23

"Well," says Tamica. "I know where we're going."

"Beeline, please," says Flynn.

Flynn imagines Nextdoor's heartfelt group grope buzz fest narration as they depart.

In a nutshell:

And don't come back, you media asswipes.

At the same time, Flynn wonders if she could call a meeting of the entire Shannon Way neighborhood and all those who might have been watching the streets on the day of the first big news conference about the Klines, ask if anyone recalls seeing an adult approaching a kid on a bicycle, asking for a favor. Flynn's fantasy neighborhood meeting is the stuff of fairy dust and talking bedazzled unicorns. Despite Peter Wright's kindness, there's no way anyone would show up, let alone assist a member of the media.

Goodman, over the phone, is a quick study.

"Good get," he says.

The highest praise.

He tells Flynn she's on at the top of the four o'clock show and leaves the choice of location to them, whether the school or sheriff's HQ.

"You do have this confirmed that he attended the school?" says Goodman.

"This came from the husband of one of the teachers."

"And Jed—*Jedidiah*—lives where now?"

"The husband thought Colorado Springs or Pueblo. Can you have Chris Casey check to see if he's had any, you know, encounters with the law?"

"Sure. You talked to the teacher?"

"Not yet."

"Only the husband."

"Correct."

"I assume the whole school is chatting up a storm."

"That's the picture I'm getting," says Flynn.

Willow Creek Country Day School asks her to leave a voicemail. The recording promises to return all calls within twenty-four hours. On her phone, Flynn finds the name of the headmaster from the school directory. Jane Emmitt. Short gray hair, forced smile, round tortoiseshell frames. And a cross on a gold necklace.

Flynn calls Tim Norton, the media relations guy for the Colorado Coalition of Private and Independent Schools. She reminds him of the helpful story she put together about a liberal state senator's legislative proposal to require all private schools to gain accreditation through one of the recognized private agencies. The legislation died a quick death, which thrilled the coalition. Sometimes the media is the cheapest form of lobbying available.

"There's only one reason you're reminding me of your credit score with us," says Norton.

Flynn explains what she's after.

"You didn't get her number from me," says Norton.

"No," says Flynn. "I think it's just floating around out there by now, right?"

Jane Emmitt is slow to answer.

"How did you get my cell?" she says.

"I'm not sure," says Flynn. "But we do keep group notes we share, including key contacts. It was in there."

Tamica rolls her eyes at the lie.

"What can I do for you?"

Flynn takes her time. Every ounce of her reporter essence wants to jump to the chase, but Flynn is building rapport. Asks how she is doing. Asks how the school is doing.

"We are hoping there's a reasonable explanation," says Emmitt.

"I know," says Flynn. "It's important to hold out hope."

What? The Klines decided that instead of taking the kids to Disney World, they would drive to Canada, find a remote log cabin at the end of a dusty back road, and turn off all their devices and connection with the outside world?

"I'm sure you've had lots of strange questions," says Flynn.

Emmitt is on speaker so Tamica can listen in. There are times that Tamica hears things or thinks of things that Flynn does not.

"More than a few," says Emmitt.

"Was there an older adopted brother in the Kline family?"

Emmitt's pause is confirmation enough. "Yes," she says.

"Jedidiah?"

"Yes."

"And he attended Willow Creek as well?"

"Yes."

"Did he graduate?"

"As a matter of fact, no." There's a new touch of coolness to Emmitt's tone. "I'm not sure how much more I can tell you."

"Did he attend four years of high school?"

"I'd have to check the records, but basically he was here—yes."

"Do you remember his last year?"

"It's been four years," says Emmitt.

"But he didn't have the credits or grades to receive a diploma."

"I do believe that's a private matter," says Emmitt.

"Can you tell me what kind of student he was?"

"I'm not talking about that today."

Flynn hears the sound of the metaphorical door closing. Guardedness crawls into the conversation, settles between them like a wary dog.

"Do you know where he lives now?"

"No."

"Have you seen him—I don't know, around? Picking up his siblings? Anything?"

"No," says Emmitt. "And not surprised about that in the least."

Flynn pulls up Sheriff Moore on her cell.

"Wait," says Tamica. "Before you ask him about Jedidiah."

"What?" says Flynn.

They are backed up, trying to get from East Orchard Avenue to the highway for the brief ride to Arapahoe Road.

"Ask him whether the Klines were known to the sheriff too. If they'd visited the home for any reason prior."

"I see what you're thinking," says Flynn.

"Right?" says Tamica.

Flynn's phone chirps.

Caller ID: Nancy Lang.

Flynn takes it off speaker, answers, brings it to her ear, gives Tamica a *sorry* grimace.

"We can make the video available," says Lang. "Our head of security wants to know what you're looking for, and our head of human resources wouldn't mind knowing if there's a bad apple on our sub list. It's not exactly protocol and we would often charge for the extra work required to pull the material, but with the newer schools and systems, it's not all that complicated."

"Thank you," says Flynn. "I mean, thank you very much."

There has *got* to be a moment when she'll spot the swamp creature who put the envelope in Wyatt's things.

"But we would like to know the gist of the story," says Lang.

"Didn't the principal tell you?" says Flynn, not wanting to reiterate the envelope detail in front of Tamica.

Not wanting to worry her.

Again.

"We haven't discussed this with her," says Lang. "This is a corporate decision."

"I will be glad to show you when we meet," says Flynn. At least, the vague generalities of the search. "How soon can I access the material?"

"The videos are saved at the school," says Lang. "We could start tomorrow."

Flynn imagines a team of school and district staff watching over her shoulder as she scans the footage, tracing Wyatt's movements throughout the day. She doesn't want that or need that, but maybe they'll all get bored. She can fight that issue when the time comes.

"I might have to do this off hours," says Flynn. "And I assume it's, what's the right word? Voluminous?"

"It's a big school," says Lang.

"Could we meet early? Seven a.m.?"

She could squeeze in an hour of screening, maybe, before heading to the station. How long will it take? What will she say to Wyatt?

Nailing down Wyatt's schedule, and knowing his likely movements between classrooms and activities, should reduce the number of feeds to review. *Maybe.* Again, thinks Flynn, better to negotiate the process once she gets the ball rolling.

Lang agrees to meet her at the school in the morning. Flynn thanks her, reminds herself to bring doughnuts or bagels, and hangs up.

"Cryptic," says Tamica.

"Sorry," says Flynn.

"What's *voluminous*?"

"Sorry again."

"I hate hearing that word."

"I hate hearing it out of my own fucking mouth."

"Why do I get the feeling I'm going to know about this sooner or later?"

Flynn takes a deep breath. It wouldn't hurt to lose her lone soldier status.

"Sooner," says Flynn.

"*Now* is sooner."

Flynn lays it out.

Envelope #1.

Envelope #2.

Her theories on the school and wanting to see the footage.

The notes and how much they read exactly like PDQ.

Bicycle Boy. Bicycle Boy's mom.

What's behind the Murder Desk concept.

Cañon City too.

"You met with that motherfucker?" says Tamica. Squeaky voice, disbelieving. Shaking her head.

"Had to."

"You got stones."

"Didn't feel like a choice."

"And you thought he'd tell you something?"

"It doesn't sound logical, does it?"

"Holy hell, Flynn, you must feel like you're tied in knots."

"Some new ones that even the Boy Scouts don't know."

"Cops," says Tamica. "Cops, cops, cops."

"No," says Flynn. "That photo of Wyatt. I'm being watched. Wyatt's being watched."

"You'll have a cop escort for Wyatt until they catch this asswipe bullshit imitator, and maybe it's someone playing with you. Maybe they used the text from the court transcript as a model, maybe they asked ChatGPT to generate threatening notes in the style of PD fucking Q."

"Doesn't feel that way. Again, the photo."

"So your plan is to analyze recent unsolved murders and try to find the link and track down our bad boy, when the asswipe has already said the pattern is no pattern? Do you hear yourself? What kind of crime scene lab and what army of technicians did you assemble without my knowing it?"

"I hear how it sounds."

"Or what's your other plan, grilling Harry Kugel until he comes clean? Under what threat or leverage will you get him to spit out anything if he is somehow behind this and, by the way, did you ever stop and think how much sheer fucking pleasure you gave him by showing up? He was salivating the whole time. He'll replay every delicious moment in his rotten head for years to come."

"I had to go. But I hear how it sounds."

"*Sounds?*" says Tamica. "How are the functioning parts of your brain coming up with the *good idea* blessing on this puppy? Do the math."

"You're not wrong."

"I fucking *hate* that expression. A bass-ackwards passive-aggressive way of saying what you mean."

"Okay, you're right."

"Cops," says Tamica. "Your Lone Ranger thing last time around?"

"Yeah," says Flynn. "I know. Give me a day to do some thinking."

"Cops," says Tamica.

"Day or two. Or three."

CHAPTER 24

"Would you care to join us on the live shot at four?" says Flynn, her head spinning from Tamica's tongue-lashing. Vituperation.

"I'll pass," says Sheriff Moore.

"Are you at the office?"

"No."

"We're heading there now. We'll be outside. The backdrop shot, you know. Flags waving, that sort of thing."

"Help yourself. Check in with comms."

"As always," says Flynn. "Have you found Jedidiah Kline?"

Moore's pause is more protracted than headmaster Jane Emmitt's. It comes with a sigh. "No comment," he says.

"Is there a reason you didn't mention that you were searching for him?"

"We run the investigations the best way we know how," says Moore.

"Is he a suspect?"

"No."

"Is he a person of interest?"

"We are keen on talking with him, yes."

"Do you know the status of the relationship between Jedidiah and his parents?"

"Part of the investigation."

Flynn jots notes on an old-school newspaper reporter's pad, the kind that fits in the back pocket of a print journalist's blue jeans or tucked inside a suit jacket.

"When did you learn that there was an adopted son?"

"I don't recall precisely, but it wasn't long after we got inside the residence."

"Are there other adopted children?"

"Not to our knowledge."

Flynn works hard to cordon off the envelopes and PDQ in separate spaces in her head, but it's really hard to think of all the questions she should be asking Sheriff Moore about Jedidiah Kline. And what if they are connected?

"Do you know his whereabouts on the night in question, at four a.m. on that Monday morning?"

"The investigation is ongoing," says Moore. "As you know."

"Are there any other new details or updates you'd care to share for the newscast?" Flynn squints to get the time off her phone. "In forty-one minutes?"

"No," says Moore.

"How do we find out when you've managed to locate Jedidiah Kline?"

"Don't forget," says Moore, not answering the question. "It's possible there's nothing to this."

"One more thing," says Flynn. "Franktown."

"That's Douglas County."

"I know—but you must have compared notes."

"The two cases are one hundred percent unrelated. There's no *there* there."

Tamica maneuvers the truck up on the highway, where traffic is hauling ass at the approximate speed of a three-year-old on his first tricycle.

"Cops," says Tamica.

"Don't start again," says Flynn. "I need time to process."

"You're not sorry you told me."

"No. I think I needed a check."

"A reality check."

"Something like that."

"Jedidiah Kline," says Tamica. "I mean, that doesn't even sound right. Kline is a Jewish name, a variation on K-l-e-i-n. And Jedidiah sounds like a Bible-thumper from a tent revival."

"Maybe Dad converted," says Flynn. "And there are definite Christian vibes at the private school too."

"Something fishy," says Tamica. "As big as a whale."

CHAPTER 25

"I can see it in your eyes."

He says nothing because he can't.

"I'm good at reading people and I'm fairly certain of this, but nod if you're afraid."

He nods. It's not much, but it's there.

"You're afraid this is the end?"

Nods again.

"You'd probably like to know why."

Nods again.

His wrists are bound tight. Maybe too tight?

"That's cyanosis, by the way. 'Cyan' like blue. And '-osis' like neurosis or narcosis—'condition of.' In this case, condition of blue. You're not getting enough oxygen in your bloodstream. Cyanosis."

Nods again.

"Most noticeable on your palms, of course, because the skin is lighter than the backs of your hands because, well, the obvious."

Nods again.

"I know, who cares? Right? In this situation? You want an explanation."

Nods again, this time eyes wide.

"I'm afraid that's not possible. Lots of people die and there is no reason at all, no matter what the priests say. No matter what any church person says or claims to say that they understand. There is no reason. Why should death be explainable when life is not?"

He says nothing because he can't.

"Do you think understanding will help?"

He shrugs.

"Probably not. I agree. Probably not. Do you know Flynn Martin?"

He nods.

"Right. Everyone knows Flynn Martin. I mean, if you're paying attention."

He cries. Both eyes. Twin silver trails trek to mid-cheek over spectacular matching malar bones. The right tear is faster, only by a moment. A near photo finish before they both stop, abruptly.

Out of gas.

"The fluid is there to clean the eye, sure, but why is *that* how we show sorrow? Regret? You ever think about that?"

He shrugs.

"No?"

Shrugs again.

"You remember, now? Years ago? Talking to Flynn Martin?"

He nods.

"I know—long time ago. You got what you wanted out of it, right? All well and good and you move on down the road, even though you switched jobs. You thought time would take care of business, for you. Am I right?"

Headshake.

"No?"

Headshake.

"But you know what you did."

Headshake.

"You know what happened, though? The consequences?"

Headshake.

"I'm not going to hurt you."

It's always a good idea to give them hope. And when it's time, the actual hurt, in fact, will be brief.

"And I can tell you're still wondering. 'Why me, why me, why me, why me?' Am I right?"

Nods.

"Don't think less of me when I tell you this."

Nods.

"Because you'll wonder even more. At least I would if I were in your shoes."

Eyes widen. Head shakes.

Confusion.

"I know. It probably feels extra weird."

Nods.

"This feels what, *random*?"

Nods.

"Because you've lived a good life."

Nods.

"You're not the message. You're the messenger."

Head shakes.

"There's a big difference."

CHAPTER 26

Wyatt wants the whole story, not generalities.

"It's now officially past your bedtime," says Flynn. "And I guarantee you that I will tell you one hundred percent of what I find *if*—and it's a big *if*—I find anything at all. But somebody used you to get a message to me."

"A scary message," says Wyatt. It's not a question. "In that envelope I brought home."

"Yes."

"What did it say?"

"That's between me and the person. The writer."

"Some troll?"

"Similar."

"Why wouldn't they leave a comment on Facebook or X?"

"They went out of their way, that's for sure."

"And you think somebody slipped it into my backpack? And now I have to wake up early, go to school early, figure out how I'm going to kill time until school starts. I hate it."

Wyatt is freshly showered. His long hair is damp. He is severely disturbed by the change in schedule. His pout doesn't hide that fact.

"It might be nothing," says Flynn, echoing Sheriff Moore's caution. She knows the envelope is not nothing as much as Sheriff Moore knows Jedidiah Kline is key. "We have to see what we see and go from there."

"What am I going to do for an hour and a half before school? An hour *and a half*, Mom."

"Read. Play a game on your phone. Bring your homework and double-check it."

"Bleh," says Wyatt. "How about Gramps picks me up? So I can sleep?"

"We ask him enough already."

"I can take the bus—this once?"

She's already banned him riding the bus. Too public. Too open. Too vulnerable. Too everything.

"No," says Flynn. "What I need is cooperation. And the longer you're awake now and complain, the less sleep you get."

"It's not the total hours, it's that morning is when you're deep asleep."

"I know you're not after logic here," says Flynn. "But right now logic is on the run. Oh, and I forgot to mention that we're picking up bagels, so we have to leave fifteen minutes earlier than I said—like five forty-five wheels up. Okay?"

On the ten o'clock show, her story remains at the top of the rundown. But now it's Chris Casey standing out by the flags at Arapahoe County Sheriff's headquarters repeating live what she had revealed six hours earlier. There are no further sound bites from the school or cops to verify the existence of Jedidiah Kline, only the cold hard facts.

Casey emphasizes that the details were confirmed by Sheriff Moore in a phone call. There's no mention of Flynn Martin's "get" of this juicy and game-changing tidbit, which seems petty and self-serving. Casey's dry delivery is as unexcited and monotone as HAL chatting with Dave Bowman as he declines all requests to open the pod bay doors.

Flynn needs her open pod bay door to escape the steady looping in her brain between Bicycle Boy, Jedidiah Kline, the school videos, and the latest envelope claiming credit for other murders but not the David Copperfield trick or whatever it is with the Kline family foursome's strange disappearance.

And Tamica's rant that Flynn take everything to the cops.

Flynn treats herself to one glass of wine, stays up through Stephen Colbert's monologue, takes half a sleeping pill, and goes to bed determined only to think about Axel Sheen, rainbows, and a poem she'd write if she were someone who knew how to express herself by other means than asking questions. Her determination works about as well as a starving feral cat left alone with an open can of tuna.

◆ ◆ ◆

The morning departure is smooth. Wyatt has opted for compliance because it's a lost cause. Or maybe he's still asleep. He doesn't say much between the parking garage and bagel shop, says even less between the bagel shop and school.

Flynn's gifts are well received by the only three people at the school—media relations princess Nancy Lang, school principal Audrey Ballard, and the district's chief of security.

Art Bay is an ex-cop. Black and Hispanic? Flynn scolds herself for never having asked about his heritage. Bay knew her ex, briefly, at DPD. Bay is also a former Green Beret, and anyone who gets him talking for more than thirty seconds will find that out. Short hair, wide face with rough and worn skin, and a large stomach he wears proudly, as if it was something he'd earned for his sacrifices in the military. Bay is proud of his efforts to modernize security systems across the district's two hundred schools.

The trio escorts Flynn to a small office normally dedicated to a school nurse. Ballard explains how schools share nurses. Today, the space is vacant. A curved, oversize monitor sits on a desk. Art Bay explains that they have taken Wyatt's schedule and matched it with the classroom, hallway, lunchroom, gym, and playgrounds. The only unsurveilled location is the locker room, and Wyatt would normally leave his things in his main hallway locker before heading to the gym to change.

"Have you scanned this at all?" says Flynn.

"Yes," says Bay. "Twice."

"And?"

"And we see nothing," says Lang, who has leaned into the corporate wardrobe with a dark blue pencil skirt and white button-up blouse. "Well, nothing that jumps out at us."

"I hope this isn't a wild-goose chase," says Flynn.

"It's okay," says Bay. "We have a hunch you have a good reason. So you think they'll find Jedidiah Kline?"

"Seems they always manage to find who they're looking for, one way or another," says Flynn. "Were there any moments in all this footage that seemed, I don't know, of interest?"

"Not really," says Ballard, "but we're all keen to see if you see more than we do."

Flynn begins with the hallway feeds. For some reason, in her mind's eye, she has imagined the moment when Wyatt received the envelope as some sort of reverse-pickpocket situation. In her mind, the anti-thief would need a crowd to pull off his deed and, perhaps, accidentally-on-purpose bump into Wyatt. But adults, it turns out, stay out of the way when it comes to the masses who move this way and that in the great classroom-reshuffling dance. She picks up Wyatt early on during his first walk into school, to science. Arrival time is a calm affair compared to the general bodychecking chaos that occurs once all the kids are on campus and the first class ends.

"Officially, our passing periods are six minutes," says Ballard, answering a question nobody asked. "But it's a big building, so there's a minute of grace before being marked tardy."

Wyatt doesn't dawdle. He's on a mission. He chats with Jeremy. He chats with a girl Flynn does not know. The footage is sharp and in color. She's Hispanic and ultra cute. They don't touch, but Flynn gets the impression they know each other well, especially when she waves goodbye. It's possible Wyatt's preteen puppy love life is better than her adult monastic one.

Having gone to all this work, Flynn feels entitled to spot Envelope Dude somewhere in these feeds. Having been manipulated and scorned by Bicycle Boy's antimedia mother, she thinks it makes sense that cold, hard facts-of-life footage will cough up a lead.

But where?

And when?

She watches Wyatt through English and art and social studies.

No adult approaches Wyatt.

Nothing is out of place.

No surprise visitors, exchanges.

At lunch, Wyatt sits in the distance. It looks as if Hispanic Girl is by his side, but Flynn can't be sure. Then it's off to gym class, and Flynn recalls that awful combination from her own days of moving up through the Denver Public Schools, when exercise immediately followed lunch and she wanted to hurl. Part of it had to do with the stinky, dank locker rooms and the unforgiving concrete playground. There wasn't much she liked about physical education, but running around after eating never made sense. Shouldn't there be a law about that?

The classroom footage itself doesn't take long to spin through. Once Wyatt is seated, it's easy to fast-forward. There are a few group activities here and there, but it's early in the school year and the kids are still getting to know each other. Public schools start the school year earlier and earlier in August, while private schools like Willow Creek Country Day take the old-fashioned approach of waiting until after Labor Day. Is it possible that if the Klines had been a public school family, they wouldn't have been jetting off to Florida on that morning and wouldn't have encountered whatever trouble they'd found? Do such random "what if" questions ever pay dividends?

◆ ◆ ◆

Wyatt clearly has his strong peer group of pals, both girls and boys, and he appears to be a leader and overall good student who pays attention.

All the surveillance footage comes with audio, too, because the school is so spanking new. It's uplifting to hear her son's voice in such an earnest, engaged manner.

"When he goes to the gym, let's say, does anyone have access to his locker?"

"No," says Ballard. "I mean, we have the codes here in the office. We keep the master list of lock combinations to every individual locker. But unless Wyatt gave out his combination to a friend, and we discourage that, nobody can walk up and get inside."

"Have you looked at the hallway footage while he was at gym?"

It takes a minute, but Bay goes through a series of controls on the security system's dashboard, dials in the day and time, and lets them all watch the gleaming empty hallway. Bay points to Wyatt's locker, third closest to the camera on the south side of the hall.

Bay fast-forwards. The scene is static for the most part, save for the occasional adult and a woman guiding one of those walk-behind machines that scrub and buff industrial floors. The machine, in fact, stops. It briefly blocks the view of Wyatt's locker. The woman crouches behind her machine long enough to bend over and pick up something. She stands, studies her find, and when Bay zooms in, she's holding a two-inch nail between her index finger and thumb. She pockets it, resumes her position, and keeps walking.

"Who is that?" says Flynn.

She's medium height, trim. She's White. She wears brown overalls and heavy black boots. Her hair is pulled back. Big gold loop earrings that hardly look OSHA compliant.

"We can get her name," says Ballard. "We have a new cleaning company this year."

"Custodians were always my favorite people," says Flynn. "So friendly, right? The only ones in school who didn't give you homework."

"We're an enterprise school," says Ballard. "We get a budget, and the district keeps its hands out of our decisions. At least, *allegedly*. You know how that goes. One of the things we decided was to contract out the cleaning. Much cheaper."

"Can I watch that again?" says Flynn.

This time, she counts the number of seconds that the woman is out of sight. *Six.* Which seems like a long time to crouch down and pick up a nail.

"Bit strange the way she's holding it," says Flynn.

"Almost like it's for our benefit," says Bay.

"Is she here?" says Flynn.

"Not sure if today is a floor day or not," says Ballard. "I can check with the company. They all have to go through background checks to work in the school."

"Can you text or call me when you have the name?" says Flynn, feeling crushed by the fruitless search. Besides, Wyatt said the envelope was in his backpack, not a random thing he found in his locker. Right?

"I'm sure it's nothing," says Flynn.

CHAPTER 27

"You're in early," says Goodman.

"Because I know what's up," says Flynn.

"And who is missing."

"Bagel?" says Flynn. The school took only half her stash. "Sesame and onion the only options. All the everythings are gone."

"Sounds like an album title," says Goodman. "For some hippie-dippie Scottish folk act from the sixties. 'All the leaves are brown. All the everythings are gone.'"

"Hope you're entertaining yourself," says Flynn.

"To the max."

Goodman settles on an onion, helps himself to a mini container of artichoke Parmesan cream cheese.

"I mean, shouldn't the person who even *thought* of that combination be fired?" says Flynn.

"Don't knock it until you've tried it," says Goodman. "Ever had artichoke dip? Same thing. You some kind of fucking purist? You got some secret New York Jewish blood in you that I don't know about?"

"Speaking of Jewish," says Flynn.

"You're thinking what I'm thinking?"

"Tamica too."

"Yeah?"

"She was right on it."

"Maybe strife in the Kline family household over religion?" says Goodman.

"Kline doesn't have to be Jewish, though," says Flynn. "Thus New Hope Church."

"'Jedidiah Kline' still doesn't sound right, you know?"

"I don't know," says Flynn. "Kind of rolls off the tongue. Not as incompatible as artichoke and Parmesan."

"Delicious," says Goodman. He raises his twice-bitten bagel like a cocktail glass at happy hour, wipes a smudge of cream cheese off his lip with the back of his hand.

"Adopted doesn't mean trouble," says Flynn. "Come on now."

"Of course not," says Goodman. "But *missing* does. Cops have had a head start for days, and they still need our help?"

"I'm not jumping to conclusions," says Flynn.

"No, you're jumping to Colorado Springs."

"Really? Can't I stay put? Isn't my reward for yesterday to *not* have to sit in traffic for four hours?"

Goodman ignores her. "Jedidiah Kline was not a stranger to law enforcement. Chris Casey found an arrest for shoplifting and, get this, two arrests for assault."

"Simple? Aggravated?"

"Both simple, but still."

"Jesus," says Flynn. "And I reference that name ironically. Guess the Christian values didn't stick."

"We have the last known," says Goodman.

As in *address*. Which means trying to find Jedidiah Kline's ex-neighbors in a scuzzy, sad part of town. She flashes forward to herself talking to strangers on the street to see if anybody claims—key word "claims"—to know him. Know or knew. Flynn's still got a touch of PTSD from yesterday's bout with Bicycle Boy's antimedia mom and won't be surprised to hear a few more "Fuck offs" if she can't wriggle out of this waste of time. Still, it's the traffic slog that bugs her the most.

"I'm sure the stations in the Springs are all camped out at the address," says Flynn. "Can't we use their stuff, give them credit? Getting neighbors to offer deep insights on the character of people they didn't know? Really? That's my day?"

"I'm not looking for beige wallpaper and reasons to yawn," says Goodman. "I'm looking, at this point, for a great cup of coffee to go with the second half of this tasty bagel, and I'm looking for true enterprise reporting. That's why Flynn Martin is going to Colorado Springs. Nobody else brings that special essence."

"Butter my biscuits," says Flynn. "Keep talking."

"You get them all chasing you since yesterday. I expect nothing less today."

With Flynn's scoop about the hunt for Jedidiah Kline, all the local media are carrying the sheriff's plea for the public's help with his whereabouts. The gods of media buzz quickly elevated the Kline Family Vanishment to the elite level of sensational true crime cases worthy of the nation's time to gawk and ponder every incremental development as it happens.

The search for Jedidiah merited a mention on the national network news, but there's no guarantee that the saga will remain as a large or small blip on the national scanner that monitors developing situations no differently than a Doppler radar evaluating whether a low-pressure system has the potential to turn into a category 5 hurricane. One thing is for sure, however—the scanner gets really excited and especially happy if the victims are rich and White, White, White. The Klines tick a lot of boxes, but if Jedidiah Kline either is hard to catch or looks a wee bit crazy, it'll be *Case closed he did it* and the vast national audience will shrug and hope for something juicy with the next candidate for conspiracy theories, salacious details, and second-guessing.

"What about my idea of spending less time focusing on this rogue wave and more time on all the little waves that lap ashore with barely a mention?"

"Snelling," says Goodman.

"Ah, the surname that is the equivalent of unrocked boats and calm waters, speaking of surf. Which means nothing will change."

"We don't typically lurch around with massive staff reassignments without running it by the general manager," says Goodman.

"Who will make a decision after he smokes all the cigars in Havana," says Flynn. "Good Lord."

"In the meantime?" says Goodman.

CHAPTER 28

"Seventy-two minutes," says Tamica. "Door to door."

"Do not under any circumstances tell Goodman," says Flynn. "Pinkie-swear?"

"Do I look like a snitch for the man?"

"Good point," says Flynn.

"Now what?"

"I wish to hell I knew."

The address on the arrest records for Jedidiah Kline is an apartment building off Circle Drive on the north end of town. Half the building is two-story. The other half cantilevers out over a dozen parking spaces below, propped up by poles that don't look strong enough for the job. Four cars huddle there, getting blasted by the sun. Another half dozen parking spaces are empty. The building is cracked brown stucco. The apron around the building is cracked black asphalt. No grass, no trees. An orange banner is draped over the front. First month free. Above it, steel letters fastened to the stucco spell out The Oaks.

To the south, another apartment building of similar vintage. To the north, a heavily gated storage complex.

Flynn gets that distinct feeling of equal parts useless and pointless after ten minutes in a paint shaker. No cops. No randos. No fellow journalists to commiserate with. Her head is in Denver, wondering what she missed on the school videos. Her body feels heavy and resistant, as if it also preferred to stay in Denver and keep worrying.

"Spray and go?" says Tamica. "Camp by the front door and wait for someone to go out or come in?"

"Sounds *sooo* productive," says Flynn.

"Head to the cop shop? Get a sound bite about the hunt?" says Tamica. "Try the landlord?"

A website is listed below FIRST MONTH FREE: www.springs-apartments.com.

"Placing any bets?" says Flynn.

The link is basic, but a telephone number is prominent.

"You got this," says Tamica. "Clear your mind of unwelcome thoughts. You know, positive head, positive outcomes."

"Fuck off," says Flynn.

"Like that right there," says Tamica. "Totally unnecessary."

The man who answers the phone stops Flynn the second she identifies herself.

"You're the fifth today," he says. "All I can tell you is that he did live there for a grand total of four months, and he is no longer one of our tenants, and before you ask, no, I have no idea where he went, and nobody asked us for a reference. We manage twenty-five properties in Colorado Springs, around Fort Carson, and in Pueblo too. Same thing I told the cops."

"When were those four months?"

"Recently."

Flynn opens a file in her laptop, takes notes. The phone, on speaker, sits in a mount attached to the dashboard.

"Like last week recently or last month recently?"

"One of those."

"Are you month to month?"

"No. He had a six-month lease, if that's what you're asking."

"But you knew he had, what, moved out—in all the properties you manage?"

"Yes."

"And feel free to tell me off the record, but how did you know?"

"Off the record?"

"Yes."

"Because he wanted his security deposit back, like, that day. Which is not how we do it."

"You need time to inspect the unit and then your bookkeepers mail out a check?"

"Correct."

"Which could take a few weeks."

"And usually does."

"How long ago was this?"

"You've already asked that."

"How much are your security deposits?"

"One month's rent."

"In this case?"

"I'd have to look it up for that building, that unit. A thousand. Twelve hundred."

"Was he, I don't know, belligerent?"

"You could say that."

"Worse?"

"It was a concerning conversation."

"In person?"

"He came here, yes."

"Threatening?"

He pauses. "Very unhappy."

"Could you describe him?"

"I'd rather not."

"Any idea where he said he was going?"

"No."

"Did he list a place of employment on his application?" says Flynn. "Did you verify his work history?"

"Yes," he says.

"By the way, sir, what's your name? You've been helpful."

"I really don't think that's necessary," he says. "Happy to answer a few basic questions, but we are not the story."

"And I'll leave you out of it," says Flynn. "One hundred percent all the way out. I only wanted to know who I am talking to."

"Mike."

"Mike what?"

"Mike is fine."

"Mike, we're trying to gather a more complete picture of this young man, and of course he may have nothing to do with what happened to his family, but if you could see clear to passing along where he worked when he filled out the rental application, that would be very helpful."

"Sorry," says Mike. "The authorities might share that information with you. Not me. That's all I got."

The subtle sound of a phone connection going from live to dead is one that Flynn and Tamica are both keenly familiar with.

"Cop shop?" says Tamica. "Wait and watch here?"

"I suppose I should at least make the effort here," says Flynn.

"Camera? No camera? I'm happy to wait here and work my crossword, check Instagram, and take a nap."

"And miss all the fun?"

CHAPTER 29

Tamica films as Flynn walks across the parking lot, pulls open the heavy door, and steps inside. Flynn loathes being a character in her own news stories. She finds it repulsive. The story should tell itself. She even hates the de rigueur two-shots and reaction shots. See the journalist at work! See the journalist's sincerity! Her ability to empathize! Or the ever-popular *Here's a look of skepticism.*

The reporter hogging screen time is the ego element of her business, but that doesn't mean she has to love it. There are times, however, when it's almost necessary. Today? The pickings might be slim in the editing room. They need video wallpaper to fill the void. So Flynn plays along. Today she's wearing a white linen blouse with a Peter Pan collar for casual authority, tight gray slacks slightly cooler than her black ones, and walking shoes the color of fired brick that mean she's ready for any race that needs to be run.

The vestibule is tiny, cramped.

"Smells like a week-old cat box and Pine-Sol," says Tamica. She's got on her cute purple jeans and a dark blue oxford short-sleeved shirt like she works at an accounting firm. A simple silver necklace hugs her throat. She's got the overall figure of a mechanical pencil, and thus can easily leave two shirt buttons unbuttoned, but whatever pheromones she pumps out into the atmosphere, like the cloud of dust that follows Pig-Pen in the *Peanuts* comic strip, is an equal-opportunity scent for both boys and girls. And Tamica, from all that Flynn can gather, is open to all hits, even if she's currently got a steady girlfriend going.

The apartment directory is three-quarters full. KLINE is scrawled in black Sharpie on a white piece of paper shoved into the slot next to apartment 206. Tamica takes a shot of the name, props the outside door open with a large rock that is there for that purpose, and takes a distant shot of Flynn inside the vestibule playacting the bit where she's scanning the list of residents.

Flynn leans on the buzzer for 206, expecting nothing.

The inside door immediately buzzes alive. Flynn leans on the glass.

"Okay," says Flynn. "That was weird."

Inside, a long hallway. A faint odor of Indian food.

"Turmeric," says Tamica. "Cardamom. Better than the cat box. And I'm officially hungry now, boss lady friend of mine. We could go plan our next steps over a steaming-hot bowl of chicken tikka masala."

The stairs are marked halfway down the hall. Flynn leads.

"Who let us in?" says Tamica.

"Does it matter?"

"No."

"Are you rolling?"

"Sorry," says Tamica. "I forgot the plot."

"Never too late."

"I'll get everything from the landing to the top of the stairs, and then I'll go down the hall and you walk toward 206. Pretend like you're checking apartment numbers."

"Genius."

"My inner Hitchcock," says Tamica. "I'm an auteur, hope you know. Trapped in the body of a photojournalist."

"Well, I'm sure it's scintillating days like this that prevent you from taking Hollywood by storm."

"True," says Tamica. "They might never know what they're missing."

The Indian food aroma is more pungent upstairs. It's an alluring scent, but Flynn wonders if the residents love inhaling it all day.

Halfway down the hall, sunlight slices through the darkness where a door is propped open. Dust dances in the yellow-orange beam. A flatbed cart sits in the hallway, piled with boxes.

"Kill the Hitchcock stuff," says Flynn.

"Check," says Tamica.

A man walks out of the room. Overalls. Red headband. Black. "Miss Martin," he says.

"Hi," says Flynn.

"You want to see what we have to go through?"

"What do you mean?"

Chatting as if they have known each other for longer than two seconds.

"When someone decides to send a message," he says. "He tore the place apart."

"This is Jedidiah Kline's room?" says Flynn. "Was?"

"He took it all out on the room. His things too."

Tings. A touch of Jamaican. Or something Caribbean.

"When?" says Flynn. "And, by the way, what's your name?"

"Akeem."

"You're the . . ."

"Super," says Akeem. "Three buildings all together. Akeem Belafonte, and please don't start with the 'Day-O' business, okay?"

"Got it," says Flynn. "Did you know him?"

"Not *know.*"

Akeem's face glows with sweat. He takes off his headband, unfolds it, wipes his face, stuffs the cloth in his pocket. He is built like a power forward.

"You saw him around?"

"Some tenants are more memorable than others. Let me show you."

The room looks like a bomb went off. Dresser drawers, smashed. Table and chairs in pieces like cheap props for a movie fight scene. The apartment is a studio, so the "kitchen" is part of the whole main room.

Someone has taken a hammer or baseball bat to the stovetop and the oven door. The refrigerator is on its back, exhaling mold and rot.

"In here," says Akeem.

Tamica, rolling, leads the way into a tiny bathroom. Toilet seat, ripped off. Toilet tank, in pieces. Mirror, broken. Shards in the sink. Water covers the tile floor and has seeped out, explaining the squishy sensation from the carpet.

"I guess he wanted his money's worth for the damage deposit," says Flynn.

"And?" says Akeem, gesturing to the bathtub.

Clothes float in water. The tub is 100 percent full. Jeans, underwear, shirts.

"You don't know when?" says Tamica.

Flynn always appreciates Tamica jumping in. And she hates even thinking the thought, but maybe the Black-to-Black conversation automatically means more trust from the get-go.

Akeem shrugs. "Middle of last week. Wednesday."

"Night?" says Tamica.

"Daytime," says Akeem. "Neighbor heard him. Called police because of the noise, but he was gone by the time they arrived."

"Were there other reporters here earlier?" says Flynn, knowing the answer.

"Outside," says Akeem. "Two television news. One newspaper."

"Did you talk to them?"

"No. I sat in my truck and watched from a distance. Waited for them to leave."

"You didn't let them inside?"

"No."

"Did they talk to anyone?"

"Half the building is empty," says Akeem. "As you can tell, the building has seen better days. And nobody wants to, you know, get involved."

He flashes a big smile with a thousand perfect teeth.

"So why did you buzz us in? Show us in?"

"Because of the soucouyant."

"Excuse me?"

He says it slowly, again. It sounds French.

"In Jamaica," he says. "The soucouyant appears by day as a reclusive old woman. Sometimes, a man. But, mostly, a woman. At night, they strip off all their wrinkled skin and fly like a fireball across the dark sky. They can get in your house through cracks. Even keyholes. Anything. They suck human blood from arms and necks while you sleep. If they take enough blood and you die, they take your skin."

"Lovely," says Flynn. "I'm hoping that's a folktale."

Akeem shrugs. "Who is to say?"

"So, why me?"

"You took down the soucouyant. In Denver. My mother cheered you on. We both did. We know you. My mother listens to true crime podcasts. She wants you to write a book about the monster. PDQ. When I saw you outside, I wanted to give you something extra. To say thanks."

Is it possible Akeem would want to know Soucouyant II is fluttering about?

Probably not.

"Much appreciated," says Flynn. "You don't know if any of Jedidiah's fellow tenants knew where he was going?"

"No," says Akeem. "Very doubtful."

"Let me get a few more shots of the room," says Tamica, "without you two inside."

"She's telling us to scram," says Flynn.

"I heard her," says Akeem. Another big smile.

In the hall, Flynn looks at the top layer of boxes on the cart. They all have matching UPS labels. They are book size and untouched by the hurricane of destruction. Flynn picks one up. It's empty. So is the next. And the next.

The labels are all addressed to Jack Kline.

"Tamica?" says Flynn. "Could you take a tight shot right here?"

CHAPTER 30

The closest library is Pikes Peak East. Flynn gives directions while flipping back and forth to the browser on her phone, searching for Jack Kline. She never seems to find anything or have a calm mind about searches until she's sitting in front of her laptop or a good desktop. She'll never succumb to the belief that something that fits in her hand works as well as a big machine.

The library hums with patrons, the Wi-Fi is open, and they get one of the last computers where Tamica can work, fifty-five minutes at a stretch per library regulations.

"Video of you browsing the web?" says Tamica.

"Hell no," says Flynn. "You take the surface web, I'll take the dark. I've got Tor on my laptop."

"Look at you."

"My father taught me how to use it, if you must know."

"The coolest of all dads," says Tamica.

"Just a guy who wants to know every tool available to go where the bad boys hide."

"Does he know about the envelopes?"

"Not yet."

"Or the threat to his grandson?"

"I probably need to fix that," says Flynn.

"If your camera lady knows more than your father, a father who might be able to help you think this through, then yeah. Big time. And go to the cops."

"No thank you," says Flynn. "Not yet."

"You're hoping what? It's a prank?"

"I'm hoping to figure out what's going on first. What's really going on."

"By your lonesome."

"No," says Flynn. "The two of us."

"Oh, like the Beatles? The two of us? Don't forget the next line, 'riding nowhere.'"

"You were negative thirty when that song came out."

"More like T-minus twenty-five, the T standing for Tamica."

"Then how do you know that, you know, kind of lyrical detail?"

"God only knows," says Tamica. "And that's a Beach Boys song. But the brain works in mysterious ways."

◆ ◆ ◆

"Got him," says Tamica.

"That quick? I've barely opened Tor."

"On Facebook."

Flynn rolls her chair over to Tamica's cubicle. Jack Kline peers out from his profile pic like an underfed Harry Potter, wire-rim glasses and bangs dangling into his eyes. But Kline's pic looks more mug shot than Hollywood headshot. Acne scars. Sweaty. Even through the glasses, he's squinting.

"How do we know it's him?" says Flynn. "Is there anything under About or Friends?"

"Empty, empty," says Tamica. "But one of his posts is an image of the Black Sun business. And another with Thor's hammer. And a photo of someone's chest with Thor's hammer straight down the sternum."

"God of thunder."

"And symbol of White supremacy," says Tamica. "Robert Rundo and all that crap."

"But do we know it's our guy Jedidiah?"

Flynn watches as Tamica scrolls. She stops on a photo of Willow Creek. The picture looks like a screenshot from the school's website.

Caption: "Whiter than white, but woker than woke and softer than soft. Avoid at all costs unless you don't believe in your God-given heritage as the rightful heirs to this earth. Rise above."

"Holy fuck," says Tamica. "Is 'woker' a word?"

"Don't think so. When was his latest post?"

Tamica scrolls back to the top. "Twelve days ago. So a few days before the rest of the family was due to fly off for vacay."

The most recent entry is a photo of a blue plate with bacon, hash browns, scrambled eggs.

Caption: "Carl's Café, best cheap breakfast around."

"Food critic too," says Flynn. "I guess we'll need some footage of his social media."

"On it," says Tamica, heading to the truck for her gear.

Flynn's phone pings. Goodman. Who rarely calls to check on progress midday.

"How was traffic?"

"Like the River Styx turned to quicksand." Sotto voce.

"Really?" says Goodman. "Because when you left, Google Maps told me it would take seventy-five minutes."

"You want conjecture from an app or an actual eyewitness? Anyway, how's it going?"

"Why?"

"You rarely bug me midday. And let me step outside."

Flynn finds a trim patch of shade, doing her best to ignore the oven-like sensation of Colorado's great outdoors. Tamica heads back inside with her camera. Flynn jerks a thumb at the sky to indicate who is on the phone.

"We got a look around his apartment," says Flynn. "Pretty sure we're the only ones who got inside. He tore his place apart. It was a wreck."

"Good work."

"And it's Jack Kline we're after, not Jedidiah. From social media, it looks like Jack fell in with the far, far White-is-right crowd."

"Another productive day," says Goodman. "You got enough for what you need?"

"We were going to swing by the breakfast joint he touted online, see if they remember him coming in. Why do you sound so, what? Tentative?"

"Need you here."

"What is this, Ping-Pong?"

"I know."

"We're checking his social media, and I haven't even touched the dark web yet. And now that I've got it, I want to run 'Jack Kline' by the cops to get their reaction. I mean, they're probably on it, but—"

"Flynn."

"What?"

"The cops want to talk to you."

"What the hell for?"

"Something about a note."

Note? Did the chatter from the folks at Wyatt's school reach DPD? Did the neighborhood-watch crazies near Shannon Way call the authorities?

"Denver? Arapahoe County?"

"Denver. Something going on in Athmar Park."

"And you told them I was indisposed?"

"That you were seventy-five minutes away and would be returning soon."

"So now we jump whenever the cops need us?"

"This has to do with a murder."

Murder muttered like a nasty curse or something rare—which it should be.

"The Klines?"

"No. I asked. And they wouldn't tell me much. They want to speak to you."

"Why haven't they called me? I don't get it."

"Institutional sensitivity," says Goodman. "Protocols."

"Something I *did*?"

The last time she ran afoul of the DPD, her station had felt compelled to place her on suspension and make her feel like reporter non grata. That brief exile was nothing compared to the loss of innocent life that day, which sits in Flynn Martin's memory bank like high-def freeze-frames: 1.5 million of them. All the awful, dreadful feelings that went with each one too. She is intimately familiar with a thousand different places where she could have said something different or done something different and the outcome would have been all positive and upbeat.

But no.

Of course it was her time in professional limbo that had led PDQ to her literal fucking doorstep and, as a result, increased notoriety. The pursuit of PDQ meant more people recognized her name. More people felt the need to comment. For every feel-good encounter that made her feel slightly rock star–*ish*, there were plenty of sideways looks that basically translated as *Were you nuts? Are you still?*

But the last thing she wants or needs now is another trip down PDQ Lane and/or entanglement with a copycat. If the cop's query to her is about the envelopes in any way, shape, or form, Tamica's been right all along. She'll detest having to say so, and she'll dread what it will mean for Wyatt and keeping him safe. Maybe, Flynn thinks, she should burn all her comp and vacation days and take her son on a long road trip north to Glacier National Park or maybe Alaska.

"As far as I know, it's nothing you did," says Goodman. "Of course, what do I know? All I get is the good show you put on when you're here."

"Hey now," says Flynn.

"Facts," says Goodman.

"Why don't you give them my number and tell them to call me?"

"They said it's an in-person thing."

"I'm confused. Heck, call me flummoxed."

But not really?

"I could record a stand-up here, make it clear we made the effort. Then I'll head back north."

"I don't know," says Goodman. "Something tells me you knew to make sure you got video of you walking into the apartment building, that kind of thing. Am I right?"

CHAPTER 31

Detective John Jasper holds a supersize ziplock, large enough to hold a gallon of water and a plump trout. Or two. At least she had the same idea as the cops about the best way to protect it.

A familiar gray envelope sits at the bottom of the pouch. The sight of it is like a magic trick, some fluke in the earth's gravitational force.

DPD HQ. It's not an interrogation room, based on what Flynn has seen from hundreds of clips of police questionings. Those rooms are tighter. Sweatier. This one has bulletin boards and a decent window with a view of the hazy Denver air. Maybe it's a room for initial jousting with potential suspects. A place to feel comfortable so you fuck up and screw yourself.

Which is precisely what Flynn is deciding how to handle. On the drive from Colorado Springs, Tamica pressed Flynn to get the cops on board. The only break from Tamica's heavy lobbying was when she called her father and gave him the details about the envelopes. And Michael Martin promptly locked arms with Tamica.

"Inside the envelope is a piece of paper," says Detective Jasper.

"Okay," says Flynn.

Detective Jasper has a smoker's glazed eyes. An accompanying tobacco stench wafts across the table. White shirt, no jacket, maroon tie. A black piece of artillery sits in a high-ride shoulder holster. Jasper's nose and heavy brow remind her of Christopher from *The Sopranos*. Tony's protégé. Dark hair slicked back. Penetrating eyes. Flynn is pretty sure she's interviewed Detective Jasper at some point, doesn't want to ask.

Doesn't want to bond.

Jasper is joined by Wendy Yamamoto. Size XS. Straight dark hair to her jawline like a shimmering skullcap. Small, calm features. Unblinking dark eyes. Flynn wonders if Yamamoto has grown used to all that nicotine pollution.

"And you're mentioned," says Yamamoto.

"I mean, what is it? I mean, I can see it's an envelope. Where did it . . . turn up? I take it there is something, what, worrisome?"

The meandering ramble of guilt.

Of the guilty.

"It was found this morning in Athmar Park," says Yamamoto.

Tumbling down the street? In someone's trash?

"Do you recognize it?" says Yamamoto.

"Do I know *that* envelope?"

"No," says Jasper. An ounce of exasperation. "Have you seen others like it?"

"No," says Flynn.

Thinking one name—Wyatt.

Can she have a month to think this through?

Two?

"I'm going to show you a photo of the words," says Jasper.

He Face ID's his phone to a functioning state, puts it on the table, twists it 180, and one-finger pushes it across the table like the last poker chip.

Flynn looks, doesn't touch it.

> #1?
> #2?
> Maybe #3?
> More?
> The Prototype Rules.

Ask Flynn.
Flynn the reporter. That one.
She knows.
The pattern is no pattern.

"There aren't any other reporters named Flynn," says Yamamoto.

All of the city's reporters, both print and electronic, could meet in an elevator. Flynn says nothing.

"Ask Flynn what?" says Jasper.

"I don't know."

"Have you seen messages like this one?" says Yamamoto.

Would the cops quickly see something in the school video footage that she missed?

Would the cops quickly locate Shannon Way Bicycle Boy, tell his mother to fuck off, and get a good description of the person who paid the boy to run an errand?

Are the cops perfect? Max, Tamica, and Michael want her to get all the reinforcements she can muster. They want the professional analysts all over every scrap of evidence so far. They want her to take the most cooperative route.

But they don't comprehend the degree of difficulty behind the envelope tricks.

Tricks or worse.

It will be a bitch when she has to come clean. She's not stupid enough to think that will never happen. But when the time comes, she'll lean on the Wyatt Defense. All for Wyatt. She was protecting Wyatt. Over and over in her head, she sees the paper photo of Wyatt fluttering to her lap from Envelope #2.

"What about Athmar Park?" says Flynn. "Where was the note found?"

"We are not releasing those details yet," says Yamamoto. "Maybe soon."

"Today soon?"

Jasper and Yamamoto consult via squint.

"Today maybe," says Jasper.

"Getting late in the day."

"Murder investigations don't run on a clock," says Jasper. "It's a tweet on X. It's putting out a news release. Any time of day will work."

"I'm aware," says Flynn. "Definitely murder?"

Hearing her own thin voice. Tasting the acid drip on the back of her throat.

"Yes."

"Female?"

"No," says Jasper.

"Age?"

"Not yet," says Yamamoto.

"When was the victim found?"

Is she playing this wrong? Should she come clean? *Fuck.*

"Details to come," says Jasper.

"Who found the victim?"

"Details to come," says Yamamoto.

"And where was the note?" says Flynn.

Jasper sighs. "Adjacent. Let's say. For now."

"Give me the whole story first," says Flynn. "The writer of that note clearly wants me there. We can send a signal. 'Message received.'"

"We?" says Yamamoto.

"Us working together," says Flynn.

"There's an implication in the note that there has already been communication," says Jasper.

Flynn ignores the assertion. "If I'm one of the reporters in a pack at the scene, it won't be the same."

"You have not received other messages? Notes?" says Yamamoto.

Flynn answers by staring again at Jasper's phone. "I'm trying to wrap my head around all of this."

"If you're being pressured . . ." says Jasper. "Threatened, maybe? Warned? We can help."

"And you need to tell us," says Yamamoto.

The easiest thing to do is stay in reporter mode. "I want the Athmar Park story," says Flynn. "Now."

It would be weird to break the news about Jack Kline and his White power leanings and have a scoop about a new murder case in Denver on the same day.

And what she really wants is for a quick wrap on Jedidiah/Jack Kline and maybe assign herself as full-time bodyguard for Wyatt. Take up Krav Maga.

She's sick about not taking that step already.

She'll need Goodman on her side.

What would Goodman say if he saw this performance?

Goodman texts as if he heard her thoughts.

Updates?

Axel Sheen's text lands like a one-two punch after Goodman's.

I enjoyed Tuesday evening. Hope we can do it again.

"The whole point is to put me in the middle," says Flynn. "For whatever reason."

"Does the style of this message remind you of—"

"Of course it does," says Flynn. "It's spot-on copy. So it feels like unfinished business."

"How?" says Yamamoto. "Harry Kugel is in prison."

"Isn't the *how* your job?"

"Of course," says Jasper.

"And?"

"And that's why we want to talk to you."

She won't tell them about her trip to Cañon City. It would sound so foolish. Harebrained. Madcap. But she had to go.

"Of course the words are familiar. The tone, the wording. Everything."

"We agree with that," says Yamamoto. "Similar."

"Too matchy," says Flynn. "Too matchy to not be connected."

"Or a heck of a mimic," says Jasper. "The messages from PDQ were in the public record, were they not?"

"Unfortunately."

"And you could have gone to the cops back then?" says Yamamoto. "When you were also getting messages like this one?"

"In theory." *But the cops were the problem.*

"And you could do the same this time," says Jasper.

"We need a strategy. You need bait."

"Bait is for the movies," says Jasper. "Potboilers."

"The message seems like a come-on," says Flynn. "An invitation. If you want me to do anything, let me know. In the meantime, I need the details on Athmar Park. And you want to give them to me first, as a sign you got the message."

CHAPTER 32

"So does the sheriff have any indication where Jedidiah Kline, a.k.a. Jack Kline, is now?"

Sitting next to anchor Sara Cornette on set feels antiseptic, clinical, and disconnected from the streets. Cornette's heavy makeup adds to the feeling of pretense. But Flynn has never not fussed over her own appearance, although less today due to a bad case of pinwheel brain.

"If they do, they are not sharing that information with us," says Flynn. "Anyone with information about Jack or Jedidiah Kline's whereabouts is urged to call either the Arapahoe or El Paso County Sheriff or your local police."

"Thank you, Flynn Martin. Incredible video from inside his apartment. I'm sure you'll stay on the story?"

"As best we can," says Flynn. How big is Athmar Park, and can she drive all the streets until she spots the crime scene van? Why has nobody called the tip line? "We know there are still more questions than answers around this tragic story."

"And we understand that there is other breaking news this evening, here in Denver?"

"Details are still coming together," says Flynn, "but we got word that police are investigating a murder on the west side of the city. In Athmar Park. We know the victim is male and the crime was discovered last night. We expect a full briefing from Denver police no later than tomorrow morning."

"More sad news," says Cornette.

"I'm afraid so," says Flynn.

Flynn gathers her things to head to her father's and collect Wyatt.

Phone: Detective Jasper.

She lets it go to voicemail, finishes packing.

Listens: "That was not public information."

Texts Jasper: You never said it was off the record.

Return text: Do you want us to provide copies of the note to the media and how you're involved?

Texts Jasper from a stoplight halfway to Michael's condo: Let me know what time tomorrow.

◆ ◆ ◆

Take-out Thai, courtesy of her father, in her father's condo. Tom yum goong, pad see ew, crispy spring rolls.

Glum Wyatt. He knows something's up. He hates not being told. He's also not a fan of getting picked up at school by his grandfather and having his options limited while he waits for her workday to end.

Michael is close to sprightly. He's received a briefing by a group of liberal legislators who are working on a plan to fix Colorado's patchwork of varying sales tax rates created by several hundred tax jurisdictions. The lawmakers have given him the first chance to write about their proposal and how they've garnered bipartisan support for the concept, which they plan to bring to the General Assembly come January.

Michael's detailed, happy ramblings are amusing. There's a problem being solved! Flynn knows she should wrap her head around the issue, how different goods are exempt from sales tax. But she also knows this is all a smoke screen. They can't discuss the real issue with Wyatt hovering about.

On the ride home, Wyatt is as quiet as a mouse.

On Valium.

Wyatt heads off to bed with a book. There are days she can see the moody eighteen-year-old to come. There are days when it's easy to remember the cheery, eager eight-year-old who relished each day's dawning. Tonight is one of the former. Flynn resists every urge to be critical. The kid is justified. He hates being left out of the loop. Like his mother.

Phone: Michael Martin.

"Did I wait long enough?"

"He just went to bed. I'm not in the mood for a scolding."

"And you met with the police?"

"There's a third note."

"Jesus," says Michael. "Where this time?"

"Did you watch the five o'clock?"

"Sorry, I was busy transcribing interviews. Well, I was busy watching Microsoft Word's dictate function do it for me."

"There was a murder in Athmar Park," says Flynn. "Male. The body was found last night, with a note telling the police to 'Ask Flynn' and mentioning the whole 'pattern is no pattern' business and again with the Prototype Rules, whatever that means."

"And you pretended to know nothing."

"I guess it took me by surprise. I don't want to be all tangled up in the public's eye. Again. Okay? And whoever is behind this crap has made it damn clear Wyatt is in trouble if I do."

"Even more to the point." Michael has strapped on a forceful tone. "The first two notes weren't connected to anything. They were free floaters. They could have been a prank. Now, with a note and a body, he's taking credit."

"Possible."

"You know at some point you'll have to backpedal on all the dodges you pulled today, the fine hairs you split. And Max?"

"He'll overrule me. And it should be fifty-fifty."

"Why the hero business, Flynn?"

There's a bluntness to Michael's interrogation that makes her feel like he's playing eight games of simultaneous chess against expert players and she's playing Go Fish.

"It's about protecting my boy. And I'm being watched."

"You need Max."

"And then I may as well do exactly what the note-writer butthole is telling me *not* to do."

"Which will be worse?" says Michael. "Backpedaling when it comes time to tell the cops or dealing with Max when he finds out about today?"

"It's him, Dad. It's him."

"He's in prison," says Michael. "Three life terms."

"Plus twenty-four more for attempted murder," says Flynn. "But it's him. I can smell it."

"How?"

"I don't know. That's the thing. I don't know."

Max is apoplectic. He uses the word "Wyatt" as much as she thinks it. But he comes to the opposite conclusion with force and conviction.

It's a gentle berating, if such a thing is possible. Max knows she doesn't respond well to mansplaining or *cop*splaining or male power asserting itself. Max takes the logical approach, but he's as sure as Michael and as certain as Tamica.

Flynn feels pummeled.

Score?

Three to one.

She's playing defense with no hope of getting the ball in whatever sport is being played. She's cornered. It's easy to flash back to those hours when she was tangling with PDQ. When Wyatt vanished for those excruciatingly long hours and her heart wanted to climb out of her chest and her lungs sipped oxygen because she couldn't find a breath. Hours of thinking the worst. Hours of terror. She can't go through that again.

"Athmar Park is yours, right?" says Flynn.

"Yes. Athmar Park is four."

The city is carved into six police districts.

"Have you heard of this one?"

"I heard it called in."

"Know anything more?"

"No. And I'm not playing that game."

"What game?"

"Of being your back channel of information. You need to call those detectives back. Crack of dawn."

CHAPTER 33

She had no idea I was special.

She had no reason to—*then*.

And she will never know.

◆ ◆ ◆

Yes, Harry Kugel made mistakes.

Hell, even Harry Kugel knew Harry Kugel made mistakes.

He could have avoided the end. He could have gone down in history.

One of the ones.

He could have kept quiet. He could have kept his head down.

But he had to protect his reputation.

His *rep*.

Sounds like something on a wheel.

It comes around. And comes around. And comes around again.

Harry doesn't know it either.

Harry Kugel has looked me in the eye.

And yet has no clue.

Same thing—not yet.

Maybe never.

If all goes well.

◆ ◆ ◆

And there's no reason to think it won't.

The city that Harry Kugel made famous is about to deal with a new level of anxiety.

There were lessons to be learned from Harry Kugel and, really, all you had to do was pay attention.

And show interest.

After all, it's a craft. Like any other craft, you must practice. And it's always a good idea to read about those who have come before you.

The Evil That Men Do.

Killer on the Road.

Journey into Darkness.

The pattern is no pattern.

CHAPTER 34

Goodman text: See The Post?

Flynn is groggy. She's barely slept.

Checks the time—5:30 a.m.

Goodman text: Athmar Park.

Flynn pulls up *The Denver Post*.

Headline at the top: Police Investigating "Curious" Murder in Athmar Park.

A Judy Hayes byline, the Good Housekeeping Seal of Approval when it comes to coverage of anything dead or bloody in Denver for the past quarter century.

Story:

> Denver Police announced late last night that a long-time resident of Athmar Park was found murdered in his home, and a "curious, unusual" clue was found at the scene.
>
> "It was a message," said Detective John Jasper in an exclusive interview with *The Denver Post*. "And we will be announcing the specific details unless those with information about this specific message come forward immediately. We need the public's help."
>
> Detective Jasper said the message was on a sheet of paper. He would not say if the message was typed or

handwritten. He also declined to say if this murder is connected to any others.

The victim was 52-year-old Robert Waller, an employee of the US Post Office. He was found by a female neighbor who noticed Waller's border terrier, a dog named Caesar, wandering around outside. She also noticed that Waller's front door was slightly ajar.

Detective Jasper said Waller, who apparently lived alone, had been stabbed. He added that there was evidence of robbery and potentially a "substantial" amount of missing cash. The precise time of the murder is still being established, he said.

Detective Jasper added that the matter is "urgent" and that investigators will be in the neighborhood today looking for witnesses or anyone who saw anything unusual.

◆ ◆ ◆

"It's me," says Flynn.

"Up early," says Goodman.

"Up a lot," says Flynn.

"You talked to the cops yesterday?"

"Yes."

"And they didn't give you this?"

"Of course not."

"Why'd they give it to Hayes?"

To smoke me out?

"I think I know."

"And?"

"It's complicated."

"Do you think I'm capable of understanding?"

"Of course."

"And?"

"Can we do this at the office?"

◆ ◆ ◆

Over cornflakes, Wyatt resists.

"No school?" he says.

"Not today."

"I have a social studies presentation. And a math test."

"We'll get them made up."

"This has to do with why you came to school."

Wyatt's blue wireless headphones dangle around his neck. He stabs at his soggy flakes with an uninterested spoon.

"Yes," says Flynn.

"What did you find?"

"Not what I was looking for."

"And the whole day with Gramps? What am I going to do?"

"He'll have something fun."

"I don't understand."

"I know."

"I hate this," says Wyatt.

"I know that too."

◆ ◆ ◆

Flynn hand-delivers Wyatt to Michael's front door. There was a time when she'd let him out at the curb in Cheesman Park and not bother to watch him walk all the way to the entrance of Michael's building. Wyatt announces in the elevator that he's "officially creeped out" by the extra attention.

Outside, Flynn stands by her car. She checks her phone as pretense, takes an inventory of the joggers and those out for a morning stroll. The park is parched, grass smudged brown in broad patches. She glances at Michael's balcony on the eighth floor. Wyatt is leaning over the railing, watching.

He holds both hands out, palms up. *Whatcha doing?*

Flynn blows him a kiss.

◆ ◆ ◆

The last thing Flynn wants is her name splattered all over town.

The last thing Flynn wants is her name splattered all over town again.

"Fuck you, Jasper," she says out loud to the empty interior of her car, snapping off a radio report covering the same turf as *The Denver Post* about Athmar Park.

Flynn drives to the pavilion overlooking Cheesman Park. She parks on a nearby street, climbs out, walks through the dehydrated garden, and leans against one of the marble pillars. A Black man sits on the steps, bopping his head to the music from his white earbuds. He's shirtless. His expansive hairless chest and riffles of chiseled abs glisten in sweat. An elderly man, barefoot and tiny, moves silently through his martial arts moves—maybe tai chi. A young couple clutch their giant cups, giggling maybe about the night before. Each sip comes with a coffee kiss.

Flynn feels the weight in her heart. A stale doughnut filled with lead. Something squeezes it like a fidget toy. She scans the joggers and walkers, imagines at some point that her father will take Wyatt out for a spin around the park and discuss their options. Michael will treat Wyatt like a friend, not a burden. And maybe Wyatt will remember this day and recall its lessons: "How to grandparent."

Or should she text Michael and ask him, discreetly, to keep Wyatt inside?

The erstwhile grass is freshly trimmed. The park was once a cemetery and who knows if they got all the bodies moved? Flynn always imagines the answer is no. Someday, if it ever rains again, a flood will show them all the bodies and the stories that they missed the first time around.

The sky is haze and burnt umber. Somewhere out there in Colorado there might be a bluebird sky, but it's likely melting. Flynn promises herself to do what's right for Wyatt, imagines how she'll roll things out for Rick Goodman, a guy so by-the-book that he'll hug the right lane heading east from Colorado because he's got a right turn coming up in Indiana.

"Miss Martin?"

The woman's dog is the size of a softball. The animal is a white clump of fur. It's keen about Flynn's shoes. A leash attached to a bright pink collar connects to a woman wearing a tight purple tank top over sleek gray slacks. The woman lowers large dark sunglasses that cover half her face, as if a quick glance will mean instant recognition. The tightness around the woman's eyes screams *work done.* So do her eyebrows, which could be laminated. Or microbladed.

"Yes," Flynn says.

"You don't remember me."

Flynn says nothing.

"Grace Underwood," she says. "I mean, there's no way you'd necessarily recall. All the stories you get involved with, am I right?"

"Sorry," says Flynn.

"Well, you were enormously helpful."

"I'm glad," says Flynn.

"It was a delicate situation."

Flynn says nothing. "I'm sorry, I'm a bit distracted. I don't mean to be rude."

"It's okay," says Underwood. "About fifteen years ago. There was a new principal assigned to our elementary school. You know, after the previous one, the one we liked so much, had been fired. Like, *poof*, gone. Great guy, out on his rear end. Some big cone of silence dropped over the whole thing like maybe he'd been caught with a minor or some creepy stuff like that."

"What school?" says Flynn.

Curious not curious.

"Highland Elementary," she says. "Oh, this was out in Jefferson County before I moved downtown—I'm probably out of context, now that I've moved to the city."

Flynn can't picture the school, doesn't recall the story.

"Anyway, the district never told us what was going on and expected us to take this new guy, this lying doofus, who'd fabricated his degrees."

Flynn's memory pings off a vague recollection. *Barely.*

"Well," says Underwood, "your coverage helped get the new guy fired two weeks later. Led to a whole thing around the district's HR process, you know? I mean, where was the background check?"

"I'm glad it worked out," says Flynn.

"You were the only reporter who cared," says Underwood, "and then the newspaper had to jump in, of course."

"Of course," says Flynn. "I'm afraid I have to run."

"Sure," says Underwood. "Good to see you. You know, you really made a difference."

"Good."

"And everyone knows what you did with that, that, that—*monster.*"

CHAPTER 35

Flynn asks Goodman if they can meet in the conference room. Goodman gives her space. Coffee, which he'll drink steadily until noon, is to the brim in his oversize cup. She's got a bottle of water. She starts with Wyatt's backpack envelope, has no trouble conjuring the intensity she felt in the moment, and knows right off that Goodman gets it too.

She explains about her skepticism. That is, about how incredulity lived side by side with instant dread—two sides of the thinnest coin ever stamped. Next, she tells Goodman about cajoling the school district, reviewing the footage, and then the whole second note and how it had materialized on Shannon Way.

Then, the story of Surveillance Capital, USA.

Next, Bicycle Boy's mom.

And everything she knows about the third note.

Goodman is a good listener, asks questions to clarify tidbits. He doesn't challenge her decisions. As she goes, she feels better. Calmer. She feels supported.

But as she walks through everything, happy with her pace and happy with her sense of owning the story and imparting the mighty heft of it all, she's thinking overtime whether to tell Goodman about looking Harry Kugel in the eye and whether telling Goodman about that detour would instantly invalidate everything else. Because certainly that whim, that necessary fucking whim, would make her look like a nutjob.

"And now Detective Jasper wants me to tell him everything about the first two notes," says Flynn. "Which means, of course, a mountain of worry about Wyatt."

"And now we know what you were trying to do with your little murder project here at the station."

"Not so little," says Flynn. "And it's not a bad idea on its own merits."

"You were going to see if you could figure out which murders belonged to Envelope Dude."

"When you say it like that, it sounds preposterous."

"I didn't say it in any particular way."

"Whatever," says Flynn.

"You can't yank the whole station around for your needs."

"It's a black-and-white good idea, whether inspired by something that's happening to me or not. Get a chart together of all our murder coverage for, say, the last decade. Income level on the vertical axis, screen time awarded on the horizontal. You know it. I know it. Straight line up. And up."

"Maybe," says Goodman. "That can't be your main concern right now."

"What if it's already started?" says Flynn. "The question mark next to number one on the third note. *The pattern is no pattern.* Holy hell."

The pressure of walking through the muck tightens her breath. Matching minuscule droplets flower like dewdrops on her eyelids. She scares them away by flashing on the cold nothing in Harry Kugel's gaze. It's an easy conjure. Letting Goodman see weakness is not what she needs.

If Goodman senses the moment, he says nothing. Flynn swallows a hard bite of air. Goodman chugs coffee.

"How was that going to work, exactly?" says Goodman. "How were you going to figure out which murders belonged to Mr. No Pattern?"

"I'm not sure, but putting the list together of recent cases seemed like the place to start and then, well, asking questions of the investigators. Isn't asking questions what we do? There are dozens of true crime podcasts all built around asking questions of unsolved cases, turning up the heat."

"May as well boil the ocean."

"It doesn't seem that impossible to me. Not with a team."

"Cops," says Goodman, as if one word explains all. "You have to pull them in."

Flynn says nothing.

Text from Axel Sheen: Don't mean to be pushy. Just checking in.

"Have you shared this with Tamica?" says Goodman.

"We've talked."

"She agrees with me?"

Flynn says nothing.

"Wow—Tamica Porter couldn't convince you? You are stubborn."

"Wyatt," says Flynn.

As if one word explains all.

"And Max? Do you think Wyatt's father gets a say?"

"Max's take was predictable."

"And your father?"

"Okay," says Flynn. "All right already. I give."

"Finally."

"What about Shannon Way? What about Jedidiah Jack Kline?"

"There are other reporters here at the station, notably Chris Casey."

Mr. Give-It-His-Best 79 Percent.

"By the way," says Goodman, "the last time I checked, the job title was reporter, not criminal investigator."

CHAPTER 36

"I've got terms," says Flynn.

"We don't do terms," says Jasper.

"You opened negotiations," says Flynn. "I'm countering."

"Negotiations?" says Yamamoto.

"You're not in charge of this investigation," says Jasper.

"I'm aware," says Flynn. "You wanted me back; your little trick worked."

"I think you're overthinking," says Jasper.

"You gave Judy Hayes the story as a signal. You want to bargain, and you've got me in a hammerlock."

"We like working with people who will work with us," says Jasper. "That much is true."

"I don't want to come across as uncooperative," says Flynn.

"Then let's get to it," says Yamamoto.

Today, Jasper's tobacco fogbank is mixed with a citrusy aftershave. Yamamoto wears a button-up shirt the color of eggplant, topped by a priestess-like white collar. Same conference room, same chairs, same awful feeling twisting her guts. Why doesn't she want the cavalry?

"I want an agreement," says Flynn.

"Did you lie to us?" says Jasper. "There were previous messages?"

"If I walk you through everything, I want this to stay in a tight loop, not splashed around."

The mere indication of a serial murderer will mean the DPD pulls in the FBI to help with behavioral analysis. What then? If there's a war room and a conspiracy wall, who will be in charge of what the public is told and whether her name gets dragged into the spotlight?

"I'm not sure we can make guarantees," says Yamamoto, "until we know what information you withheld from us."

"I didn't—" Flynn stops. *Yes she did.* "I'm worried about my son. I'm worried about anyone in my orbit. You know? I'm being watched. It's obvious I'm being watched. I need to know that my name doesn't get out there."

"We may need the public's help," says Jasper. "It's likely."

"We can't sit here today and know what we're going to need," says Yamamoto. "We need to know what else you know."

Flynn begins the night Wyatt brought home the first envelope. She's peppered with questions. What she did with the envelopes. Who she talked to at the school district. And the school. What she thought she saw on the videotape with the custodian and her floor machine. Name of the guy with the video near Shannon Way. Name of Bicycle Boy's mom.

They skip around. They ask about Tamica, and they ask about what else Flynn might have shared with the "upper ups" at the station. They ask what Wyatt knows, and they mention her father too. Flynn wonders if they'll ask about her date with Axel Sheen.

Finally, a discussion about Wyatt. "I can't have him out there, free-floating around the city," says Flynn. "And he hates missing school."

"Where is he today?" says Yamamoto.

"With my father," says Flynn. "In an eighth-floor condo at Cheesman Park."

"We'll see if we can get some resources to help," says Jasper. "We can work with school district security too."

"I don't want to scare him either," says Flynn.

"We need those envelopes and messages," says Jasper.

"And I want regular updates on what you're finding—at Wyatt's school and from Bicycle Boy."

"I don't know about 'regular,'" says Jasper. "We'll likely have more questions of you—and you need to promise to call us the second you encounter any more, let's call it, 'activity' along these lines."

"Fine. Tell me more about Athmar Park." An idea pops out of the blue. It involves Max. It might work. "I've earned that, haven't I?"

Jasper and Yamamoto share a cold glance.

"There's not much more to say beyond what was in Judy Hayes's story this morning," says Yamamoto.

"Do you have any witnesses?"

"Not yet," says Yamamoto.

"Where was the message found?"

Jasper says nothing. Yamamoto shrugs.

"Off the record. *Come on*—I'm right in the thick of this."

"Off the record," says Jasper. "It was right with Mr. Waller."

"With?" says Flynn.

"It was in his grip," says Jasper. "At least, it was made to look like he still had one."

CHAPTER 37

"We're underway."

"Who is 'we'?" says Harry.

"Me, I guess."

"And you felt the need to tell me."

This time, Harry took forever to show up in the room. He looks tired and, unfortunately, unimpressed. A tall, skinny White dude guard sits behind Harry and off to the side. Two tiny cameras watch from the corners of the ceiling. Three tile walls the color of Dijon. The fourth, heavy green bars.

"I thought you'd want to know."

"Not really," says Harry. "I don't remember saying anything that would have suggested another visit was welcome. Or warranted."

"We all know you shouldn't be in here."

"Now *that* is some fucking truth right there."

As if he's mainlined a quart of espresso, Harry sits up.

"You were trapped. Unfairly trapped."

"Correct!"

"You know I'm not the only one who knows that to be true."

"It's reassuring," says Harry. "But doesn't change anything about my predicament."

"Which is why I thought you'd get a little pleasure—little to be sure—knowing that things are rolling."

Harry looks at the ceiling. Stretches out the fingers on his hand, stares at his palm like he wants to tell his own fortune. Rubs his eye hard with a knuckle.

"You said the first time you cared about the loose ends of my *campaign*."

"Yes."

"It's a funny word, you know? 'Campaign'?"

"What?"

"It means open country. Or field."

"Really."

Harry smirks. Or it's a smile stirred gently with disdain. "Soldiers would go on a campaign—an organized course of action, if you will."

"I'm nothing if not organized."

"Today the word 'campaign' implies you're selling a level of bullshit. A public relations 'campaign.' And it's the public's job to determine the degree of stench."

"Right."

"And what word goes with 'campaign'?" says Harry.

"I'm not sure."

"'Trail.' Campaign 'trail.' Every campaign leaves a trace of slime. Like a snail. Do you know researchers found that when one snail crosses another snail's trail, that their heart rate goes from forty-six to fifty-one beats per minute? Can you imagine being the researcher? 'How was your day, honey? What did you do?'"

"Unless you can figure out how to avoid leaving a trail."

"You left a trail coming in here, right?"

"Yes."

"Got the third degree?"

"Everything short of a blood sample, but it's okay. Like you said, it's about paying close attention to details. And patience too. You said it was possible."

"Landing a man on Mars is possible. Bringing him back? Forget it. Tell me why you came back. I have places to go, things to do."

"I wanted you to know the work is underway."

"So I'll sleep better or some bullshit like that?"

"You only care about results."

"Results or reasons. That's all we've got. Are you capable?"

"More than."

"The mindset is key, of course."

"You made that clear the first time."

"Can you imagine being Tchaikovsky? You write *Swan Lake* or the '1812 Overture' but you are so afraid of conducting an orchestra before a live audience that you talk yourself into thinking that your head is going to fall off?"

"Seriously?"

"One hand under his chin while he conducted with the other. For years like that."

"Strange."

"Calm mind, calm work."

"And no trail."

"You want me to help you?"

"That's what I've been getting at."

"Then you need to help me," says Harry.

"Quid pro whatever it is?"

"Quo. Something for something."

"I'm listening."

"Finish. And I mean in both ways—noun and verb."

"Yes. You need not worry."

"You're doing it for me?"

"Of course. We all know the system didn't give you credit for your self-rehabilitation. But I may also have my own reasons. Good ones."

"Then get the fuck out of here."

CHAPTER 38

Some conversations are better in person, but Flynn can't afford the two-hour round trip.

From her car, she FaceTimes Max.

He's in street clothes, out of uniform. Max is male-model handsome with Tom Brady cheekbones. His blue eyes would sparkle in a coal mine. He's outside. A black T-shirt hugs his chest in defiance of the heat. He explains that he's in a hardware store parking lot. "Leaky faucet—what's up?"

She puts the phone in the mount on her dash, heads around Civic Center Park and down Fifteenth Street to her condo.

"Are you working on Athmar Park?" she says.

"I can't tell you." Max isn't a detective, but he could have been given a task related to the investigation.

"Can you get yourself involved?" says Flynn.

"Way too obvious," says Max. "And, no."

"Do you think my name is, you know, out there? Among the cops?"

Flynn imagines cops chattering about cases like one big stinky locker room.

"Hard to say," says Max. "But nothing has come back to me."

"Can you find out?"

"Again, too obvious. The main thing is, did you talk to Detective Jasper?"

"And his partner," says Flynn.

"Which exposes Wyatt."

"'Exposes' is the wrong word," says Flynn.

"You know what I mean. And that means you've got an idea."

"How do you know?"

"You've got that look. You're going to ask me something."

Flynn spells it out. It's simple. Max takes a week off for starters. Maybe two. He'll be Wyatt's bodyguard. She realizes that Max, if he goes for the plan, will want to begin and end each day smack dab in her condo and not in the lobby. And that might complicate her vague and selfish but quite necessary plan to entertain Axel Sheen in the most personal way possible, not that Flynn hasn't encountered her fair share of Max's breakfast-munching conquests. But, at the same time, it's a really bad idea to put anyone else in her current orbit of doom. Are there books on the joys of celibacy? And how the hell can she be thinking of sex when she's come all the way out here to manage Wyatt's safety?

Max, to his credit, doesn't reject her out of hand.

"I don't love losing the time," says Max. "But I get it. Wyatt will hate it."

"He already hates it."

"I'm sure Jasper couldn't say what information was going public. If your name was going to get out there."

"No," says Flynn. "He couldn't. But imagine the number of chatterbox cops and then add the FBI. It won't take much for my name to slip out, and then whoever is behind all of this, well, you know."

"Wyatt could stay with me out here," says Max. "I could get him to school every morning, pick him up, and still put in a few hours each day, if they'd let me."

"That's a lot of driving." Wyatt's school is at 1:00 p.m. on the distant tip of an elongated, misshapen Salvador Dalí clock; Southwest Denver, where Max lives and works, is at 7:00 p.m. "You really think he'd be okay? I mean, that first message came home from school. That's way too close."

"We can alert district and school security," says Max. "You want me to follow him from social studies to math?"

"I want him safe." Flynn's throat tightens. She fights to keep her composure. "I want no problems. No remakes. I want the asshole behind all of this to know Wyatt isn't a target. And I think that message gets sent if the bodyguard is obvious and if that bodyguard is you."

CHAPTER 39

Back at her condo, Flynn retrieves the two envelopes in their plastic bags and drives back to DPD headquarters listening to the repeat news on the whole business at Athmar Park.

Nothing new.

Jasper meets her out front. She hands over an innocuous-looking grocery bag with the evidence inside. "Thanks," says Jasper with the tone of *What were you thinking?*

◆ ◆ ◆

Parked in the lot at work, Flynn senses relief. Again with the tears, and this time she lets them have their way for a minute because it feels so good to sit in her car and let the anguish flow. It might be premature. It's certainly self-indulgent. She hates herself for letting the moment carry her away. The facts don't justify what she's feeling. But now it's not just a ball in the cops' court; it's a dark star.

You figure it out.

You go stare into Harry Kugel's dead eyes and get him to show you the puppet strings.

Flynn imagines the police making quick work at Wyatt's school, figuring out how the envelope made its way into his backpack. She imagines them finding Bicycle Boy lickety-split, vacuuming up all the neighborhood spy cam footage from around Shannon Way, drawing a bead by sundown on the individual who needed the kid to carry out the weird errand. And maybe Athmar Park and the whole Twinsie PDQ thing will come to a brisk conclusion.

Certainly much faster than she could manage.

And, yes, *What was I thinking?*

◆ ◆ ◆

"That took longer than I thought," says Goodman.

"Anything new on Shannon Way?" says Flynn.

"You're not going to tell me how it went?"

"They had a lot of questions, and they asked them all five ways from Sunday."

"It's six," says Goodman.

"Six what?"

"Six ways from Sunday because there are six ways *to* Sunday."

"Okay," says Flynn. "You're correcting my metaphors?"

"It's more like an idiom. Implying endless possibilities."

"Jesus," says Flynn. "Real cops in my business over the envelopes and word-usage cops here at the television news station watching my tongue."

"You're welcome," says Goodman. "And now?"

"And now they know everything I know. And we wait."

"What about our dead post office worker in Athmar Park?"

"I'll check in with the detectives," says Flynn. "Every minute or two. I'm not sure I've got the inside track, but I think I elbowed a few ribs. What else is going on? Any word on the search for Jack Kline?"

"Matter of fact, Chris Casey got a tip that cops might be on Jack Kline's trail in Pueblo. He's heading there now."

"*Our* Chris Casey?"

"Stop it," says Goodman. "Turtles have their merits, you know."

"I can help," says Flynn.

The thought of going south again, to a town forty miles south of Colorado Springs, is unwelcome. It's already past noon and she wants to see Wyatt, to explain how things are going to work with his dad. Leaving now would mean an open-ended assignment in Pueblo, especially if the cops haul in Kline. It's not impossible to imagine live shots until the late news and then a motel room with one of those child toothbrushes they give out at the front desk, the ones you can't really grip, because you traveled with nothing but the clothes on your back. Morning live shots, too, in the same getup.

"Tamica's with Casey," says Goodman. "They've got it."

"What?"

"Tamica Porter is allowed to work with other reporters," says Goodman. "You know, teamwork? Flexibility? It's a thing."

"I can go anyway. Another pair of eyes. Ears."

"It might be a false lead," says Goodman. "And just because Jedidiah Jack is on the run does not mean he knows how to make a whole family disappear or had anything to do with it."

"Right," says Flynn. "Sure."

"You're not in the mix today as it is," says Goodman, "so cut yourself some slack."

Emails with a dozen story pitches. Voicemails with five more. Politics. Environment. Education. A potentially corrupt mayor in a mountain town she's never heard of. A charter school where student phones are banned from classrooms and the parents are up in arms, so to speak, because they don't think it's safe in case of, well, every parent's worst nightmare.

Flynn flags a few emails for follow-up, takes notes on two of the voicemails in case Goodman asks if she's got anything. A quick check of social media shows no indication that Jack Kline has been located. Judy Hayes and *The Denver Post* have nada. *Bueno.* She vibes a few positive thoughts to Chris Casey. He's a decent reporter, but she can never tell when he really cares about something. It's as if he's a soulless reporter robot with no point of view about how the world works or how to make it better. Reporters like Chris Casey take the powerful at their word, have no edge.

She calls her father to check on Wyatt. She explains the new plan with Max, though not certain of the launch date until Max secures leave.

"You know I don't mind," says Michael.

"I know," says Flynn. "But you have your life."

"And what's the latest?"

"I gave the detectives every scrap I had," says Flynn. "That's all I know. And between us—"

"As if I have anyone to tell."

"I know," says Flynn. "But it looks like they're closing in on Jack Kline, so maybe this whole Shannon Way thing is about to wrap. That will be a huge relief."

"You're sure he's the one?"

"Sure? No. Pretty sure?" Why is there no *ugly* sure? "But he's got to know something."

"Are you jumping to conclusions?"

"His flight tells me what I need to know."

"Okay," says Michael.

"It sounds like you've been poking around."

"I don't know."

"You don't know if you've been poking around, or you don't know if you're onto something?"

"I really shouldn't mess around with crime stuff," says Michael. "I feel like a sleazy true crime podcaster."

"They're not sleazy," says Flynn.

"They're enabling the gawkers. It's like rubbernecking accidents on the highway, only everyone gets to play along with the whodunit game. All the Sherlockian conversations at watercoolers across the land. What's the point?"

"There are no watercoolers, Dad. You're forgetting nobody goes to the office anymore."

"Then they text each other all day. Whatever."

"It's another medium for telling stories," says Flynn. "And you shouldn't be opposed to having more reporters out there doing their thing."

"Imagine if they took all that energy and spent time reading government contracts or analyzing the basic metrics of a healthy society—education rates, child wellness, rural isolation, suicide rates. You know? And then pressing our so-called leadership about why places like Iceland or Singapore are so much healthier, happier?"

"You can't put a stop to the voyeurs," says Flynn. "Or the interest in learning how to avoid those scenarios for yourself."

"Maybe."

"But you're still not telling me what you found."

"How about stories about how much professional sports teams make from promoting gambling? How about the true cost of college sports or how the state's highest-paid employee is the coach of the university football team?" says Michael. "What message does that send?"

"You don't need to prove your curmudgeon credentials to me."

"This isn't me being grumpy pants. These are things we should all be concerned about."

"I know," says Flynn. "Those are all good issues. What have you got?"

"This goes back a few years," says Michael. "There was a legislator who wanted to try and tighten how nonprofits are audited by the state when it comes to taxes. Nonprofits and churches."

"Okay."

"It's a thing these days, churches managing sizable bank accounts," says Michael. "And when Patrick Kline's church popped up in the news, I got a call from Cillian Doherty. Remember him?"

"Maybe a touch Irish," says Flynn.

"As in very," says Michael. "He's eighty-five years old now, but back in 1996 he managed to gather enough signatures to put an amendment on the ballot that would have put seventy-five hundred properties around the state back on the tax rolls—properties owned by churches, nonprofits, arts organizations, et cetera."

"Cillian Doherty." Flynn rolls the name around in her head.

"You were starting college, of course."

"So many crazy citizen petitions ago."

"Anyway, Doherty's idea got trounced," says Michael. "Eighty-two percent of the voters basically said go to hell."

"Not a nice thing to say to a man who sounds like he just got off the boat from Dublin."

"Ex-Catholic. Very ex-Catholic. He kind of went underground after that humiliation on the ballot, but during all the priest sex abuse scandals, he's been active with websites publishing information about cases being reviewed and prosecuted. And he's never stopped watching churches and their money."

"New Hope Church," says Flynn. "Patrick Kline was a church leader."

"Exactly. And that's a massive church. An empire."

"And what did Cillian Doherty tell you?"

"To look into their holding companies."

"That sounds like a corporate thing," says Flynn.

"I know," says Michael. "But churches are sitting on all this cash, and there's no set, firm rule on how much they have to spend on, you know, ministry. On helping people. They've got staff to pay and building maintenance, of course. And a parsonage allowance can balloon into some pretty fancy digs."

"You said plural—holding 'companies.'"

"Cillian Doherty gave me the name of four," says Michael. "He's got a mole in New Hope who leaked the names to him."

"And the holding companies do what?"

"They hold," says Michael. "That's all. They own interest in other companies. They own stocks or bonds. They're a shell organized to protect assets."

"Sounds like we need a CPA," says Flynn. Thinking she doesn't need a reason to call Axel Sheen, but now she's got one. Something in her reporter's bones suddenly tells her the Jedidiah Jack angle isn't it. She smells greed and feels as if she's going to need to school herself on nonprofit tax regulations and how much government oversight is brought to church organizations. Heck, what defines a church? She needs a full list of all those who run New Hope Church, and she needs to figure out who is not going along with the program. Rats are rarely alone in their thinking.

"Wasn't there a holding company something or other rock band?" says Flynn.

"Before your time," says Michael. "Big Brother and the Holding Company. Janis Joplin's band at first. But I do believe back in the day that the 'holding' they were doing had to do with weed and acid, not stocks or bonds."

"And Big Brother?"

"George Orwell, of course. *1984*."

"Weird mix," says Flynn.

"No stranger than a church with four holding companies."

"Will Doherty talk to me?" says Flynn.

"I already asked him. He can guide you. Or us. But nothing on camera."

"Who is his mole?"

"Someone who is going to stay anonymous," says Michael.

"But open to talking off the record?"

"Cillian told me there should be enough there for you to pick up the threads and pull on them yourself. He's willing to help if you get stuck. Maybe he can tell you what rock to turn over. That's about it."

"And he thinks that's what Shannon Way is all about?"

"Apparently there's a ton of money involved," says Michael. "And he did leave me with one wee Irish bromide."

"I'm always down for advice. Or up. Or both."

"You'll never plow a field by turning it over in your mind."

CHAPTER 40

Texts Axel Sheen: Time for a quick call.

Texts again: Forgot to add "?"

She finds Goodman in an edit bay. He's watching a piece about an older lady in Wheat Ridge who had accused a neighbor of stealing her cat. The cat was later found in the basement. The two neighbors are making up over a pot of tortilla soup. The accuser is White. The neighbor is Hispanic. Footage of the hiding spot in the basement reveals a homeowner who is a hoarder in training. It's no wonder the cat couldn't be found.

It's a charming piece. Flynn works hard to dismiss the idea that the reporter encouraged the hug or waited around long enough to get one solid "meow" sound bite out of the large-eared Devon rex. But finds herself pushing back an uninvited tear over the sheer beauty of the homeowner's heartfelt apology and also dreaming of a day when she can parachute in and out of a story and head into her evening totally clueless about what the next day might bring.

"Nailed it," says Goodman to the reporter, Andrea Morgan. "I got all warm *and* I got all fuzzy. What's up, Flynn?"

"A tip on New Hope Church. And maybe trouble in paradise. I've got a friend who is a CPA, and I want to run some things by him."

"Sounds like you're asking for a hall pass."

"It's complicated stuff," says Flynn. "Better in person. Don't worry, I'll check in on Athmar Park."

Axel texts: Say the word.

◆ ◆ ◆

"Do you know enough about nonprofit taxes that I could ask you a few questions?" says Flynn.

"In person?"

"That's what I was thinking."

"Not exactly the next date I had in mind," says Sheen.

"Well, that's two of us."

"Is there any reason we need to hold this conversation in my office? Unless you've never seen the dull landscape of a few hundred waist-high cubicles all gussied up in a fetching shade of pewter."

"I can probably picture it." She can also picture his firework eyes. "Can you talk now? Sounds like you're driving."

"You're good."

"I try. Where to—or from?"

He hesitates. She hears a clatter, the drone of traffic. "Leaving a client's," he says. "Heading back to the office."

"That's so 2019."

"Old-school owner who believes in the quote-unquote 'power of office camaraderie.' We get to work from home two whole days a month."

"Lucky boy."

"I try to keep that fact to myself."

"Your secret is safe with me."

She gives him the address. It's better this way. It's no-risk. If she's being followed, then Axel Sheen could be any one of the hundreds of other tenants coming and going. And it's also not an immediate invitation to her condo, only a deliberate and thoughtful Emily Post progression of their relationship and not the racy video in her mind that has occasionally fought for screen time amid the other clips that have replayed images of Wyatt's safety, the envelope creep, Harry Kugel's vapid gaze, and all the sadness at Shannon Way.

"Eighth floor," says Flynn. "It's the common area. Like a giant coffee shop with a ton of workplaces for those who have jobs with twenty-first-century owners."

"Do tell," says Sheen.

◆ ◆ ◆

Two cold IPAs. Crackers. Slices of cheddar cheese.

And a shady spot on the outdoor patio. City oven set to braise. Invisible traffic hums below.

Axel Sheen knows about nonprofit taxes. He knows how infrequently churches get audited. He remembers seeing a *60 Minutes* piece about how the Church of Jesus Christ of Latter-Day Saints invested in holding companies and how one of those holding companies bailed out a for-profit insurance company, not exactly what you think of when the word "religion" comes to mind.

"You're a church, aren't you supposed to be out there helping folks?" says Flynn.

"I'm sure they have plenty they can point to for their core mission," says Sheen. "And they have savings, like any business or family. And they get to choose how to manage their money. Believe me, nobody's watching."

"Nobody?"

Axel Sheen wears a light blue pullover with a shallow V-neck that somehow looks dressy but also looks easy to remove. He's unaware of his understated appeal.

"The IRS opens a handful of cases each year," says Sheen. "Six or seven. The odds are pretty good that you can do what you want with your tithings."

"So a church owning a holding company, even though that sounds a little whack on the surface, doesn't surprise you."

"Not really, no," says Sheen. "There are three words in play. 'Not,' 'substantially,' and 'related.' If the business is not substantially related to the organization's exempt purpose—say, helping the poor—it might be subject to UBIT."

"Oh, you must know how much I love a good IRS acronym," says Flynn.

"You don't speak IRS?"

"Work hard to avoid speaking in government lingo every hour of every day."

"Unrelated business income tax."

"Sounds like a wide berth," says Flynn.

"Room for the *Titanic* and *Queen Mary* to park in the harbor of tax freedom," says Sheen. "Hell, throw in the whole US Navy. In general, and I paraphrase from the IRS guidelines, rents from real property, royalties, capital gains, and interest and dividends aren't subject to the unrelated business income tax unless financed with borrowed money."

"You could be quoting Shakespeare right there," says Flynn. "Or Maya Angelou."

"I know," says Sheen. "Inspiring stuff."

"And churches aren't required to publish their financials?"

"Not even to their own members."

"Jesus," says Flynn. "And I mean that quite literally."

"Who wants to be the politician that goes after church tax exemption today, when you need the church vote?" says Sheen. "And, by the way, what's this all about? A backdoor way of checking my religious leanings?"

"Well?" says Flynn, giving him "earnest reporter face" with the dead eyes.

"Not my cup of tea," says Sheen. "Or even my tiny cup of grape juice substituting for Christ's Blood. You?"

"Ditto," says Flynn. She raises her bottle of beer, clinks it against Sheen's. "And cheers to that."

Doesn't she deserve an hour in bed with this good-looking man, even as a form of stress relief? Or relaxation? Doesn't the world owe her a touch of its generosity from the pleasure side of its gifts? On the other hand, how can she even contemplate those needs when a dead postal worker was gripping an envelope addressed to her?

"And what's this all about?"

"Patrick Kline and his family," says Flynn.

"What a tragedy," says Sheen. "You had that story about the missing son."

"You watch the news?"

"I could say 'religiously,' but that wouldn't be quite true. Maybe I'm paying a bit more attention since meeting you. Is that okay?"

"We'll take all the viewers we can get, for whatever reason."

"I mean, it sure looks like the son will know something, right?" says Sheen.

"I was thinking the same thing," says Flynn. "And then I got a tip that there might have been something going on, a struggle over church finances."

"Which led to this debriefing."

"Debriefing?" says Flynn. "And I went to all this trouble with beer and cheese."

"I don't mean to be ungrateful," says Sheen with a sly smile. "What are the chances of a real second date?"

"Chances are good," says Flynn. "I'd rate them excellent, in fact. But now I need to figure out if there was some heavy-duty church infighting. And how the hell am I going to do that?"

"I don't know," says Sheen. "Go to church?"

CHAPTER 41

"So I get it correct, say and spell your first and last name, please."

"Meg Hart. M-e-g. H-a-r-t."

"And you're a parent here at Stoneham Elementary."

"Correct."

"How many children do you have here?"

"Two. Liam is in fourth grade. Emma is in second."

"Any other children?"

"No."

"And you've lived here in the neighborhood for—?"

"Ten years," says Hart.

Story from a telephone tip. Instant green light from Goodman. To Flynn, following an uneventful, catch-your-breath weekend that was jam packed with things Wyatt wanted to do, feels like a one-day palate cleanser. This is a perfect Monday story, a dish of lemon sherbet between the hearty soup and filet mignon.

"Your husband?"

Hart pauses.

"I'd rather leave him out of this."

"What does he do?"

"He works at an investment firm, but I'd rather this be about the bomb threats."

"What do you mean leave him out? Not mention you're married?"

"I mean, that's fine," says Hart.

She's nervous. Most people get the jitters when a camera is pointed at them for the first time. The interview is being conducted on the sidewalk across the street from Stoneham Elementary on Denver's west side. Vince Tajira has set the shot to capture students romping on the playground over Hart's shoulder. If Tajira were a chef and not a photojournalist, he'd count the grains of salt. He works at half the speed of Tamica.

"Does your husband not share your concerns?" says Flynn.

"I mean, can we stop for a second?"

"Don't worry, we won't use this," says Flynn.

"Well, he thinks I'm being an alarmist. I'm only trying to get the school's attention, but he thinks we should trust the system more, that kind of thing."

"Okay," says Flynn. "That's fine. We won't mention him. But could I get his name?"

"What for?" says Hart.

"Strictly for the record. It's a background detail."

"You're recording."

"Yes, and ninety-five percent of this hits the editing room floor, but I'll make a note for my files. Just being thorough."

"It's Aaron Hart. A-a-r-o-n."

"Thank you. Are you involved in the school?" says Flynn. "Parent committee or anything?"

"No. I'm a parent who cares about her kids' education. I check the online portal every day for homework assignments. I attend every school function, even though of course I'm always never that comfortable inside, thinking about what might happen."

"And now tell us about the bomb threats," says Flynn.

She is a tall, short-haired brunette. She's wearing sage high-waisted pants and a loose white pullover. Minor makeup, no earrings, dark eyes, all business.

"We know for a fact that the school has received bomb threats," says Hart, "and the school has not informed parents or done anything about them. In fact, the teachers have kept right on teaching."

"How many?"

"Three that we know of," says Hart. "Two last week and one the week before."

"Threats saying there was a bomb?"

"Yes."

"And how did you find out about this?"

"All I can tell you is that one of the women in the neighborhood is a paraprofessional at the school, and she overheard the principal discussing it with the office staff."

"Do you know if the police were called? Or school district security?"

"I know they consulted with district security," says Hart. "Yes."

"So you have taken your concerns to the school?"

"I talked to the principal, and he told me they know when a bomb threat is legitimate and when it's a prank, which I think is crazy. In this day and age?"

"But the first threat turned out to be nothing, correct?"

Hart shrugs. "Doesn't every threat deserve serious evaluation? And shouldn't parents be notified? We get alerts on our phone about school plays and school fundraisers; shouldn't we know when our children's lives are in danger?"

Flynn locks that sound bite in her head. There's the opening quote for the piece or the tease for the top of the newscast.

"Do you know if it was the same person making the threat?"

"I don't."

"Do you know what time of day the threats came in?"

"I heard they were left as messages overnight," says Hart. "Not sure if that's true."

"And what days specifically did these come in?"

"You'd have to ask them, but I doubt you'll get anywhere."

"How does this whole situation make you feel, you know, as a parent?"

"It makes me feel like I'm not being listened to."

"Do other parents feel the same way?"

"There's a group of us, yes," says Hart.

"You know you can take it to the school board?" says Flynn. "Sign up for a public hearing and let the board know your concerns?"

"Yes," says Hart. "Of course. And get swept under the rug."

"Is there anything else you want to add? Something I'm not asking you?"

Hart ponders this for a moment. She takes a breath. "I think the principal is controlling. Overly so. He thinks he knows what's best. He wants to keep a tight lid on everything, and he's only concerned about test scores. But what do test scores matter if our kids don't come home?"

"Okay," says Tajira. They've shot B-roll of Hart walking with Flynn on the sidewalk. Hart has departed in her shiny black Acura. "Now what?"

"Let's shoot exteriors," says Flynn. "Then I'll go see if the principal is around."

Tajira is a calm, old-school pro. He's an Afghan by heritage and Muslim. He's a tireless photojournalist, but he's tied to his tripod and uncomfortable without it. The setups take longer. Flynn's dance with Tamica is fluid. With Tajira, Flynn always feels like every collaboration is the first.

"I'll get a shot of you going up the steps to the school," says Tajira.

"That's okay," says Flynn. "No theater today, okay?"

Tajira is six feet tall with a long face and weary eyes. He's got five kids and he's happy to tell anyone about their skills.

"Why don't you set up on the sidewalk, and I'll go ask the principal to step out?"

"You don't want to check with the school district honchos?"

"What are my chances of getting through, or getting approval? I mean, isn't it a simple question?"

"Go for it," says Tajira.

Gaining access means an intercom chat. Flynn presses the buzzer on the metal box.

"Yes?"

Flynn wonders if she has ever heard a male voice in this role of invisible doorman.

"Hi, it's Flynn Martin. I'm a reporter." Flynn isn't sure if she's supposed to talk to the red metal box or face the steel door. "I'd like to talk with the principal, please?"

"May I tell him what this is about?"

"I've been chatting with one of your parents, Meg Hart. About the threats that have been coming in by phone."

Flynn gives herself credit for not saying the word "bomb" out loud.

"You'll have to put your request through downtown," says the voice. "School district HQ."

"Why?"

Now Flynn wishes Tajira were rolling, to capture the welcoming sounds of a fleet-footed bureaucracy in responsive mode. Flynn pulls out her phone, opens the record function.

"Because it's a matter of security," says the voice.

"I'd like to know about your school's policy for communicating with parents," says Flynn. "And how you know when a threat is something you can ignore."

"Please check with the district's media relations office. We are in the middle of the school day and focused on teaching and learning."

"I've interviewed a parent who is concerned about the threats and how you're handling them. I'd like to balance her concerns with someone from the school in question. It would be much more meaningful from those here at this school."

"Again, Miss Martin, our policy on this one is that you speak with the media relations office."

CHAPTER 42

"I'm not airing it without a response."

Goodman is adamant.

"I gave them all afternoon," says Flynn. "I called them the second I got back in the car, waited an hour, and called them again. Called again around four p.m. and started writing. Nada. Zipola."

"It needs a comment from the school or the district. A statement would work."

"We say all the time, 'So-and-so couldn't be reached for comment.' We got bomb threats and parents in the dark on one side, and all the school district has to do is ignore us, and that means no story?"

Goodman gives her a hard look. Like a father deciding if he can extend a curfew. She's standing in his office. Goodman, who is seated, wipes an invisible crumb off the side of his mouth with a thumb.

"It'll wait a day, won't it?"

"But why let them win? I mean, Nancy Lang has like six people working for her. All media relations or internal communications, and it's not that hard to give us a callback."

"You told Nancy Lang what the story entailed?"

"Of course," says Flynn. "And I told them the story was running today."

"You called the school back?"

"After the greeting I was given out there?"

Goodman sighs, thinks.

"We can run this today and follow up tomorrow," says Flynn. "And we don't always need to defer to the bureaucrats."

"I'm feeling abraded," says Goodman.

"Huh?"

"Worn down."

"Good," says Flynn. "Flexibility is good for the soul."

"When they do call back, ask for district-wide numbers on bomb threats. Maybe this is a bigger story about how they assess the calls and decide when to take them seriously."

"Deal."

Flynn sits on the set as all 105 seconds of the story run. In some ways, this is the way it's supposed to work. The story is simple. It's one voice reaching an audience. It's Meg Hart slicing through the bureaucracy. It's Meg Hart getting her school principal's attention. It's one mother with strong parental instincts pointing out something about the way the world works and saying, "Look, over here. This is a problem."

Flynn doesn't feel bad about running the audio from the intercom box. Tajira, it turned out, shot video from the street of her at the school door. His camera picked up enough audio that it was easy to sync with her crystal-clear recording of the office staffer telling her to go to hell.

"Well," says anchor Sara Cornette when the piece wraps. "I guess most of us assume that they clear the building each time a threat is called in, to make sure."

"We called the district to understand their policy and how they handle these threats," says Flynn. "So far, no reply. We expect to hear back soon."

"As always," says Cornette, turning back to the camera, "this story came in through our tip line, and you can see on the screen the various ways to get our attention via email, our online form, and social media. We need you. And appreciate you."

◆ ◆ ◆

Flynn packs up, decides at the last second to check her messages and the reaction. There's always reaction.

Spewing takes is what we do.

Spewing takes is who we are.

◆ ◆ ◆

On X: Test scores so much more important than sending students home at the end of the day ALIVE. How the hell do they know when a threat is legit?

On X: Just another example of a school district that really listens to its parents. Insensitive jerks.

On her station's Facebook page: I guess any parent can pull the pin on a hand grenade and lob it over the wall, try to shame a school. Sorry for the violent imagery, but let's keep in mind that school districts deal with this stuff all the time and if they took all the students outside every time there was a threat, the scum out there who call in these threats wouldn't stop.

An email from Nancy Lang: Wow, Flynn, did not expect that from you. I know you called today about the Stoneham Elementary School parent. You never mentioned once that this would run today, that there was a deadline. You said you had talked to a parent, but I assumed you were doing in-depth reporting on the subject, not doing a surface-level one-off. Come on, Flynn, you know these matters are complicated. Here's a little fact for you—as soon as a school that receives a wave of these threats so much as whispers the idea of extending the school day or adding days to the school year, the threats stop. Did you know that? That's because the vast majority of these are not credible and if you want to really do an in-depth story on the issue that shows some recognition of what our security team faces every day—and many of these school security officers are also parents with kids in school and not insensitive, faceless bureaucrats—let me know. I mistakenly thought when we went WAY out of our way to help you with your issue at Wyatt's school that we could expect, maybe, a little grace back from you and your station on these kinds of cheap, easy stories that are only designed to give parents and taxpayers more reason to think we, somehow, are heartless functionaries.

CHAPTER 43

"Did you write back?" says Michael.

Her father also thought the bomb threat story was of the flawed, skipping-stone variety.

"Can we go?" says Wyatt.

"I feel awful about burning Nancy," says Flynn. "I didn't think she'd take it so personally, and it didn't seem to be an attack on her. It was more about the school."

"What was the rush?" says her father.

Was she trying to fill her brain with something other than the grim Shannon Way scene, the murdered post office worker? Had she dropped her standards in the process?

"I'll call Nancy back tomorrow," says Flynn. "And come in crawling."

"Can we *please* go?" Wyatt tucks his thumbs under the straps on his heavy backpack. "So I get to my home, where I can be locked up in my prison cell condo bedroom?"

"Let's thank Grampa for keeping you safe," says Flynn.

"Thanks." Wyatt's effort is weak. "Safe from what, I'd like to know."

"And Max is taking over," says Michael. "Right?"

"Starting tomorrow," says Flynn. Max had a work "thing" that delayed moving Wyatt's base camp.

"May as well be Arizona," says Wyatt. "You know sleep is good for kids, don't you? Brain development? Mental health? Teenagers who don't get enough sleep are prone to getting involved with risky behaviors? Have you ever done a story about that? I'm going to have to get up at like five in the freaking morning to make it to school on time."

"It's temporary," says Flynn. "It'll be over soon."

Frozen veggie burger patties, sesame seed buns, sliced red onion, all the trimmings and bagged salad.

"Did you know how much water they use so you can eat salad straight out of a plastic bag?" says Wyatt.

"I know. The things we do for convenience."

"It's like a triple wash, and one of them is with chlorine to kill bacteria."

"We have to pick our battles," says Flynn.

Wyatt nibbles at his burger. He won't finish it. He stabs at a piece of romaine lettuce with his fork, studies it like a scientist.

She asks him about school, trying to sound like a chill friend and not a probing mother. Wyatt tells her about an art project, how he's writing a story that will be turned into a graphic novel that involves a bunch of lost students on a mountain camping trip who encounter vampires.

Wyatt retreats to his room. Flynn pours a glass of cold white wine to help her with the cleanup and dishwasher loading. She composes apologies to Nancy Lang in her head, wonders if groveling will be enough. It's not as if she can let the school district off the hook *that* easily.

How hard would it have been for Lang to call and ask for another day to respond?

Flynn pours another glass of wine, closes the curtains of her floor-to-ceiling windows with the push of a button, settles on the couch, and realizes she left her phone in her car. She taps on Wyatt's door.

"What is it?"

"I'm running to the car. Your space-head mom left her phone."

"I think I can manage."

Wyatt sits up in bed, the room dark other than the glow from his laptop.

"Wanted you to know."

She gets a thumbs-up reply.

Flynn decides her condo neighbors will have to deal with her slightly disheveled appearance in loose sweatpants and a braless dark blue T-shirt. It's possible to make the long walk to the elevator and to her car without running into anyone.

This time, however, is like rush hour on I-25. Each stop requires offloading and onloading like a cargo ship in a port with striking dockworkers.

Her garage floor, however, is devoid of humans. A distant car door slams. The lighting is weak on the brown end of the spectrum. The spot for her Kia is at one of the ten reserved for vehicles that need charging stations, about halfway down the row of cars on the north side of the building. A warm breeze through the open-air garage carries garlic and ginger from a Chinese restaurant down the block.

Flynn clutches her keys, ponders how she'll approach Nancy Lang and whether to leave a reply voicemail tonight, and already wonders if she should say anything at all. The *lack* of a district reply in her piece doesn't invalidate Meg Hart's facts or concerns. Isn't that where she should start with Lang? Confirm the bomb threats and lack of parent communication?

The envelope sits erect and perky on her driver's side window, only a corner shoved down between the glass and weather stripping.

Flynn stops.

Impossible.

Completely utterly fucking impossible.

Looks around.

Looks around.

Listens.

To her heart pound.

Steps closer.

Her name is handwritten. This time, in blue ink.

Flynn Martin

The envelope isn't gray, but maybe the weak light is playing tricks. It's not as big as the other ones.

She doesn't touch it, thinks *Forensics* and *How the hell* in the same jumbled thought.

Has it been ninety minutes since she parked?

One thing is certain. This one is way too close to home. Way too fucking close.

Flynn unlocks the car with the remote. She goes in from the passenger side, using a finger wrapped in her T-shirt to open the door. She grabs her phone from its spot next to the cup holder without touching anything else.

Pulls up Jasper, hits the button, wonders if she should risk the trip back up to change. Worries about leaving the scene. Worries she's being watched.

A billion cars. A billion places to hide.

"Flynn Martin," says Jasper.

Her night climbs aboard the hellscape express.

CHAPTER 44

Back up the elevator, needing to change. Knowing it won't be quick. Thinking *Fuck, fuck, miserable fuck.*

"Mom?"

"It's me."

Wyatt is out of bed.

"What took so long?"

"I ran into a friend," says Flynn. *Forget it. Nice try. No way. Won't fly.* "The police are coming."

"What? Here?"

"To the garage," says Flynn. "There's another one of those messages. This time they left it on my car. I need to go back down. I have no idea how long—"

"I want to come."

"No."

"I want to see."

His tone is matter of fact. It's easy to hear a touch of Max, the declarative inflection.

"You want to see?"

Buying time.

Her phone chimes. Jasper.

"Yes?"

"Tell your building's security team we are coming," says Jasper.

"Of course."

"Three vehicles and we'll need the gate up."

"I'll tell them."

"And then we'll close the whole garage until we're done. No more coming and going."

Hell, the ruckus. Commotion. The unwanted attention and all the whispers.

"Are you with your car?" says Jasper.

"I ran back up to tell Wyatt what was happening."

"We're five minutes out."

The phone drains itself of life.

"Please, Mom."

Again, bonus points for civility.

And why not? The kid has a right.

"Get dressed," she says.

"I am."

Shorts, Glass Animals T-shirt from Wyatt's first live concert this summer. She took Wyatt and Jeremy to Red Rocks in July. They gawked at the beauty and amazement of ten thousand people hanging on every note. Mid-concert, a saffron moon rose over the eastern plains.

"Shoes or slippers too," says Flynn. "Give me two minutes."

Olive jeans. Bra—*because.* Blue-striped button-up shirt. One last long glug of room-temperature wine.

Down the long hall and in the elevator, Wyatt says nothing.

"There's not much to see," says Flynn, prodding conversation.

"I know," says Wyatt.

At the garage level, they step out through the entryway.

Flynn thinks how easy it might be to wait, make it look like you belong, and slip in the building through one of these garage-entry vestibules. If, say, you walked up the ramp around the security gate. If you risked being spotted on camera. If you picked your moment and waited for someone coming out, you could pretend you're a regular and could get through the buzzered door, especially if you were dragging a wheeled suitcase or some such.

They're halfway between the vestibule and her Kia when Flynn hears the urgent rumble of the caravan. The size and heft of their vehicles feels like an invasion, and the third one, a tall van, looks like it should be scraping the overhead beams. The vehicles park. Jasper climbs out of the first one, gives her and Wyatt a wave to come his way.

Carter pops out of Jasper's vehicle too. Carter from the building's ninth-floor courtesy desk. That's all she knows. Carter. He's Black, young, easygoing, and wears the maroon jacket uniform of the building's security team. He likely met the cops at the street-level gate to ensure access and then they gave him a ride up.

"I'm sorry there's a problem," says Carter.

"Me too," says Flynn. "There are security cameras on the garage entrance, the gates?"

"Detective asked me the same thing. Yes, for sure."

Jasper. Dark slacks, white oxford shirt loose at the collar, blue-and-orange-striped tie.

Once he's walked close enough to see the envelope, he explains the drill. He tells them they'll set lights. They need to process every "minuscule tidbit of jetsam" they can find within twenty yards of the Kia. They're sending two uniforms to review all comings and goings on the security camera at the garage gate and all the foot traffic in and out of the vestibule. They need a complete list of all the tenants who came and went between the time when Flynn parked and the time she returned, and, in fact, the footage of her trips will help establish the parameters for the search. As they get names of those who came and went, they will knock on doors and ask if anybody saw anything unusual or useful.

Whispers. Commotion. Ruckus. And rumors.

Three light stands placed in an arc, knee high. A photographer. Four Tyvek-suited ghosts in a practiced dance of evidence observation, evidence collection. Three uniforms head off with industrial flashlights, searching those one billion hiding spots.

"What did you touch?" says Jasper.

Flynn tells him.

"What shoes were you wearing?"

"These," says Flynn, standing on one leg to show him the thousand-dot tread pattern.

"Size?"

"Eight."

"Bold MF," says Jasper under his breath, leaning down to her ear. "I'm sure your son has heard the word, but, you know."

"The surface looks like it wouldn't hold an impression," says Wyatt.

"It does appear that way," says Jasper, treating him like he belongs. *Good.*

"There's no sand, no dirt," says Wyatt.

"Even a patch of oil, something, we might get lucky."

"Is that like the other ones?" says Wyatt.

Not quite. Flynn doesn't say it.

Maybe *the pattern is no pattern.*

Except the envelope itself, even if a different color and size, is a pattern.

"We'll see when we get closer," says Jasper.

The techs crouch in a huddle near the Kia's left-rear bumper like archaeologists studying the first exposure of an ancient bone after hours of gently scraping dirt with a pastry brush. At some invisible signal, they all stand. A marker goes down. Paparazzi pop-pop photos low and high. Around and around and around.

Good.

Flynn's phone chimes.

Chris Casey.

Flynn steps away out of earshot, keeps an eye on the conductor Jasper and his Tyvek quartet. Wyatt is transfixed, arms folded, mouth open an unconscious crack.

"Where are you?"

Several times over the weekend, Flynn thought about whether Casey's long stakeout was paying dividends.

"Pueblo," says Casey.

"Any luck?"

"They've marched Jedidiah Kline out of the trailer park here. He'd shaved his head and looked like he could have tumbled off a boxcar after a cross-country ride."

"Were you there?"

"The only ones. Close enough to ask a question."

"And?"

"I asked him why he left home, why he was on the run."

"And?"

"He said 'Fuck you,' which I am going to take as an indication that he was not interested in a formal chat. Tamica was in close. God, she's good. Aggressive, you know? Cops didn't seem to mind. They wanted to show off their trophy."

"Arapahoe County cops?"

"Pueblo too."

"You've been, what, waiting?"

"I had access to the guys leading the hunt, and they didn't want anything out there about the chase coming to Pueblo until they had him. He was using his dad's credit card, and I guess the first thing he did was take out a bunch of cash. He went to a strip mall off Academy in Colorado Springs and kept asking people to take him south to Pueblo. He offered five hundred dollars cash. The guy who drove him thought it was weird, called the cops, and showed them the spot where he'd let Jedidiah out, by the Arkansas River along the train tracks."

"And if Jedidiah Kline had his father's credit card, that puts him back at the family house up north."

"Correct," says Casey.

"And then he's in the Springs, trying to hire a driver."

"Right."

"Did he withdraw the cash near the family home in Centennial or later in Colorado Springs?"

"Centennial," says Casey. "Next question."

"The only next question is when."

A tech lifts the envelope from its perch on the window of her Kia with giant tweezers, places it in a black tray held by a second tech.

"Friday, before the Klines evaporated."

"Not good," says Flynn.

"For him?" says Casey. "Not good at all. For us? This might be a wrap."

"You've got this, obviously, for tonight?"

"Goodman considered a cut-in at nine, but we'll be all over the ten. We'll beat everyone in town."

"I'm sure," says Flynn.

"We'll stay here for the morning news conference, head back."

"Good work," says Flynn. She means it. It's not easy to wait for days for a payoff and wonder if anything will come of it.

The problem, and it's not *really* a problem, is that if Jedidiah killed his family in a rage, that means there's nothing to the business with the holding companies or foul infighting over church finances.

Or maybe the church money is a story in its own right? And does she follow up even if the church is reeling and wounded?

Or wait a few weeks and then come circling around?

With the big news out of Pueblo, Flynn gets an idea. She calls the station and gets the late show producer on the phone.

"Can you not rerun the Meg Hart bomb threat story?" says Flynn.

"It's in the rundown for a quick sound bite."

Producer Linda Newton is a veteran. Unflappable.

"It would be a big favor," says Flynn.

The thought of a clean finish to the Kline family grisliness isn't unwelcome, but how the hell would one rabid son get the drop on his whole family? Was he in the car when it drove off to the airport? Could he have been driving? Were they *all* in the car?

If Jedidiah Jack confesses or if the evidence is so overwhelming that the trial will be a formality, she can devote 1,000 percent of her anxieties to being simultaneously furious and worried about PDQ2.

A huddle around Jasper's vehicle. A white mat sits on the hood. The black tray is on the mat, the envelope next to it. The paper inside has been extracted and sits, unfolded, next to the tray like a rare specimen. Flynn catches only glimpses through the man trees.

Jasper looks around, gives Flynn a *Come here* nod.

The Tyvek crew peel off their suits.

A laugh.

Really?

What's to laugh at?

Jasper says "Stand down" into a walkie-talkie.

Flynn comes up behind the gaggle of cop beefiness. They're like a thicket.

The note is in a beautiful, clean longhand.

Flynn reads:

> Miss Flynn,
>
> I'm a neighbor here in the building and I've seen you coming and going. I know this is highly unusual but I wanted to let you know I think you do a fantastic job. So thank you for what you do for the city, for the community of Denver. I'm a believer in quality news and of course it's terrible that we have to qualify what kind of news we like because, by definition, news should be just that. Anyway, yes, this is a fan note. I wanted to brighten your day. And ask you a favor. I respect your privacy and I want you to know that I don't mean to complicate your life or add to what I'm sure is a stressful job. However, if you have time and the inclination, I have a daughter at CU Boulder in Journalism. I was wondering if you might be willing to meet with her for coffee and give her encouragement? If I don't hear from you—understood. I'm

sure your hands are full. However, I'll leave my phone number just in case.

Thank you.

Tom Rosner / Apt. 1837

393-555-8974

CHAPTER 45

"I'm the reporter who cried envelope."

"You're the woman who did the right thing."

Detective Jasper, even at this hour, remains so freaking starched. Put together. Like he must move about his day with a portable dressing room for quick touch-ups. Tonight the Jasper eau de tobacco comes with a whiff of stale sweat.

"I feel like a fool."

"How could you have known?"

"Logic doesn't work when you feel the way I do," says Flynn. "Drink?"

He looks at his watch, a fancy gold number. No wedding ring. It's the first time she's noticed.

"One couldn't hurt," says Jasper.

"It's the least I can do, though I should have your whole team here if I was doing it right."

Jasper arranges himself on the couch. He chooses a vodka on the rocks from her brief verbal menu of hard stuff. She's got the TV on, muted, and explains about wanting to watch Chris Casey's report from Pueblo.

"They got him?" says Jasper.

"Chris called me about the same time the envelope was being plucked from the car window."

"Have to say that's not a good look for that kid. What was his name again?"

"Jedidiah Kline," says Flynn. She sits next to him, on the edge of the sofa, with a fresh glass of cold white wine. As if she's the guest, not the owner. "He was going by Jack."

"But if you think about it—hurting your younger brother and sister too?"

Jasper scooches back in his seat, deflates like a few pounds of pressure released from a rock-hard tire. She can almost hear the exhaling hiss.

"You have your doubts?"

"I swim in a sea of doubts," says Jasper. "It's not over until the verdict is read. Would you like to hear what Tom Rosner had to say?"

"Wait—did you call him, or did you go to his place?" Cops at your door inside the tower, with no advance notice, would deliver a serious jolt. "And how did you explain why his envelope would draw such a response?"

"Called first, then went up," says Jasper.

"Just you?"

"Yes."

"And?"

"And I told him you've been getting threats, that's all. Kept it vague."

"And?"

"And he confirmed the note was legit. Gave us the name of the daughter in college, all of that."

"How did he react?"

"Um, confused? Rattled. I mean, embarrassed, too, I guess."

"What's he like?"

Jasper stares at her, cracks the faintest of smiles.

"Oh, you think the favor request is some sort of ruse?"

"I'm good at questioning everything too. Young? Old?"

"He turned fifty last month."

Bingo. Within range.

"You checked his ID."

"Had to."

"And you made note."

"That was five minutes ago," says Jasper. "I think my brain is capable."

"And what's he like?"

"I'm not your wingman, okay?"

"Divorced?"

"As a matter of fact."

"In shape?"

"Jesus, Flynn Martin, that's not why I came to your place. You've got his phone number."

Tom Rosner's note sits on her kitchen counter.

"Then we can talk about Robert Waller."

"No," says Jasper. "We—"

Flynn holds up her hand. Her station's dramatic theme music plays. A brooding, offbeat riff like a first draft of the *Mission: Impossible* ditty. 10:00 p.m. anchors Lee Rosen and Oliver Garrett. Rosen's got bushy dark hair and a bookish look. Garrett with the blond buzz cut and ever-present cheeriness looks like he's ready for a kegger at the drop of a hat.

"Sheriff's deputies and local police tonight in Pueblo have located and arrested Jedidiah Kline, the son of Patrick and Victoria Kline, who vanished, along with their two children, from the family's Centennial home in a story that has gripped the city and state," says Rosen.

"Our own Chris Casey is in Pueblo tonight," says Garrett. Heavy sincerity. "Chris was there when the work paid off, and he joins us live from the scene."

Casey. Madras short-sleeved shirt. Dark background with one unreadable neon sign. He could be anywhere.

"As you can see, all is quiet here tonight at Westside Court near downtown Pueblo." *No, we can't see that.* "Residents here said they had no idea one of the homes was harboring a fugitive—the older, adopted son of Patrick and Victoria Kline."

Roll video.

Jedidiah Kline sandwiched between three cops, being frog-marched to a waiting vehicle.

Casey's voice off-camera: "Why did you leave home?"

Kline, shaved head and dead eyes, says nothing.

Casey: "Why did you run?"

Kline says nothing.

Casey: "Do you know where your family is?"

Kline's lips move, but the words are trapped under two grating bleeps.

Next, shots of the unit where Kline was found and Casey's voice-over about the length of the hunt and the fact that authorities were able to track his movements, in part, because Jedidiah had his father's credit card and had used it to access cash at ATMs as he headed south, bribing one driver with $500. Casey's package includes shots of the Kline family, their Shannon Way home, and the church where the congregation is "devastated by the tragic loss. Guys?"

Guys—question mark. The universal toss back to the studio.

"When exactly did we women agree to be lumped in as guys?" says Flynn to the TV.

Rosen: "And we understand that there will be a news conference tomorrow?"

Casey: "Correct. In Arapahoe County."

Garrett: "Was there any indication about why he headed to this particular location in Pueblo?"

Casey: "I'm sure that's one of the questions we'll be asking tomorrow."

Garrett: "Thanks to you, Chris Casey, on the exclusive reporting tonight for a story that has kept the city fretting for many days now, and also thanks to photojournalist Tamica Porter for her work today as well."

Flynn mutes the TV. She wants to keep an eye on the rundown to make sure the Meg Hart bomb threat story doesn't run, per her request.

"He didn't do it," says Jasper.

"What?" says Flynn.

"If I was placing bets."

"Why so sure?"

"He's too slight, too timid. Did you see the size of him next to the cops?"

"Then why the stolen credit card? Why did he run?"

"Panic does crazy things. He would have come home to an empty house, right? At that point, nobody knew they were missing."

"So why is Patrick Kline's credit card still at home?" says Flynn.

"Exactly," says Jasper.

"If they were heading off on vacation."

"Exactly."

"Why doesn't he call anyone? Nine one one? Alert a neighbor if he thinks it's strange? Maybe the whole wallet was left behind?"

"Maybe he knew nothing about the planned trip," says Jasper. "Or maybe he did, and maybe he's got a key to the house, comes home to crash for a night or two, and comes across the credit card. And there's always the chance the dad's got multiple accounts, multiple cards, and he left one at home on purpose. There could be a reasonable explanation."

"Can we go back to Robert Waller?" says Flynn.

Why not take advantage of the crazy reason that Detective Jasper is inside her condo drinking her vodka? Plus, she doesn't want to give Jedidiah Kline a reasonable explanation. She wants the Kline saga to wrap.

Jasper sighs. Sips. Sips again. "I take it Wyatt is asleep?"

"If he's not asleep, he can't hear anything," says Flynn.

"Doesn't matter," says Jasper. "Not here. We have questions."

"Questions for me?"

"We have a process," says Jasper. "And we need to go through it. And do it the right way."

"Can you give me a vague helpful idea of what you're going to ask me?"

"I'd rather not."

"I don't know any post office workers from Athmar Park."

"Okay," says Jasper.

"And I'd like to not stare at the ceiling tonight while I'm trying to fall asleep."

"I understand," says Jasper. "But I want to do this by the book. With Detective Yamamoto. And in a good place where we can all think together."

"What about the two envelopes? The one in Wyatt's backpack and the one left in my car?"

"With Yamamoto."

"How bad was it?" says Flynn.

"It?"

"The murder of Robert Waller."

"There was rage involved."

"Any links to PDQ?"

"Harry Kugel is in prison."

"You know what I mean—how Waller was killed, anything. Posing the body."

"Not now," says Jasper.

"How was he killed?"

Sip. Ice cube rattle. Sigh. Sip.

"You don't give up."

"I try not to."

"Are you capable of sitting on information?"

"Not one of my sharpest talents," says Flynn. "There's always this clear voice whispering in my ear about the public's right to know."

"It's that easy?" Jasper sits up, shows her his empty glass. Asks, "Do you mind?"

"Help yourself."

She waits. The ice dispenser grinds. She hears him pour a generous second drink, tells herself not to try and keep pace. A Monday night. *Ooof.*

"I didn't say it was easy," says Flynn.

"Then how do you determine?"

"We discuss it. It's never my decision."

Well, rarely.

"Discuss," says Jasper with extra venom on the *ess*. "I think that's what people want to know. How do you reach a decision about what gets airtime or how much resources to throw at a story?"

Flynn squelches the urge to show Detective Jasper the door, to spool out a ruse about fatigue, or an early start, or how she would really rather go to sleep thinking about Axel Sheen than to cover the same old ground she's covered a gazillion times with Max. She trashes the cautionary thought about another drink, makes tracks to the refrigerator, finds a fresh bottle of wine there, thanks her lucky stars it's a screw-top and she doesn't have to go through the fussy uncorking stuff, and pours another glass.

Jasper's electric field of cop*ness*, in fact, reminds her too much of Max, and that must explain why she hasn't thought once about him in any sexual context or flash of fantasy. If Jasper said he was a high school teacher and if he looked the same as he does tonight, would that change? Most likely. Somehow the job of cop comes with a worldview that permeates your marrow, gaze, mannerisms, essence. Unfortunately, Flynn's internal scanner failed to ping on the cues about Max's hardened *Weltanschauung*—a word her father taught her on the day she told him about the pending divorce—until about five years after she had tied the knot with Max. Deep down, she thinks that if she had gone for a long drive in the mountains and really thought it through, say a month before the wedding, that she could have seen the trouble ahead.

On the other hand, had she pulled the plug on the wedding, there would be no Wyatt.

That thought is unacceptable.

So, in the end, she would do it all again. And maybe having developed a hyper nose for cop mentality is a good thing for her work.

"Well, deciding on what gets broadcast is not a science," says Flynn. "And I've often thought that if our newsroom had a staff twenty-four times as large, we could run an all-day local news show and never repeat anything. There are a thousand individuals out there every day in government and private business and in communities who are happy we have not yet been tipped off on their schemes, failures, screwups, mismanagement, sloppiness, or full-system failures."

"A thousand?"

"Easily," says Flynn. "Size of Denver? Given all the issues? Given all the people and communities who feel left behind? And that's before we get to the crimes and murder."

Jasper shakes his head. Drinks. "An awfully cynical view of the world. You start with the default mentality that those in office are taking advantage, cutting corners, whatever. Or that a corporation automatically means greed?"

"I don't start there. Sure, there are plenty of good people doing their jobs, but shortcuts are tempting. So is feathering your own nest."

"Do you ever take a complaint and put it on the news?" says Jasper. "Take it, air it, run with it? Without getting the other side?"

Did Nancy Lang and John Jasper share notes?

Did he catch the Meg Hart bomb threat story before she phoned in the false alarm envelope waiting on her Kia?

"I try to get both sides," says Flynn. "Kind of Journalism 101. But it happens. Especially if the school district, government agency, or private business is playing hide-and-seek."

"You're saying the exact opposite things that would put me in a sharing mood."

Late-night weatherwoman Marcia McNeil delivers the forecast. The red-hot graphics say it all. So do the triple digits.

"I know," says Flynn. "But I'm telling you what I know, and now you should do the same."

"And you could immediately put it on the morning news and we would lose an advantage—plus we'd give Mr. Waller's killer a ton of satisfaction."

"And you might also help a few million citizens of Metro Denver be more alert and wary," says Flynn. "You might save a life by making sure the public knows the threat level is high."

"But you aren't willing to let us decide what facts we want in the public domain."

"I can't make any promises."

"You could if you wanted to," says Jasper.

"If I wanted to be co-opted? Sure."

Jasper studies her.

Or looks through her.

She stares back, gives him nothing.

"We all know what you've been through."

"Don't—under any circumstances—cut me an ounce of slack," says Flynn.

"And you're in the quagmire again."

"Because *fuckwad* Harry Kugel is doing something," says Flynn. "Manipulating something."

"You don't know that. We certainly don't know that. His communications are monitored."

"He's behind it," says Flynn.

"Robert Waller was stabbed."

"So you're giving me this information?"

"I'm telling you all of this," says Jasper. "Because of your connection. It's not for public consumption."

"So not strangled like how PDQ did it?"

"Are we in agreement here?" says Jasper.

"I guess."

"Think of another word."

"Agreed," says Flynn.

CHAPTER 46

"So not strangled?"

"Correct."

"Were there signs of a struggle?"

Jasper nods.

"Did he live alone?"

"Yes. Divorced. His wife and two kids moved to Northglenn."

"What did he do for the post office?"

"He worked maintenance," says Jasper. "Mechanical work—fixing machines and that sort of thing. Graveyard shift."

"How long?"

"About ten years."

"What time was he murdered?"

"Early in the morning. We believe his killer was waiting inside when he got home."

"Any witnesses at all?"

"We're still looking," says Jasper. "It may be a case of someone not knowing that they saw something important."

"I've always wondered," says Flynn. "Has that *ever* worked? Same as the Kline issue in Centennial—'Everybody think back.' Are memories that good?"

"All we can do is ask people in the neighborhood if they recall anything from overnight and the day before."

"You've got the neighbor who spotted the open door and the loose dog," says Flynn.

"But she didn't see anything else."

"He was stabbed more than once?"

"Nine times."

"Jesus," says Flynn. "Did you recover the knife?"

"Yes," says Jasper. "And the killer left the sharpener out on the kitchen table, next to the knife."

"One of Waller's knives?"

"Yes."

"Doesn't sound so rage-like," says Flynn. "If the killer is leaving his tools out."

"Eye of the hurricane. Something."

"Fingerprints? DNA? Anything? Leads?"

"We're looking."

"Motive?"

"Robert Waller was employee-of-the-month material," says Jasper. "Lived modestly. Home and work, home and work. One-or-two-beers-on-the-weekend kind of guy. Broncos fan and not a big believer in banks."

"You got that from his ex-wife?"

"She said he liked the 'feeling' of holding all that cash," says Jasper.

"How much?"

"Tens of thousands, most likely."

"So robbery could be the motive."

"If word got out, sure, but that level of violence? More than robbery."

"And Mr. Waller?" says Flynn.

"I was about to ask you if you can think of any possible connection."

"Between?"

"Between you and him."

"You mean, other than the envelope with my name on it?"

Jasper slides a five-by-seven color photo from a notebook.

"He's Black," says Flynn.

Jasper says nothing.

Why did she default to White in her pathetic predictable head? *Why?*

The photo is head and shoulders only. It's got the random-expression quality of an employee badge or a DMV auteur. First shot, only shot. Waller's eyes are at half mast, but he's got a wide friendly smile with teeth like a white stone fence disappearing off to the horizon. Short hair, a fleshy nose with large nostrils.

"I don't think so," says Flynn.

"Don't think so what?" says Jasper.

"I mean, I don't recognize him. I can't imagine why I would. The poor man—he looks so happy."

"By all accounts, he was just that."

"Was his body posed? Anything? Where was he found?"

"In his living room."

"Fair amount of blood, I assume."

"Can you hold off on putting this out there?"

"I will talk it over," says Flynn. "I'll guarantee that."

"If you don't bring the topic to your folks at the station," says Jasper, "then there's no discussion. Can't you make it your decision?"

"Not quite that easy."

"Sounds easy to me. I'm extending confidence here, you know?"

"I do," says Flynn. More than before, she wants Jasper gone. She hopes she's out of vodka. "And I appreciate it."

"And you feel safe?" says Jasper. He loosens his garish blue-orange tie, unbuttons the top button, rattles his ice cubes as if a cocktail waitress will appear out of the ether and save him the effort of standing.

Please no, Flynn prays.

"Of course," says Flynn. She's feeling bludgeoned by the evening, but she's not going to let on. "Suddenly very tired."

"And you think Wyatt is going to be okay?"

"With Max? Of course."

Did she tell Jasper about that plan? *When?*

She can't recall.

"I need to ask you a question," says Jasper.

"I'm not sure I've got any more answers in me."

She stands, walks to the sink, rinses her glass. She walks back to the couch, sits a few inches farther out of reach. She wants to take his glass and say *Time to go*.

Jasper sucks on an ice cube, spits it back in his glass. Doesn't move.

"Are you seeing anyone?" says Jasper.

"Excuse me?"

"Seeing anyone." No question mark.

"Oh, no," says Flynn. "Not—*not*—going there. Let's keep this aboveboard."

"Of course I'd be interested," says Jasper, ignoring her. "I'm putting it out there. Maybe when all this is settled."

"You're ten years younger. At least. And—"

"And one cop was enough?"

"Maybe," says Flynn. "And I am seeing someone."

Does one date count? Two dates?

"Well, *that's* a different story," says Jasper. "Must be pretty recent, then?"

Flynn stares at him, hoping he can read the *Fuck you* freshly tattooed on her forehead.

"Pretend you never brought this up, okay?" says Flynn. "Hit the erase button on the last minute."

"No," says Jasper. "I don't mind if you know. Do you ever wonder, you know, when someone calls you out of the blue and suggests that you come out and cover a story, that what they really want is to chat you up for other reasons?"

"I'm really not going down this road," says Flynn. "This topic."

"Do you?"

Flynn has been hit on plenty, but not by detectives working a case that's pulling her into its murky whorl. At the same time, getting curt and defensive may not be the best path to getting Jasper gone, especially with Wyatt asleep in the next room. Wasn't there a woman who survived a serial killer's rampage by changing the mood, by saying she liked it rough? By getting him to let his guard down?

"I think I've been around the block a few times." Flynn thinks she sounds chatty, more at ease. "And fully capable of sorting out what's what."

"But I also ask because of your safety. Does your new guy know what's going on?"

"No," says Flynn. And why is it necessarily a "he"? Jasper is 1,000 percent correct, of course, but why the assumption? "Not at this level of detail."

"At any level?"

"I don't want to scare him off," says Flynn, realizing the use of "him" confirms her solidly heterosexual yearnings.

"Because you need to be alert," says Jasper. "More than getting Wyatt's home base moved to Max's."

Flynn says nothing.

"Because there's one more detail about Robert Waller we don't want out there. So this is off the record."

"Whatever." Flynn feels sweaty and dry, underhydrated. Her head throbs. "A holdback for investigative purposes. I'm familiar with the concept. What about Mr. Waller?"

"He was decapitated. His head was propped up in front of the living room TV."

CHAPTER 47

Rich leather. Thick carpets. Books galore. Not one spine-crinkled paperback in the bunch. All the rigid volumes are stuffy and stiffly bound.

Flynn and Tamica sit at a boat-shaped conference table large enough for twenty-four people. Flynn has counted the seats. *Twice.* They've been instructed to wait.

In the middle of the table, a sculpture of praying hands in white marble. Flynn is no expert on conference table wood, but she has a hunch this one is cherry, and she's pretty sure you could buy an electric car for less money. The chairs are comfy, and if she has to wait much longer, there's always the option of moving her ass over to one of two expansive leather sofas and taking a power nap.

◆ ◆ ◆

She barely slept.

She worried about transitioning Wyatt out to Max's, wondered if she was doing the right thing.

The grisly image of Robert Waller.

Jasper's mansplaining protectiveness of his investigation coupled with his overt, yucky come-on. How the hell is she going to deal with that?

Her betrayal of Nancy Lang's trust.

And her reporter-cries-wolf bit when she spotted the envelope, even if she did the "right" thing and even if the false alarm led to the insightful, ghastly, and repulsive chat with Detective Jasper.

At 6:00 a.m., after an hour of sleep at best, she texted Nancy Lang.

> Nancy: You're right. I was wrong. I jumped too fast. You have my sincere apologies. It probably doesn't mean all that much but I made sure they didn't rerun the piece at 10. I would like the opportunity to tell the district's side of the story when it comes to managing bomb threats. Can I buy you coffee and apologize in person?

At 8:00 a.m. she dropped Wyatt at school and made promises that his commute from the hinterlands wouldn't last long. It was a promise based on precisely zero facts.

◆ ◆ ◆

"Jeez-*us*," says Tamica.

"I know," says Flynn. "Power move."

"In a church, making us wait?"

"The request was kind of last minute, but they agreed to it."

It's 11:20 a.m., twenty minutes past the appointed hour. The room's antique stuffiness gives Flynn the willies. Too quiet. Too padded. She can't stop thinking about what kinds of big decisions would require New Hope Church to build a meeting room of this magnitude, deep in the inner sanctum of the church. Brief research on the drive out suggested a sprawling religious operation with a large staff.

A giant door whooshes open, led by a youngish woman who holds the heavy door for Pastor Levi Bergeron.

"Sorry, sorry—please excuse my tardiness," says Bergeron.

Flynn stands to shake hands. Tamica too.

"It's okay," says Flynn.

"I know you're busy," says Bergeron. "I'm sure there's a lot going on out there. You won't be needing the camera."

Tamica's rig is ready to go on the tripod.

"Why is that?" says Flynn.

"We have nothing to say."

Bergeron is medium height and trim with heavy eyebrows and dark eyes. He's wearing a dark green blazer over an open-collar powder blue shirt. Country club casual. He doesn't look a day over forty. The effect is unassuming, but also a rabbit man watching the clock. He doesn't sit.

"I'm afraid not," says the woman.

"And you must be Romy Glover?" says Flynn.

"Yes, you spoke to me. Communications and marketing."

Glover is *hip? Fetching?* She looks like she belongs at an art gallery or trendy bar. Cute dark hair is parted mid-skull and falls to her shoulders in perfect straight whooshes that capture every movement. An inch of hair on her left side is dyed lime green. Cranberry eye shadow. A tiny gold loop pierces her right brow. Tight black jeans. A teal pullover blouse made of something equally shimmery. She's five ten in brown flats and carries an open, carefree vibe. If there's an antithesis of the stodgy church lady caricature, she's it.

"You haven't heard my questions," says Flynn.

Glover glances at notes on a legal pad. Says, "We think it's best for the community to let the judicial system take this one step at a time."

"This isn't about the arrest," says Flynn.

"No?" says Bergeron. "We kind of assumed—"

"Why did you agree to let us come out here, then?" says Flynn. It was a forty-minute drive out to Parker Road, where the houses are massive, the shopping malls sprawl, and the church buildings and their parking lots repeat like cheap background scenery in old cartoons.

"My mistake," says Glover. "I should have checked with Pastor Bergeron first. I am sorry for the inconvenience."

"We would like your thoughts on Jedidiah's arrest," says Flynn. "I assume you knew Patrick Kline? The family?"

"We *know* Patrick Kline and the family."

"Present tense," says Flynn.

"Yes."

"You think he'll be found? *They'll* be found?"

"Our prayers begin with that assumption. We have to hold on to hope."

"Can you describe their roles at New Hope?"

"Again, we'd rather let the police handle all of this."

"It's a simple question," says Flynn. "Patrick is listed on your staff page. Senior warden?"

"*Everyone* knew Patrick and everyone knew them," says Bergeron. "His wife was a pillar in the community too. She managed our coffee and breakfast bar. And those kids, of course—"

Pastor Bergeron inhales, puts a fist to his mouth, squeezes his eyes shut.

"It's been a difficult time," says Glover. She reaches a hand to console Bergeron, changes her mind, and withdraws.

"Why the kids?" says Bergeron. "Why?"

"Were their vacation plans well known?" says Flynn.

"I don't know why that matters."

"I'm curious," says Flynn. "That's all. Seems like a logical question. I mean, does it feel like a random thing to you?"

"We don't think along those lines," says Bergeron. "Amateur crime analysis."

"I assume taking the family to Orlando was a pretty big deal," says Flynn. "Patrick might have said something."

"We certainly knew about it, especially because Patrick was careful with his money, not prone to splurges, but again, this is irrelevant for right now until they turn up."

"I know," says Flynn. "The whole city is trying to understand. But we would also like to ask you about other issues too. Do you mind?"

Flynn gestures to Tamica and the waiting camera.

"We don't mind," says Bergeron. "But we like to prepare. Our lawyer—"

"Lawyer?" says Flynn.

"Yes," says Bergeron. "We need to be careful about what we say, given the stakes involved and suggesting anything prejudicial about the case as it moves forward. By the way, Miss Porter, I know you were right there when Jedidiah was arrested, and thanks for all you do."

"Um, sure," says Tamica. "No big deal."

"What other issues?" says Glover.

"And keep in mind that this is all off the record," says Bergeron.

"Really?" says Flynn. "We're not recording."

"That doesn't mean you couldn't use the information." Bergeron stands behind one of the high-backed chairs. He scoots it in an inch so it's in perfect alignment with the twenty-three others. "We're quite familiar with how the process works."

"What would help," adds Glover, "is if you would send us an email with your questions in writing."

Flynn turns to Tamica, who may as well be a figure in a wax museum. All the right details, yet stone-cold inscrutable.

"These questions aren't necessarily, as far as I know, about what happened to the Klines."

"That seems," says Bergeron, "a bit coincidental?"

"Maybe," says Flynn. "Maybe not. But doesn't writing questions and emailing them over seem unnecessary? Excessive?"

"We need to be careful," says Bergeron. "That's all."

"You don't even want to know what kinds of questions we've got?" says Flynn.

"An email," says Glover. "That would get the ball rolling."

"If you'll excuse us," says Bergeron.

◆ ◆ ◆

"Jeez-*us*," says Tamica once they're settled back in their SUV, where the August heat has taken a quick toll on the interior despite the cracked windows.

"No red flags there," says Flynn.

"Not a one," says Tamica.

New Hope Church's parking lot is a uniform sheet of black asphalt, white striping. The building's facade is a massive frame of concrete around tinted glass, four stories tall.

"What a fucking waste of time," says Flynn.

"Now what?"

"Do you want to do me a favor?"

"Depends."

"Let's give them a little jolt," says Flynn.

"What have you got in mind?"

For the next twenty minutes, Flynn shoots mock stand-ups in the blazing-hot parking lot.

Take after take. Flynn walks and talks. Flynn gestures. Flynn talks to the camera, points back at the church. They pretend to watch screenings of their work, then set up again. The acting is top notch.

"It's working," says Tamica.

The verb is a two-note song. *Whirrrrr-king.*

Flynn's got her back to the church. "Which one?"

"Marketing and communications."

"I figured," says Flynn.

"We still got a minute till she gets here."

"Poor thing had to come out in the heat. Okay, well, let's pack now that the bait has found its prey."

"Sounds good, boss."

"Fuck you with the 'boss' business," says Flynn.

"You know, after how many days with Chris Casey? I really missed you."

"I'm sure," says Flynn. "What did you do all that time?"

Tamica gives sly eyes, slips her camera into its case. "What happens in Pueblo, stays in Pueblo."

"Here I always thought that was a Vegas thing. Well, hope you showed him the world and all its glorious wonders, perk him up out of his malaise."

"Oh, we *malaised*, all right," says Tamica. "All day. All night."

"That particular thought is, I don't know, unthinkable?"

Flynn opens the passenger-side door, plucks a bottle of cold water from a cooler, and passes another one to Tamica.

"You need to lower your standards, boss lady friend of mine, or you may as well join a convent."

"*Ew,*" says Flynn.

"He's got stamina," says Tamica.

"Double *ew*."

"I'm talking about his persistence with the cops," says Tamica. "He's got a really good way of making them feel comfortable. He comes across as a team player."

The line stings. First, because Flynn hasn't heard back from Nancy Lang. And second, it's possible Tamica is commenting on her tactical skills. There was a time in Flynn's career when she defaulted to trusting everything she was told, even the public relations brush-offs. She's not going back to being a puppet on anyone's string.

"Excuse me?"

Flynn turns around in mock surprise. "Oh, hey," she says.

Romy Glover looks exasperated. And overheated.

"Can you tell me what you're doing?"

"Well," says Flynn. "No, not really."

"I mean, it looks like you're saying something about New Hope and our conversation—but we didn't tell you anything."

Flynn drinks from her bottle, shakes her head slowly. "That's true," she says. "You didn't give us much."

"So what are you saying, then?" says Glover.

"We were shooting stand-ups," says Flynn.

"But what do they say?"

"I don't think we're required to share that information," says Flynn.

"You're on our property," says Glover.

"And you invited us out," says Flynn. "On the general assumption that there would be an exchange of information. That is, we have questions—you have answers."

How would Chris Casey handle this? Maybe with a tenth of the tart tone?

"I know," says Glover. "At first when you called I thought it would be fine, but then I went to Pastor Bergeron and told him you were on the way."

"And?"

"And he didn't want to engage," says Glover. "But please don't use this. You're not secretly recording this, are you?"

Flynn looks at Tamica, who pats herself down, shrugs. "No," says Flynn. "No tricks."

Except for the one I just pulled that drew you outside.

"What did you want to know?"

Glover clutches a brown leather portfolio to her chest, arms locked around it like she's bracing for a blow. Flynn wants to ask if she needs to *have* religion to work at New Hope Church, because everything about her suggests edgy urban groovester.

"We wanted to ask about the holding companies," says Flynn. "We—that is, *I*—heard there were some concerns, internal struggles?"

"Holding companies?" says Glover.

"Please," says Flynn. "You're marketing and communications?"

"Okay. What about them?"

"Well, how many holding companies are there? What do they do? What's their purpose? How do they advance the cause and purpose of the church? Are they financially successful?"

Glover takes a breath. "I figured," she says.

"Figured what?"

"Figured it had to do with that."

"Why?"

"I don't want to be the rat."

"Nobody does," says Flynn. "Unless it's the right thing to do."

"And I know I'm being watched right now, and they're thinking that I'm doing a terrible job of getting you two to leave the premises."

"It's true," says Flynn. "You are. Are we making them nervous?"

"You could say."

"Would it help if it looked like we were arguing?"

"It's taking too long. I must be unconvincing."

"Meet me later? Call me later?"

"I need to think this through," says Glover. "You can protect me?"

"I'll do everything in my power," says Flynn. "Everything."

CHAPTER 48

Tamica drives.

Tamica, at least, stops and goes.

From this far end of Parker Road way out in the southeastern sprawl, it's a million stoplights back to the station and a jillion cars reminding her that the world is a busy, frantic place and everybody is going nowhere in a big hurry and Wyatt is right that this isn't the beginning of the end, it's the end of the beginning, and even decapitated postal workers and internal fights over church finances will pale in comparison with the ongoing floods and droughts, hurricanes and melting polar caps, and all the climate change refugees looking to find new homes that aren't threatened by one disaster or another.

"The lights are perfectly timed so we can stop and admire each one," says Tamica.

"You're feeling me," says Flynn.

"You're awfully quiet is what I'm feeling."

Flynn flips through her phone—emails, texts, X, Google News, *The Denver Post.*

The surprise email is from Annie Baker: I hope you're reconsidering this book idea. I think if you would commit, then everything would open up. You know, if you say "yes" then others would agree. Like how getting an

A-list actor attached to a movie sends a signal, you know? Anyway, glad to discuss.

Flynn scrolls to her options, hits Trash.

"Any word on the news conference about Jedidiah Jack's arrest?"

"Nothing," says Flynn.

"Text Chris Casey and ask?" says Tamica. "He'll know."

"Will he?" says Flynn. "Really?"

"He'll know what the plan is, and he'll know why they didn't hold it this morning like they said they would."

"You seem awfully sure of his reporting prowess."

"He's got more *prowess* than you know."

"Please don't start with the pretend sickening fantasy that you turned a Pueblo Quality Inn into a pleasure palace," says Flynn. "Unless this airplane comes with barf bags."

"Okay," says Tamica. "But you gotta stop judging books by their covers."

They're stopped behind a dozen cars and trucks at another stoplight with its own evil schemes to keep the world from running on time. Tamica's phone is propped in a holder on the dash. She pulls up Casey's number, presses call.

He answers before the first ring finishes, on speaker.

"What's shaking, T?"

T? Flynn gives Tamica a creeped-out frown.

"I'm here with Flynn," says Tamica.

"Oh, hey." Casey's tone goes from fizz to flat. "What's up?"

"Wondering if you've heard from Sheriff Moore?" says Tamica.

"Rescheduled," says Casey. "They're waiting a day. At least."

"Do we know why?" says Flynn.

"They're going through his story," says Casey.

"Meaning?"

"Meaning Jedidiah Jack has *got* a story and an alibi for the Sunday in question and all night into the early hours of Monday, when the family car pulls out of the garage. But they have work to do to check it all out."

"Are you reporting on the delay?"

"Of course," says Casey. "I'm outside sheriff's HQ in Arapahoe County. We're going live at noon."

Back in the newsroom, Flynn fills Goodman in on the cold shoulder from Pastor Bergeron and the wary approach from a timid Romy Glover.

"Keep stirring," he says. "Looks like Jedidiah can account for his whereabouts. What about following the bomb threat business, how school districts decide?"

"I'm waiting to hear back from Nancy Lang."

"There are other school districts besides Denver," says Goodman.

"I'm well aware," says Flynn. "I also have an interview with Detective Jasper on Athmar Park."

Good Lord, if Goodman only knew about the tense moments and small army of cops in her building last night. She needs to thank the Gods of Random News Tips that none of her inconvenienced building neighbors felt the need to let a newspaper or television station know about the pointless *CSI: Denver* takeover of her parking garage. There might be a strange TikTok or odd tweet out there, but those electronic puffs of smoke got lost in the ongoing hurricane of haphazard hogwash.

"Okay," says Goodman. "You'll take Tamica?"

"No camera," says Flynn. "It's background."

"What's on background about a murder investigation?" says Goodman. "They know what information they want to put out there. They've been through this a thousand times before."

"I need to tell you something," says Flynn. "Conference room?"

"Sit or stand?" says Goodman, a minute later. He's cradling a coffee cup as if he knows a Hogwarts spell that conjures one in a blink.

Flynn closes the blinds. "Sit," she says.

"Must be good."

"Robert Waller was decapitated."

Goodman's expression changes so little he could be a deaf-mute.

"And his head was left in front of the television."

"Source?"

"We can't use it."

"Source?"

"The lead detective."

How does she know Yamamoto isn't the lead?

"Of course we can use it," says Goodman.

"They want it held back."

"And you must have cut a deal. You and your bargains."

"It's temporary," says Flynn. "I'm going back over there to negotiate, but I made inroads, put it that way, and he trusted me enough to tell me. I'm sure it's some sort of test after, you know, my rogue ways."

"We need that detail," says Goodman. "When did you get it?"

"Last night."

"Working late?"

"I had something come up that gave me a reason to talk to one of the detectives."

"Mighty cryptic."

"And we had a good chat."

"Kissed and made up, did you?"

"We're back to level ground," says Flynn, not wanting to think of the word "kiss" and John Jasper in the same sentence. "Good enough for me."

"I want that detail on the five o'clock news tonight."

The whole sickening process of dismemberment is something she can't think about for more than a few seconds without an acid eel slithering in her stomach.

Making the city aware feels both necessary and evil at the same time.

"I want it out there too," says Flynn. "The whole town needs to know."

CHAPTER 49

It was the floor machine woman.

They pulled her in for questioning. At first, she denied it. But she wasn't good at lying. She was "as nervous as an unbalanced load on spin cycle," says Jasper, whose greeting was straightforward, ordinary, vanilla.

The floor machine woman's problem, he explains, was $5,000 she'd deposited in the bank. Cash. She thought she was being smart by depositing the money in a variety of odd amounts, but two of the deposits preceded when Wyatt had brought home the envelope, and three occurred after. The bank quizzed the woman, whose name Jasper declines to offer, but she claimed it was pay from a temporary side job.

Partially true.

The deposits equaled a fat round number. "And she said she thought she wasn't doing anything wrong, and she wanted the money so she could go to San Salvador and visit her parents for Christmas," says Jasper.

The question, says Yamamoto, is who hired her, "and that's where things get murky."

The floor machine woman was approached by a man in the school parking lot. She gave them a "pretty decent" description. Mid-forties. Medium build. Sunglasses. Purple Colorado Rockies T-shirt, blue jeans. The man had a photograph of Wyatt, the envelope, and he showed her the cash. He told her, however, that he'd been paid to ask her for this "small, easy" favor. She was told to make sure nobody saw her slip the envelope into the vents on the locker door once she spotted Wyatt Martin and once she figured out which locker was his. And she was told to do it during class, when nobody was around. The man told the floor machine woman, who was a contractor and not a direct school district employee, that she would get half the cash up front if she agreed to take the job and half once she'd signaled the job was done.

"What sort of signal?"

Flynn has a notebook out. It's not like she needs notes. Every moment of the story will be seared in her brain like a cauterized scar. The one outstanding issue is how the envelope goes from being a loose item in Wyatt's locker to an item that came home in his backpack with a field trip signature form, but it's not hard to imagine Wyatt innocently scooping up the envelope and putting it with Other School Crap for Mom.

"The signal?" says Jasper. "During her afternoon break, she would go out to her car, open the trunk for exactly half a minute, close it, and then leave the car unlocked for the afternoon—the remaining cash would be waiting for her under the driver's seat at the end of the day."

"Is there closed-circuit TV on the parking lot?"

"We can see a figure approach the car, but it's way off in the corner of the lot," says Yamamoto. "Only have a general sense of size and height."

"And we all think it's another hired hand."

"Not the Rockies T-shirt guy?"

"Maybe," says Yamamoto. "Maybe not."

"But you think delivery person or delivery boy because of what happened with envelope number two."

"Exactly," says Yamamoto.

Finding Bicycle Boy had not been difficult. A still photo from Noah Gifford's video surveillance led police to him and his mother. Yamamoto declines to add names. The boy was paid to deliver the envelope. This time, $100 in cash.

"Less complicated," says Jasper, "but an eye-opening amount for a kid like that."

Bicycle Boy was approached by a man who told him to deliver the envelope to a Kia EV9 parked three blocks away. The boy was given the license plate too. He said it took him five minutes to complete the task and pocket the money.

"That was a weekday," says Flynn. "How old a kid?"

"Fourteen," says Yamamoto. "I know what you're thinking, but he's homeschooled."

"That's rough," says Flynn. "His mother is a piece of work."

Jasper's squinty eyes translate as *Holding out on me again?*

"The guy who had the video of Bicycle Boy approaching my car put it on Facebook," says Flynn. "He asked anyone with information to contact me. His mother reached out and I drove to Shannon Way, only to have her tell me that all reporters are scum and that I could try some anatomically impossible physical act and that I was never talking to her boy."

"She wasn't much more cooperative with us," says Jasper. "Although the kid was impossibly happy-go-lucky."

"Go figure," says Flynn. "And?"

"And the boy didn't remember much. He thought the man was dressed like a UPS driver—brown short-sleeved shirt, brown shorts, and maybe a brown baseball cap. He thought at first he was helping a UPS guy for some strange reason, but he didn't see a truck. And you're going to ask if he remembered where this exchange happened, and the kid did not remember—he had been out bombing around on his bicycle and had gone to see the big commotion with the news conference that day at the end of Shannon Way. He was cruising around."

"Hard to believe it wasn't captured on someone's doorbell camera."

"It's a massive neighborhood," says Jasper, "and the kid rode everywhere, up and down the greenway—the same one that goes along the back of the Klines' home."

"And you think the UPS look-alike driver is our guy?"

"Or another go-between."

"But you'd have to know I'd be there," says Flynn. "I mean, it would have taken a bit of planning to distance yourself that much from the actual delivery of the envelope."

"Maybe," says Jasper. "But the Kline family story was a pretty big deal. Still is."

"You're saying it was assumed I'd be there?"

"Pretty good odds," says Yamamoto. "Right?"

"We're that predictable? *I'm* that predictable?"

"I'd call it patterns," says Jasper.

"The pattern is no pattern." Flynn mutters it.

"Your presence that day could be anticipated." Jasper arches an eyebrow. "Leave it at that."

"I assume you're still looking for Mr. UPS?"

"We're canvassing," says Yamamoto. "Yes."

"And Robert Waller?" says Flynn.

What she wants to ask is how you "prop" a head? If you cut through at the neck, how do you get it to stay upright? Do you bring a handy holder along, like an oversize eggcup, to keep it vertical? The grisly question was one of her late-night torments.

But the second she switches topics, she realizes she has no clue if Jasper has told Yamamoto about last night. The impostor envelope. Their chat and all its slimy drippings. Wouldn't he tell Yamamoto he'd answered a string of her questions about the case? Why would Jasper keep that to himself?

She assumes Jasper has shared so many details because he wants to ask if she recognizes Waller. But he didn't have to provide a glimpse of Waller's murder scene, or anything else, to ask her that simple question.

"We have nothing new to release," says Jasper.

"Any witnesses?" says Flynn.

"Off the record?" says Jasper.

Jasper looks at Yamamoto, who gives a mini headshake. *Don't.*

"On," says Flynn.

"The case is under investigation." Jasper's eyes are dead. "We won't stop until we find whoever did this, and we need the public's help. Somebody must have seen something."

"Okay," says Flynn, "that was useless."

"What did you expect?" says Jasper.

"Something other than pablum."

"Can you think of any connection between you and Robert Waller?" says Yamamoto.

"The only connection I see is Harry Kugel. Have you sent someone to ask?"

Jasper takes a chest-deep breath like an irritable father. "As I have mentioned before, all his communications are monitored."

"And you didn't answer the question."

"We're not getting into that," says Yamamoto.

"What did he tell you?" says Flynn. "How is he doing it?"

"This is not a road you want to go down," says Jasper. "Is it?"

"Why the hell not?"

"Maybe you would like it widely known that you raced to Cañon City at the first opportunity." Jasper flips pages in his notebook, slides his finger down the page. "And spent thirty-eight minutes alone with Harry Kugel at a time when you could have been bringing information to authorities? Should we publish this time-stamped photograph of you walking into the Colorado State Penitentiary on the internet?"

Jasper slides an eight-by-ten color glossy across the table. The shot is fuzzy, but not fuzzy enough.

"Should we count the days between when Wyatt brought home the first envelope and Mr. Waller's murder?"

"He was threatening *me*. He was threatening *my son*. And now you're taunting me with what, embarrassment?"

"How do you think it would look?" says Jasper.

"And what would you get out of doing that?" How long has Jasper been waiting to pull out this attempted gotcha? "Get me to fall in line?"

"Why are you so certain it's him?" says Jasper.

"We've been over this—the tone, the style. I'm deeply familiar."

"What did he tell you?" says Yamamoto.

Flynn sits back. "Nothing useful, but why would he?"

"Well," says Jasper, "I'm relieved to hear that you're not sitting on some grand insight about his involvement."

"Of course not. *Jesus.* But you're the one who knows his incoming and outgoing messages. How he might be manipulating this."

"He's alone," says Jasper. "The rare occasional visitor, but he declines as many as he accepts. He's alone with his tablet, streaming classical music."

"It's impossible," says Flynn.

"On the surface, it would seem that way," says Jasper. "And yet those are the facts."

CHAPTER 50

"I'm glad you were available on short notice," says Flynn. She has showered, changed, and driven to his town house in River North. His place is tidy. And sorely lacking in personal touches. Oak floors. Quartz countertops. A whiff of lemon Pine-Sol. "That's the way things roll with my gig. It's rarely a punch-the-clock kind of situation."

"I get it," says Sheen. "I do."

"Photography fan?"

"Oh—you mean the posters?"

Thinking, *Ansel Adams? Really? And isn't four of them overkill?*

"I know, not very cutting edge. They were on sale online."

"No family pics?"

"No real family," says Sheen. His lips tighten. "Although I didn't think we were getting into this, well, yet."

"Oh, I'm sorry."

"It's okay."

"Well, the basic brushstrokes are I was a toddler when my parents were killed by a drunk driver. I was raised by my mother's second-youngest sister, and let's just say she really didn't relish the opportunity."

"Axel, I'm so sorry—"

"There's a lot there. I try not to wear it on my sleeve."

"You don't. At all. And, well, I need to tell you something too."

She has weighed the pros and cons of simply telling him, one grown adult to another grown-ass adult, that she would like to spend the night.

She came *this close* to texting him that fact in case he wanted to spruce up his quarters or tend to the care of his personal hygiene. She opted for playing it cool and then congratulated herself on her restraint.

"Is this about the church again?" says Sheen. "Holding companies?"

"No," says Flynn. "I have a source coming through soon. I mean, *may*. May have a source. This is more along the lines of, well, *awareness* about my current situation."

"Doesn't sound good."

She's wearing casual blue slacks and a loose cream-colored split-neck blouse. He's in tight blue jeans and a short-sleeved yellow Hawaiian shirt with hula girls and coconuts. Take-out tikka masala and butter chicken, delivered by DoorDash, sits on his kitchen counter, waiting. Waiting for what? It's too late to eat. The thought of food makes her queasy.

"It's not bad," says Flynn. "But it is a thing."

"I'm listening," says Sheen.

"If we see each other, which I hope we do, we can't be seen together in public."

Sheen sips beer from a pint glass. "Cuts down on all my creative ideas," he says. "Bowling. Amusement parks. Red Rocks."

"Bowling?" says Flynn. "Really?"

Flynn pulled over and stopped three times on the drive over, taking inventory of every car, truck, and pedestrian. North, south, east, west. Scan and repeat. She parked three blocks from his address and walked with the same wariness, stopping occasionally to observe on foot.

"Bowling is one idea. But that's why you came over?"

"It seemed like an in-person thing," says Flynn. "To me."

"So you're saying all our dates are confined to your place or mine?"

"Not even that much variety."

"Then by the power of deduction that comes with my CPA training, I assume you mean that we're confined to your quarters?"

"Yes," says Flynn.

"But you came here?" he says.

"I was careful. And I'm sure it's temporary. I mean *this*. This restriction."

"And now comes the explanation? And, by the way, why was Botanic Gardens okay?"

"That was before." *Not completely true.* "Before I knew I had someone watching me way too closely. And I have reason to believe this *someone* is interested in using the people I'm seen with. Maybe hurting them too. I can't say for sure about that. But this *someone* went to the trouble of using Wyatt to get a message to me."

Sheen takes it in, blue eyes staring. Half smile. Sideways, tenuous look. "Well, I'm sorry," he says. "I assume we—*you*—don't know who he is?"

"No," says Flynn. "And I know you'll ask, but the police are on it."

"But you can go out and about by yourself?"

"I have to."

"This person, enigma, whatever—doesn't approach you?"

"Not directly."

"Which is why Wyatt is staying with Max?"

"Extra cautious, but yes."

"Your stalker knows about Wyatt?"

"But my ex is a cop, and my 'stalker,' to use your phrase, would be making a big mistake to try anything."

"Well," says Sheen. "I'm sorry about what you're going through."

"Don't be. Like I said—it's temporary. And I would enjoy the company until this all gets sorted."

Sheen shrugs. "I guess bowling will have to wait."

"I'm afraid so."

"It's only our second date," says Sheen. "I mean, third."

"Are there rules you like to follow?"

Sheen thinks. "Can't think of one."

CHAPTER 51

"You're still awake," says Sheen.

"Brain like a whirligig in a wind tunnel," says Flynn. Was it worth it? What exactly was the rush?

"Worried?"

"It's a state of being."

"I thought we took your mind off things."

"In the nicest way possible."

In the last twenty minutes, she realized how much she missed a man's form. His bed is firm. The sheets smell stale. She yanks a pillow back off the floor, pulls up a blanket to cover herself. His spare bedroom comes with blank walls, not even one Ansel Adams poster up here. She's experienced more charm from a hotel room. A modest balcony protrudes from the south wall. Shades open. Downtown building nightscape fills the view.

"I'd love it if you spent the night," says Axel.

She pulls him closer, kisses him full on the mouth. Deep, hungry. His kisses, with a taste of Indian spices, are as good as everything else. Ginger. Cinnamon. She crawls on top, crouches, knees tucked on both sides of his chest. Kisses him on the neck, stares at his eyes in the dark. The room is warm. He smells faintly of summer grass and leather. It's been forever since she's tried to fall asleep in a strange bedroom.

"What are you worried about?"

"I don't think you have the time."

Flynn reminds herself to be careful on the return trip home too.

"Give me one thing," says Axel.

"Door number one, door number two, or door number ninety-six?"

"That's a lot of doors."

"They all lead to the same place—my fucked-up, busy head that plays back all the crap I said and all the weird things I did all day long."

"Start at the beginning."

"I can't."

"Try."

Sheen rolls her over so they're side by side.

"I'm too sharp at times. Too brusque. Prickly."

"Doubt that," says Sheen, hand on her breast.

"I screwed a source."

Why hasn't she heard back from Nancy Lang?

"And you just finished screwing another one."

"You're not a *source*."

"That second so-called date?" says Sheen. "I thought I was helping you with that church holding company business."

"That's background," says Flynn. "Consultation. That's schooling the reporter who flits from story to story and barely stops long enough to get into any depth and really see how the world works."

"But you work in a business that moves pretty fast, true?"

"Too fast for its own good, I think."

"Switch to print?"

"It's occurred to me," says Flynn. "But they'd never have me. Believe me. And I'm getting into old-horse territory. 'Old gray mare, she ain't what she used to be.'"

"I don't think *old* moves like you were moving a few minutes ago. You must work out."

"Now that's a knee-slapper."

"Get out of here. Yoga? Pilates? Something?"

"My body eats itself from all the nerves," says Flynn. "It's called autophagy. Constant state of anxiety."

"Well, on the bright side, you're limber and enthusiastic."

"I had good inspiration," says Flynn, reaching to see if he might be in shape for round two. "And you're wide awake."

"Ignore him," says Sheen. "He only thinks of himself."

"I don't mind a narcissist."

"He's terribly needy."

"Sometimes need meets want."

"Let's talk about you first."

"We'll be up all night."

"You know what I do about late-night monkey brain?"

"Does a CPA have anxiety?"

"All the freaking time," says Sheen. "I mean, sure, our lives aren't very public or anything like that, but the potential for mistakes is all there, you know, making a mess."

"Okay, so what's your trick?"

"I acknowledge each thought. I articulate it in my head. I honor it. And then I walk it to the edge of a cliff and watch it drop like one of those stupid Instagram videos where some nutjob jumps off a cliff with a wingsuit. I watch it fall until it's out of sight, and then I go back to the next thought. And repeat."

"Fascinating," says Flynn. "Your little guy found it enthralling too."

"And of course if you don't like that approach," says Sheen, "the other thing to do is to dig into the particulars of what's really bugging you. Take it by the horns."

"Okay," says Flynn. "If I'm trying to find out if there's a holding company connected to New Hope Church that is having, say, a crisis. Or ran into trouble. Or something. Where the hell do I start?"

Sheen rolls over on top of her, brushes her hair back with his hands, kisses her forehead, nose, and lips. "I don't know," he says. "But we can start over again right now."

CHAPTER 52

The mea culpa bomb threat explainer comes together easily, even without the help of Nancy Lang.

Via Zoom, with Tamica shooting, Flynn interviews the head of security for a school district in Colorado Springs. With a mustache so bushy you can't see the guy's mouth, he walks her through how they train front office staff in schools to know what questions to ask when a bomb threat is phoned in. Tamica set the interview up in the conference room to capture both the Zoom image and Flynn's questions. Since the pandemic, online interviews have saved driving time and prevented unnecessary contributions to the warming planet. But Flynn always thinks the approach makes it easier on the interview subject. In-person interviewing makes it easier to get a sense of someone's essence. Their pith.

"I mean, it doesn't mean it won't happen, but the actual number of bombs that go off in schools?" says the security chief. "We all know we need to be way more concerned with kids carrying assault rifles than we do about some high school freshman who doesn't feel prepared for a test and thinks a phoned-in claim of a bomb will buy him the time he needs. Always dudes, by the way. Always the dudes."

Clicking off the Zoom connection, Flynn recalls a story from years ago, in the suburbs. A quick online search helps her remember the high school, in Thornton, and how the whole building had been evacuated while a bomb squad inched down the hall to a locker with a scary buzzing sound inside. Only to discover a switched-on electric toothbrush scrubbing the air.

She pulls the clip, studying images of her much more fresh-cut and innocent self. She's standing outside the high school treating the incident as if the students inside had dodged an actual bomb and not a battery-powered personal hygiene device.

"Before you were hired," says Flynn, looking at her poufy hair and fake concern.

"Before I was born," says Tamica.

"We were all newbies once," says Flynn.

"You dripped drama," says Tamica. "Acting school too?"

"That was a jumpy time—a few years after Columbine, and that was during the PDQ round one too."

"Were you like, a summer intern or something? They let you do live stand-ups?"

"You can fuck all the way off," says Flynn.

"Fine with me. Sounds pleasurable in its own weird way. Speaking of which?"

Flynn smiles. "We had a really nice time."

"Oh, give me a break." Tamica shakes her head. "Speaking of seventeen years old, you sound like you just got home after your first cheek-to-cheek dance at the high school prom."

"He's terrific, okay?" says Flynn.

"A little morning-after floaty thing going on?"

"I wouldn't go that far," says Flynn. And checking herself. *Is the morning brighter?* Maybe. "But it feels good to know I remember how all that stuff works."

◆ ◆ ◆

Flynn pulls statistics from an online search, relies on an old connection through Chris Casey to find someone in the Jeffco Sheriff's Office to discuss how they prefer school districts to manage bomb threats, and goes back through her interview with Meg Hart to pull sound bites again for her new script.

Texts Nancy Lang: I left you a message earlier this morning. We are putting together a piece today about the bigger picture regarding bomb threats. Welcome your comments/insights via phone, Zoom, in-person, anything. Especially around the issue of communicating threats to parents. How often, when? Etc. Tks.

Nancy Lang doesn't get a second apology if she's not going to reply to the first.

Texts Meg Hart: We are taking a look at the bigger picture of bomb threats. Did you ever hear from your school? Ever talk to your principal?

Texts Romy Glover: Glad to meet anywhere, anytime about whatever is going on at the church. I've protected sources for years and years. You need not worry.

Texts Axel Sheen: I had a great time.

Is it weird he hasn't texted *her* yet?

Or is that a game for high schoolers and Gen Z?

"No notes," says Goodman after screening her piece. "Except if Denver Public Schools cares to weigh in on their policies. Sounds like they owe our parent over at Stoneham Elementary an explanation. No?"

"Makes sense to me." Flynn's tight bond with Goodman means that unlike with most reporters, he, not the executive producer or managing editor, checks her stories. "I think every parent has a right to know about incidents at their kids' school."

"But we don't know if anything changed at Stoneham since you first interviewed Ms. Hart."

Goodman stretches in his chair, issues a massive yawn with sound effects.

"She didn't text me back and the school district isn't playing. Sorry to put you to sleep."

"Kind of leaves them hanging out to dry—*again*."

"I can add a line that says we haven't heard back from Stoneham or the district, and it won't sound accusatory. Just the facts."

"Let's give it a day," says Goodman. "Maybe head to HQ and find Nancy Lang in person?"

"Does she deserve that kind of effort?" says Flynn. "She knows she's ignoring us."

"We'll wait a day—the rundown could use some breathing room anyway. There's nothing here that won't wait," says Goodman. "What's happening with Robert Waller?"

"And what's happening with Jedidiah Jack Kline?" says Flynn.

"Chris Casey thinks the Arapahoe County folks are about to release him," says Goodman.

"Then I'll bear down there."

Text from Romy Glover: Too risky.

"Speaking of which," says Flynn. "There she is now."

"What's she got?"

"I'm not sure exactly," says Flynn. "Something to do with infighting. Money. Dunno. She's getting cold feet, though."

"That won't last," says Goodman. "The Flynn Martin touch is on the way."

Text to Romy: I've protected hundreds of sources.

Text from Romy: There are so few people who know about this. I'm one of them.

Meet me somewhere to discuss? Much easier.

I could be spotted.

I'll come to your place?

There are eyes and ears everywhere. Even these texts . . .

Where do you shop? Are you running any errands after work today?

Probably.

Tell me what kind of car you drive, tell me the shopping center.

Still sounds scary.

Do you have documents? I have secure ways you can get me documents. No digital or online trace. Nothing.
I shouldn't be texting you.
Think about the Klines. You're doing the right thing.
How do I know?

An hour later, Flynn sits in Romy Glover's well-worn green Subaru in the parking lot at the sprawling Park Meadows Mall.

"You don't know for sure," says Flynn.

"I thought you said—"

"I know it's hard to step out of line," says Flynn.

"*You* did," says Glover.

"Kind of," says Flynn. Does everyone know? "That was different. But sometimes you have to take risks, right? Over what's right and wrong?"

Glover's car idles. The air-conditioning is lame. Flynn feels droopy. Congealed.

Glover wears a red blouse with a tiny matching bow, cinched tight. Again, black jeans. She looks lanky behind the wheel of her car, seat pushed all the way back, but her demeanor is tight. She keeps glancing in the rearview mirror even though they are going zero miles per hour.

"'Thou shalt not bear false witness.'"

"Against thy *neighbor*," says Flynn. "Not sure where I pulled that from because I'm not exactly a church person."

"I think 'neighbor' means 'anyone.'"

Flynn wants to know how a book full of myths and parables, one that asserts a man named Jonah was swallowed by a whale but managed to pray and repent his sins, draws more credibility than the evening news. She also wants to know how a thirtyish woman with a Subaru that looks like it's used regularly for weekend hikes in the mountains also catches flak for a megachurch. A carabiner dangles from the keys in her ignition. Maybe some terrifying moment on a cliff face brought her religion.

"And I doubt what you have isn't anything but true," says Flynn. "So it's not false."

"I'm not sure," says Glover. "I only know what I know."

"Have the police come around? Detectives?"

"For days."

"Interviewed your pastor?"

"And everyone."

"You?"

"Of course."

"Not fun, is it?" says Flynn.

"My heart tried crawling out of my chest."

"But you didn't tell them everything."

"No."

"Why?"

"Because I was right there—at work."

"Are they still asking questions?"

"Not like at first. One whole day went by, and we didn't see them."

"Tell me what you feel comfortable telling me—what this has to do with? And maybe a few of the names involved. There's money involved?"

"And everything that goes with it."

"Meaning?"

"Meaning the usual."

"Like an affair," says Flynn, flashing for a moment on Axel Sheen. The warmth and comfort that came with having him there.

"Entanglements," says Glover.

"Always a dicey combination," says Flynn.

"You can protect me?"

"Yes."

Stated with authority. Stated as if *whatever* comes out of Romy Glover's mouth is gold. As if her motivations are innately pure. As if

Flynn knows that whatever Romy Glover is about to impart is bound to make the world, not only her personal universe, a better place overall.

"And what will you say when people ask where you got the information?"

"That my sources are confidential."

"There aren't that many likely suspects, you know, inside."

"Give me the right rock to pick up—shape, size, general location. I can take it from there."

CHAPTER 53

Glover's hands shake. A hand goes to her chest.

"Dennis Mencher," says Glover. "There's your name."

"Good start," says Flynn. "Who is he?"

Flynn reaches for her notebook.

"Two *n*'s Dennis. And then 'men,' like asshole M-e-n and c-h-e-r like the singer."

"Bit harsh," says Flynn. "Got it."

Glover lays it out. About two years ago, Mencher was hired to work at a ranch called Diamond Creek, east of Elizabeth. Fifty acres and a small herd of Black Angus cattle.

The ranch was run by a couple who went to New Hope Church, but the husband was getting "up in years." Mencher was one of three hands. He mended fences, repaired vehicles, kept the barns tidy, earned his keep. He moved into a small outbuilding. "Played John Prine songs on guitar and read Dostoyevsky." He earned his CDL so he could drive the ranch's big trucks. Took on any task. Kept his head down.

"He made everything easy," says Glover.

"Before you get too far, is there a connection between Diamond Creek and New Hope Church other than the couple were members?" says Flynn.

"The church bought it," says Glover. "The church thought it might be a good long-term investment because of all the growth out in Elizabeth. The owner was a longtime elder at New Hope. And a longtime, generous donor."

"Nice to have friends," says Flynn.

"There are multiple holding companies," says Glover. "One invested in an insurance company. And another invested in a downtown office building."

"Lot of money."

"It's a successful church with wealthy parishioners."

"Sitting on piles of tax-free money. What's the name of the holding company?"

"Some gobbledygook," says Glover. "Meaningless initials."

"Who knows about the ranch?"

"You mean, at the church?"

"Yes."

"It's a small circle."

"But you're in it."

"Around," says Glover. "Not really in. Because I'm not a guy."

"The rancher's name?"

Glover takes a moment. "Arnold Wilkins. And here's where it gets juicy."

"It's saucy already," says Flynn.

"Arnold was seventy-six. Belinda Yates is forty-nine."

"Second wife, I assume?"

"Third," says Glover. "Younger each time."

"You said 'was' for Arnold and 'is' for Belinda."

"I did," says Glover.

"Because?"

"Because Arnold Wilkins died mysteriously four months after the sale went through. Last January."

"How mysteriously? Cops involved?"

"No," says Glover. "He'd had four small strokes in the year prior. He was incapacitated and confined to the home on the ranch, so the coroner signed off. Natural causes. But it became apparent that Belinda and Dennis were involved at least from a business perspective and maybe more. Dennis Mencher attended all the meetings."

"Meetings?"

"When Arnold died, the church turned around and decided to sell."

"Because?"

"One of the other ranch hands at Diamond Creek grew suspicious about Mencher. They thought he was running into town too much. When he ran an errand, he was never back in the time you'd think. There was always a story. So the church dug into Mencher's background. He'd falsified his application. He gave them a fake reference who spoke glowingly. The rest was crap too."

"I'm listening."

"Dennis Mencher was three years from a stint in prison for first-degree assault. Dennis Mencher was really Denis one *n* Mincher—capital M-i," says Glover. "Eight years in Cañon City. Beat the hell out of a guy in Alamosa. Sentenced to fifteen years. Released early for good behavior and, who knows, reading the classics."

"Belinda's got all this cash?" says Flynn.

The sale of the property will be registered with the county and easy to find.

"I'm not sure," says Glover. "I think I heard something like two or three million, yes."

"Which would have proved mighty enticing to our Mr. Mincher. Were they, you know?"

"Not sure," says Glover. "We only know Belinda started traveling. Nice spots. Mexico. Costa Rica. Sun, surf, et cetera."

"I assume if the church owned it, the church was watching the books?"

"The trips were with Arnold's cash, not on the company books. But once Arnold died, the church knew it needed somebody in there who could run the ranch. Get the value up, the quality of the livestock and everything. And that's when Patrick Kline was called in."

"Patrick was a CPA." And a stingy one, from Bergeron's description.

"Right," says Glover.

"And?"

"And he couldn't find anything solid."

"Drugs," says Flynn. Not a question.

"Patrick was worried about that. Couldn't find anything substantial."

"Evict them?"

"That idea was broached," says Glover. "But Belinda Yates had an ace in the hole. Something."

Already Flynn is wondering what she'll need to corroborate in order to put something on the air there about this line of investigation. The town of Elizabeth is in Elbert County; the Kline family was killed in Arapahoe County. One detective who can confirm they are looking into Denis Mincher and Belinda Yates will give her the opening she needs.

"Patrick agreed with me." Glover stares out her window. Away. "Spill it all. Own the story. Admit mistakes. Move on."

"But you lost your argument?"

"The directors were adamant. The whole situation kind of went static. The pressure was building, but they couldn't reach a decision."

"Even after Patrick disappeared?"

The question triggers sobs. Glover tries here and there to enunciate a word. But fails. Her chest heaves like an accordion. She unties the bow at her collar, unbuttons the top button on her blouse. "I'm sorry," she says.

"Don't be," says Flynn. "Sounds like you were close to Patrick."

"We were allies," says Glover. "That's all."

"Was Patrick the one who thought Arnold Wilkins's death was suspicious?"

"Not *thought*."

"How?"

"He was sitting in the office out at the ranch looking through records, and I guess Belinda's text app on her phone mirrors on her computer. She was sending messages back and forth with Denis about how there was no way the 'nosy church asshole'"—Glover adds air quotes to the last three words—"would ever find or figure out anything about what happened to Arnold."

"So why not go to the cops?"

"It was discussed," says Glover. "But there was no hard evidence, and most of the directors wanted out. Pronto."

"So Patrick was meeting with Belinda."

"He believed weapons used to fight evil have divine power. That's Bible stuff. Second Corinthians."

"So he met with her?"

"*Them,*" says Glover.

"Where?"

"At their house."

"Shannon Way?"

Flynn hears the incredulity in her voice. If so, there must be neighborhood watchdog video of them arriving, parking, getting out. The cops must have reviewed every scrap of footage from every doorbell camera and followed every license plate on every car that parked near the Klines' home on the day of and day before their departure.

"They couldn't meet at the church," says Glover. "Pastor Bergeron didn't want them anywhere near that place. So Patrick made them park blocks away and come down the greenway and through the back gate. I mean, this is Patrick's volunteer work for the church, so it was after work, in the evenings."

"How many meetings?"

"Two that I know of. Patrick thought they were making progress, that the divine power thing was working."

"You weren't there?"

"No."

"Patrick didn't mind meeting with an ex-con who might have helped murder Belinda's husband?"

"He told me that Denis was reasonable, polite. But Patrick didn't tell me everything," says Glover. "To protect me."

No forced entry . . .

Not impossible to imagine that the negotiations go south . . .

Denis goes berserk . . .

Mayhem follows . . .

Then how about the timely vacation departure? What gives with that?

"I didn't mean to sound so callous," says Flynn. "But the investigators must know about the holding companies, about the ranch."

"We all thought it was Jedidiah," says Glover. "I mean, it sounds crazy, but we all *hoped* Jedidiah had flipped out. Patrick said Jedidiah was a wild card, that Jedidiah had punched him in the face and threatened to kill them all. So when it happened—"

"But now Jedidiah can apparently account for his whereabouts."

"And the investigators are starting over."

"And?"

"And I don't know what to do," says Glover.

"Because if you go public, the church will know it was you."

"In two seconds. So how are you going to get this out there and give me cover?"

Does she trust Glover's story? Trust Glover? Flynn's confidence meter is in the green zone.

Yet she knows to be wary.

"I've got my ways. Do we know where Denis Mincher is now?"

"No."

"Belinda Yates?"

"No idea."

"Does a Dostoyevsky, John Prine guy sound like a killer to you?"

"I know," says Glover. "It's all so weird. Sad first and then a whole lot of weird."

CHAPTER 54

At home, Flynn pulls up the details from the Alamosa newspaper about the assault that landed Denis Mincher in prison. His victim was in a coma for three months. Traumatic head injury, broken nose, busted shoulder, ruptured spleen, internal bleeding, lost an eye. When arrested, Mincher was twenty-nine years old.

Mincher's unnamed victim, left for dead in the street, was twenty-four. The fight began inside and finished outside a bar downtown. Eyewitnesses identified Mincher and he was arrested, with a scratch under his left eye, at his trailer an hour later. With eight years in prison and a three-year gap since being released, that would make him nine years younger than Belinda Yates.

Another search finds one sad, unused Facebook page that looks as if Mincher tried to get active on social media shortly after being released. The page contains two posts. The first is a quote by Fyodor Dostoyevsky, white letters on a black background, about how the right given to one man to inflict corporal punishment on another "is one of the ulcers of society, one of the most powerful destructive agents of every germ and every budding attempt at civilization, the fundamental cause of its certain and irretrievable destruction."

The second is the rollout of his profile pic, backlit and blurry. And useless.

◆ ◆ ◆

The Belinda Yates trail yields a touch more three-dimensionality, including a stream of selfies on Instagram.

Vegas in early December; Cancún in late December. Costa Rica in January.

Colorful drinks. Splashy food. Beaches. Sunsets.

Belinda is short. Curly brunette hair, full figure, a straining smile like it must hurt. Like she's trying way too hard. So many bikinis. Purple, green polka dots on white, yellow. Max cleavage, tight tummy. Belinda getting outfitted for parasailing. Belinda getting outfitted for snorkeling. Belinda standing by a swimming pool getting her resort certification to go scuba diving. Belinda in fancy-schmancy evening wear on the way out for dinner.

The captions are short. "Blessed" is used again and again. Flynn stares at the beaches, the oceans, the carefree life.

But no Denis.

The feeds produce nothing about Wife #1 or Wife #2, but there are shots from outside church with husband Arnold. The age gap is a monster. She could be his sparkling, vivacious daughter.

And then a post about how she auditioned for the job of hosting the church's weekly news shows—updates on various church-related events and activities, along with interviews with members of the staff, including visiting pastors and regular check-ins with Pastor Bergeron.

From the church's website, Flynn follows a link to the YouTube page: "The New Hope News." Belinda hosts from a black leather chair, playing reporter-anchor. A giant fern sits in a pot between guest chair and host chair, with the massive New Hope logo dangling against a black curtain behind them. Belinda wears solid-color dresses, like she's fresh from the sanctuary, and flashes plenty of leg. Segments on the winter coat drive, the Easter canned food drive, an interview with Pastor Bergeron about the importance of donating to the church. "When you donate," says Bergeron, "you're expressing your faith in God and your thanks to him, too, for providing for you and your family."

"What do you have on the church, Belinda Yates?" Flynn says out loud. "Why not take your money and go? Huh? And, Romy Glover, do you think you could have mentioned Belinda's fake anchor gig to me?"

Flynn texts her father: I've got my hands full but if you have time could you track down the name of the holding company that owns a property in Elbert County called Diamond Creek Ranch? And find out anything else that pops up?

Michael Martin is a whiz with TruthFinder. PeopleLooker too.

Texts again: And anything you can dig up on an ex-con named Denis Mincher, once lived in Alamosa. And a 49-year-old woman named Belinda Yates, was married to Arnold Wilkins and owned Diamond Creek Ranch with her husband. Appreciate the help. I'm running.

Texts Axel Sheen: Hope you had a good day. Good night.

Add a heart emoji, yes or no?

Flynn adds two.

CHAPTER 55

"I'm a bit surprised you didn't want to chase this last night," says Goodman.

"I poked around online," says Flynn, deciding not to reference the help from Michael Martin via an early-morning email. "I've got more documents to look through. I got the address, of course. I could go out there, see what I find."

"Or talk to the pastor?"

"Doubt that would be productive. He was not wanting to engage. At all."

"And you feel good about Romy Glover?"

"Her story fits pieces together."

"The cops have to know about Diamond Creek."

Goodman is studious, professorial. And painfully careful.

"One would think. They would have asked about all of Patrick Kline's work-related business and his role at the church. Emails, et cetera."

"And right now if the church was that afraid of the story coming out before, they've got to be really nervous that they led a bad actor to Patrick Kline's doorstep."

"They haven't officially cleared Jedidiah," says Flynn. It would have been so much cleaner, simpler, more streamlined a story if Jedidiah Jack Kline were the culprit. "And on track two, we've still got all those questions about Robert Waller and Athmar Park."

"And it's going to be a hundred and five degrees today," says Goodman. "If our weather team is right, that's a new Denver record for August."

"Are we frying eggs on the sidewalk or tracking two bizarre crimes?"

"It's not frying eggs, it's the whole melting planet and the demise of *Homo sapiens*. You know, we had a good run until the last century and decided to burn everything in sight and all the stuff we could pull out of the ground. We're about to get shrugged off the planet, all eight billion of us. Mother Earth says *Thank U, Next* like Ariana Grande."

"You sound like Wyatt."

"Everyone should sound like Wyatt. That's the problem."

"Diamond Creek or Athmar Park?" says Flynn.

"The cops are keeping a tight lid on Athmar Park, and you're compromised."

"I'm *not* compromised."

"You're entangled," says Goodman. "It's all going to come out at some point, so you should steer clear of Athmar Park and Robert Waller."

"I disagree. I can make calls and feed Chris Casey what I find."

"Sounds like you wrote your ticket to Diamond Creek. Start with the Elbert County cops?"

"Or go out there and see what's what?"

"Helluva long way to go if you don't know if you're welcome on the property. And another wasted automobile trip heating up the planet and contributing to our collective demise."

"Someone's gotta be out there," says Flynn. "Cattle ranches don't run themselves. Do they?"

CHAPTER 56

There's a place southeast of Denver where the hopscotching growth of suburban tracts finally gives way to the steady, unending stretches of farmland that run clear out to the Kansas border. It's not a defined line. It's a mood, a decompression.

The drive to Franktown takes an hour. And driving through Franktown reminds her she needs to dig into the double murder there—also unsolved. And then east for the short ride to the small exurb of Elizabeth, through the town, and follow GPS directions south and then east again. The road turns to dirt and dust.

Patches of dense pine trees here. Expanses of harsh, fallow ground there.

The ranch is guarded by a modest entryway. The Diamond Creek Ranch sign dangles between two tan vertical logs, black metal silhouetted against a sky of haze and pale, weak blue.

"No trespassing," says Tamica. "Guess that settles that."

"I wish I spoke ranch," says Flynn. "Or cattle. Or irrigation. Or pickup trucks. Or antelopes. See any antelopes?"

"I see the sign that says *scram.*"

"That's for amateurs," says Flynn. "No gate means we're allowed to access the driveway and knock on the door."

"What exactly is the plan?"

"Ask to talk with whoever answers."

"Am I shooting?"

"Seems like a good idea, seeing as we came all the way out here."

"Think it might, you know, be a bit friendlier to not be rolling in gotcha mode right from the get-go?"

"That's fine," says Flynn. "I'm easy. The main thing is to find out who's here. See what they know."

"And come face-to-face with a guy who might know something about the disappearance of a whole family."

"Those true crime reporters on *48 Hours* do it all the time," says Flynn. "They walk right up to the husband who thinks he got away with it. Like in the parking lot at a grocery store. Broad daylight. 'Did you kill your wife? Why did you buy that nineteen-inch machete with the serrated edge the day she disappeared?'"

"No thanks," says Tamica. "Outside my job description."

"Where's all your bravado from the Jedidiah Kline arrest in Pueblo?"

"We had cops *right there*. Big burly uniformed dudes—lots of them—with guns. You see any cops? You see anyone?"

A two-story white house with green shutters sits at the end of a quarter-mile dirt road fenced on both sides. The fencing is heavy duty and new. The driveway wraps around a large wood gazebo. Tamica follows the loop around and parks. A grove of pine trees guards the house from the south. No vehicles are parked in front.

Wide stairs lead to a broad porch, front and sides. Eight steps. In the distance, an unpainted barn looks drafty, lists to one side. Smaller outbuildings, a tractor, an old teal school bus with cinder blocks for wheels, a two-story chicken coop with a plywood ramp to the roost, one shiny red pickup truck with four doors, one faded brown pickup with a mismatched driver's side door that's black, dozens of dots of cattle off in the distance trying not to move in the scorching heat. The land they're grazing appears to have little left to offer in the way of nourishment.

"Notice something?" says Flynn, opening her door to step out.

"Such as?"

"No dog. Or dogs. You have a ranch like this, you get border collies watching everything and sounding the alarm at newcomers."

"Is it a law or something?"

"Yes," says Flynn. "Heavy fines for disobeying too. Here goes nothing."

"You hope," says Tamica.

The first knock on the door goes unanswered. Same with the second. Same with the third. Flynn gives Tamica a shrug, walks down the porch to what's likely a living room window, and peers inside.

The phrase that comes to mind is "still life." As if the composed scene is ready for a Dutch painter's detailed strokes over weeks of work ahead. Maybe cattle ranches do run themselves.

A shaft of light from a side window catches an old brown leather couch that sits low and long. A coffee table, made from a slice of a tree trunk, sits in front of the couch. Side chairs, a large fireplace, walls of old green wallpaper with a faded floral pattern. A giant dark red rug. A swinging door propped open to a kitchen. Flynn's angle allows only the view of a small section of wood counter and two metal cabinets. Like the lack of dogs outside, the interior is deficient in one aspect—the detritus of daily life. No coffee cups, no magazines strewed about, no books being read, no abandoned clothes or hats, no shoes, no unwashed glasses, no half-burnt candles. The space is showroom ready if there are any buyers looking to transport themselves back to a Colorado ranch during the Eisenhower administration.

For the heck of it, Flynn raps on the window with a bit more emphasis than she used on the door. The rap reverberates with a piercing ping.

Nothing.

Feeling a touch of relief, Flynn gives Tamica a shrug, holds up one finger, walks around the porch, and takes in the view again, hoping to spot an ATV racing across the fallow fields.

Chickens cluck. A hot breeze brushes Flynn's face, carrying the vigorous aroma of cows and manure. Would Denis Mincher's secret drug lab be in the barn? One of the windowless metal outbuildings?

The going-nowhere school bus? She wants to stroll out, walk around, find indications Mincher was running fentanyl or meth.

She opts for discretion.

◆ ◆ ◆

Flynn suggests they shoot exteriors from across the road. She's been around long enough to know that if they get footage from close up that it will appear as if they had permission to do so on the property, should someone come along or if they get a call later from the pissed-off lawyers of New Hope Church.

Tamica drives out to the county road, puts two wheels in the scruffy shoulder, and parks. She scrambles to a spot with a few extra feet of elevation so the fence doesn't block her view of the house, barn, cattle, whatnot.

Flynn switches on the hotspot-sharing function from her phone, pulls up the link from a text from her father: Cost me $13. I'll keep poking around.

She forwards the link to her email, opens it on her laptop, downloads a report. A PDF document comes complete with aerial photographs of the acreage and purchase history.

Most recent owner or resident: CHN Holding Company, 01/21/2023

Some gobbledygook, as Glover had said. *Is CHN "New Hope Church" backward?*

Next:

Most recent owner or resident:

Arnold Wilkins and Belinda Yates, 04/15/2022–01/20/2023

Next:

Most recent owner or resident: Arnold and Stacy Wilkins, 07/02/2009–04/14/2022

Next:

Most recent owner or resident: Arnold and Julie Wilkins, 10/21/1981–07/01/2009

Younger each time, as Glover had said.

"Check and check," says Flynn to herself.

Each owner listing is accompanied by a "View Report" button that includes address history, possible phone numbers, possible emails, possible criminal and traffic records.

"Got enough wide shots for a Ken Burns documentary," says Tamica. "Unless you're going back across the road and inspecting the barn and other buildings, can we find someplace cool? Freshen up?"

Tamica guzzles from a bottle of water plucked from a cooler, hands her another. Water so cold it stings.

"Did you see anything?" says Flynn.

"I got an orange excavator chugging across the prairie and somebody by the barn loading stuff into a pickup. One of those pickups with a camper shell. Way off in the distance."

Downtown Elizabeth is tiny. There are two coffee shops. They pick one and settle at a table by the window. The coffee shop is half full. One table hosts two cops, their flat-brimmed hats taking up the empty spots at the table. Giant plastic cups in front of them hold drinks that look like caramel milkshakes with frothy coronas of whipped cream. Barring an emergency, the cops aren't going anywhere soon. A glance outside at their burly SUV tells Flynn they are county cops, not city.

"Wassup?" says Tamica.

"Checking out Romy Glover's story via public information. There's like a thousand threads."

"I've got an idea."

"Fire away."

"We could call Chris Casey and ask what he'd do."

"You trying to press my buttons?"

"You wear them on your chest," says Tamica. "And they're bright red. It's so easy."

"I need to find Denis Mincher or Belinda Yates."

"So we have our iced coffees, go back to Diamond Creek, and maybe this time they're back from Costco or the feed store or a trip to Bora-Bora."

"Could that have been Mincher loading the pickup?"

"Entirely possible," says Tamica. "But I was zoomed in and he was still a blur in the shimmering heat."

"I feel like I'm in the wrong place," says Flynn. "I don't know. I should have insisted on working on the Robert Waller story. Finding his neighbors or family or something, but if Glover is right—"

"So the holding company checks out?"

"I've got the name of it," says Flynn.

"And it's tied to New Hope?"

Flynn pulls up the secretary of state's business search page, punches in "CHN Holding." The address matches with New Hope Church. The "true name and address of the incorporator" is listed as Levi Bergeron, but the name of the person who filed the document is a new one, Jessica Griffith.

"Shots of you working?" says Tamica. "Or the state records online?"

"Dear god, no," says Flynn.

"Might need some wallpaper."

"I'm not that desperate. Yet."

A call to the Elbert County Sheriff's Office is answered by a woman who patches Flynn through to a man who identifies himself as Deputy Kerrigan.

Flynn gives her name and station. "I'm calling because I'm working on a story that may have a connection to Diamond Creek Ranch, about five miles southeast of Elizabeth."

"Flynn Martin?"

"Yes. Can you help me?"

"I'm familiar with it," says Kerrigan.

"In what way?"

"In the way that we drive all over the county and I've seen the sign."

"Is the property a source of concern?"

"In what way?"

His voice jumps through the phone like it's on speaker. But it's not.

"You know, source of trouble?"

"Such as?"

"Anything," says Flynn.

"What's your story?"

"I'm working on a story about the murder investigation over in Arapahoe County—the Kline family."

"I know it. Is it a murder investigation?"

"Okay, disappearance."

"Words matter."

"Yes, they do. And Patrick Kline was a church leader, and the church owns Diamond Creek through a holding company."

"Is that right?"

Again, the voice seems overly close, the best tin can and string of all time.

Tamica taps her shoulder. She nods in the direction of the table with the two cops. One is on the phone. Staring at Flynn.

"Why don't you join us?" he says.

CHAPTER 57

Deputy Sam Kerrigan and Deputy Mike Cage return their hats to their heads to make room for Flynn and Tamica as they sit—boy, girl, boy, girl. Flynn introduces Tamica. Nods are ample greeting.

Kerrigan is older than his partner, with gray at his temples, a prominent crevasse down one side of his face, weary eyes, long face. Cage is baby pink with plump cheeks and a stovepipe neck. One gnarled ear suggests Cage was a high school wrestler.

"Kind of you," says Flynn.

"Well, a bit less awkward," says Kerrigan. "But I can't tell you anything. You'll have to get with the sheriff."

"Remind me?" says Flynn.

"Rose," says Kerrigan. "Sheriff Richard Rose."

"Is he around today?"

Kerrigan shrugs. "'Around' covers a lot of ground."

"Available, I guess."

"Probably depends on what you want."

"I told you what we're looking into," says Flynn.

"Yes, you did."

It's clear that Kerrigan will handle the talking. Cage is a newbie.

"I need simple confirmation that Diamond Creek Ranch was on your radar. That's all."

"Again," says Kerrigan. "Sheriff Rose. He'd put our asses in a sling for not going through channels."

"I know there's a connection between the ranch and the church," says Flynn. "I know there were issues. I'm wondering if the property drew your attention for the wrong reasons."

"I can repeat myself," says Kerrigan.

"Or if the name Denis Mincher floated up?" says Flynn. "Ex-con? He's worked out there for a couple of years?"

"You're working on a big story," says Kerrigan.

"Correct," says Flynn.

"We don't get big stories very much."

Kerrigan takes a sip of his muddy drink through a bright red straw.

"Does the name Denis Mincher mean anything to you? Or Belinda Yates?"

Kerrigan finishes the sip, winces like he's got a brain freeze. "Protocols," he says.

"I don't need anything on the record," says Flynn. "I'm not going to stick a microphone in your face. No cameras. I only need an acknowledgment that you were looking at Diamond Creek or that the sheriff folks over in Arapahoe County had asked for permission to come out and do the same. Could you possibly raise Sheriff Rose on your radio and check on his whereabouts? Availability?"

"Today? Like, now?"

Text from her father: Call me when you get a sec.

"Today would be good," says Flynn. "Right now would be fine."

"Just a tip," says Kerrigan. "Don't sound so desperate when you talk to the sheriff."

"I'm not desperate. It's eagerness to find out what happened to that family."

"I get it," says Kerrigan. "But Sheriff Rose is not a big fan of reporters. Especially foreigners."

Outside, Deputy Kerrigan climbs into his vehicle. He sips at his adult milkshake. The heat is oppressive, all-consuming, demands attention like a petulant child.

Kerrigan starts the engine, closes the door for cone-of-silence purposes, waits a minute for god knows what other reason than to prove who's in charge or to let the AC come up to speed.

Flynn stands with Tamica and Deputy Cage on the sidewalk.

"There was nobody at the ranch house itself," says Flynn. Making conversation. "Otherwise I would have asked somebody directly if you all have been around."

"Is that right?" says Cage.

"And the main house didn't look like it was being used."

"Could only speculate, you know?"

"Am I on safe ground to say that you all know about Belinda Yates and Denis Mincher?" says Flynn.

"Know about?" says Cage.

"Looking into."

"Isn't that what Kerrigan is checking?"

"Seems to me it's obvious that the answer is yes," says Flynn. "You wouldn't bother with this runaround if the answer was a clean no. But since the answer is yes and since you're surprised we found out, well, you gotta run a simple question up the flagpole, and that question is attached to a bright red flag."

Cage slurps at the last of his drink, shakes the plastic container, slurps again. Says nothing.

"And when your colleague gets out of the car and tells me Sheriff Rose won't even confirm or deny my basic little question, then I'll know for sure the answer is yes because you know they're debating the pros and cons of letting me in."

Cage winces. He scratches his forehead. He puts his back to Kerrigan like he's looking for a trash container. Mutters, "You're not wrong."

"Tell me more," says Flynn, matching the mutter.

"Can't," says Cage, back to his fellow deputy. "But you're on the right track. There's some shit going down."

"Does it deal with the death of Arnold Wilkins?"

Cage gives her two wide eyes like he's seen a ghost.

Kerrigan opens the passenger-side window, signals Flynn over.

"I have the official word," says Kerrigan.

"Lay it on me," says Flynn.

"No comment."

"Back out to the ranch in the blazing-hot sun?" says Tamica. "Shoot a stand-up out there? Or maybe Goodman will want you on live at four so the people can watch a television news reporter melt like the Wicked Witch of the West right before their collective eyes?"

"Find some shade," says Flynn. "Not sure what direction we're going."

Tamica pulls out slowly, takes her first right, and loops around back to the main drag. Flynn grabs her phone, scrolls through the recent calls.

"Romy," says Flynn. "It's your reporter friend."

"Don't call me here."

"I came through a virtual receptionist. Nobody knows."

"Still," says Glover.

"The cops are looking into Diamond Creek."

"Good."

Romy whispers it.

"Why didn't you tell me about Belinda's gig with church TV?"

The question catches Glover off guard. "Is that relevant?"

"Everything is. How often do they record them?"

"Twice a month. You know, it's content. The whole PR thing. Tell your own story."

"I'm familiar," says Flynn. "Is she there today?"

"I haven't seen her."

"What day do they tape, record, whatever?"

"It's not a set deal," says Glover.

"Seems like an odd coincidence."

"How?"

"That the woman whose decades-older husband was quietly murdered has a high-visibility gig for the church on YouTube. How long has she been doing the videos?"

Glover thinks. "Almost a year. The videos were *my* idea."

"And?"

"And he didn't think I had the right look."

Flynn imagines Glover's piercing and offbeat styling. Her artsy outdoorswoman vibe.

"Who is *he*?"

"The pastor."

"Bergeron?"

"Yes."

"What? Did he hold auditions?"

"No," says Glover. "She was suddenly there. Done deal."

"Interesting."

"Tell me about it."

"And you, what, write the scripts?"

"And all her questions too," says Glover. "She doesn't know how to make it a conversation."

"Could I leave a message for her to call me?"

"She's not calling a *reporter*." Said like *the devil*.

"Don't tell her who it is, just give her my cell."

"I can't do that."

"Maybe I'm a viewer with a suggestion. Or a compliment."

"That would be a trick."

"So?"

"Then they would know," says Glover.

"Not if you didn't know who left the message." One good interview or even a run-and-gun on the street with Belinda Yates would be priceless. "Tell her my name is Edith or Mabel and give Belinda my number. She comes in, right?"

"Yes."

"And what about Denis Mincher?"

"Never seen him here."

"Have you ever asked her about him? About anything?"

"No," says Glover. "Belinda barely sees me. I'm not on her radar, you know? But I know her day is coming. Remember Proverbs? 'Pride goes before the destruction. A haughty spirit before a fall.'"

Flynn takes it in. "You're a real believer, aren't you?"

"I know you're thinking I don't look the part," says Glover. "But I don't have to explain it. That's the mystery of our faith."

CHAPTER 58

Goodman wants them on live at four. He doesn't care if they're in downtown Elizabeth or at the sheriff's office or out at Diamond Creek, but only out at the ranch so long as they are not on the property itself. Flynn assures him there's a spot on the side of the road by the ranch, explains that the road was quiet when they were out there earlier in the day.

"You feel solid about this?" Goodman is on speaker via Bluetooth from her phone. The engine idles so they can stay cool, even in the shade. Flynn sips from another cold bottle of water, wonders if she'll ever pee again. "Even without the sheriff's official confirmation?"

"Rock solid," says Flynn. "But I'm only going to mention that Wilkins died. I don't have enough information that they've opened an investigation."

"The church and the holding business stuff is a lock?"

"That's in the state records and we'll get video of that."

"But no official comment from the church itself?"

"They aren't playing ball."

Flynn tells Goodman about the clips they'll use of Belinda Yates hosting the church's video channel.

"So she's *really* got something over them," says Goodman. "She's got all the church's cash, jets around, keeps up appearances."

"So maybe Patrick Kline was about to go to the cops with everything," says Goodman. "And since Denis Mincher hasn't been located, maybe the best thing would be to do your live shots from Elizabeth."

"I'm agnostic on location," says Flynn.

Well, everything . . .

"Oh, and Chris Casey is looking for you."

"I don't have a message." Flynn suddenly remembers to call her father back.

"This was a few minutes ago." The last thing Flynn wants to hear is that Chris Casey has made significant progress on the murder of Robert Waller. "He's right here. I'll punch you over to his line."

"Flynn?" says Casey.

"What have you got?"

"Does the name Belinda Yates mean anything to you?"

Flynn steels herself. Has she mentioned that name to anyone in the newsroom other than Goodman? Or Tamica?

Flynn looks at her partner, who holds up both hands and waves them madly back and forth.

"Yes," says Flynn.

"I got a source who says she's being interviewed by the cops right now."

The Elbert County Sheriff's Office is seven miles east on Highway 86, farther out in the farm country in the small town of Kiowa.

"So you and Chris Casey don't talk?" says Flynn.

"You know I was yanking your chain," says Tamica.

"Yes, I did. But I was still having a hard time, you know, imagining."

"Imagining what?"

"Oh, tangled sheets in a scuzzy motel and the two of you."

"I'm afraid my tastes run a bit more exotic than plain vanilla. And doughy. I like taut. Tight."

"That's enough," says Flynn. "Thank god."

The town of Kiowa isn't in Kiowa County, which is farther south and east, by the Kansas border. That would make too much sense.

Flynn thinks the Kiowa people are probably shaking their heads to this day. And also at the fact that the sheriff's office, located in a one-story, newer building a block south of the highway, is on Ute Avenue.

"It's been a long time," says Flynn. "And brings it all back—though the sheriff's office wasn't in the same place back then."

"What's that?" says Tamica.

"Karen Schultz."

"Karen Schultz, PDQ Karen Schultz?"

"Victim number one," says Flynn. "Of course nobody knew she would be part of a pattern at the time. There's an old stone church on the edge of town. I was out here for her funeral. Saddest day of my career to that point. Gloomy and weepy AF."

"She's buried here?"

"Yes," says Flynn. "And you could tell from the tight-lipped people in town that the real problem was that she moved to the city, that she put herself at risk with all the looney bins in the city. The church was packed. People milling around outside. I couldn't get anyone to talk on camera. Coldest shoulders ever."

◆ ◆ ◆

What quickly confirms Casey's tip is the presence of two black Arapahoe County Sheriff SUVs. Tamica pulls into an empty spot next to the two visiting cop cars. *Foreigners,* thinks Flynn. *Like us.*

Tamica says she'll grab a shot of the vehicles.

The receptionist, in full cop uniform, sits behind a low counter. She's talking on the phone, gestures Flynn to a hard bench along the wall.

Flynn remembers a trip to Kiowa to look for a response after the Colorado secretary of state sued the county clerk over a breach of voting security procedures. The county votes 90 percent Republican, but there were shenanigans around vote-counting conspiracy theories. The earlier effort produced nothing in terms of official comment. Flynn hopes the same doesn't hold true now. Whatever happened to the election-related squabble? Flynn can't recall.

Tamica is next through the door, camera in hand, slung low.

"Anything?" she says.

"I'm worried that us being here means they'll try to slip Belinda Yates out a side door," says Flynn.

"Roger that. You want me to stand in the inferno outside? Am I catching your drift?"

Flynn holds up a fist. So does Tamica.

The first throwdown is paper-paper.

The second is scissors-scissors.

"Fuck you," whispers Flynn.

Tamica gives her best Clint Eastwood clenched jaw. Stares back.

The third is rock-scissors.

"Gotcha," says Flynn.

"I'm watching with windows rolled up and the AC cranked," says Tamica.

Flynn paces. She reminds herself to reply to her father, but she's afraid to jump on the phone in case Belinda Yates comes strutting around the corner.

The receptionist hangs up. Stands. She is trim, angular, middle-aged. A gold rectangle on her chest says R. BROWN. She says, "To what do we owe the honor?"

The question is commonly deployed by individuals who are thinking the word *scram*. Flynn smiles.

"I'm Flynn Martin—"

"I know."

"We understand the investigators from Arapahoe County are interviewing a woman named Belinda Yates."

"I'm sorry," says Brown.

"Sorry how?"

"We don't discuss ongoing investigations."

"Let me put it this way: Would it be worth my waiting?"

"Depends on what else you have to do with your time," says Brown. "I really don't know."

"Is she here on a cooperative basis?"

"Nice try." Smarmy smile. "Let them do their job."

"So she's here."

"I didn't say that."

"Yet, somehow, you did."

"That went well?" says Tamica.

"As cooperative as a brick wall," says Flynn. "But she's in there."

"You're sure?"

"Dead."

Flynn calls Goodman.

"You're sure she's in there?" he says.

"Dead," says Flynn. "Arapahoe County has two vehicles here. And god bless Chris Casey for the tip."

"Excuse me," says Goodman. "Can you repeat that?"

"No thanks."

"Thirty-five minutes till four," says Goodman. "Gabriella is anchoring the four today."

Vasquez is unflappable. Perfect for this. "I'll send you a script in fifteen and the edited B-roll."

Vasquez in her ear: "And now we go live to Elbert County, where Flynn Martin is standing by with a major new development in the story of the strange disappearance of the Kline family. Flynn?"

"That's right, Gabriella, we have confirmed that sheriff's deputies from Arapahoe County are here and interviewing individuals based on a new angle in the investigation that involves New Hope Church, where Patrick Kline was a prominent member. New Hope Church, we have learned through sources and a confirmation with state records, is the owner of a holding company that recently acquired Diamond Creek Ranch in Elbert County."

Flynn pauses briefly. Per the script, this is where the B-roll of state records fills the screen.

"The property was owned by the late Arnold Wilkins and his wife, Belinda Yates, before the church bought it. Wilkins, a longtime church member, passed away earlier this year. From what we have gathered, there was a dispute between the church and Belinda Yates. Patrick Kline was leading the talks on behalf of the church."

Looking squarely at the camera, from memory: "Our sources tell us that Belinda Yates is here now at the Elbert County Sheriff's Office as part of what may now be a joint investigation between the two counties. We hope to ask authorities—"

Flynn stops. "Wait," she says.

A woman is being escorted by two sheriff's deputies across the parking lot. Flynn turns away from the camera.

"Sorry for the interruption, but. Well. Shall we?"

Tamica unsnaps her camera from the tripod, puts it on her shoulder.

"Let's see where this goes," says Gabriella. "Is that in fact Belinda Yates?"

The two deputies on either side of Belinda are familiar enough.

Kerrigan.

Cage.

"No," says Kerrigan, waving Flynn away. Cop hands clutch Yates by the biceps. "Not now."

Flynn ignores him. "Belinda Yates?"

Whatever polish and perkiness Belinda showcased on the church's YouTube work is drained and gone. Her eyes are weary, her mouth is tight. She's been crying. Or is about to. She's wearing a fitted gray tank top over blue jeans. And sandals. She's short and chesty. Her mousy brown hair is a frenzy.

"Belinda Yates?" says Flynn again.

The cops and Yates are on a beeline to an old pickup. Flynn keeps walking, extending the microphone.

"We are going to cut away," says Gabriella. "And let you get back to us with anything that—"

"Wait," says Flynn. That could be for Gabriella. It could be for Yates. Flynn is two steps behind. Feels Tamica behind her. "Belinda Yates, do you know anything about what happened to Patrick Kline and his family?"

Belinda Yates stops. Kerrigan pulls at her arm, but Yates plants her feet.

Turns. Stares.

"Me?" says Yates. "You want to know what they asked me about?"

"Yes," says Flynn. "And we are live right now. And also, what did you tell them?"

"We're live?" says Yates.

"Yes."

"On the TV?"

"Yes."

"Well," says Yates. "Let me keep it simple. Fuck off all the way back to Denver. You and your Black camera bitch. Okay? Is that clear enough for you?"

CHAPTER 59

"Fair?"

"Nrrrt farrrr."

The response is a blurt. A splutter. A clack.

Behind all that tape.

Her eyes are glass. Fear pours from them.

What would Harry do?

"I'm not going to hurt you."

Say things like that, that's what he would do.

It helps if they're calm.

"I'm not going to hurt you. Oh, I already said that."

"Nrrrt farrrr."

"I'm sending a message. You're the vehicle."

Her eyes scream.

It was easy getting in—sympathizing with her cause.

So easy.

The door flew open.

Getting the drop on her while she poured iced tea.

And—what great timing.

The second she was subdued and getting comfortable with her new reality, which wouldn't last long, here comes Flynn Martin doing one of her Valiant Journalist bits.

Right there in the living room on the wall-mounted flat-screen.

They watched together.

Flynn Martin with that badge of certainty. Every question a flame-thrower torching the shrouds surrounding the truth.

The Klines.

Always the Klines.

"Can you promise to not scream if I take the tape off?"

A furtive nod.

Still, lots of fear.

"Can you?"

A better nod.

"In fact, if you say one word, the tape goes back on."

Nod.

"We can do this in civilized fashion, if you want."

No nod.

"That was a question."

Nod.

"Okay, but not one word."

CHAPTER 60

Gabriella in her ear: "Our sincere apologies to viewers. We certainly don't know what to expect from these unscripted moments, but also thanks to Flynn Martin and photojournalist Tamica Porter for staying with this story."

Belinda Yates climbs into a demolition derby Ford pickup that could be thirty years old. It's aqua. The door moans on the open, gets slammed shut.

Yates flips them the bird as she backs up, pressing her stubby middle finger against the window. Flynn can't help but wonder how she must feel, knowing that this is the beginning of the end.

Kerrigan and Cage head back inside.

Flynn's phone chirps. Goodman.

At the same instant, a text from her father: Watched that. Good work. Call me. No giant rush.

Flynn answers the call. "Boss."

"I think you caught a live one."

"By the looks of it. The sound too."

"Can I talk to Tamica?"

Flynn hands over the phone. Only hears Tamica's side of the conversation. "Yes." "I'm fine." "Doesn't bother me." "Thanks for the concern, but I've heard way, way worse."

Tamica hands the phone back.

"Stick around for the five o'clock," says Goodman. "And then we'll get you back in the studio for the ten."

"I'm going back inside to ask for a formal statement from the sheriff. It will be a media cluster by morning."

"Call Arapahoe County too?" says Goodman.

"Two of their cars are still here. By that I mean we're parked right next to them."

"Sheriff Moore is out there?"

"Maybe."

"We'll need the church too," says Goodman.

"On it."

"They can't hide forever."

"On it."

"Good work."

"Thanks. And tell Chris Casey thanks too."

"Excuse me," says Goodman. "Can you repeat that?"

"I'd really rather not."

"Whoa," says Tamica. She's editing on a laptop in the back seat.

"Whatcha got?" says Flynn.

"In the background. Look."

The image is frozen seconds after Flynn and Tamica abandoned the tripod and began moving across the asphalt.

Belinda Yates, given her height compared to the two sizable cops on either side of her, could be a distraught toddler. Over Yates's shoulder, a man makes his way across the parking lot. He's alone. Gray, long-sleeved business shirt. Dark slacks.

Tamica shuttles the video ahead one second, when he disappears off frame, and back two seconds when he first comes into view.

"Bergeron," says Flynn.

"And earlier, after I shot the video of the two Arapahoe County cop cars, I walked the parking lot to see who else might be here," says Tamica. "I didn't recognize anyone else, but there was a bumper sticker on a spiffy new Acura."

"And it said?"

Tamica pulls out her phone, shows Flynn a photo. White letters on a burgundy background:

DO YOU FOLLOW JESUS THIS CLOSELY?

Flynn shakes her head. "Good," she says. "They're onto the whole stinking mess."

CHAPTER 61

"One-word answers only. Yes or no."

Nod.

"I need a verbal."

"Yes."

"You're scared."

"Yes."

"Do you know why I'm here?"

"No."

"And you probably wouldn't. Do you watch Flynn Martin a lot? Her station?"

"Yes."

"She's done big things, right?"

No answer.

"That was a question."

"Yes."

"Brought down PDQ."

"Yes."

"He was scary."

"Yes."

"That *wasn't* a question."

"I'm sor—"

"One word!"

She nods.

"Don't be scared, okay?"

Nods.

"I'm going to undo the rope around your wrists. I'm going to free one hand and tie the other one back to the chair. Your ankles will stay tied. I want us to sit here and have a conversation. Okay?"

"Yes."

She stares at the kitchen table. She could be staring at the center of the earth.

"Okay, then. Here we go. Real easy like. No sudden moves, okay? Are you with me?"

"Yes."

CHAPTER 62

Flynn asks receptionist R. Brown for directions to a restroom, washes her hands in hot and then cold water, daubs at her forehead with a cool paper towel, checks her hair and makeup, and amuses herself thinking how many times she's been live and never had one f-bomb dropped on her and the viewers.

Flynn asks R. Brown if there's a vending machine handy and gets begrudging directions down the hall to an alcove, buys herself a lemon-lime soda and one for Tamica too. Flynn drinks two sodas a year, but this one hits the spot. She lingers inside the sheriff's office, hoping to bump into somebody, checking her phone to kill a few minutes.

Her station has quickly posted the story:

> New Development in Kline Investigation Leads to Elbert County Ranch

Her station switched off comment opportunities years ago, but X is alive.

> Looks like another megachurch is taking a tumble. Greed is a bitch. #NewHopeChurch #wherearetheklines

> Jeezus. And I mean that literally, New Hope better start praying. Hard. #KlineMurders
>
> This is like that 60 Minutes piece about those Mormon Church holding companies a few years back. Thanks for your tithing, we are going to invest it in big business and see what happens. Help the needy ha ha fucking ha. #shameless #NewHope #gotsomeexplainingtodo

Flynn wanders back to R. Brown.

"I'd like to ask Sheriff Rose for an interview."

"I was told two minutes ago that all media requests will be handled tomorrow."

"One on one, do you know? Or big news conference?"

"Yet to be decided."

"Is Sheriff Moore still here?" says Flynn.

Blank face. "I didn't see him leave."

Back outside, Flynn delivers the cold soda.

"Feels like it's getting hotter," says Tamica. "Almost five and that doesn't feel right."

"Well," says Flynn, adopting a professorial tone. "Even though the sun is straight overhead at noon, the earth's surface is still heating up, and then in the afternoon it's radiating all of that back, so it can feel hotter."

"Look at you. You need to get your own show. *The Science Chick*."

"All Wyatt all the time. I need to call my father, and then we'll set up for the five. You got the video edited with a fat 'bleep' over Belinda's salty talk?"

"All set."

Flynn finds a patch of shade from her truck, calls her father.

"Did you know Arnold filed for divorce?" he says.

"*What?* When?"

Maybe Arnold figured out Belinda had taken up with Denis Mincher?

"Two months before he died," says Michael.

"But two months after they sold the property to the church," says Flynn. "So they're swimming in cash."

"And theoretically the holding company is paying them a salary to keep managing the ranch."

"I assume there's no detail with the petition?"

"Only the filing—right."

"That says plenty about the state of affairs between Arnold Wilkins and wife number three," says Flynn. "Did you get a copy of the document?"

"Check your email in about thirty seconds."

CHAPTER 63

"It's *your* iced tea. Come on. A civilized afternoon chat."

A tear rolls out of her left eye. She has short brunette hair. There is something sleek and appealing about her unfussy look.

"So freaking hot out there. Here, I'll take a drink. Now it's your turn."

She stares at it.

"Don't be scared. We've been over this. I will be out of here very soon. I'll walk out the front door the way I came in, and nobody will know a thing. A neighbor leaving a friend's house. But you need to drink. That's what makes this civilized."

She takes one sip.

"See? It's fine. Now drink."

A better sip.

"Why Flynn Martin?"

"I don't know."

"Was she your first choice?"

Nods.

"And she just came running."

Nods.

"Because you're a rich lady from a nice neighborhood."

"No, I . . ."

"Wasn't a question."

Nods.

"Rich lady. Nice neighborhood. And you go on TV and make someone look really, really bad."

Chin quivers. Eyelids flood.

"Is that what you wanted? To make all those school people feel wretched about themselves?"

"No."

"Wrong answer. Why else would you call Flynn Martin?"

Shrugs.

"You know why."

Shrugs.

"Because it's so easy. So easy. So fucking easy. And you wanted to humiliate all those people. The principal, everyone."

"No."

"You call, she comes running."

"No."

"Admit it."

"That's not why—"

"Humiliation made you feel good."

"No."

"You wanted to see them suffer."

"No."

Tears coat her cheeks.

She won't look up.

"Easy target?"

"No."

"Easy pickings."

"No."

"Make you feel important."

"No."

"And then you take your precious little clip and put it on your social media. Write up some more nasty things to add to it. Window dressing."

"No."

"Extra juice."

"No."

"No? Want me to read what you wrote?"

Tears in a torrent. Sobs. "I'm sorry."

"But not really. You blast it everywhere. Hope it goes viral."

"No."

"And you're wondering why I'm here?"

Nods.

"It's not always a straight line, you know? A to B?"

CHAPTER 64

Throat like a dust kitty crawled in there for a long nap.

Goodman in her ear: "One minute."

"And right on cue," says Tamica.

Flynn turns.

Taupe Stetson, sunglasses, black shirt—Sheriff Moore. And two other Arapahoe County deputies, with Elbert County Sheriff Rose propping open the door. Handshakes. *Adios*es.

"We may have a live guest," says Flynn to Goodman. "Scrap the script. I'll recap after."

"You don't think his timing is a coincidence, do you?" says Goodman.

"Not for a second."

Flynn waits until Sheriff Moore is halfway across the parking lot. Four steps. "Sheriff Moore, can we speak with you for a minute? We go live in thirty seconds."

Moore stops. He takes off his aviators. Says nothing.

Flynn hears the dramatic theme music, and Gabriella tosses it to her with a lightning introduction. Flynn tells herself: *Ignore the drama. Ignore the gear. Ignore the moment. Keep it simple. What does everyone want to know? Cops and reporters are on the same side. Except when they're not.*

"Sheriff Moore, what brought you to Elbert County today?"

Moore clears his throat, hangs his head like a preacher at a grave site, lifts it back up. "Well, the investigation into the Kline family, you know, situation."

"Can you confirm that Jedidiah Kline is no longer a suspect?"

"That's correct."

"Why?"

"He can account for himself on the key dates and times."

Each word chiseled from granite.

"Even if he had his father's credit card."

"Yes," says Sheriff Moore. "Both can be true."

"And now, why are you out here in Kiowa?"

Moore takes the question in. Rolls it around.

"We're looking into a piece of property owned by New Hope Church."

"Are there specific individuals you are talking with?"

Again, a pause. Moore wants to be in charge of the pace. *Fine.*

"Yes."

"We saw Belinda Yates leaving here. And we believe we saw Pastor Bergeron as well?"

"No comment."

"Can you explain the connection between the church and a cattle ranch in Elbert County?"

"That's the church's business, and we're following leads, no matter where they take us."

"Was there a church dispute over Diamond Creek?"

Moore puts his aviators back on. "Again, that would be church business."

"Are the four missing members of the Kline family the only crimes that are part of this investigation?"

The question is not only from left field. It's from another ballpark. Moore's headshake is minuscule, but it's there. "That's all I've got."

"Thanks for your time," says Flynn. She turns back to the camera, races through her recap of the items she mentioned an hour earlier. "And of course we will be out here early tomorrow morning to provide you with any updates on a story that's moving in a new direction tonight."

Vasquez wraps the segment, thanks Flynn for her hard work.

Moore stands by his vehicles. Conferring. Huddling.

Or waiting?

Flynn wanders over to thank Moore for his cooperation.

"What else do you know?" says Flynn.

"Are we off the record?" says Moore.

"We can be."

"First, what did you mean 'only crimes'?"

Flynn mulls the pros and cons of playing along. Doesn't see a downside.

"My sources tell me Arnold Wilkins didn't die of natural causes."

"Your sources are?"

"It's one person."

"And the name?"

"I'll ask," says Flynn. "I'll ask if they're willing to talk with you."

"When?"

"Soon."

"Tonight would be good."

"I can try," says Flynn.

Moore pulls out a business card, jots a number on the back. "Personal cell," he says.

"How do you prove that an elderly man with health issues was murdered if he wasn't, say, shot or stabbed?"

Moore shrugs. "That's our job."

"Did you know Arnold Wilkins had filed for divorce?"

"You've done your homework."

"And no question it's all balled up?"

Moore opens his car door. "At this point, it would shock the hell out of me if it wasn't."

CHAPTER 65

Pure hunch.

But if you do the math, it's a long fucking drive in from Kiowa, and even if Flynn Martin was wheels up at the exact same moment after her last interview with the cops way the hell out there, at the same moment the last of the iced tea was going down the hatch, there is no way that Flynn Martin is already tucked inside her parking garage at her fancy-ass condo.

Plus, Flynn has got to drop the SUV at the station and switch over to her funny little Kia. She probably drives it like a badge of honor. *Look at me, saving the planet.*

The same way she must feel after chasing a "big" story, even if it's only the rotten, decaying half truth. *Look at me, exposing issues.*

And ripping people's lives apart.

◆ ◆ ◆

It would be hard to sleep anyway.

So much success.

The pattern is no pattern.

It would be ideal to take Wyatt off the map for an hour.

Or two.

For the scare factor.

The fuck-you.

The fact that you threatened Wyatt and then showed you can deliver, even if Max the Ex is his personal bodyguard?

Too good not to contemplate.

Of course, would never hurt the boy.

The boy doesn't fit the bigger story.

But with some careful planning?

The other thing that needs to be planned is finding out her unit number and getting inside her condo fortress fucking tower without her knowing.

There's got to be a way.

Need to think.

Need patience.

◆ ◆ ◆

Observe.

Analyze.

Observe some more.

◆ ◆ ◆

Harry Kugel had better be paying attention.

How can he not?

He should take comfort in knowing that, at least in some ways, he's still out there.

Doing his thing.

Through his new rep.

CHAPTER 66

Text to Romy Glover: Call me?

Text to Axel Sheen: Can you meet me at our date spot? You know the one? I won't be much fun. I'm whipped. But a drink or two?

◆ ◆ ◆

Tamica drives west after Franktown to pick up I-25 rather than deal with the hundred stoplights on Parker Road. It's a gamble they both agree to take. It's a gamble they both lose.

The highway is the proverbial parking lot. No retreat. Nothing to do but endure the pain. The problem isn't too many people in the world. The problem is too many machines.

Flynn calls Goodman. She wriggles out of doing a live segment on the ten. There's not much that her presence on the set will add in terms of substance.

◆ ◆ ◆

Sheen text: Time?

Text to Axel: 8 pm? I'll leave your name with the guard in case I'm running late. Use my name and they'll get you up the elevator.

◆ ◆ ◆

The building has its own security app. It takes a minute to figure out the bells and whistles because Flynn doesn't use it often. She calls the building security desk anyway to double-check she did it right and to review that Axel Sheen is the only one allowed up.

"Is this, by any chance, Carter?" says Flynn.

"Yes, ma'am."

"I wanted to apologize for the cops and all the commotion the other night in the parking garage."

"You can't be too careful, ma'am."

"I'm sure it all looked a bit silly."

"If you thought it was serious, Miss Martin, we're good with that."

They are 100 percent, all-the-way stopped. So stopped that Tamica puts the vehicle in park.

"So we know why both Denis Mincher and Belinda Yates might not have been at the ranch," says Flynn.

"They were talking to the cops," says Tamica. "Right. Except we didn't see Denis."

"But that doesn't explain why the house looked lifeless."

"Maybe we should have gone back to the ranch," says Tamica. "At least, given it a drive-by."

"Damn it," says Flynn. "Now it's forty-five minutes or more the other way. Back. *Fuck.* Should have thought of that."

"Tomorrow?"

"Maybe. Sure."

"Or go find the pastor."

"Mr. Do You Follow Jesus This Closely?" The traffic creeps forward. "I mean, like a bumper sticker is going to win you converts?"

"I expect the pastor was more forthcoming with the cops than he was with us. Seems kind of strange that he was out there at the same time?"

"Or does it seem kind of strange they paraded Belinda Yates in front of us?"

"Maybe our pastor saw his pickle, you know? And asked if there was another way out of the building. Asked the cops to create a distraction."

"Does our family-man pastor have a sidepiece?" says Tamica.

"I wish I spoke ranch," says Flynn.

"You said that," says Tamica. "Already."

"You got cattle, and they graze, right? What else? Water?"

"We all need water," says Tamica.

"But if you get them water and food—pretty simple business, right? Watch for diseases? Buy sheepdogs to move them around. What else?"

"You're thinking Diamond Creek is a front?"

"It crossed my mind," says Flynn. "And maybe right this minute there's a swarm of DEA vehicles out there tearing apart a meth lab."

"You think we might be beat on that angle?"

"Always worried."

"Maybe ask Casey to see what he's heard?"

Flynn punches up Casey, asks a favor. Casey compliments her and Tamica on the work out in Kiowa, asks if it's a rush, a "now thing," because he's already headed home. Flynn realizes she knows precisely nothing about Chris Casey's homelife or even the part of town where he lives. Is he, in fact, single? During the whole running joke about Tamica's fling with him, it never occurred to her to even wonder whether Casey has a stable homelife or if he goes home every night to video games and ramen soup, alone. Flynn tells Casey that if he's got time for a quick call or two, that would be great, but only if it's not an inconvenience.

"How's my boy," says Tamica when she hangs up.

"Funny," says Flynn. "Do you know where he lives?"

"Are you being serious?"

"Yes."

"I have no idea."

The cars ahead of them suddenly rocket forward. It's as if they've been inching up to an invisible starting line at the Daytona 500. There are no cop cars, no wrecks on the shoulder, but the cars start flying.

"Why are you asking?" says Tamica.

"Curious," says Flynn. "Feeling like I need to pay more attention to that sort of stuff. That's all."

They're doing sixty-five, climbing the hill near Castle Pines Parkway. Soon, they'll get a glimpse of downtown Denver off in the distance in the summery haze.

"Wait a minute," says Flynn. "Did you say 'sidepiece'?"

"Yeah, why?"

"Belinda's travel photos. Aw hell, right there."

"What travel photos?"

"Who was *taking* the photos? Not who's in them."

"Were the photos selfie distance?"

"I'm pulling up her feed now," says Flynn. "But I know before I look. She was hopping in a boat to go parasailing or standing on a hotel balcony holding a glass of champagne. Not selfies."

Flynn goes back to Belinda's Instagram.

"What's her handle?" says Tamica.

"At belindaloves—all one word," says Flynn.

"Sounds like OnlyFans."

"Sounds like a teenager."

"Or both. What do you got?"

Flynn scrolls. "Not selfie. Not selfie. Not selfie. Maybe selfie. For sure not selfie because she's in the water and she's got her arms wrapped around her chest like she accidentally—*yeah, right*—lost her bikini top. Not selfie. Maybe selfie. Maybe she asked strangers to take them?"

"Of yourself half naked in the water?" says Tamica. "I don't think so. Any videos? All stills?"

"Wait, here's one."

"Where are we?"

"A hotel on Saint Kitts."

"Where the hell is that?"

"In the Atlantic. That's all I know."

"And?"

"Belinda standing on a balcony in a loose green dress. More like a wrap. She's holding out a flute of champagne, so it looks like the sun is dropping into her glass. Cliché city."

"Sounds like she had company."

"Wait," says Flynn. "What the hell was that?"

"What?"

"Right at the end, the camera comes off her, and for like a second, less than that, we get a reflection in the door leading out to the balcony. I gotta play it again."

"Hold your thumb down when you want to pause it. Don't tap—press and hold."

"Here we go with the champagne, the sunset lining up. Big, huge wonder-what-the-poor-people-are-doing smile from Belinda, and now the camera is going to move, and fuck, there he is."

"Who?"

"Our pastor," says Flynn.

"Not mine," says Tamica.

"Hairy chest. Powder blue boxer briefs."

Tamica gives her a look. "Guess I know who *he* was following closely."

"Yeah."

"Are they getting ready to pray?"

"Or something."

CHAPTER 67

"Why is it always the sex?" says Flynn.

"I feel like any answer I give will be the wrong answer," says Sheen. "Shall we talk about this Thai food I brought over? Or the weather? The weather is a good topic."

"It was right there in front of me," says Flynn. "It wasn't Denis Mincher, though god only knows where he is."

"Can you use the Instagram video? I mean, is that enough to put on the news? Wouldn't that get the ball rolling?"

"I talked with my news director. Long talk. We're going out there tomorrow to ask for an interview."

"That makes it sound like there's a reasonable explanation."

"I agree," says Flynn. "At the same time, it will be interesting to watch his reaction."

"If the pastor was out there in Kiowa being interviewed by the cops, they must know about it too? All the travel? The affair?"

"That's our fear."

"What?" says Sheen.

"That we'll get beat. The cops might leak something to stir the pot."

"Why wouldn't they leak it to you? You were first."

"That's not the way it works," says Flynn. "The cops can use whoever they want. And there's this newspaper reporter, Judy Hayes, who knows everything and everybody. And as soon as I went on the air, they were all scrambling to catch up."

Flynn takes a bite of cold pad thai noodles, a long glug of white wine, needles herself for not staying out in Kiowa or Elizabeth. Now that she's sitting on her couch with the drapes closed and MSNBC on mute, Diamond Creek Ranch feels like a distant planet. She should have stayed out there to see who was around the ranch in the twilight or stayed in a motel and headed out there at dawn.

"You said 'use,'" says Sheen.

"That's what it is."

"Is it that obvious?"

"Sometimes," says Flynn. "Not always."

"Do reporters know when it's happening?"

"They should. A big corporation calls a news conference to announce some new whizbang project. Everything is all spiffy and sharp, talking points honed like a razor—they're not there to tell you about how much they pollute or how they mistreat women on the corporate ladder, or how their products are manufactured by child labor with horrible working conditions in China. They want you to take their spiel and run with it. You know you're being spoon-fed, but it's still some giant business that's providing jobs and making something people use or like and you roll with it. At least for the day. You might circle back. But, yeah, you know you're being used. You can't play the mean asshole every day. It's exhausting."

Sheen takes it in with another scoop of gaeng keow wan and white rice. "We don't have those issues over in CPA Land."

"Enjoy the lack of theater."

"By the way, when was that hotel-balcony video taken? And how do you get to Saint Kitts?"

"June," says Flynn. "I checked. You fly through Miami. It's a full day both ways."

"Then this was before the Klines disappeared," says Sheen. "I mean, if you're the face of a big church like that with thousands in your immediate congregation, your face is all over YouTube and billboards; are you really going through the airport with your girlfriend?"

"Private jet? Separate flights? Or maybe separate seats? You know, build the sexual tension? Rendezvous once you're both checked in? Separate rooms as the ultimate precaution and cover story?"

"In that case, posting photos or selfies seems careless," says Sheen.

"If you think you're high-quality Teflon, you don't think it through. Happens all the time."

"Aren't you going to ask me what I found out?"

Flynn looks at him. Those magnetic eyes. She thinks he must not realize the overall allure as he moves through the world or how the combination with his dark hair and dark complexion makes the eyes jump out like two juicy blueberries.

"Oh my god," says Flynn. "Sitting here the whole time. All about me and my day. I am so sorry."

"It's okay. I don't have much."

"I feel so crass. Self-absorbed."

"It's okay," says Sheen. "We all know where Patrick Kline worked. That's out there. I realized I had a classmate who worked at the same firm, so I took him out for drinks. Not unusual. You know, few-times-a-year kind of thing. Chatted him up a bit, and he told me that back in June, the firm was about to get fired."

"By the church."

"Yeah."

"So maybe Patrick Kline had found something?"

"Wouldn't take much."

"Is that kosher?"

"Wrong religion," says Sheen. "But, yeah, if Kline was being too nosy, CPA firms get fired all the time."

"Could your guy find out more?" says Flynn. "Would he talk to me?"

"I doubt it. We don't air dirty laundry. There might be a stiff penalty in the contract for terminating early, but if there's a problem you want buried, that's cheaper than the public relations mushroom cloud."

"Patrick Kline was sitting on a bomb," says Flynn. "He knew."

"What's our pastor's situation in terms of wife and kids?"

"The church website said he moved here from Wichita. Graduated from a seminary in Kansas, got gigs at smaller churches in Missouri and Arkansas. I searched online to confirm the website's facts about his past, and it checked out. He's married to a woman named Beth Hackett, now Beth Bergeron. She's a teacher at Willow Creek Country Day School, where their kids go and where the Kline kids went."

"How many?"

"Three," says Flynn. "Amy, Tommy, and Christian. Oldest is twelve, Christian is five."

"And your story will wreck it all."

"The marriage? One would assume."

"You're okay with that?"

"The cops are right there too. Or will be in a minute. And I'd much rather be first on a story than eating the day-old crumbs from other reporters."

Sheen sips wine, takes it in.

"Don't look at me like I'm some kind of monster," says Flynn.

"Do you get used to this?"

"I don't love seeing a family ripped apart, but it's also easy to see the good that comes out of it. I'm not going to worry about the shame and humiliation that Levi Bergeron has to go through compared to Patrick Kline and his family. In fact, you're making me think I'm in the wrong place."

"What?" says Sheen.

"I shouldn't have left the ranch. It's all about to break. The cops are right on it."

"You're leaving—now?"

"I don't know," says Flynn, reminding herself to pack overnight needs. Toiletries. Undies. Fresh top, socks, phone charger, backpack, laptop. And charger for that too. "I need to think."

"I could come with."

"Sweet idea, but no."

"Do you think going alone is the best plan?"

CHAPTER 68

Patience is a dependable bitch.

Where to now, Flynn Martin?

Show me your guile.

Show me how you get it done.

Show me the way to Diamond Creek.

CHAPTER 69

Flynn climbs out of her car. Her car ticks, exhausted from the surprise race. Stars pixelate the moonless sky, and not for the first time does she reject the use of the word "firmament" because there is no temporary barrier between god and his people because there is no god if Levi Bergeron is one of his many dudes on earth.

The warm breeze is redolent with cattle poop.

An upstairs ranch house window glows. Signs of life? The light could have been burning all day, too, and they wouldn't have noticed.

And coming down the road, behind her, a pair of headlights bumps along. They disappear in a dip in the road, surface again at the top of the next crest, and vanish once more.

The sheer timing of another vehicle out here feels strange, too coincidental, but maybe it's someone coming home to Diamond Creek?

Flynn moves around to the passenger side of her Kia, ducks to keep her body and face out of sweeping headlights, realizes her Kia will be in the spotlight.

But there's no time.

The car sails past.

Oblivious.

Small. Silver. Hatchback.

As cars go, a runt. Not new.

And gone, dust billowing in the taillights, flecks of flying grit sprinkling on her windshield like dirty rain.

"You fucking wimp," says Flynn to herself. "Get a grip."

She was half hoping Diamond Creek would be swarming with cops and she could raise a ruckus, get a crew out, and ask questions.

She was also half hoping *this*.

Status quo.

Unruffled, so far, feathers.

But now?

It's one thing to drive onto a ranch property and knock on the door during the day.

It's another thing at night.

11:13 p.m.

In the distance, two bright bubbles of light far behind the ranch house. So small, she can block them both with her index finger—arm extended. Searchlight hot. They appear to flicker.

The long driveway feels deader than it did the first time. A bit closer now, she sees that the lights are propped on stands. A tiny figure walks in and out of the glare, a sharp silhouette. But only a flash.

Flynn walks to a spot where the lights are about to disappear from view behind the house. The only way to get closer is from the porch and get around to the side where she stood earlier. She'll gain another twenty valuable yards. She peeks again at the upstairs window. It's inscrutable, soulless.

A glance around. Flynn puts one foot on the stairs, half worried she'll trigger a motion detector and the porch will come alive with light, and how does she know whether all this isn't being recorded by a camera like the watchful buzzards back on Shannon Way?

Flynn's heart rams her chest. She tiptoes up the steps, hugs the outer edge of the porch as she makes her way around, tamps down that exploding feeling in her lungs that wants her to scram.

Flynn tries to settle herself, but it's no use. She opens her camera app, disables the flash, steadies her phone on the railing, and zooms in with a pinch of her shaky fingers. At max zoom, the lights fill only a quarter of her screen. One man, a shimmering apparition, walks back and forth into the field of view. A flatbed truck sits nearby. The side of a barn looms in the shadow—something she can't see with the naked eye. The man loads something heavy onto the truck. And comes back into the light wearing a Darth Vader welding helmet, and soon sparks fly near the ground a few feet outside the zone of brightest light.

A shout riffles her way. It's guttural, sharp. Is he shouting to someone out of view? It doesn't seem aimed at her. Vader squats. Sparks fly.

Flynn snaps a photo, the fake shutter sound jolting her like an electric prod, and buries herself behind the railing as if she'd accidentally launched a flare.

Waits.

Looks.

And realizes the sizzle of a welding torch is plenty of insurance against the mechanical baby burp from her device.

She stands, puts her phone on silent, zooms in, and snaps a dozen photos because who knows what might show up on her computer when she can look more closely, and then she decides a minute of video wouldn't hurt. And isn't that her medium?

She's fifteen seconds into recording when she realizes the phone light has come back on of its own fucking accord and she slams it on the railing, then brings it to her chest, already backing away from her spot on the porch and starting to run.

A glance tells her she's done it now. Headlights snap on in the far distance. The next shout is louder than the first, still indecipherable. Flynn has no trouble putting together cause and effect. The croaky rumble of an ATV is unmistakable.

Her awkward footfalls thump the porch. She scrambles down the steps and hits the driveway at full tilt, which isn't saying much, except fear is extra fuel in the tank and she realizes again that the driveway is a nightmare mousetrap because she's got a hundred yards remaining and there's no way she's going to outrun a racing machine to the entrance, let alone all the way to her car.

And if she tries to hide, where? And if she hides, they'll find her car and know someone is still out there and all they have to do is wait her out, smoke her out.

And then?

She stops.

Waits.

Listens.

Calculates the odds of her pinprick of light being detected by a couple of dudes, one wearing a welding helmet, working under two Hollywood searchlights pointing at the ground. Like picking out Pluto while floating next to the sun.

Flynn crouches.

Watches.

Gives it a minute and feels her heart come back to normal. She thinks about going back to the house, but maybe the ATV was on a run for beer or sandwiches.

And maybe she's pushed her luck enough.

She walks, looking over her shoulder now and then, but she's soon alone under the vast sea of stars, wondering again if she's in the right place and if she should have maybe texted Goodman her plans. At least done something more than make a casual reference to Axel Sheen that she might come back out here and see if anything was about to go.

Sitting in her car, Flynn checks her messages.

Text from Romy: I can't talk to the police. You told me you'd protect me.

Flynn checks the time of the text—11:15 p.m.

It's thirteen minutes old.

Text to Romy: You still up?

Text from Romy: I can't sleep. It's going to be a mess.

The sheriff thinks you could be helpful.

No.

The sheriff wants to talk with you.

You don't realize.

Realize what?

Writing bubbles percolate.

Stop.

Percolate again.

Text to Romy: There's a lot at stake. Can we talk rather than text?

Text from Romy: Rather not.

Is Romy, maybe, *not* alone? Flynn tells herself to stay vague, though she wants to ask whether Romy Glover knew that Pastor Bergeron and Belinda Yates were on a fuck-buddy tour of exotic beaches across the Caribbean.

Did they come to you?

Everyone is getting questioned.

Then they're clueless.

He might ask to see my phone.

Who?

Pastor Levi.

Say no. And delete these exchanges. Is he the one who questioned you?

Yes.

Not happy?

More than that.

You can help.

I can't.

Think of Patrick, his wife and kids.
I've cried. And cried.
What should I tell the sheriff?
I'm out.

◆ ◆ ◆

Flynn checks X, Facebook, Bluesky, the *Denver Post* website, TikTok. Looking for reactions and takes on New Hope Church, Diamond Creek Ranch, Levi Bergeron, church holding companies, and anything new with Robert Waller because she really doesn't want to get beat on anything to do with a story that's connected to her with an electric, fiery tether.

Scrolling turns up drivel, blather, and drool. Speculation and conjecture have run away together and produced folly and insipience. The gutter overflows with muck.

Flynn watches the video of the grainy pixelated ghost and wonders if it means anything at all, except it seems odd to be welding so late.

"Are you Denis Mincher?" she says out loud.

◆ ◆ ◆

Flynn forwards the video to Axel with a text:

I drove out here and spotted this. Probably means nothing. Wonder if you see anything. No biggie, no rush.

Forwards another copy to Tamica.

Text: This is out at Diamond Creek late tonight. Not sure it means anything. Welding? WTF? Also I'm texting Goodman right now to see about getting you out here tomorrow morning, knock on the door again here and also keep an eye on New Hope Church. I know it's late. Sorry. Also, bring the drone.

Sends Goodman a copy.

Text: Every bone in my body tells me we need to be at Diamond Creek at crack of dawn. I'm out here now. There's people up and about. Not sure if a hornet's nest is getting stirred or just another night. Sorry to text so late. What the hell are they welding at this time of night?

Forwards another copy to Max:

Text: I know this is completely random but do you see anything here I don't see? Welding something, right? Thanks for everything, BTW. Say hi to Wyatt. Sorry to text so late.

Staring at her phone, half hoping one of the four is up, Flynn finds Sheriff Moore's business card and sends him a text: Talked to my source. Not willing to come forward. I tried everything I could. Regrets.

Flynn can't even think how she would have handled anything like this when she was a newbie, when the television cameras were beasts and pagers were cool and her second BlackBerry, nothing more than an email pager, was also capable of a phone call. Big whoop!

In her rearview mirror, in the far distance, she catches the red-and-blue flashing lights of a cop car coming her way.

It's hauling ass.

CHAPTER 70

Stay put?

Drive straight?

Turn around and head back?

And . . . *are they coming for me?*

Flynn pulls a U-turn. She's far enough off the road that it's easy to get going in the other direction. When her headlights sweep around, the cop car has dropped out of sight into a dip in the road.

She guns it. The Kia leaps forward, happy to strut its electric stuff.

Flynn tops a modest rise. The cop car screams down the other side of the same dip. They cross at the bottom a second later, Flynn ceding most of the road to the behemoth SUV. Flynn is right at sixty-five. She eats dust. Visibility drops.

In her rearview, brake lights bloom. *Fuck.* Flynn punches it to seventy-five for a five-second sprint, then settles back at a steady forty-five because it seems about right for the road and she doesn't need to get busted for a bullshit speeding charge.

The cop car closes the gap. Flynn slows. There's no shoulder. She stops in the road. The cop car pulls in so close it could be sniffing her tailpipe but there is no tailpipe because electric vehicles don't produce waste and Flynn is sure that driving an electric vehicle means extra demerits or full treatment as an alien, invasive species.

Flynn's interior throbs with flashing light.

She rolls her window down. Props an elbow out as if she's relaxed and chill, which is the precise opposite of the current vibe.

The cop makes her wait.

And wait.

Finally, his door opens in her side mirror. Boots crunch on the gravel road. A howitzer flashlight beam dances across her rear window, tires, road. He stops to touch her taillight. Not for the first time does Flynn thank her White fucking luck.

"Ma'am, please step out of the car."

The voice is familiar. Or simply ubiquitous.

A red light blinks on his chest.

Body cam.

For all the world to see.

"What did I do?"

"Ma'am, please step out of the car."

"Is that really necessary?"

The cop says nothing.

Flynn pops the door, climbs out.

"Officer—Kerrigan?"

Why couldn't it have been the other one, Cage?

"Do you know why I pulled you over?"

"No," says Flynn.

"License and registration?"

"You know who I am."

The officer says nothing.

"Pulling long hours?" says Flynn.

"Short staffed for sure," says Kerrigan. "License and registration."

Flynn's phone chirps with a text. She half sits back in her car, reaches across to her glove compartment for the registration, digs the license out of her wallet. Stands. Hands them over.

"Why are you out here?"

"I know for a fact that isn't any of your business."

"Did you drive or walk onto the Diamond Creek Ranch property?"

"No."

"Were you watching the Diamond Creek Ranch property?"

"Not against the law."

"Were you with someone else who drove or walked onto Diamond Creek?"

"Yours is the first vehicle I've seen tonight."

Kerrigan snaps the flashlight off. Says, "Wait here." He returns to his vehicle, powers it down, gives the berries and cherries a rest too.

"Thank you," says Flynn.

"What are you doing out here?"

No light blinks on his chest. The night turns worrisome in an unwelcome way. Shades of Jasper. Residue. That icky feeling.

Kerrigan towers over her, a shadow against the stars.

CHAPTER 71

Flynn thinks about pulling out her phone, recording a video. But that could rile him up.

"What are you doing out here?" says Kerrigan.

"I wanted to be here when it started."

"It?"

"Activity."

"It's the dead of night—really?"

"Why not?"

"So you were watching the property?"

"I didn't say I wasn't."

"But you stayed in your car?"

"That wasn't the question."

"You didn't go on the property?"

"Was there an intruder? Something damaged or stolen?"

"You know what's really hard for people in situations like mine?" he says.

"Maybe."

"We want to trust reporters, right?"

"And we want to trust the police."

"But reporters *lie*."

He draws it out like a four-syllable word.

"Is that where this is going? Who is cleaner?"

"I already know the answer," says Kerrigan.

"Well, that's a big leap. And I don't know about 'lie.' At least, you can't get away with one for long at the good organizations. But cops lie too."

"Not the good ones."

"But it happens," says Flynn. "They fabricate evidence, destroy evidence, look the other way, succumb to political pressure. And then there's beating the hell out of suspects and/or killing innocent people too. Want me to go on?"

"And sometimes reporters take the smallest crumb of a complaint and blow it up into this big story without even getting the other side. And you have no idea how much damage you've done."

"Look," says Flynn. "It's late. You're pulling a double shift. Probably not the right moment to negotiate a truce. You got bad apples, we got bad apples. Well, every now and then. You have good apples who play it straight and clean all day, every day, and make the world a better place. We got good apples who check every fact five times before they put it out there. And, by the way, we check each other. The truth, over time, comes out. But it seems to me you've got something to tell me, and you'd rather not tell me with your body camera on because you think it's something that I can help you with, to nudge this story down the road. Am I right?"

Kerrigan says nothing.

"Because what you and I should be doing is thinking about the Kline family and how Diamond Creek Ranch plays a role in their disappearance, not to mention what happened to Mr. Wilkins."

Kerrigan shuffles in place, clears his throat.

"Is something going down?" says Flynn. "I could be home in an hour, comfortably in bed, if you tell me I'm wrong. I'll trust you."

"Did you walk or drive onto Diamond Creek?"

"I've already answered that question."

"And I'm giving you another chance to answer it."

Flynn's phone chirps with a text.

"Why don't you tell me what you need to tell me?" says Flynn. "I protect sources all the time."

"If I tell you something, you can't use it for anything else than for your own—let's call it—'planning.'"

"Okay," says Flynn. "Tell me why you're going to help me."

"Why does that matter?"

"Because I want to know why you're going to help me after you told me all reporters are scum."

"I didn't say 'all.'"

"It was a pretty broad brush."

"I know they're not all bad."

"Then why help me?"

"Because in high school I dated Karen Schultz."

The name smacks like a flying two-by-four to her chest.

"I was at Karen's funeral," says Kerrigan. "There were lots of reporters."

"I was there."

The words sound meek, distant.

"Well," says Flynn. "I mean. I stood around outside."

"We don't trust the city out here," says Kerrigan. "We don't get the appeal, the craziness. You know? But then we saw what happened years later and how Harry Kugel ended up in Cañon City—we know that was all you."

"Not all."

"And this town, you need to know, well, we held another celebration-of-life kind of thing, not quite that formal, but the day Kugel was found guilty in court? We all got together. It was as if Karen could finally rest in peace. You know?"

"I do."

"Thanks to you."

Flynn wipes at a sudden tear.

"Karen seemed like a really good person. I am so sorry."

"I was her first boyfriend," says Kerrigan. "She was shy, then. Into art. Really into music. She moved to Denver the day after she graduated and I visited her once or twice, but she was trying to leave something behind. Including me."

"Again. I'm so sorry."

Flynn walks a small circle, takes in the sweep of starlight. Comes back. "I would love it one day if I could come back and we could have a beer, and you could tell me all about her."

"Deal," says Kerrigan. "And it's not like I pined for long. Got married two years later. Three daughters now—the oldest getting ready to go to college."

"I'd like to hear more about them too."

Flynn's phone chirps with another text.

"You got people trying to reach you? This time of night?"

"The news doesn't sleep. Neither do cops, right?"

"It's true."

"And what about Diamond Creek?"

"We're off the record?"

Flynn's phone chirps again. She long ago disabled the repeat-alerts function. Each chirp is a fresh text.

"Off the record," says Flynn.

"The sheriff would have my head if this gets out."

"I get it."

"Tomorrow? Nothing. It's the day after."

"At Diamond Creek?"

"Right."

"Why the wait?"

Kerrigan takes a moment. "Ducks. Row. That kind of thing."

"Doesn't sound urgent."

"Not my call."

"Focused on the Klines or Arnold Wilkins?"

"Yes. All of that."

"Day after tomorrow?"

Is it possible he's trying to get her out of the way?

"Correct."

"Can you text me if they change plans?"

"No, not a good idea."

"Even from a personal cell?"

"I don't want that responsibility," says Kerrigan. "I'm sure you'll figure it out."

"So I'm free to go?"

"Unless you want to tell me about walking around the ranch house at Diamond Creek."

"Yeah," says Flynn. "I think we already covered that ground."

CHAPTER 72

Stopped by a cop!

Oh, the irony.

If the cop only knew.

From this distance, impossible to tell if it's one cop or two.

No doubt someone heard Flynn scuffling around on the porch, called it in.

What is she talking herself out of now?

What is she lying about now?

Did she tell the cop—or cops—she didn't walk around Diamond Creek?

Would the cops like to have the record set straight on that very important point?

And *what the hell can be taking so long?*

CHAPTER 73

Flynn watches as Deputy Kerrigan's vehicle rolls out of sight in the direction of Elizabeth.

Text from Tamica:

That's not welding. That's CUTTING. Where do you want to meet? What time? Will bring drone.

Text from Max:

Cutting torch, kiddo. You can see the extra oxygen supply line. There's a flash of green hose. That's the oxygen. The fuel line is red. And if you look closely around the trigger on the handle, you can see the trigger for the oxygen. They're not melting metal together, they're ripping it into pieces. And let me know when you have time for an update on everything. Wyatt wants to get things back to normal as soon as possible. So do I. BTW, where are you?

Text from Goodman:

I'm no expert on welding. If you grab a hotel in Castle Rock, of course, keep your receipts. Be careful.

Text from Axel:

Have a hunch that's a cutting torch. I took shop in high school but it's been a long time. What can I do to help?

Doesn't anyone sleep any longer? Flynn shakes her head at the responses. She's all alone in the middle of nowhere in Elbert County and she couldn't tell anyone the number or name of the road where's she's parked, but she's rarely felt more like she's part of a team.

CHAPTER 74

No motels in Kiowa.

None in Elizabeth either.

Coming into the lit-up interchange with I-25 in Castle Rock takes twenty minutes. And, already, that weird feeling that she should have stayed put and slept in her car out there, to watch.

Trust Kerrigan the cop? Or no?

The sleepy receptionist at the Hampton Inn recognizes her, doesn't want to say anything.

12:49 a.m.

The room is cool. Flynn feels proud of her go bag, only wishes she thought to add a bottle of wine. The sheets are fitted so tight to the bed, she feels like she's crawling into a tight cocoon. Reverse birth.

Sleep comes quick.

Until it doesn't.

3:13 a.m.

Flynn watches Darth Cutting Torch Vader on her phone.

And feels the horror pool around her like night sweats.

Like bloody, sticky, gummy, cold night sweats.

Cutting.

Flynn AirDrops the video to her laptop, pulls it up on the larger screen. She sees now what Max told her to look for—the oxygen trigger, the green hose.

All there.

The question comes flying at her: *Where are you burying the pieces?*

Better: *Where did you bury the bodies?*

Texts Tamica: I'm at the Hampton Inn in Castle Rock. Wheels up at 6 a.m.? I'll leave my car here. Sorry to text so late. Um, so early.

Texts Sheriff Moore: I have questions. Can you tell me where to find you? Anywhere.

Flynn figures Sheriff Moore from Arapahoe County is calling the shots. He's got four victims. Sheriff Rose in Elbert County has only one and, so far, Arnold Wilkins isn't on the public radar. It has to be Sheriff Moore's decision on timing. Maybe they're organizing their own flyovers, something less threatening and less obvious than a drone. Maybe a simple single-engine plane making a pass or two high above. Cruising across the plains. Taking photographs.

Looking for fresh scars in the dry fucking dirt.

CHAPTER 75

Tamica is outside, waiting, at 5:55 a.m.

"You rock," says Flynn. "Thank you. I need to throw my go bag in my car."

"Look at you—the planner!"

"I know—there's a first time for everything." Flynn hands her a cup of coffee from the hotel's courtesy thermos. "And only the best for you."

"Gee, thanks," says Tamica. "Hope you didn't go out of your way or anything."

Her Kia is parked two rows over, eight cars back. It's dawn. The Castle Rock air smells like precisely nothing. One day the whole world will smell of nothing. All developed. All paved over.

Flynn bleeps the car open with her remote, throws her bag behind the driver's seat, and hears the world screech to a halt. Feels her tennis-shoed feet rivet to the spot.

The envelope pokes from the rubber weather stripping on her driver's side window.

Right color.

Right shape—though she only sees half.

Flynn looks around. Tamica sits behind the wheel of the station's truck, sipping coffee.

She scans the parking lot.

Inert. *Deadsville.*

She knows the Detective Jasper protocol. She knows the scene it would make. The hoopla. The embarrassing CSI whoop-de-do.

She knows how it would set her whole day back.

She pinches a corner with two fingers, pulls it up.

It's evidence . . .

It's fucking evidence . . .

Means I was followed . . .

Last night . . .

She tugs the envelope up.

No name.

Plucks the paper out from inside, trying not to shake.

Unfolds it.

Blank.

See—?

Nothing.

Except it's not nothing.

Flynn glances around again. There are a hundred cars, maybe more. And someone could be sitting in the dark in a room overlooking the parking lot, waiting for this moment.

To study her reaction.

Flynn stares one by one at the front block of windows. All the shades on the rooms are drawn except for one. Flynn mutters *motherfucker* at the outlier window and wonders how the hell you would request a room with a specific view overlooking a certain section of parking lot.

Envelope Asshole could be long gone, anyway.

Long gone.

And why didn't she notice anyone last—

Wait.

That one car. The puny little fucking runt car that blew by her when she first parked out at Diamond Creek.

Coincidence?

Not coincidence?

Where did it go?

Did she see it all-the-way go?

◆ ◆ ◆

"You think what now?" says Tamica.

Flynn explains her theory, about the Kline vehicle being cut into pieces.

"So the video of the car leaving Shannon Way predawn for the airport?" says Tamica.

"Someone else was driving."

"And they're already dead."

"Yeah."

"And who was driving?"

"Denis Mincher is my guess."

"Where's the other vehicle?"

"Maybe they parked it blocks away, knowing one of them would slip out the back and down the greenway."

"And you think Bergeron was there?"

"I know they let someone inside. Someone they trusted and recognized. And Belinda's fuck buddy makes the most sense. Maybe he's there with one last plea to ask Patrick Kline to chill out, calm down. They've already fired the big CPA firm because those guys were raising red flags."

"And Pastor Levi knows the vacation plans and what time to make it look like the family is leaving for DIA."

"That could have easily come out during the chitchat portion of the evening," says Flynn. "I mean, you'd see the packed suitcases, ask about the flights and that kind of thing."

"But if you're Patrick Kline, you have to be worried about the sudden arrival of Pastor Levi the night before you're leaving."

"Not if they had been meeting," says Flynn. "If they'd been trying to work it out."

"What's to work out?"

"Maybe Levi was asking for forgiveness, claimed he would clean things up himself?"

"You mean fakey-fake ask for forgiveness."

"Yeah. And what better place to make their car disappear?"

"Which means?" says Tamica.

"I know," says Flynn. "It means they're out there too."

"And you're thinking the drone will show what?"

Flynn wonders if she should have left the envelope in her car instead of shoving it in her handbag. And should she tell Tamica? Or anyone? And when? The question makes her think of Robert Waller and again that unsettling feeling.

Wrong place.

Going the wrong direction.

Fucking PDQ.

"What?" says Flynn.

"Did you sleep?"

"Couple hours—yeah."

"You seem distracted."

"Long night."

"You keep looking in the rearview mirror."

"General paranoia. Sorry."

"What time did you get to Castle Rock?"

They're coming down the long hill into Franktown, the sun about to crash the pastel grays and blues on the eastern horizon. Flynn reminds herself to go back and look into the details of the Franktown double murders. A forgotten stray crumb. *Crumbs.* But how can any murder or murders be reduced to something you sweep off a floor? It's always bugged her that those deaths didn't draw the cop and media attention they deserved. Did she miss something? Was someone arrested? She doesn't even know the victims' names.

"It was late," says Flynn. "My presence out there meant I had to do some fast-talking for our cop—you remember the older one from the coffee shop?"

"Does fast-talking mean lying?"

"Maybe."

"You were on the property when you shot that video."

"Guilty," says Flynn.

"But you told him you weren't."

"Correct."

"How did he take it?"

Why a blank envelope? Why no message?

"I don't think he believed me, but I think Deputy Kerrigan and all the other cops have bigger burrs under their saddles."

"And it was Deputy Kerrigan who told you nothing was happening today."

"That's what he wanted me to believe."

"And you think the drone will show what?"

"Fresh, I don't know. Something. Activity?"

"And you want us sitting out there in the station's truck on the edge of Diamond Creek while we fly a drone over private property? You think if they were watching closely enough last night to call the cops that they won't spot us in broad daylight?"

"I'm thinking we send the drone up from the county road. Use the height to give us an angle."

"Over a scene involved in a quadruple murder? See any issue there?"

"I've been after the sheriff for an interview," says Flynn. "Sure, I'd like him to confirm they see what I see."

"And?"

"And so far no word from Sheriff Moore."

"Which I hope does not surprise you."

"Of course not," says Flynn. "He might not answer my calls, but I'm hoping for the same kind of reaction this morning as I attracted last night."

"So the drone is for added, what, irritation factor? Cop magnet?"

"And to see what we can see."

CHAPTER 76

"I'm not going out there."

"Excuse me?"

They've stopped at the same coffee shop in Elizabeth where they ran into Deputies Kerrigan and Cage. Breakfast burritos, giant black coffees. Flynn balked at wasting the time. But remembered the golden rule of television journalism. *Always feed your crew.* Tamica insisted they sit for a minute, not grab and go.

Now Flynn knows why.

"Makes no sense," says Tamica.

"You went in with Chris Casey, chasing Jedidiah to Pueblo."

"We were with the cops. We were riding with the fucking cavalry."

Tamica's gaze is flat.

"We'll be on the county road," says Flynn. "Where we have a right to be."

"And put yourself in the head of Pastor Levi Bergeron or this butthead Denis Mincher."

"They don't know that we know."

"Correct," says Tamica. "They know more."

"They're not going to make it worse."

"You sure about that? And you want to shove a microphone in their face? Out there? Might as well be a cattle prod."

"Maybe."

"Why risk it?"

Nothing worries Flynn more than being the last straggler reporter to the scene.

"Risk what?"

"Risk *us*."

"All I know is to keep asking questions."

"Then as far as we know, Bergeron works at the church. Not out here."

"He was so forthcoming last time," says Flynn.

"At least get Goodman's take."

Tamica's burrito is unwrapped. It's been drizzled with Cholula in a zig-zag pattern, but she hasn't taken her first bite. Flynn is half done. Balls the remainder in the tinfoil wrapper. She wants to smack it with a fist, watch it explode like a bean hand grenade. She's not sure how to budge a brick wall.

"We were out there yesterday—nothing happened," says Flynn. "And I was out there last night—nothing happened. All we're doing is flying a drone."

Tamica shakes her head.

"Then why did you come out here?" says Flynn.

"That was before I heard your theory."

"And?"

"And." Tamica lowers her voice. "It makes sense. Which means these are violent motherfuckers. And you don't have to be first."

"We might be *last*," says Flynn.

"You really think there are reporters out there?"

"I won't know until I see. And there could be a swarm of cops out there right this minute," says Flynn. "We could be missing the whole scene."

"Or we drive out there in the middle of nowhere, and we're the instant target."

"You saw the place," says Flynn. "It was lifeless."

"Until they all come out at night."

"One guy."

"Cutting up the car he used to drive four dead bodies to a place where he could bury them," says Tamica. "Last I looked we were reporters, not SWAT."

"You're scared."

"Damn right. And I'm trying to save your unforthcoming ass."

"That's a big word."

"You're holding something back."

"Oh really?"

"Something happened back at the hotel."

"I got a lot on my mind," says Flynn. "Isn't that okay?"

"Which means you need protecting."

"From?"

"From yourself. You don't always have to be leading the charge. We'll get the story. We always get the story. But we don't have to shove our hands in an electric meat grinder to get it."

Flynn's phone chirps.

Text from Sheriff Moore: Where are you?

Flynn holds the phone for Tamica to see.

Tamica shrugs.

Return text: Elizabeth. Coffee shop. Why?

Where were you heading?

Diamond Creek.

Stay put.

For how long?

Do you want the story?

Of course.

Stay right there.

Give me an ETA?

No typing bubbles. No reply.

"I feel betrayed," says Flynn.

"Call Goodman. Get his take."

"This is a reporter thing. Reporter instincts."

"I got instincts too," says Tamica. "Good ones."

"Sheriff Moore wants us to stay put."

"Good."

"Which should tell you we need to do the opposite."

"You're wrong."

"I'm not a goddamn golden retriever in obedience school," says Flynn. "Call Goodman."

"Give me the keys."

"No."

"You're not doing this."

"I am, in fact, doing this. I'll go if you get the green light from Goodman."

"I don't need Goodman to know where the story is."

"There you go," says Tamica. "The Lone Ranger rides again."

Before Flynn can say *Fuck you*, the coffee shop fills with flashing lights.

One car.

Two.

Three.

Flynn goes to the window, looks to the west. It could be a motorcade for a fellow fallen sworn officer. Arapahoe County. Elbert County. SUVs, bigger SUVs, unmarked black ones. Fifteen? Twenty? An ambulance. A van marked ELBERT COUNTY CORONER.

No sirens. All lights.

A crime scene lab truck brings up the rear.

No—the last vehicle is a flatbed truck toting a shiny red hunk of major farm equipment.

"Backhoe?" says Flynn.

"Excavator," says Tamica. "Three-hundred-and-sixty-degree range of motion. Much better than a backhoe."

"I didn't think you spoke ranch."

"*Je parle un peu,*" says Tamica. "And the *merde* is about to hit the fan."

"Does that mean we're good to go?"

"Don't you feel better knowing we're not trapped between the ranch and all of them?"

CHAPTER 77

On the outskirts of town, the motorcade turns off the highway, bumps its way onto the dirt county road, maintains its methodical pace.

A slow tsunami of *This shit ends now*.

The army of vehicles spews a fog of dust. Tamica flips on the headlights. Somewhere above, the persistent buzz of a helicopter matches their pace.

"Sound like ours?" says Flynn.

The stations all share the use of one airborne eggbeater.

"No," says Tamica. "Cops."

Text from Detective Jasper: Where are you?

Elbert County.

We need to see you.

Urgent?

Wyatt? Better not be.

But thinking about Wyatt gives her an idea she needs to check.

Text: It's not good.

I'm tied up. The Klines. Coming to a head. Wyatt okay?

Nothing to do with Wyatt.

I don't know how long this is going to take.

Have you had any other contact?

Flynn doesn't reply. She's got two bars. Has no excuse.

◆ ◆ ◆

Max answers on the first ring.

"Is Wyatt okay?" says Flynn.

"Fine, why?"

"Thanks for your help with the video." Flynn puts Max on speaker. Showing Tamica a bit of trust. "You know—realizing what was there."

"Sure."

"I'm sorry I texted so late."

"That's okay," says Max.

Text from Jasper: I asked a question.

"Did you forward the video to anyone else?"

"Of course," says Max. "Where are you?"

"Elbert County. With Tamica."

"Are you going back out to that ranch?"

"Yes."

"Cops there?"

"In force."

"So they figured it out."

"What?"

"They have tools. Analytical tools."

"And?"

"They can analyze the shape of the metal he was cutting, and I'm assuming it came back as a 2013 Ford Expedition. Quarter panels. Hood. Tailgate. A door. Something. And maybe there was an emblem or molding on there that gave it away."

"Jesus," says Flynn.

"It's not going to be a happy ending."

"Who did you send it to?"

"A friend who transferred to Arapahoe County. Works homicide. I think they were already spinning up a good case to go out there, but your video cinched the deal."

"So you told him where the video was from?"

Text from Jasper: Call me ASAP. I'm calling Rick Goodman now.

"You'll get full credit," says Max.

"I don't want it," says Flynn. "I don't want to be the reason."

"Might be a little late for that. I know they were impressed. And appreciative."

"Thanks, Max. Is Wyatt okay?"

"You already asked that."

"I know."

"Well, nothing has changed in the last two minutes."

Flynn calls the station, asks for the morning news producer, explains what's happening.

"You're how far out?"

Bonnie Ashburn is a chill veteran.

"Ten minutes," says Flynn.

"Worth disrupting the network feed?"

"Maybe," says Flynn. "They're not bringing this much machinery out here to sit around and wait."

"Our cut-in is in four minutes," said Bonnie, referring to the lightning-quick break for local stations in the national feed.

"We won't be there by then."

"Maybe for the next one at the top of the hour?"

"In my opinion, this will be something everyone wants to see," says Flynn. "And watch unravel. They've got an excavator. It's grim as fuck."

"Ten-four," says Ashburn. "Don't disagree. Our competition?"

"Unless they were already out there this morning ahead of this massive cop convoy," says Flynn.

"None of them have gone live from the scene yet if they're there," says Ashburn. "Seems unlikely."

"Good," says Flynn.

CHAPTER 78

Dust settles. The chopper whirs. Cop cars clog the county road on the perimeter of Diamond Creek Ranch.

Tamica parks, plucks her gear from the back of the truck, emerges with her camera and tripod.

A cop spots them. Gives them the universal sign, ten fingers spread, to stay put. Flynn gives the requisite thumbs-up *gotcha* signal, waits a moment for the cop to ignore them, and leads Tamica behind a wall of heavy black unmarked cars to a better spot with a clear view of the gate and the ranch house in the distance.

The Diamond Creek gate is pulled shut and chained tight. The house looks dead. Flynn scans the barns and outbuildings, watching for movement. Nothing.

Sheriff Moore scans with binoculars. Retrieves a phone from a clip on his hip. Calls. Listens. Shakes his head. Says nothing. Gives a *go* signal with a flick of his hand.

Bolt cutters and a sledgehammer make quick work of the chain and padlock. Two cops swing the gate open, lash it to the fence. Radios squawk. The helicopter thrums. The excavator belches piercing beeps as it backs down the ramp from the flatbed. Cops line the fence in SWAT gear, chests puffed out with ballistic vests, eyes hidden behind visors on their protective helmets. Faceless bugs.

Shotguns. Tear gas guns. Rifles, rifles, rifles.

Flynn calls Ashburn. "A wild scene out here," she says.

"You ready in two?"

"Ready now."

Tamica rigs her with an IFB.

Flynn waits.

Four cops climb into a vehicle like a steroidal armored jeep.

"The BearCat," says Tamica. "They had one in Pueblo too. They're not fucking around."

In her ear: "Once again this morning, our own Flynn Martin is at the scene of a developing story that is, we believe, bringing questions about the Kline family disappearance to a critical juncture."

The voice is morning anchor Jayla Taylor, the single most articulate anchor in town. Black. Cheekbones for days. And a big believer in prep, unless there's no time.

"We have breaking news in Elbert County this morning, where once again our own Flynn Martin is at the scene. Flynn?"

Flynn stands to the side of the camera, gives it a moment for viewers to take in the scene and the sounds.

"I'm here this morning with photojournalist Tamica Porter southeast of Elizabeth, where a substantial number of police vehicles, at least two dozen, have descended on Diamond Creek Ranch, the property that has become the center of the investigation into the disappearance of Patrick and Victoria Kline and their two children."

Going for a steady, even pace in her narration.

"Officers have already made their way through the chained-up gate and are preparing to go in. I don't want to leap to conclusions, but a few moments ago, Arapahoe County Sheriff Gates Moore appeared to be trying to make contact with those inside. Based on what we could tell, we don't think he was successful."

Taylor in her ear: "Do we know why they've brought an excavator?"

"We can theorize, and I want to be cautious about making assumptions. But law enforcement authorities believe that the Ford Expedition that the Klines were driving the night they disappeared may have ended up here and is being dismantled and, perhaps, buried in pieces on the ranch."

Flynn desperately hopes that Taylor doesn't ask her to draw conclusions about the fate of the Kline foursome, that the viewers will be smart enough to fill in the blanks.

"Do we know who the sheriff believes is on the property this morning?" says Taylor.

"No," says Flynn. "The property is owned by New Hope Church. We haven't seen any sign of anyone, but we've only been here a few minutes."

Bad news bubbles in her gut. Apprehension. A raw flash of fear from the convenience store. The hostage taker. Debbie Ernst. *Dead* Debbie Ernst. The day that led Flynn to PDQ. That led PDQ to *her*. That same nauseating angst. The uncertain script. The evil unknowable variables of going live.

And now that they're live, how long will they give it? Flynn gets an urge to pull the plug, kick over the tripod.

She flashes on Wyatt, feels a burning need to hug him hard and never let go. Images tumble of Patrick and Victoria Kline getting jumped in their own home. The terror. The realization. Bergeron and Mincher with Patrick in a basement den, negotiating. Voices raised. Voices ebbing and flowing, Bergeron wanting Patrick Kline to forget whatever he found. Bergeron trying to get Patrick Kline to buy whatever weak explanation he might have had for the beach trips, get him to overlook all the evidence that Bergeron was fucking Belinda Yates and to overlook the indication that Belinda Yates might know the reasons why her husband Arnold suddenly took ill and died.

Bergeron trying to negotiate.

Or even better, Bergeron trying to repent. Asking for forgiveness. Maybe the asshole went to his knees?

And maybe Victoria is listening. Maybe she senses the dread. And suddenly the conversation stops. It's way too quiet. Too quiet for too long. Victoria comes to check on the silence, and when she opens the door, her heart pounding and she's trying to convince herself it's not the worst, but it is the worst, they are waiting.

She stands no chance.

Two against one.

And then the kids. Zachary and Adina. The kids are entangled too. They were up late, too excited about their trip to Disney World and maybe it was after their bedtime when Bergeron and Mincher arrived, but one of them comes downstairs and sees the men. One or both. Saw too much. Saw anything. Or maybe that was the plan all along.

To kill all four.

Maybe the hole had already been dug at Diamond Creek.

How long does it take to strip down and deconstruct a Ford Expedition?

Four cops climb in the BearCat, which has pulled to the entrance while Flynn pursued her dark reverie. How long has it been? A minute? More?

The four cops with vests, helmets, rifles. The BearCat doors snap shut, and the vehicle chugs up the long driveway.

Text from Romy: What the heck is going on?

Text from Goodman: Cops here very eager to talk to you as soon as this is over. They claim it's unrelated to Diamond Creek. Chris Casey on the way for support with second crew. Keep up the good work. Holy hell.

Taylor: "Do we know the plan here, exactly?"

"Only what I can surmise," says Flynn, "and that's to notify anyone in the house that a search of the property is underway. And here comes the excavator. From what we can see, the entire driveway is lined on both sides with fencing that leads all the way to the ranch house itself, so I'm not sure how the—"

Flynn stops.

The excavator treads up the driveway, wraps the teeth of its digging bucket around the third fence post, and yanks it from the ground as easy as plucking a wild hair. Moves to the next, does the same, calmly drives over the flopping chain-link fence and trudges toward the barns and outbuildings on its giant treads, beeping all the way.

"If you'll give me a moment," says Flynn, "I'll let the pictures tell the story, and I'll go ask Sheriff Moore if he's willing to give us a bit more insight."

Flynn hands the microphone to Tamica, scoots around out of the shot, and makes her way to a loose huddle of cop quarterbacks near the entrance.

"Sheriff Moore?" she says.

"Not now." He's watching the BearCat through binoculars. "And if you want our advice, not that you'll take it, we really don't think going live is a good idea."

"Why?"

"I think you know why. And you two need to back way up. Like a mile."

"Do you have any indication that someone is inside?"

"Yes. But let's not do this right now, okay?"

"I'm trying to understand the plan," says Flynn. "Off-camera."

"Thank you," says Moore, "that's all."

Flynn makes her way back to Tamica, takes the microphone, repeats what little she learned.

Texts Goodman: Only relaying what Moore told me but he thinks LIVE is a bad idea. He's worried.

Text: Not his call.

Taylor in her ear: "If they think there is a person or persons on the ranch, they must have been watching the property carefully."

"Agreed," says Flynn. "Another likelihood is that they had initial contact by phone with someone on the premises who made it clear they were not coming out willingly. Again, lots of reasons why they believe this show of force is needed."

The BearCat reaches the steps to the porch. Unless the machine is going to crab up the steps as well, the vehicle has served as nothing more than an armored troop transport.

Four cops emerge and quickly mount the steps. Two hang back at the top of the stairs, rifles up. The other two approach the door with a battering ram. A shout comes floating across the cow-poop breeze. One cop pounds on the door with his fist, steps back. The cop with the battering ram pulls it back like a playful dad ready to throw a giddy toddler into a pool, smashes the door in one heave, and all four cops disappear in a burst of smoke and flame and violent disintegration, accompanied by a bone-rattling wallop that sends Flynn spiraling to the ground.

CHAPTER 79

Oopsie.

◆ ◆ ◆

Oopsie fucking daisy.

The picture goes to a frozen shot of horizon, except the horizon is vertical and then the shot fills with black snow.

The picture flips back to the shiny anchor in her safe-ass bunker studio. She looks stunned.

"Flynn?" she says. "Flynn, can you hear me?"

◆ ◆ ◆

You better not die on me, Flynn Martin.

Probably a scratch.

A shock wave.

Your ears might be ringing. Big-time ringing.

But now you have to get up.

I have other plans for you.

◆ ◆ ◆

"Obviously," says the anchor. She listens. She stares, flustered. Unsure. Panicked. "An explosion at the Diamond Creek Ranch. We are trying to reestablish contact. Flynn? Flynn? We will step away for a minute and come back and reset the scene. Flynn?"

◆ ◆ ◆

No.

Not good.

Too much work has gone into everything.

It will be pointless if Flynn Martin dies now.

Dies prematurely.

Dies before I say so.

Dies without knowing all she's done.

Dies without knowing the carnage she's left in the wake of her half-baked truths.

◆ ◆ ◆

Fuck.

CHAPTER 80

Rain as dust and shrapnel.

Flynn eats the ground.

Tries to come up to her hands and knees.

Can't.

Rolls.

Lets the ground take her back in its arms. *Feels so good.* She can't fight it.

Tamica???

A leg shakes. It's tangled around the tripod.

"Tam?"

Reaches for her.

"Tam?"

"Yeah. Fuck."

"You okay?"

"My ears."

"Mine too."

"Ringing."

"What?"

"Ringing."

"Yeah."

Flynn coughs. Coughs again. Coughs harder. Spits. Spits again.

"You okay?" says Tamica.

"I'm checking." The ground rises and falls like she's riding a cockeyed playground swing.

"Those cops," says Tamica.

Those cops.

A million acid-spewing gnats hatch in her stomach.

Those cops.

Flynn staggers to her feet, leveraging herself off the bumper of a cop's SUV.

The sky is opaque.

Fragments of house and shingles and crap flutter like wounded birds. The sky is dark.

Flynn pulls Tamica to sitting, checks for blood, brushes debris and crud from her hair. And face. And shirt. Tamica coughs, hugs Flynn. Says, "You've never called me Tam."

CHAPTER 81

Text from Goodman: You OK?

He calls a second later.

"We're okay," says Flynn.

"Tamica?" says Goodman.

"Yeah, she's okay."

"Jesus."

"Yeah." Tamica's full body weight presses Flynn back into the cop SUV. "I know."

"You need medical attention."

Text from Axel Sheen: Flynn?

Text from Max: Call me, call me.

Tamica drops to her hands and knees. She coughs, spits, rolls on her back, puts her arm over her eyes.

"Who was that?" says Goodman.

"Tam," says Flynn. "There's a lot of junk in the air."

"You need medical."

"No."

"That wasn't a question."

"We need a few minutes."

"Chris Casey is on the way," says Goodman. "He can pick it up."

"We'll check the gear. See if we get back on. Give us a few."

Flynn hangs up.

She stagger-walks to the truck, digs out two bottles of water from the cooler, and careens her way back. Tamica leans against the front tire of a cop SUV, coughing.

Tamica sips the water. Coughs. "Better," she says.

Two cops squat next to them. Helmets, visors, vests—two massive human beings.

"You okay?" says one.

"We're getting there," says Flynn.

"There are EMTs here." A voice from behind one of the visors. "We'll get around to you, okay? They're busy."

"Those four on the porch," says Flynn.

"Yeah," says the cop. "We know."

CHAPTER 82

"You scared the hell out of me."

Goodman's voice is so close. It's a surreal connection. Is he on the phone?

Or?

Or what?

Flynn opens her eyes to a blur of green plastic, bright sunshine, and a nurse making notes on a laptop. Cords, beeps, tubes, a gurgling sound, a funny smell.

And Rick Goodman in the flesh.

"Tamica?" says Flynn. Her tongue is thick and imprecise. Her mouth is rocks.

"Next room."

"She's okay?"

"About the same as you."

"How long has it been?"

"Not even lunchtime," says Goodman. "Couple or three hours."

"Smells like rubber."

"I'm sorry," says the nurse. "That's oxygen."

"How'd I get here?"

"Ambulance," says Goodman.

"Where are we?"

"Sky Ridge in Lone Tree."

"You could have blast lung," says the nurse. Fifties, tall, trim, matter of fact. "An air embolism. You could have a blockage in your bloodstream and not even know it. Are you feeling any shortness of breath?"

"I don't think so."

Is she naked under the bedding? Flynn reaches down, feels no clothes. "I don't remember losing consciousness," she says. "My car is in Castle Rock."

"There's a non sequitur if I ever heard one," says Goodman. "Your car will be fine."

"What day is it?"

She has no clue.

"Friday."

"My head aches."

"I'm sure."

"Otherwise?"

"We'll want to watch balance issues," says the nurse. "And your lungs. And all fluids. But it's likely temporary."

"By the way, Max is here and Wyatt too," says Goodman. "Dang, that kid has grown."

"Wyatt," says Flynn. "I need to see him. Those four cops?"

Goodman shakes his head.

"Fucking hell. Names?"

Words come hard, like she's learning how to talk.

"Not yet."

"All four?"

Goodman nods.

"I need to get back out there."

"Casey's got it. Casey and Tajira. They've been going live off and on all morning. Half the reporters in the state are out there. Network is on the way."

"Anyone else killed?"

"Everyone else was wearing riot gear. The helmets helped with the blow from the shock wave."

"Booby trap?"

"With the bomb material hidden, maybe in the basement or out of sight somehow from the windows."

"Anyone inside?"

"They're still putting out the fire. Then the search."

"They thought someone was inside," says Flynn.

"They did?"

"Sheriff wouldn't confirm, but he must have thought that was the case. What showed on video before the signal went poof?"

"One second of black cloud racing your way."

"Where's Wyatt? And Max?" says Flynn.

"Cafeteria," says Goodman. "Back in a few minutes, I'm sure."

"I'm not staying here," says Flynn.

"You're staying as long as the doctors say," says Goodman. "And when you're up for it, the next piece of business is with Detective Jasper."

◆ ◆ ◆

The blank envelope . . .

Being followed . . .

And the motherfucker PDQ someway, somehow behind all of this . . .

◆ ◆ ◆

"What does he want?" says Flynn.

"He wants to talk to you. Today."

"Can you get me home?"

"We can check with the doctors."

"I want to see Tamica. I want to see Max and Wyatt. I want a plan to get my Kia back to my building if you're not going to let me drive."

"Terrible idea," says the nurse. "We have to watch for internal bleeding, organ damage. Kidneys, of course, but it's mainly those lungs. It might not feel like anything at first, but believe me when I say you're better off here. We're talking minutes if something goes wrong."

CHAPTER 83

Four dead cops—really bad fucking news.

The discovery of the bodies of the entire Kline family? Double the really bad fucking news.

Well, it's not yet *official* official, but come on. Everybody and their parakeet can put two and two together, and it's not going to be long until they come out and say what we all know. It's not going to be long until we get the video of the bodies being unearthed and even now we have the news chopper in the air, circling and circling, and it's pretty easy to see why the excavator is digging where it is, because of the fresh scab in the earth. Where there was a "recent disturbance," as one news anchor put it, out on the ranch.

◆ ◆ ◆

Four dead cops.

Four dead Klines.

And two injured *journalists*?

If that's what they call them.

Is that what they call them?

Is that what they call themselves?

Well, you put all that together—eight total dead plus two wounded soldiers in the fight for truth and journalistic justice—and you got yourself wall-to-wall coverage on all the stations and easy-peasy tracking of Flynn Martin's location because the other stations have reported the name of the Lone Tree hospital where she was taken and—

Well, *fuck* . . .

Did she get the envelope, or is it still waiting with her car at the hotel in Castle Rock?

Hmmm?

◆ ◆ ◆

The main thing is she's alive.

◆ ◆ ◆

Flynn fucking Martin is going to want a medal.

That's for sure.

You don't put yourself next to an explosion in a valiant search for a whole disappeared family, a *religious* one no less, and not want a medal pinned to your chest.

Not want the credit.

The heated block of calcium oxide. I.e., the limelight.

The warm air blowing up her skirt.

◆ ◆ ◆

"Non-life-threatening."

Just come out and say it.

She's not going to die.

She's not going to die, and neither is her video girl, the cool Black one.

Tamica.

But all the reporters have the standard patter at the ready. There must be a song sheet somewhere. A playbook. All the reporters must master the basic phrases.

◆ ◆ ◆

Stay tuned.

Time will tell.

Back to you.

Our top story tonight. (Says who?)

As you can see.

We'll have more on this urgent cataclysmic story tonight at fucking whenever after you watch three hours of fucking crappy commercial television.

◆ ◆ ◆

And the ever-popular . . . *were taken to the hospital with what is believed to be non-life-threatening injuries.*

Does anyone ever notice that the reporter never says *They were taken to the hospital with life-threatening injuries*?

May as well say *They're going to die.*

And you can't say that.

◆ ◆ ◆

Go check on Flynn's fussy woke-as-shit e-car in Castle Rock?

Or go wait for her to arrive back home at Altair Tower?

What would PDQ do?

◆ ◆ ◆

Four dead cops.

Four dead Klines.
And even more to come!
Iced tea woman.
Taken to the hospital with . . .
How would a good reporter phrase it?
. . . no visible life-threatening or non-life-threatening injuries.
Because she was already dead.

CHAPTER 84

The day drifts in and out of the mental murk.

Wyatt. Max. Axel Sheen with a surprise appearance.

Chat, questions, chat some more.

"I'm fine" ad nauseam.

Recite your birth date.

Recite your birth date.

Recite your fucking birth date.

Tamica sits in the chair next to her bed for twenty minutes before they scurry her away for more tests. Stethoscopes galore. This doctor has to listen, that doctor has to listen. Lungs from the front. Lungs from the back. Deep breaths. A CT scan. A chest x-ray. Name. Birth date. Name, birth date, name, birth date. Scan the ID bracelet. Try to get comfortable on the bed, try to find a relaxed position with the doll-size unforgiving pillows.

Flynn stops whining about wanting to be released. She gives herself over to the process. They wheel her out for a transesophageal echocardiogram.

Dizzying hallways, weak food. Gulps of high-flow oxygen.

Water, water, water.

You need to drink.

We'd really love a urine sample if you're up for it!

At midafternoon, finally, a conversation about setting her free.

It's a fifty-fifty proposition, but Flynn doesn't put her thumb on the scale. She wants points for good behavior. On the test hallway walk, she steels herself for an Oscar-worthy performance despite the mental fuzz and balky legs.

Finally, a plan emerges. Rick Goodman will drive her back to her condo, and Axel Sheen, who has lingered all afternoon, volunteers to take a Lyft to Castle Rock and drive her car downtown. Flynn gives Axel a general description of her car's location. She can only hope to hell that Axel doesn't find another envelope, blank or not, stuck in her window weather stripping. Flynn tries to sell them on the idea of letting her drive. They immediately make a big fuss of Flynn passing the keys to Axel Sheen and watching him walk away.

"What about Tamica?" says Flynn. "What about the station truck we left out at Diamond Creek?"

"All sorts of things you don't have to worry about," says Goodman. "And Tamica went home an hour ago."

"What?"

"She passed all her tests with flying colors."

"And didn't say goodbye?"

"You were dozing."

On the ride, with an anxious feeling like she's been marooned on a desert island, Flynn scrolls for news. Her station. *The Denver Post.* Socials.

"Give me the highlights," says Flynn. "Have they found a body in the rubble? Inside?"

"One body," says Goodman. "That's it so far."

"ID?"

"Not yet."

"What else?"

"They are digging in an area that looks like they wanted a fresh ditch for irrigation, but there's no water on the property, no creeks or anything."

"Car parts?"

"The sheriff said they found pieces from a 2013 Ford Expedition, and now they need the bodies."

"How awful does it get? No sign of Pastor Bergeron or Belinda Yates?"

"Unless the dead body inside the house is one of them."

"It's not. Do they know to watch the airport?"

"Why?"

"Check the airport," says Flynn. "They could have easily seen the trouble on the way and hightailed it."

"Sheriff Moore held a presser at noon and emphasized that they were looking for both of them," says Goodman. "He also said they have reopened an investigation into the death of Arnold Wilkins."

Text from Romy Glover: I hope you are okay. I can't believe all of this.

Text from Axel Sheen: Got your Kia. Now back north to you.

Text from Tamica: You were sleeping comfortably when I left. I'll touch base soon. Take it easy.

Goodman walks her inside, past security, and to the concierge desk on the ninth floor, being manned by Carter.

"So good to see you," says Carter. "Are you okay?"

Flynn assures Carter that she's fine, thanks him for his concern, introduces her boss, and wants reassurance that nobody else will be cleared to come to her condo without a personal green light from her.

"Yes, of course," says Carter. "But Detective Jasper is here—you remember him from the other night? And he's with another detective, Yamamoto. Wendy Yamamoto."

"Where *here*?"

"I sent them down to the common area and told them I would come get them as soon as I knew you were here."

"It's okay," says Flynn. "I can find them."

CHAPTER 85

"We would rather do this in your apartment," says Jasper. "More privacy. And we would rather talk only with you, no disrespect to Mr. Goodman."

"No on both counts," says Flynn. "I would like Rick to hear this, whatever it is. But if we could make this quick, you know, I'm afraid I've had a bit of a day."

"Indeed you have," says Jasper.

They are outside. They sit on matching outdoor couches with those firm plasticky cushions that will survive the apocalypse. The city hums. It's the last few minutes of dusk. Flynn feels a cool breeze on her face, tries to connect this moment with the bomb at dawn and realizes that it's all been the same day. A lingering dentist's-drill ring gnaws at her ears from deep inside.

"I'm very sorry for your fellow officers," says Flynn. "No IDs yet? Were they all Elbert County?"

"Yes." Jasper looks at Yamamoto, who nods. "Still unconfirmed."

"But that's not why you're here," says Flynn.

"No," says Jasper.

"Have you received any other contact?" says Yamamoto.

"Maybe," says Flynn. *This is for you, Tamica. No more Lone Ranger. At least tonight.* "Probably."

"I asked you earlier," says Jasper.

"It was a busy day," says Flynn. "Overnight at my hotel in Castle Rock, there was an envelope waiting for me on my car. Shoved in the weather stripping on the driver's side."

"And?"

"It was blank. Outside and inside."

"And it's where now?" says Yamamoto.

Flynn digs through her handbag, pulls it out, hands it over. "I know, I probably ruined evidence. I didn't really have a choice this morning to wait three hours to get out to Diamond Creek."

"Did you drive your car out to Diamond Creek?"

"No," says Flynn, immediately realizing the implication. She could have left the envelope in place and alerted them about its existence. The Denver cops would have had all day to process the scene and see if they could come up with something. Anything. "Spur-of-the-moment thing."

"Did you know you were being followed?" says Jasper.

"Not until then."

"And once you knew, were there any other moments that jumped out at you?"

"Out at Diamond Creek—the night before. I went out to the ranch, and a car was on the road a few minutes behind me."

"And?" says Yamamoto.

"And it kept going, but it seemed strange, you know? The timing."

"Type? Color? Anything?" says Jasper.

"Silver. Small. And the more I think about it, not a new car."

"But it kept going?"

"Yes," says Flynn. Did it? Did she watch it go all the way? "There's been another—?"

"We'll be announcing it in the morning," says Jasper.

"With a message?"

Grim expressions say it all.

Flynn feels like she would crawl on hands and knees all the way to the elevators and down the hall to her place if she could sleep for twelve hours straight. Or maybe slump to the outdoor carpeting right this second and curl up in a hedgehog ball.

"I can't manage this right now," says Flynn.

"I'm sure," says Yamamoto.

"It's PDQ," says Flynn. "Harry fucking Kugel, and I don't care if he is behind bars a hundred and twenty miles away, he's right in the thick of this shit."

"We don't see it that way," says Jasper. "But we are monitoring his contact with visitors. And his mail."

"It's him," says Flynn. "Okay, who is the latest?"

"We don't want this out there tonight," says Jasper. "We want this to be a coordinated release in the morning."

"Why?" says Goodman. "Then why come here?"

"Because there is a specific connection," says Yamamoto.

"What did the message say?" says Flynn.

"Do we have an agreement on not rushing this on the ten o'clock?" says Jasper.

Goodman shrugs. "Okay."

Jasper fusses with his phone for a second, hands it to Flynn. It's a photo of the message.

◆ ◆ ◆

Maybe #3?
Maybe #4?
Maybe even more?
Does this one help you understand, Flynn Martin?
What you do?
How you do it?
The Prototype Rules.
The pattern is no pattern.

◆ ◆ ◆

"I'm ill," says Flynn. "Seriously, I need to lie down somewhere. This is bullshit. I mean, why me? It was me last time with PDQ and it's me now with this asshole."

"Unfortunately," says Yamamoto. "There's more."

"Who was the victim?" says Goodman.

Jasper waits. Yamamoto looks at her colleague, defers.

"The woman you interviewed recently about school bomb threats," says Jasper. "Meg Hart."

CHAPTER 86

"When?" says Flynn.

They're in her condo. Twenty minutes of angry sobbing begins to subside.

She doesn't want any more details.

She wants all the details.

The day swallows itself. Gloom equals misery times the speed of loneliness.

"She was found by her husband yesterday evening," says Jasper.

"Where?"

"In her kitchen," says Yamamoto, "on the floor."

"How was she killed?" says Goodman, able to form full four-word sentences without choking up even though he looks plenty perplexed and disturbed by all the implications.

"At first her husband thought it was natural causes. Not a scratch on her. As if she'd stretched out and taken a nap. The autopsy is pending," says Jasper. Still looking crisp and unfazed. Some part of his brain able to cordon off the dreadful dreck of it all as nothing more than a problem-solving exercise.

"Of course Mr. Hart was distraught," says Yamamoto.

"Mr. Hart," says Flynn. "Aaron Hart. Right?"

"How did you know?" says Jasper.

"I remember asking Meg for his name," says Flynn.

But why did that random morsel stick?

"That's him," says Jasper.

"Two little kids. One boy, one girl?"

"Emma and Liam," says Yamamoto.

"So the envelope wasn't with her?" says Flynn. "Like Robert Waller?"

The pattern is no pattern.

"There's a fair amount of commotion," says Jasper. "The neighborhood is alarmed. It's a nice area, you know? Neighbors come over, and the sadness, well, you can imagine. The kids are despondent. In fact, we believe it was Liam who first ran from the garage into the house and tried to wake his mother. At first Aaron thought maybe his wife was pulling a prank, and then reality hit. Aaron tried CPR and everything, but to no avail."

"The police get Mr. Hart to review his story a few times, and it all checks out and there is talk of what to do with the children," says Yamamoto.

"There are options to let the kids try and sleep at friends' houses, and Meg has a sister, the kids' aunt, who lives in Boulder," says Jasper. "But they decide, hours later, to keep the kids at home, the place they know best. And by then the aunt has arrived and she plans to spend the night. To help."

"It's about eleven p.m. when Mr. Hart goes into the master bathroom," says Yamamoto.

"I mean, the cops have given a general once-over walk-around to see what they see," says Jasper. "But there is no reason to think it was anything other than natural causes."

"The envelope falls out when he opens the medicine cabinet," says Yamamoto. "It's like a small cupboard on the side of the vanity. The envelope tumbles out and he wastes no time. Doesn't touch it but calls the cops, and, well, the next thing we know we are out there confirming that it's, you know, the same."

"And then?" says Flynn.

"And then we treat the whole thing like a crime scene, of course," says Yamamoto.

"But as you can imagine, there's been a fair amount of traffic all over the property," says Jasper. "Regrettably."

"What time was all this?" says Flynn.

"They arrived home around six," says Jasper. "They are in an after-school, extended day program at the school. Closes at five, but when Meg didn't pick them up, Aaron left work and came to get them."

"She could have been dead for—?"

"Hours," says Yamamoto.

"And working to see, again, if anybody saw anyone coming or going?" says Goodman.

"Of course," says Jasper. "We've been out there canvassing all day."

"And nobody called in a tip to the newspaper, the other stations?"

"We have had a few queries," says Jasper. "Judy Hayes calls from the *Post* about every hour. But all we are saying at this point is that we are being thorough, given the investigation into Mr. Waller. That will change tomorrow morning. We need everyone's help."

"The public needs to know," says Yamamoto.

"So," says Jasper.

"So *what*?" says Flynn.

"What do you think it means?" says Yamamoto.

"What?" says Flynn.

"Does this one help you understand, Flynn Martin?"

"No, it doesn't help me understand," says Flynn. "Except we know it's him. PDQ him. Somehow. He's got a puppet, or in this case a marionette, I guess, because they're the ones on strings. Directly controlled."

"But can you think why killing Meg Hart sends you a message?"

"Of course not," says Flynn. "I mean, I'm ill about those four cops, I'm sick as can be thinking about the Klines. And now I have to add in Liam Hart unable to wake his mother? What did I do? I did an interview."

"We'll keep you off air for now," says Goodman.

"What?" says Flynn. Burning now. "*That's* your solution? Now?"

"They're going to suggest it anyway," says Goodman.

"We were—" Jasper starts. Stops. Pauses. "We are, in fact, asking that. Urging that. Strongly urging that."

"That *what*?"

"We think you stay here," says Yamamoto.

"What? Lock me up? Confined to quarters?"

"Along those lines," says Jasper.

"Absolutely not," says Flynn.

"Do you think anyone will go on camera with you, after tomorrow?" says Goodman.

"Like what, I'm picking victims for a serial killer? That is fucked up."

Everybody says nothing.

"Jesus," says Flynn. "Really? Why does my name have to get out there?"

"Because it's part of the story," says Jasper. "And it's not like a reporter from the *Post* or one of the other stations won't put it together. Anyone who saw the clip would remember her."

Story, thinks Flynn. Not a fucking *clip*.

"But why the hell would you have to mention that my name was on the message from the killer? Can't you make that a bit you hold back?"

"Whether we do or don't, you're part of the story."

"Only if *you* agree that's a possibility," says Flynn.

"It won't be up to us," says Jasper. "And we have already thought this issue through because, ultimately, it will come out. We need to play all our cards in getting the public's help."

"Which is what the killer wants," says Flynn. "Don't you think?"

"We've consulted with the FBI," says Yamamoto. "All day. While you were dealing with what happened this morning and while you were getting checked out at the hospital—and we are so glad you are okay—we came at this issue every way imaginable."

"Ultimately," says Jasper, "we think this moves the case forward in the best way possible."

"By making a splash out of my name."

"By being an open book," says Jasper.

"By punishing *me*," says Flynn.

How can this not feel like a backhanded penalty for outright rejecting John Jasper's invitation for personal entanglement?

Bleh.

"The person behind these murders is very angry," says Jasper.

And so are you, Flynn wants to say. Doesn't. "A beheading?" she says. "I think I knew that."

"They want to know they're being heard," says Yamamoto.

"They?" says Flynn.

"The killer," says Yamamoto.

"What about Robert Waller?"

"What about him?" says Jasper.

"There's no connection."

The pattern is no pattern.

"You're not thinking about the appearances," says Goodman.

Flynn's phone chirps.

"Axel?" she says.

"Remind me of your parking spot number," he says. "I'm pulling in now."

She gives it to him, asks him to plug in the car for the night too. Not that she's going anywhere ever again. "Use the fob to open the door in the vestibule," she says, "and then come up to—"

"I know how it works," says Axel. "I've been watching."

"And switch elevators, use the fob again on the panel by the buttons in the elevator or it won't go anywhere."

"Yeah," says Axel. "Got it. You okay?"

"Not really."

"You alone?"

"Not even close."

CHAPTER 87

"Who was that?" says Jasper.

"Boyfriend."

Flynn gives Jasper a high school lunchroom drama queen stare.

That's right, motherfucker. You're about to meet the guy who was approved for takeoff and is currently dating the bumbling reporter who drags misery around like a sack of woe.

"Coming up here?" says Jasper.

"You have to be careful," says Yamamoto.

"I recognize his voice," says Flynn. "He's got my car keys. He's got my car. He's been here before. How much more careful can I be?"

"He might not be aware of someone following him," says Jasper. "Showing someone else the way."

"You can't roam around this building without attracting attention," says Flynn. "Layers of security."

"We are adding a detail to this building," says Jasper. "Plainclothes. We could tell you or not tell you and you wouldn't even know the difference, but we wanted you to know."

"What? Outside my door?"

"There's an empty unit on your floor," says Jasper. "In fact, there are several units for sale right now, but this one is on the other end of the hall. We'll rotate two people in and out, and occasionally they will walk around outside to see if anyone is watching. The folks here who run your building are being extremely cooperative."

"You've already talked to them," says Flynn. "This was all a done deal?"

A soft double knock at the door.

One-two.

Bop-bop.

Precise and clean.

Flynn goes to the door, peers in the peephole, opens the door, and gives Axel Sheen the body hug of his life.

"You're welcome," says Sheen.

"You could have unlocked the door yourself," says Flynn.

"I didn't want to be presumptuous," says Sheen. "Or give you a jolt."

"Found my parking spot okay?"

"Of course. Who all is here? What's going on?"

Five minutes later, Axel Sheen has the horrifying gist of events. As soon as he does, the cops make their exit but not without uttering a heap of admonishments, cautions, and warnings.

Cop-free again, Flynn pours red wine for herself and Axel. Goodman accepts a splash of whiskey, neat. From her bedroom, letting the two men get to know each other, Flynn calls Wyatt, who wants this all to end, and gives Max the overview of the bombshell to be dropped in the morning.

"I heard about the investigation," says Max. "You know, another Westside murder, and they were pulling out all the stops going door-to-door talking to people who might have seen anything. But I had no idea it was connected to you. Well, you have to follow their advice. You know that, don't you?"

"Kind of," says Flynn.

"You okay? After this morning?"

"What is 'okay'? And is it a good thing?"

"You're angry."

"You bet I'm angry. It's him. It's fucking him. But nobody wants to figure out how he's doing it."

"Let the cops take the lead," says Max. "They know what they're doing."

"They do?"

"I know they've got a profile."

"That's hocus-pocus," says Flynn. "Reverse engineering character traits from a crime scene? What about when there is no pattern? Pissed-off White male, because it's always a White male. Late twenties or early thirties, because after that you're tired and run out of gas unless you're nutjob psychopath Harry PDQ Kugel. Loner. Drives a Volkswagen because it's always a Volkswagen. There you go. There's your profile."

"It's more scientific than that," says Max. "Hundreds and hundreds of cases over the years. Tons of data to look at. Look, why don't you come stay out here with me and Wyatt?"

"Maybe," says Flynn. It's a reasonable thought and a decent offer, but hard to imagine fitting Axel Sheen into that scenario. "I don't know. When Wyatt's at school and you're at work, I think I'd feel quite isolated, you know? All the way out there?"

Her father also wants her to toe the line.

"You have to follow their lead," says Michael. "Especially if you were being followed and didn't know it."

"I kind of knew it."

"Not the same."

"Maybe."

"You're doing okay? Feeling okay?"

"What is 'okay'? Is that the low-bar threshold for our existence or something we should all feel proud and satisfied that we have reached, the mighty plateau of resignation and acceptance for our lives?"

"It was a simple question," says Michael.

"I know," says Flynn. "I feel fine. Thanks for asking."

Tamica picks up. Flynn decides to hold the chat in the living room, on speaker for Goodman's benefit.

"The on-air talent always gets the news director's in-person empathy," says Tamica. "The way it goes, I guess."

"I'm coming there next," says Goodman. "Provided it's not past your bedtime."

"Being second means I was the first loser," says Tamica. "Too late. Besides, I've got company. While I got you, need me anywhere tomorrow?"

"You feel up for it?" says Goodman.

"Of course."

"There's going to be a follow-up out at Diamond Creek. Any hesitation about going back out there?"

"My hunch is all the bombs are done exploding," says Tamica.

"No residue?"

"I don't believe in that shit."

"Once a cowgirl, always a cowgirl," says Flynn.

"Something like that," says Tamica. "You're going back out there too, FM?"

"I'm afraid she's not," says Goodman. "Due to this new situation."

CHAPTER 88

"They're all going to want interviews with you," says Tamica, still on the call. "Every one of them."

"Well, they can't," says Flynn. "And what do I know anyway? But if one of them wants to shove a microphone in Harry Kugel's face and get him to tell us how he's doing it, I'll consider it then. But only then."

"If she's doing any interviews, it's with us first," says Goodman.

"My favorite," says Flynn. "The reporter becomes the story. No way. We should be focused on Meg Hart. And the search for Levi Bergeron and Belinda Yates. Or find an angle with the Kline family. Or the four dead cops. As if that's not enough options, there's also the murder of Arnold Wilkins."

"We?" says Tamica.

"Someone," says Flynn. "And me being grounded like a fucking teenager who crashed the family car doesn't mean I can't make calls."

"We've already had requests to interview both of you about being out there when the bomb went off," says Goodman. "I declined on your behalf."

"Good," says Flynn.

"Good," says Tamica.

◆ ◆ ◆

The ten o'clock news begins with the last ten seconds of footage before the bomb went off and the fifteen seconds of walloped-to-the-ground blackout footage when the blast wave reached them.

"Have they played that enough today already?" says Flynn.

"They?" says Goodman.

"Us," says Flynn.

"First time I've seen it," says Sheen. "Jesus."

Anchor Lee Rosen: "That was the tragic scene this morning as four sheriff's deputies lost their lives when a bomb exploded inside a ranch house in Elbert County. Authorities were conducting a search for the bodies of Patrick Kline, his wife, and two children. And, as this devastating day has progressed, law enforcement appears close to finding remains, even as the hunt continues for two key figures in connection with the Kline family disappearances, both prominent members at New Hope Church. We begin tonight with reporter Chris Casey out at the scene, where the sheriff has released the identities of the four fallen officers."

The shot is so close that Elbert County Sheriff Richard Rose's mug fills the entire screen. The video starts with the sheriff gathering himself. *Getting emotional,* as the saying goes. As if the only emotions that truly count are the ones connected to sorrow and grief.

"The four fallen warriors." Rose's voice is thin and distant, dry. It's night. He looks up as if for guidance from a star. "The four fallen warriors whose names will never be forgotten here in Elbert County are Deputies Alan Travers, age forty-one, from Elizabeth; Nicholas Walsh, twenty-nine, from Agate; Peter Lake, thirty-eight, from Simla; and forty-year-old deputy Sam Kerrigan, from Kiowa. All together, they leave behind three widows and seven total children, and our hearts, thoughts, and prayers are with all of them tonight."

A chill flashes from Flynn's right arm to her left, flies down her back, turns her guts queasy. She hangs her head. Feels a hand on her back.

"Flynn?" says Sheen.

"Sam Kerrigan," says Flynn. "He stopped me last night out at the ranch. We met first at the coffee shop. Elizabeth. Then in Kiowa at the sheriff's office. We have footage of him escorting Belinda Yates to her car. He was the high school boyfriend of Karen Schultz."

"You're kidding me," says Goodman.

"Who?" says Sheen.

"PDQ's first victim," says Goodman. "It's like the impossible Venn diagram. It shouldn't be a thing."

"What does it mean?" says Sheen.

"It means I'm a curse," says Flynn. "Meg Hart and now this. *Fucking* this."

"One thousand percent coincidence," says Goodman. "Two completely separate stories."

"They overlap in one minuscule aspect and point a big arrow at me."

"And if you weren't out there," says Goodman, "you never would have found that out. It never would have come up."

"Point proven."

Chris Casey: ". . . as you can see tonight in the far distance, the sheriff's department has brought in lights to work through the night, and they have erected a large screen to block our view, but clearly they are finding something in the field and you can make out the top of the excavator occasionally as it moves, ever so slowly. In the last ninety minutes tonight, we've seen one coroner's vehicle arrive, depart, and then return and drive back out across the field to that same spot. It could be a long, somber night."

Anchor Oliver Garrett: "In addition to the four deputies, were there other victims inside the house?"

Casey: "Yes. One additional victim, and he has been identified as Denis Mincher, who apparently had been working at the ranch for some time. He has a record for felony assault, and we are working to get more details tonight."

Anchor Lee Rosen: "Police are also searching tonight for Pastor Levi Bergeron, the face of New Hope Church, and a woman named Belinda Yates?"

"Fuck buddies," says Flynn. "Check the goddamn airport!"

"Yes," says Casey. "Authorities are seeking the public's assistance tonight for any information. Both Bergeron and Yates are persons of interest. Of course we have contacted the church and requested an interview and expect to follow up there in the morning, as the church controls this ranch through a holding company. Lots to untangle out here at this very sad scene."

CHAPTER 89

Errand boy.

So easy to spot in Castle Rock.

So easy to follow all the way back to Flynn's condo tower.

Errand boy.

Clueless.

Probably didn't think once about being followed.

Errand boy is a boring driver.

Never the right lane. Always #2. Never considered the two other lanes with the much better flow. Drove her Kia like it was made of untempered glass.

And if he had Flynn Martin's car, that means he left his own car at the hospital and would need to complete the circuit via friend or Lyft.

The question is *when*.

The fact that errand boy didn't come out the front door of the condo tower a few minutes after the Kia was swallowed up by the entrance to the parking garage suggested that he was more than a gofer.

Errand boy with benefits.

Part of the inner circle.

And errand boy, one way or another, will have to get back to Lone Tree to retrieve his vehicle.

Tonight?

Doesn't seem likely.

At this hour, they are tucked in for the night. Maybe. Probably. With what she's been through today, she's toast. Maybe. Probably. An all-night vigil feels unnecessary.

Should errand boy have company when he drives back south?

Maybe, by morning, Flynn will feel like driving him on the return.

But she's likely, under doctor's orders, to lie low for a few days.

Yes?

No?

Maybe?

The big problem is keeping an eye on the front of the condo tower and the side entrance, where the cars come and go. In order to see both, the only spot is across the intersection diagonally, and it's almost too far, especially at night, to make out the needed detail.

No.

Let errand boy go.

Errand boy isn't the problem.

Errand boy is a distraction. He would be, as they say, low-hanging fruit.

Errand boy would be too easy.

◆ ◆ ◆

The real prize is Flynn Martin.

The real *gotcha* will be figuring out how to get inside Flynn Martin's condo tower and sauntering—yes, *sauntering*—right up to her door.

But which fucking door? How would PDQ figure it out? And then get inside?

But when the news breaks about iced tea lady?

And it's got to come out tomorrow . . .

Will they let Flynn Martin go anywhere?

Do anything?

And on the flip side . . .

Who would want to be interviewed by her?

CHAPTER 90

"Should I stay or should I go?"

"Stay," says Flynn.

"You don't have to think about it?"

"I don't have much here in the way of breakfast."

"I don't need much."

"And I'm going to be zero fun, if you know what I mean."

"I'm not even thinking about that."

"You're not? What kind of man are you?"

"I try and read the room," says Sheen. "That's the kind."

"Well," says Flynn. "The decent kind. My type."

◆ ◆ ◆

Flynn finds him a new toothbrush, courtesy of a dentist appointment she can't recall. Sheen showers. His routines are comforting. She hates admitting that fact to herself, but the thought of being alone, tonight, is worrisome.

Today, hell.

Tomorrow, worse.

And what is worse than hell?

◆ ◆ ◆

Three unread messages.

Text from Romy Glover: You okay? Sorry so late. Tell police to check Albuquerque hotels. Sometimes he would drive to ABQ, fly from there. Long drive but probably not as easily spotted down there. Check the better hotels for Paul Ramon.

Reply: Paul Ramon?

Glover: The name Paul McCartney used when checking into hotels as a Beatle. Stupid, right? How The Ramones got their name. Levi thought it was hilarious.

Reply: Thank you. Are YOU okay?

Glover: In some ways, yes. In some ways, no. So sad about the cops.

Reply: I know. Believe me, I know. Hey, can we talk instead of text?

Flynn's phone chirps two seconds later.

"Thanks," says Flynn. "Easier. You're home?"

"Yes."

"I need to know for sure about Bergeron and Yates."

"What?"

"Can you call him?"

"He's on the run," says Glover.

"Exactly."

"Exactly what?"

"He might need help," says Flynn.

"Jesus," says Glover. "I think he suspects me."

"But you don't know that, do you? If you call now, the suspicion comes off immediately."

"I'm not so sure about that."

"I need to know where he is. Where they are. I don't need needle-in-a-hotel-haystack in Albuquerque."

"What am I supposed to say?"

"Ask him if he needs anything. A favor."

"He could be anywhere," says Glover.

"That's the key."

"Now?"

"Are you afraid of waking him up? I think he's got bigger problems than that."

CHAPTER 91

Flynn listens to the steady thrum of Sheen's shower. She can't think about Deputy Kerrigan. Or Meg Hart. She can only think about Deputy Kerrigan. And Meg Hart.

◆ ◆ ◆

Flynn texts the Albuquerque tip to Sheriff Moore and Sheriff Rose in a group chat. Gets back near-instant replies from both saying thanks. She turns off the lights in the main room. Slips in front of the window shades. She presses herself against the warm glass. Nose. Breasts. Hips. Legs. Pigeon toes jammed against the window too. Looks down. Looks out. Wonders if one good punch, even from a feeble arm, could do the trick. One quick tumble and *pffi.* Gulping air all the way down. Watching the street rise. Keeping an eye out for the silver runt car. Waving back up at Axel, standing where there was once a window. Waiting to smack the asphalt.

Sweep up the glass, call it a night.

Wyatt's face—*right there.*

Knees shiver.

She backs away, head light and dizzy.

Stands in the shower. Bomb soot. Ranch dust. Hospital grunge. Driving-around sweat. City grime. Flynn washes, washes again. Hot water. Hotter. *Sorry, planet.* Shampoos. Shampoos again.

Hears Tamica over and over:

Last I looked we were reporters, not SWAT.

And:

And I'm trying to save your unforthcoming ass.

Meg Hart picked the wrong reporter.

Or did the wrong reporter pick *her*?

Why?

Why?

PDQ is why.

Unfinished torture.

Unfinished business.

Her own unforthcoming ass is nothing more than a loose end for a monster who wants her to pay the price.

From the shower, she hears her phone. Slams off the water, answers dripping wet.

"Romy?"

"It worked," she says. "I'm still shaking."

"Tell me."

"Do you think it's a trap?"

"What?"

"He needs me to run an errand, bring him something."

"I'm almost afraid to ask. When?"

"Right now. But I figured you need a few hours to alert whoever it is you would alert?"

"You're catching on, Romy. Where is he, and what did he want you to fetch?"

CHAPTER 92

"Late," says Sheriff Moore.

"You're still at Diamond Creek?"

"Yes. And you can tell your reporter friends to all go home."

"Would carry zero sway," says Flynn. "Care to know where you can find Levi Bergeron and Belinda Yates?"

"Goes without saying."

"I need a deal."

"Feel free to propose something. I'm not agreeing to anything."

"I want a crew there when you go in. Not watching from outside. There for the arrest."

"How do you know where they are?"

"Sources," says Flynn. "And he's holed up in your county. The source is bringing the pastor something he desperately needs. You follow her in, we follow you in."

"Hell," says Moore. "Okay, where are they? And who is the go-between?"

◆ ◆ ◆

Texts Goodman: You up?

◆ ◆ ◆

"Still working?" says Sheen.

Flynn gets dressed. Jeans, a loose sweater. "Sorry. Yeah."

"Did I hear that right? You found the pastor?"

"I think so."

"He forgot something, and your source is bringing it to him, and you used that as a bargaining chip to bring in the cops?"

"You're paying attention."

"But you're not going anywhere," says Sheen.

"Oh yes I am," says Flynn.

Reporters, not SWAT.

Lone Ranger.

"You agreed to stay put."

"This is different," says Flynn.

"How?"

"This is closed-ended. It's a known quantity. It's the end of the story, not the beginning. All of that. And there will be cops everywhere."

"How are you getting out there?"

"Lyft," says Flynn. "If my stalker is keyed on my Kia, I can't use it."

"Understood," says Sheen. "And I'm coming with."

Flynn feels the jolt instinct to reject the suggestion, slaps it down. "Okay."

"What does he need?"

Flynn picks up her phone.

"It's late," says Goodman.

"We need to reroute Tamica," says Flynn. "I've got cops and my church source Romy Glover all meeting at a hotel near Aurora City Center at five a.m. The pastor is there, and dollars to doughnuts so is Belinda Yates. Romy's got something he needs."

"What's that?" says Goodman.

"His passport," says Flynn. "He left it at church."

"Jesus," says Goodman.

"Yeah. I know."

"And, what then? Flying out of DIA? Doesn't he think he'll be spotted?"

"Not positive of the plan," says Flynn. "Romy was smart not to ask too many questions. He might be driving to Albuquerque or Dallas or Juárez."

Flynn names the hotel, gives him the address. "I got the cops to agree to one camera on the scene. Tamica can handle it."

"Of course she can."

"Can you call her?" says Flynn. "Better coming from you?"

"Sure," says Goodman.

◆ ◆ ◆

"You didn't tell him," says Sheen.

"Tell him what?"

Flynn smiles.

"About going out there."

"Because I don't need permission."

"The detective," says Sheen. "You told him you'd stay put."

"And I'll be a lone reporter bee in a swarm of Arapahoe County and Aurora cops. Safe as safe can be. Arrest at five, back here by six. I'm not letting Levi Bergeron's arrest go unrecorded. No way. No how."

"It's two a.m. We've got time to think it through."

"No we don't," says Flynn. "We're leaving now. And as much as I appreciate your being comfortable sitting on my bed in your underwear, you might want to get dressed."

CHAPTER 93

The hotel is three stories, newish. Flynn directs the driver to a parking spot with the best view and asks her to back in. Judging by the parking lot usage, the hotel is half occupied. Flynn negotiates a $100 fee with the Lyft driver, a skinny older woman named Kimberly, if she'll sit in the parking lot and give them a place to wait. Tells the driver they are expecting their friend to show up soon. Flynn tried to keep track of any vehicles following them out from downtown on the long scenic route rifle-straight east on Colfax Avenue. Didn't spot anything. The brief walk from her condo tower to the Lyft was uneventful. At least it felt that way.

"Tired?" says Sheen.

They are scrunched in the back seat of an old Corolla, windows open. Flynn counts four rooms with lights on. One on the top floor, two in the middle, one on the bottom. Moths flutter and dance in the light from three high poles bathing the parking lot in a jaundiced glow. The night hums and ticks.

"It doesn't matter," says Flynn.

"Feels like a stakeout," says Kimberly.

"I just sent you the money plus a tip. It should be there"—Kimberly's phone issues a piercing *ping*—"right about now. I'm going for a quick walk."

"What?" says Sheen.

"Two minutes. Got a hunch."

Flynn walks briskly. Purposefully. Rockies baseball cap not too low. A stretching walk. A normal walk. Mantra: *Not suspicious, not suspicious.* In case of security cameras.

In the row closest to the hotel, a silver Acura is backed into its spot. It's the only vehicle in the row with its nose pointing out, directly under one of the parking lot lights. If Pastor Bergeron is watching from a dark window, her next steps will be a giveaway. Of the dead variety.

She scoots her way across the row and glances back quickly, looking but mostly looking *around.* All she needs is a glance.

The rear bumper is message-free, but that's because the sticker is mostly gone, but not all—shards of ripped vinyl. The white square backing material holding on for dear life. No longer following Jesus?

Flynn climbs back into the Corolla, gives Sheen a nod. Doesn't want to say anything that would confirm for Kimberly that this is, in fact, a stakeout.

Text from Tamica: I'm here. Parked down the street. I figure you're here too?

Reply: What are you driving?

Tamica: My Camry. Figured we didn't want the news truck?

Reply: Bingo. Come on to the parking lot. Pint-size Corolla in the northwest corner. Park somewhere but not too close. We'll transfer over and wait with you.

Tamica: We?

Reply: Axel too.

Tamica: Party on.

CHAPTER 94

"He's here," says Flynn.

They have let Kimberly go and are tucked into Tamica's Camry. Tamica is sitting shotgun, Sheen in back.

4:00 a.m.

A Saturday that feels like Any Day.

"Now what?" says Tamica.

"There's no need to whisper."

"It feels better."

"Okay, then I'll whisper too."

"Thank you. Now what?"

Text from Romy: I'm parked down the block and I saw two black unmarked vans pull into a gas station across the street. Think cops.

"Everybody's early," says Flynn.

"Everybody's eager," says Tamica.

Flynn texts Romy to stay put, asks if she's driving her Subaru.

Calls Sheriff Moore on speaker.

"We're at a gas station a block away," he says. "Staging here."

"I know," says Flynn. "Do you see a green Subaru parked across the street?"

"Yes."

"That's Romy Glover, the go-between."

"Got it. Where are you?"

"Hotel parking lot."

"Okay," says Moore. "I'm keeping this line open."

They hear Moore walk, cross the street, introduce himself to Romy, ask to see the passport, tell her that she has to call or text the pastor and get the room number and then all she has to do is knock on the door, say "It's Romy," and then get out of the way because the hall behind her will be full of SWAT.

"You comfortable?" says Moore.

"Not really," says Romy. "But I can do it."

"Okay, then," says Moore. "Let's go."

Romy's Subaru pulls in, parks near the entrance. Two black vans slide into view, park nose to tail, blocking the exit. The vans disgorge a bevy of armed cops. A dark unmarked SUV pulls up in front of the two vans. The sight of such overkill is delicious, heartening. But Flynn's head ping-pongs to Meg Hart. Emotions knotted like a twist tie. You think it unravels one way, but you're wrong. You try the other, but you're still wrong. There is no release.

One of the four room lights goes dark. Tamica pops her door, scurries around to the back, snaps open the trunk, grabs her gear. Flynn tells Sheen she'll be back, hurries across the parking lot to catch up.

CHAPTER 95

Knock-knock.

"It's Romy."

She says it in a half whisper.

Cops line the hall like storm troopers. Twenty cops and not one burp or clatter of weaponry or squeak of bulletproof vests. Visors down.

Romy steps back. Black jeans, red cardigan with a blue pine tree embroidered on one lapel. Her dark hair is braided in two tight pigtails. Makeup. She could be going on a date. Romy's sole commandment was that she not appear in a single frame of footage.

Sheriff Moore takes Romy's spot. Also in storm trooper mode, except no helmet.

Tamica is smack behind the sheriff, on his left side to see the door open. Tamica clicks Record. Flynn hooks an index finger around a belt loop in Tamica's jeans.

No answer.

Sheriff Moore head-bobs Romy. *Try again.*

Knock-knock.

"Pastor Bergeron? It's Romy."

She steps back. The sheriff replaces her again.

The silence is heavy.

The door cracks and starts to slam shut, but Sheriff Moore puts his weight into it. Bergeron backpedals into the darkness. Tamica follows the sheriff. Room lights flood the scene. The smell is dank. An air conditioner rattles.

One bed is tossed in a tangle of sheets. Two suitcases sit on top of the second bed, ready to go. Bergeron and Belinda Yates are dressed. Bergeron in a blue oxford button-down. Yates in a short-sleeved flouncy yellow top. Yates sits between the suitcases. Sobs. The vinegar that was in her system when she flipped off Flynn on live TV in Kiowa has fizzled. Moore tells Bergeron his rights and then one of the storm troopers pops off a helmet and repeats the drill for Yates. *Female* storm trooper.

Handcuffs.

"Where are the Klines?" says Flynn. "Where is the Kline family?"

Bergeron stands, hands behind his back. Sheriff Moore grips one of his biceps. Bergeron stares. He looks small, unimportant.

"Did you plant the booby trap bomb that killed those officers? Plan it with Denis Mincher?"

Bergeron's body is there. His eyes are a million miles away.

"Why the whole family?" says Flynn. "What did Patrick Kline find that you needed to keep a secret?"

Bergeron shakes his head. "It's not what it seems."

"Are they buried at the ranch?" says Flynn.

Bergeron says nothing.

"What happened to Arnold Wilkins?"

Bergeron hangs his head, shakes it. Whispers, "Fuck you."

Flynn looks at Yates. Her cheeks are wet. She's breathing hard.

"Where were you going?" says Flynn.

"Albuquer—"

"Shush!" says Bergeron.

"We were," says Yates. "But it was a stupid plan. I know we wouldn't have made it."

CHAPTER 96

Harry: Don't tell me you haven't had your chances.

Text: How did you get this number?

Harry: Don't concern yourself with irrelevant details!

Text: How?

Harry: You left it when you signed in, you silly thing.

Text: And how the hell are you texting?

Harry: Good grief. Have you never heard of a thing called contraband? This Zanco Tiny T1 is so small I could hide it under my tongue.

Text: OK.

Harry: OK what then?

Text: I am waiting for the right opportunity.

Harry: She's running around all over the fucking place.

No reply.

Harry: Get on with it.

Text: Rest assured.

Harry: On what basis?

Text: It's not like she's often alone.

Harry: Jesus Fucking Christ.

Text: I've got her building. A condo tower downtown.

Harry: Then it should be easy.

Text: Hundreds of units. And no "Martin" as owner. On any of them.

Harry: Seriously?

Text: What?

Harry: Good fucking grief.

Text: What?

Harry: Voter registration. Public records. Are you really capable? Really?

CHAPTER 97

Tamica drives, Axel rides shotgun. The return trip was delayed fifteen minutes while Romy sobbed and gathered herself and pleaded again to make sure her name would never get mentioned forever and forever and forever. Flynn can only imagine how Romy Glover's confidence level and faith-in-Flynn level will sink when the Denver cops spill the whole Meg Hart story in a few short hours.

Flynn taps out a script on her phone, texts it to the station halfway back. Flynn watches for the silver runt car or any other vehicle being a bit too familiar, sees nothing.

She hopes.

◆ ◆ ◆

Text from Bonnie Ashburn: Stand-up where?

Reply: Nowhere. Goodman knows. It's complicated. Use script as anchor copy, roll video, wrap with a mention that we will follow every angle on this story.

Text: Helluva get, Flynn. Judy Hayes and all the others gonna be shaking their heads.

Reply: It's not going to matter by noon.

Text: ???

Reply: Today has a long way to go.

◆ ◆ ◆

11:00 a.m.

Alone, back inside her condo cell.

On the TV, Detective John Jasper is clean. Polished. Poised. Detective Yamamoto sits next to him, stone-faced inscrutable. Flynn watches from her couch.

Jasper is inside. Downtown. One of the bland rooms at police HQ. Names Meg Hart. Says a final determination of cause of death is still being determined. Runs through the detail on the envelope. Mentions that there is now a connection with the murder of Robert Waller. Talks about another envelope. "And there are also other messages from someone who is clearly trying to get the attention of a reporter we all know, Flynn Martin."

Reporter: "Other messages? How many?"

Flynn recognizes the voice of Judy Hayes. It's a rare story that gets her out of the newspaper office to walk three whole blocks to the cop shop.

Jasper: "Several."

Hayes: "Connected to other murders?"

Jasper: "Not necessarily."

Reporter: "Where was Meg Hart murdered?"

Sam Tucker. The newspaper has doubled up and ruined the weekend plans for them both, not that either would want to miss this story.

Jasper: "In her home. And that is why we believe somebody must have seen something."

Tucker: "When?"

Jasper: "Day before yesterday. We're asking people in her neighborhood to recall anything during the day. No detail is too small. Contact us."

Hayes: "The killer got inside the home?"

Jasper: "Yes."

Reporter: "Where was this envelope?"

The voice of Andrea Beamon. Even from a distance, over the television, Flynn can feel the tension in the room among the A-list reporters. The race is on, even among the two newspaper colleagues, to find out what the cops *aren't* saying.

Jasper: "That's a detail we're not divulging."

Beamon: "What else did the message say?"

Jasper: "Ditto."

Tucker: "No indication what this person wants from Flynn Martin? Or why she's being mentioned."

Jasper, after a pause: "That's one of our lines of inquiry."

Hayes: "Your advice to the public?"

Jasper: "Be alert. Don't let anyone inside your home you don't one hundred percent know. Be mindful of anything out of order."

◆ ◆ ◆

Her station cuts back to Sara Cornette, solo on the anchor desk. She recaps everything they have heard from Detective Jasper and says they have breaking news out at Diamond Creek Ranch in Elbert County, and the scene cuts to Sheriff Rose, mid-flow, announcing that four bodies have been recovered from the ranch and there are car parts, too, and a "final, positive identification" is forthcoming but they believe they have found the remains of the Kline family.

"With the sensational arrest this morning of Pastor Levi Bergeron and New Hope Church television host Belinda Yates, as reported exclusively by our own Flynn Martin after a dramatic arrest at a hotel in Aurora," says Cornette, "this tragic story appears to be reaching a pivotal moment."

◆ ◆ ◆

The wave is a rogue. It towers over her. She could go full stoic. She could harden her heart. She knows how. She knows the curtains to pull, the locks to lock.

But not this time. The wave is a crusher. There's no place to run. Maybe it's Axel. Maybe she wants him to see she's not impervious to pain. To events. To reality. Maybe she wants him to see that she is porous. She lowers herself in his lap. She puts an arm around his chest.

And lets the wave fill her chest.

And sobs.

And bawls.

And sobs some more.

◆ ◆ ◆

Flynn's phone chirps.

Michael Martin.

"Dad?"

"Yes."

"I really can't right now."

"You must feel ripped in two."

"Boy howdy," says Flynn.

"Don't let it get to you," says Michael. "You did all the right things."

"I can't hear that right now."

Her voice small, weak.

"You need to hear it."

"I can't. I have to go."

"Call me later."

"Mmm-kay."

◆ ◆ ◆

Five texts:

Goodman: Call me when you get a second.

Max: I might have something for you.

Unknown number: This is Judy Hayes. I would like to ask you a few questions if you have a minute. Please call.

Nancy Lang: I can only imagine what you're going through. Let me know how I can help you—any way at all.

Unknown number: This is Andrea Beamon. Sending my support to you, Flynn, as a fellow reporter. I'm sure this isn't easy and I'm so glad you're okay. We would love an on-camera. Are you going to be at the station?

CHAPTER 98

Where do I find the database of registered voters in Colorado?

The Colorado secretary of state.

Types: Colorado Secretary of State Voting Records.

> Enter your information as it is currently shown on your voter registration record. If you have only one name, use the last name field. Zip code and birth date are required.

Enters: Flynn. Martin.

Types: What is the zip code for downtown Denver?

> 80202

Enters: 80202.

But why the need for the fucking birth date? How many Flynn Martins can there be?

If only Flynn Martin was on social media. A robust Facebook page would cough up a birth date in two seconds flat.

Wyatt Martin? Nothing. Not a social media kid.

Max McKenna? Nothing. Typical for a cop.

Types: How do I find someone's birth date?

> www.publicdata.com

> Enter first and last name, hometown, and age.

Enters: Flynn. Martin. Denver.

Age? How old is Flynn Martin? How many years has she been doing her questionable reporter thing?

Late forties? She'd covered PDQ when he was active, but she'd already had a few years under her belt, so maybe she was twenty-five or twenty-six back then? Plus fifteen years when PDQ came back. Plus another year for the trial and another five months since PDQ was taken to Cañon City.

Enters: 48.

> Searching.
> Please do not exit this search as Public Data is reviewing millions of public records at your request.

A horizontal blue bar crawls across the screen: 10 percent . . . 17 percent . . . 23 percent . . .

> Did Flynn Martin previously live elsewhere in Denver? Yes/No?

Clicks Yes.

> Was Flynn Martin previously married to Max McKenna? Yes/No?

Clicks Yes.

> Does Flynn Martin occasionally, as they say, shoot from the hip?

Ha!! Wouldn't *that* be hilarious if publicdata.com knew her that fucking well?

Is Flynn Martin now divorced? Yes/No?

Clicks Yes.

Do you suspect Flynn Martin may have had a DUI? Yes/No?

Hmmm. Clicks No.

Do you suspect Flynn Martin has a criminal record? Yes/No?

Well, she damn well should have one! There should be a Star Chamber for journalists where their sloppy work can be prosecuted, and their reporting badges stripped.

Clicks No.

Searching . . .

What the fuck with all these rabbit holes?

Would you like Flynn Martin's birth date? Yes/No?

Clicks Yes.

Please enter your credit card information below. The $19.95 charge includes additional details about Flynn Martin and may also include arrests. Do you wish to continue?

Clicks Yes.

CHAPTER 99

"It's me, Max?"

"How are you doing?"

"Sorry I didn't call last night. How's Wyatt?"

"Fine. Well, given everything. Wyatt wants to come home to be with you."

"It'll happen," says Flynn. "Soon."

"I assume you are staying home?"

"They don't want me out there. At all."

"I mean—"

Max doesn't finish the thought. Doesn't have to. Who would agree to an on-camera interview with Flynn Martin? Someone with a death wish.

"Are you alone?" says Max.

"Yes."

After the return from Aurora, Axel Sheen wanted to stay with her, but she pushed him off for maximum self-loathing.

"You're okay?"

"Not really," says Flynn.

"Helluva night," says Max.

"Thanks for not scolding me for going out to Aurora."

"You're welcome."

"Did you say you had something for me?"

The news is on. Nothing but recaps. She's heard her name on all the stations. That fact alone is sickening enough. *The grisly murder of Robert Waller . . . the murder of Meg Hart . . . and messages at both scenes that reference well-known local television journalist Flynn Martin.* Or variations thereof.

"Something you'll have to get confirmed."

"Fine," says Flynn.

"And keep my name out of it."

"No problem."

"Tetrahydrozoline," says Max.

"What?"

"It's a form of a medicine called imidazoline," says Max. Articulated like a doctor. Probably spent an hour online to learn all about it. "That's what they're looking at with this latest victim, Meg Hart."

"Can you be a little less, I don't know, cryptic?"

"Eye drops," says Max. "Meg Hart had consumed a large glass of iced tea, and the analysis came back that it was laced with tetrahydrozoline. In her blood as well."

"Eye drops," says Flynn. "There was a murder case somewhere a few years back."

"Wisconsin. And that dentist who offed his wife right here in Colorado," says Max. "When you swallow eye drops, it's a neurotoxin. Seizures, everything. A quarter cup mixed with a glass of iced tea and good night."

"Was there a bottle found at the scene?"

"Of eye drops?" says Max. "No."

"Who is your source?"

"It will check out, believe me."

"Any sign of forced entry?"

"No."

"Any other trace? Traces? Anything to go on?"

"Not so far."

"Eyewitnesses in the neighborhood?"

"Still canvassing."

"Doorbell cameras? Anything?"

"Not so far."

"Any idea how long the killer was in the home?"

"They're working on that. Long enough to drink a large glass of iced tea."

"You don't get in and out of a neighborhood on a puff of smoke."

"I think we know that."

"So probably somebody who looked like they belonged? Innocuous?"

"Big time."

◆ ◆ ◆

Flynn calls Goodman, passes along the tip, says she'll get it confirmed.

Calls Jasper.

"We'd like to hold that detail back," says Jasper.

"You'd say that no matter what *detail* I asked to take public."

"Not true. Where did you get that?"

"You know better than to ask me that."

"I still need to ask. Your ex?" says Jasper.

"No."

"You sure about that?"

"When I was younger, I really didn't know what it meant to have sources, you know? After a few years, you make friends. Okay, relationships. People in various institutions and organizations who understand the value of fair reporting. And sometimes those relationships bear fruit."

"Where are you?"

"What does it matter?"

"Do you really think it was smart to leave home? Go to Aurora in the dead of night?"

"I did what I had to do."

"Did you go to work?"

"No. Why?"

"Because of the obvious. Because of the risk of being followed."

"You want me to go out for a long walk?" says Flynn. "Then you can watch who is watching me? Or I can go for a drive? Look for a half-pint silver car that missed its last growth spurt. Bland as bland can be. I can drive all day if you want."

"It's not a bad idea. But we would rather you stay put. Are you alone?"

"Whose business is that?"

"Do you feel safe?"

"Not sure I know what that means," says Flynn. "Once you watch a two-story ranch house disintegrate before your eyes and feel the shock wave rattle your ribs, and *then* try to reconcile how one innocent interview meant a Westside mom was marked for death? Well, not sure what safe is. Or was."

"I get it."

"How long am I confined to quarters?"

It's weird to think about not leaving the apartment for a few days. A week would be torture.

"So *now* you're agreeing to stay put?"

"That was one time."

"Careless."

"I'm home safe."

"As far as you know."

"How long?" says Flynn.

"We're working as hard as we can. And you can imagine the mayor and what he wants."

"FBI?"

"We're joined at the hip."

"Are you sending someone to Cañon City?"

"You're fixated on a bad hypothesis," says Jasper. "We're watching all the communications. Visits. Everything."

"It's his fingerprints, his style, his bullshit."

"We're working both ends," says Jasper. "But right now all I can tell you is Harry Kugel doesn't go anywhere. Seven-by-twelve cell. Thin mattress. Sunlight once a day in an outdoor cage. Meals passed through a slot in the door. Headphones and a device to listen to his goddamn precious classical music. All calls monitored, all visitors screened."

"I want the logs," says Flynn.

"The visitor logs?"

"Yes."

"Since when?"

"Since day one."

"What for?"

The idea comes screaming out of the blue. She loves it.

"I think the answer to that is obvious."

"They're not public record," says Jasper. "You know that."

"Then I'm going with the eye drops."

"I can't negotiate with something I'm not allowed to trade."

"And I might wait a week or two after you've found the silver runt car and locked up PDQ Junior, but then I'm going to have a chat with your upper ups about you hitting on witnesses in your cases."

"I did nothing."

"But you wanted something." The moment doesn't bother her a bit. Especially if it leads to the logs. "You're going to tell me that was protocol? Telling me maybe we could get together when all of this died down?"

"Putting it out there. The offer stands."

"You're not reading the room. Or the society."

"I think we got off on the wrong foot. For that I'm sorry."

"Is this like—a pattern of yours?" says Flynn. "If we go back through your cases, how often do you figure out a way to get the female witnesses alone? No Wendy Yamamoto. A cocktail in your hand and—what?"

Silence.

"The logs," says Flynn.

"I can't—"

"Wouldn't it be helpful, in fact, to see if I spotted a name? A connection?"

Jasper says nothing.

"I'm going with the eye drops."

Long silence.

"I didn't confirm anything."

"You said it was a detail you wanted to hold back. Run the logic."

"I don't have time to go around and around on this."

"It leaked to me," says Flynn. "You sure it's not leaking to another station right now? I'm going with it."

"Okay," says Jasper.

"Okay what?"

"I'll send you the logs," says Jasper. "And I'm formally asking you to look through them and see if you can recognize a name. Anything. And, at the same time, I'm asking that you not tell one fucking soul that I shared the logs with you. And you can't put anything from the list of visitors on the air. Right? Got it? Do we have a deal?"

CHAPTER 100

2875.

There it is in the voting records.

Flynn Martin.
#2875
990 15th St.
Denver, CO 80202

Of course you're a voter, Flynn Martin.

What a good girl.

Wouldn't we all like to see your blue-as-hell, sky blue, azure blue, liberal-hearted voting record all the way back to your Boulder days? Wouldn't that tell the true story of Flynn Martin?

Blue, blue, fucking blue.

Down through the years.

Even when you were married to a cop, probably canceled out each other's votes, didn't you?

There ought to be a law that reporters have to publish their ballots for the world to see. So if you get a call from someone like Flynn Martin, you know who you're dealing with.

More specifically, *what.*

So you know what they really think.

Because what they really think drives how the story gets covered.

Hell—
Whether the story gets covered.
Right?
Isn't that right?
How can it not be right?

◆ ◆ ◆

2875.

Up in the sky.
Probably licking her wounds.
Maybe even being told to lie low.
Because the people she points a microphone at tend to end up dead.
As good a reason as any to stay home.

CHAPTER 101

The agent, waiting in the lobby, is impossibly buoyant and animated.

"This is the first level of security," she says, gesturing to a silver kiosk. "Guests dial you up, and then you as the owner would be able to buzzer-in anyone. But the guest needs to stop at the ninth-floor courtesy desk, and one of the guards there uses a fob at the elevator to send you to your floor. Ninth floor because it's all parking below that. Did you say you have a vehicle? The unit comes with one parking space."

Real estate "sales team member" Bianca Morehead wears a red sleeveless top. Buff triceps and biceps like a gym rat. Minimal makeup, eager everything. Tiny purse on a long strap. Shiny black heels. Hand clutched around her phone like it's a rope and she's drowning. She hands over her business card and a brochure.

"One space works."

"So you saw the listing just this morning?"

"Right."

"And you're in a hurry?"

"I have a flight back to Chicago tonight."

"Relocating?"

Bianca isn't paying attention. *Just another customer.* She's missing out on Sales 101, forming a personal bond. She's not taking in details. And that's not good because of all the work that went into the fake mole above the right lip, the work on fashioning extra layers for the Dudley Do-Right chin, the bright hazel eyes thanks to color contacts.

"Not by choice. They made me an offer I couldn't refuse."

"I'm sorry."

"Me too."

"What line of work?"

"Insurance."

"And it will be just you?"

"Yes."

"Then one bed, one bath should work." They are in the elevator. "Even though it's technically an open house, you need a personal escort. They are careful about who comes and who goes. Nine hundred square feet. In-unit washer and dryer. Balcony. AC."

"HOA?"

"Five hundred and fourteen dollars a month. Again, security the main feature."

"Do you already have offers?"

"It's only been on the market for two days, but we do have interest."

"Good location."

"Good everything. There's a smaller unit for sale, but it's farther up. You pay for the view. Another forty K."

"For elevation? For feeling superior?"

"But that unit is in the middle of the building, and this one is at the very end of the hall. It's a corner unit. So only neighbors on one side, though the soundproofing in this building is truly unbelievable."

They stop at the ninth floor. Bianca dangles her fob for the folks at the security desk.

"Busy day," says a young Black man.

"This is Carter," says Bianca. "He's practically Mr. Altair Tower."

"Nice to meet you."

"Don't make me sound more important than I am," says Carter.

"Seems like you're always here," says Bianca.

"And pulling a double today," says Carter. "My relief called in sick."

Bianca's heels click as she struts to the next bank of elevators, waves her fob over a magic spot below the rows of buttons, and presses 23. It's hard to tell if there's a security camera inside. It would be dumb to assume there's not. A pint-size embedded television above the buttons carries a national news report about the excavations at Diamond Creek Ranch.

"So sad," says Bianca.

"Is there any way to escape the news?"

"Probably not."

Bianca leads the way. The hall sails off to infinity. No sign of security cameras. "I'll introduce you to my colleague Chloe, who can answer any questions. I think we have several people looking at the unit right now."

A bowl of shiny apples. Seltzers on ice in a dark green cooler. Wedges of sad white cheese drying at the edges. Triscuits. Brochures. And four other would-be buyers. One couple and two solos. Chloe wears a navy skirt, a white top with frilly ruffles. High heels that look painful. "Welcome, come in, ask me anything." Teeth stained with lipstick. "Feel free to drop your backpack here for a few minutes while you look around."

"That's okay."

The self-tour takes three minutes. What's not to like? Notes on the yellow lined paper in her binder because it looks good to take notes. What must it feel like to live so cushy? So high? Sunlight fills the condo like a blast furnace. You'd have to live with seeing every scrap of dust all day long. Ugh.

But Flynn must love it. To think, Flynn lives five stories higher still.

Straight above, in fact, if the system of numbering units matches floor to floor.

So close.

"Open house closes in seventeen minutes," says Chloe. "I'm glad to answer any questions. We do have other offer feelers coming in, so don't dawdle if you're keen on it."

Unlike the rest of the building, the open house bustles like it's the last condo for sale in Denver.

Perfect.

Open a few kitchen cabinets.

Run the shades with the button on the wall like a six-year-old fascinated with the idea of remote control.

Inspect the entryway closets.

Stand for a minute on the balcony.

Wait in the bedroom.

Delay.

Straggle.

Watch everyone file out.

Listen to Bianca and Chloe in the main room, where "open concept" has become the positive selling point because in the twenty-first century, cooking is performance and hosts must entertain, not be hidden away in a galley.

Listen to Bianca and Chloe thank everyone for coming.

Answering last questions.

Slip into the bathroom.

Leave the door slightly ajar.

Flip off the light.

Lower the backpack into the tub-shower.

Quiet, quick.

Stealth.

Climb in, reach up, pull the frosted door closed with a pleasing, satisfying, metallic *ker-chunk.*

Go still.

◆ ◆ ◆

And wait.

And listen.

◆ ◆ ◆

"Cheese all gone!" says Chloe. "Apples not so much."

"Did you see Chicago?" says Bianca. "I saw Chicago come back, thought we would get an offer. Did you get Chicago's name?"

"Actually, no," says Chloe.

Hears the bathroom door swing open.

Light on.

Light off.

"Guess we're clear," says Bianca.

◆ ◆ ◆

Waits.

Listens.

Waits some more.

Climbs out.

Listens again.

Stretches out on the bed and thinks about Flynn Martin, five floors above.

◆ ◆ ◆

Flynn fucking Martin shoved a microphone in my face. She asked me questions. Yes, it was random. Yes, there were others. She had other options with the run-of-the-mill believers.

Her eyes were so businesslike. All that window-dressing femininity. All that Ivory-soap wholesomeness. And yet those focused eyes. Trying so hard to be her daddy. To please her daddy. If you want to be taken seriously, why work in a business known for its smarmy fluff?

She thought we were posers. Delusional fakers. And then she interviews a self-anointed "expert" on her show to confirm her theory, to show she's right. How could she possibly think we were delusional? How could we possibly think he was innocent? That he didn't deserve to be locked up forever?

She could have been pinching her nose while she asked questions. She didn't *really* want our opinion.

We were boxes to be checked.

We were the freak show.

Because that's how reporters work.

They make up their minds.

You can tell.

You really can tell.

All you have to do is pay attention. Sure, they are good at straight faces. They fake sincerity like champs. That's part of their job. But there is always a clue. Do they ever give credence and credibility to the second point of view once they've made up their mind?

The scorn was thick.

Disdain dripped from her eyeballs.

She didn't want to be there.

We were subhuman.

We didn't belong.

◆ ◆ ◆

Tonight's the night.

But first, the city has to settle.

The building has to settle.

Denver needs to pop a couple of melatonin gummies, pull up the blanket, and head off to slumberland.

CHAPTER 102

Is she wrong about PDQ?

Flynn looks again at the Cañon City visitor logs. She shouldn't take one name or company name or law firm name for granted. Is it one of the lawyers? Pretending? An online search suggests they're all legit.

Should she question his mother? Alice Kugel?

What do you say when you go visit your serial killer son in maximum security prison? What the hell do you talk about? Do you bring him homemade blueberry muffins? Do you simply, *what*, talk about everything else? Could someone have pretended to be Alice Kugel? Why wasn't Harry's father, Richard, on the same trip?

Flynn sits at her kitchen counter.

Glass of white wine.

Notepad.

And Jasper's screenshot of Harry Kugel's visitor log.

It's late, but her head buzzes. She knows herself too well. Knows not to expect to fall asleep with her brain on hyperdrive.

She's texted with Axel. She's talked to Michael, Max, and Wyatt, and she's whined to Tamica about not being trapped. She can't imagine being confined to quarters for more than a day. She also can't imagine that the cops and the FBI don't have plenty of evidence to draw a bead on Mr. Fucking PDQ Offspring Envelope Writer.

It will all be over soon.

◆ ◆ ◆

There's one oddball name on the visitor log.

Ellie Stuffel.

Hometown: Thornton, Colorado.

An online search quickly dials it in. One of the Harry Kugel nutjob true believers who rallied on his behalf outside court during his trial.

Flynn finds the newspaper story about Stuffel and the others in the Harry Faithful Posse. Then to her station's archives and pulls up the video of ultra-nerdy Ellie Stuffel and all her facts about recidivism rates and her makes-no-sense theories about how Harry was railroaded. Stuffel is White. Plain. Slender. Dark hair cropped close. Eyes like slits, and Flynn recalls the feeling of wanting to finish the interview as quickly as possible. How can you give a second of airtime to people who can't add two plus two?

Of course Ellie Stuffel would visit Harry Kugel. Time to fawn. Time to encourage Harry to keep fighting. Maybe time to suggest one of those hard-to-fathom romances between a locked-away-for-life prisoner and one of his female true believers.

◆ ◆ ◆

In the meantime, keep digging.

CHAPTER 103

The neighbors at this end of the hall will know the condo is for sale.

And unoccupied.

So the key is to leave without being spotted. Once you're in the hall or on the stairs, of course, you can act normal because you could be a friend or a lover or an owner.

Nobody knows all the faces on their own damn floor.

So those first steps are crucial.

Same on the return.

If returning is an option.

By the time returning to the for-sale empty condo is an option, it's very possible there will be a whole lot of commotion, but it's also possible Flynn Martin won't be found until late morning or lunchtime or whenever all her so-called friends get worried.

The thought is horrific.

The thought is abominable.

This could all be over very, very, very soon.

And then what?

Well, of course, go back to PDQ.

Report.

Get a new assignment.

But, of course, lie low for a month or two and then head back, ask for an employee performance review. Knowing full well Harry Kugel will be quite pleased with the results.

◆ ◆ ◆

There are two keys.

First, she must know *why* before she dies. This will all be fruitless and pointless if Flynn Martin doesn't realize it was all her own doing. That she got the ball rolling so many years ago. And explaining it all, reminding her of everything, might take time.

No doubt she'll struggle.

No doubt she won't listen.

But when it hits, when the light bulb goes off, the look on Flynn's face will be, as the kids say, chef's kiss.

Delectable.

The other key is to not be spotted leaving Flynn Martin's condo. The few short steps across the hall to the stairwell must be clean.

And if you need the for-sale condo as a temporary hidey-hole, then how to get back in?

The door needs to *appear* to be snug and yet unlatched. A swatch of duct tape across the strike plate would be perfect, but a search of the for-sale condo yields nothing of use.

A wedge of cardboard or something in the side jamb to keep the door from closing all the way?

One of the sales brochures, folded in half, might do the trick. The door is brown, the brochure is white, but who is going to notice an eighth-inch scrap of paper in a door at ankle level at this time of night?

Who?

CHAPTER 104

Bop-bop.

One-two.

Precise and clean.

Soft.

Medium soft.

Axel?

What are you doing here?

Flynn realizes she's fallen asleep.

How is that even possible? *Sleep* at a time like this?

◆ ◆ ◆

Bop-bop.

One-two.

Checks the time: 12:30 a.m.

Jasper? Watching the halls?

One of Jasper's men?

Flynn stares at the door. Was she dreaming?

Waits.

Waits like one of those moments when a smoke detector goes off and you need to stare at it and wait for its next cry, to figure out if it's the guilty party.

◆ ◆ ◆

Flynn's heart thuds. Mouth like dust.

Fuck.

Sits up, stands up, stares at the big wooden door.

Waits.

Nothing.

Tiptoes halfway to the door.

I must have been dreaming.

Waits.

Tiptoes the rest of the way.

Tries not to breathe, sneaks up on the peephole.

Looks out.

Stares.

Stares.

Nothing.

◆ ◆ ◆

Retreats.

Grogginess racks her head.

Groggy, foggy.

Flynn sits at her kitchen counter. Prickles flash on her legs and arms.

Picks up her phone, calls security.

"Miss Martin?"

"Did you—"

Hears her voice catch, clears her parched throat.

"Did you send someone up? I know you wouldn't without—"

"No, ma'am."

"Is this Carter? Sounds like Carter."

"Yes, ma'am."

"This late?"

"Pulling a double, ma'am. I'll be right there."

"No," says Flynn. "I was asleep and thought I heard something. Probably a little jumpy."

"Yes, ma'am."

◆ ◆ ◆

Bed or couch.

Couch because it's closer to the door and if she hears it again—

Bop-bop.

One-two.

Already grabbing the phone.

Already wondering if the animal has a way to jimmy the door. Knows a secret. Knows a trick. Did she check the dead bolt? When?

Who was the last to leave?

Scurries to the kitchen, pulls the biggest knife from a wooden storage block.

Carter doesn't answer.

"Carter?" she whispers to nobody. "Where the fuck did you go?"

Listens to the ring. And ring.

Risks another stealth tiptoe one-step-at-a-time ambush on the peephole.

Creeping.

Staring.

Staying low as if the peephole goes two ways, hand gripping the knife like it's the throat of a rattler.

Hangs up the phone, puts it on the floor, wraps all ten fingers around the handle.

Hears herself whisper, "You motherfucker."

Son of PDQ.

Son of a bitch PDQ.
Offspring. Spawn. Rotten fucking fruit of PDQ.
Sneaks up on the peephole, ready for the door to come flying open.
Looks out.

◆ ◆ ◆

Nothing.

CHAPTER 105

Flynn reaches for the doorknob with her left hand, clutches the knife with her right fist, ready to flail and jab.

Ready to end this nightmare.

Yanks the door open.

Takes a ragged whack at the emptiness for good measure.

Sees the door across the hall closing by itself.

Steps out.

"Stairwell!" shouts Carter. "Black hoodie!"

Carter runs.

It's a marathon hallway.

Flynn is light-years closer.

She pushes open the door to the stairwell, sees a dark flash on the next flight down. Hears the thudding.

Starts down. Legs churning.

One flight.

Two flights.

Losing ground.

Feet getting into the rhythm.

Looks in the gap to the flights below—sees a blue hand.

Blue?

Gloved-up hand. Those blue nitrile gloves. Medical gloves. Crime scene gloves. Sees a flicker of black.

Hears Carter above her.

She's losing ground.

Down.

Down.

Stenciled red numbers on the white cinder block.

Twenty-four.

Twenty-three.

Stops to listen.

Maybe catch a glimpse again.

Nothing.

Gasping makes it impossible to hear.

Nineteen.

Eighteen.

Seventeen.

Carter closer behind now, one flight away from catching up. Flynn stops. Carter passes his phone like the smoothest relay race ever, his yellow security sport coat a mustard blur. Says "Call 911." Flynn stops long enough to press the numbers. Carter crashes ahead. The banging metal stairwell could wake the dead.

Sixteen.

Trying to grip the knife and the phone and maybe balance herself with a hand on the rail at the same time is impossible. She lets the knife go, hears it clatter.

Fifteen.

"What is your emergency?"

"Altair Tower," says Flynn. "Intruder!"

"Is anyone injured?"

"I don't think so."

"What is your name?"

"Flynn Martin."

"Your location again?"

Fourteen.

She says the name of the building again, gives the address.

"Are you injured?"

"No."

"Can you describe the suspect?"

"Wearing black. A black hoodie. He got all the way in the building. Somehow. All the way to my door. He's in the stairwell."

"Nobody is injured?"

"Send someone now!"

◆ ◆ ◆

Where does the stairwell come out?

If they lose the race to the exit—?

Or will they spot the silver runt car? Carter won't know what to look for.

Eleven.

Ten.

Nine.

Slowing. Listening.

Losing.

Gasping.

Knees angry.

Lungs dying.

Eight.

Seven.

Six.

Walking now.

Shaking.

Coughing.

Five.

Listening.

Four.

Three.

Wobbling, clutching the rail with one hand, squeezing Carter's phone with the other.

Two.

Step.

Agonizing step.

One.

Flynn pushes the crash bar open on the big heavy doors.

Staggers into the night.

◆ ◆ ◆

Carter is slumped on the curb, heaving. Crying out.

Blood gushes. Dark splotches fan out on his spiffy blazer.

"He—"

"Shhh."

Flynn presses her hands on his chest and torso, searching for the wound. Or wounds.

"Fuck," says Carter.

"Stay with me." Flynn presses gently, figuring it's got to help. Somehow. Some way. "Stay with me."

"He—"

Carter goes still. Way too fucking still. "Carter—*Carter*. Carter! Stay with me."

The fight slumps out of him.

"Carter!" Her guts roil. She wants to shake him awake, doesn't dare jostle him.

Flynn wipes at gushing tears, looks up and down through blurry vision, sure she'll spot the silver runt car.

Something.

Nothing.

"Ma'am?" The tinny voice comes from the phone. The phone lies face up in the slick of blood on the asphalt. Flynn pulls her wet hand from Carter's chest. Drips of horror trickle down her wrist. "Are you still there?"

CHAPTER 106

"Open house?"

"One of the units was for sale," says Jasper. "Five floors below yours."

"And?"

"And we think he used the open house traffic to get inside the building."

"And then what? How did he know my unit? There are hundreds."

Flynn feels washed out, used up.

The last eighteen hours a sad trudge without sleep—dealing with the double whammy of him right at her door, immediately swallowed whole by the tragic murder of Carter Melloy, who is all over the news. For now, Carter's killing is isolated news. Police aren't saying whether the incident started with anything inside Altair Tower.

Even though they know.

"Not sure," says Jasper.

"My unit is listed in the name of a trust," says Flynn. "A trust I started for this reason."

"Let me ask you this," says Jasper.

They're in her condo, at her dining room table. She stares at her door, wonders about a million different ways the previous night might have unspooled. For better. And for worse.

"What?"

"No need to snap."

"Sorry."

"I assume you vote?" he says.

And there it is. The trapdoor opens. Flynn sees down to black infinity. Her insides wobble. Her guts flex as if they want to hurl.

"Fuck," she says. "Me."

"It's only a hunch," says Jasper.

"I thought I was being so careful."

"You were."

"And now?"

Jasper opens his laptop. Explains he's loaded security footage from the building entrance. Opens full screen to a still image of Altair Tower's main entryway.

"That's Bianca," says Jasper, pointing to a fit woman in a red top and heels. "She's with the real estate agency that held the open house—two to five p.m. Three hours of coming and going."

"Three hours? I'll watch it five times if I have to."

"You can shuttle a bit when it's dead," says Jasper. "But we want you to look at everyone."

"I don't know what this asshole looks like. How would I?"

"You won't. Until you do."

Jasper is grim faced. He's tired too. He remembers Carter from the night of the bogus note on her Kia. He's glum about Carter's death too.

"You've watched it?"

"Yes."

"And?"

"And that's why we need your eyes on it too."

The footage is routine. Boring. Couples. Single men. Single women. Mostly, it turns out, single women. All shapes, sizes. Most in their thirties, Flynn guesses, and forties. Wannabe neighbors. Wannabe fellow building dwellers, more like it—"neighbors" hardly the right word for people you encounter on an elevator for polite chitchat. Bianca disappears for minutes at a time to escort folks up. Returns. Checks her phone. Paces. Studies her fingernails. Primps, using her phone as a mirror. Says goodbye to those departing, stops potential buyers on their way out to answer any last-minute questions.

"How do we know he used the open house as cover?" says Flynn, still watching.

"We don't," says Jasper. "But everyone who lives here would have a fob, right?"

"Right. I don't know what the fuck I'm looking for."

"Who," says Jasper. "Not what."

"This feels useless. These people all look like regular Joe Blow potential buyers, know what I mean?"

Flynn makes coffee. Pours Jasper a cup.

"He could have come in through the garage," says Flynn.

"True. But let's clear the open house folks first. He could have gone to the open house and then found a place to hide," says Jasper.

Or he could have paced hallway after hallway, working his way up and down the building via the open stairwell. Nobody would have said a thing.

"How about footage on the streets of the silver runt car?" says Flynn.

"You'd be surprised at the number of cars that match that description, but we are looking."

Bianca and a tall woman with an overstuffed green backpack, WTF, like she just finished hiking a fourteener. Bianca and an NFL-ready White dude with a block head and an orange T-shirt. Bianca and two women, arm in arm, one with long curly hair and the other a bit younger with a buzz cut, wearing cute black jean shorts and a tight turquoise top.

A woman dressed in black.

"Now *that's* bizarre," says Flynn.

"What?" says Jasper.

"The sticker on her binder."

"Sticker?"

Impossible.

"Yeah."

"What?"

"Rail Yard Ale."

Her mind doing backflips. Breath still. If she could hear her brain work, it would be a deck of cards being shuffled. Shuffled. Riffled. Over and over.

"Can't be," she says.

"What, what?" Jasper sounds desperate. "The woman?"

"It's her," says Flynn.

"Her?"

"It's the same fucking binder with the Rail Yard Ale sticker."

Flynn stops the video. "How do you zoom in?"

Jasper spins the laptop his way, goes to the View tab, clicks "Zoom in" twice from the drop-down menu.

Standing erect, the woman is fit and buff. Black tracksuit top with hood. Black tracksuit pants. Black running shoes.

"The fucking wheelchair was a prop," says Flynn.

"Wheelchair?"

"There's something off about her face." Flynn's whole body feels like it's racing to figure it out.

"You know her?"

"When was the last time you saw a Rail Yard Ale sticker?"

"The Wynkoop beer?"

"Yeah. Early days of Denver brewpubs."

"You met this woman?"

"She came to see me. In a wheelchair."

"Came to you where?"

"Right at my fucking station," says Flynn.

"When?"

"Middle of last week? Something like that. She didn't want to work on a book with me or work on a fucking podcast." Flynn's back zaps with a wave of chills. Her legs follow suit. "She wanted to get me alone."

"What's her name?"

The paper-thin website. Background detail as sketch. Probably a website built by AI.

And Flynn's own failure at due diligence.

"It's not a name that's going to matter."

"Hit me anyway."

"Annie fucking Baker."

"Who is she?"

"The offspring."

CHAPTER 107

"You helped her."

"Her?"

"You know it's a woman."

"Why would I help?"

"Because you're in here. And she's not."

The meeting took two days to arrange. Two agonizing, angry days.

"Why did Ellie Stuffel come see you?"

Harry Kugel seems chipper, if anything. Jovial and upbeat.

"I don't keep track of names."

"Or Annie Baker?"

There was no such name on the visitor logs, but it's worth asking.

"Ditto."

The two names like a wacko puzzle, a knotty thrombosis. Over and over on the mental loop—Stuffel filling out the visitor log, Baker posing as would-be condo buyer. Whom should she fear more?

"Ellie Stuffel was a member of your fan club. *Is*, I suppose."

"Some come for the thrill of it, you know? Some want me to repent. Some want to breathe my sweat. Get their jollies. But the name doesn't ring the proverbial bell." He smiles at a distant thought. "Did you ever hear the bells in Hector Berlioz's *Symphonie fantastique*? The last movement, 'Dream of a Night of the Sabbath'? Classic. It's almost midnight!"

"If you could think back," says Flynn.

"For what reason?"

"She wants to eclipse you," says Flynn. "Is that what you want?"

Harry puts one finger to his cheekbone, scratches it. "Not much I can do about that."

"There is."

"Humor me."

How do you shove a single thin thread of hope and kindness through the eye of a hot needle that's on fire from all the hate and loathing? Why would Harry help? Does she really need him? This in-person time with Harry fucking Kugel is over every objection from Jasper, Axel, Max, and Michael.

"By helping me."

"I don't even see how that's possible."

"You know her."

"I may have met her. I don't know her."

"This is different, Harry." She hates using his name. "You were reformed, all your own. And your reasons for doing what you did? Well, they are your reasons, and I'm quite sure they are very private and that's the way they will remain."

Harry inserts a fingernail into his central incisors, pretends to dig for something, studies his finger once he's pulled it back out. "You wouldn't want to know."

"She's not you, Harry."

"Her reasons are more—elemental. Like learning 'Chopsticks' on the piano."

"Explain."

"She's prosecuting a vendetta."

"Oh, really?"

"A big one, if you ask me."

"What did I do?"

"How would I know the long and tangled career of Flynn Martin? You might head to the store and buy a body-length mirror, perhaps."

Revenge? For what?

"She's bound to make mistakes," says Harry.

"Why?"

"Revenge can be a sloppy business. She's not for long out there on her own."

"Why are you so sure?"

"Little old you found me," says Harry. "I'm sure the police and all their skills will have no trouble with her."

"You're following along?"

"Who can deny the entertainment?" says Harry.

Entertainment.

"When did it start?"

"You're right about her," says Harry. "She's out of her league."

"She's a weak imitation."

"A few points for variety. I suppose."

"When did it start?" says Flynn. "Where?"

"You think I can help you?"

"We'll see." Impatience drains out of her.

"Franktown," says Harry. "You might start in Franktown."

ACKNOWLEDGMENTS

Thanks again to the dynamite editing team of Jessica Tribble Wells, Kevin Smith, Bill Siever, Elyse Lyon, and Angela Vimuttinan. Thanks also to my terrific agent, Josh Getzler, for his editorial insights and to early readers Christine Carbo, Kelly Werthmann (for all the technical television news details and much, much more), Mark Eddy, and Jody Chapel.

ABOUT THE AUTHOR

Photo © 2019 Tom Sandner

Award-winning author Mark Stevens was raised by librarian parents in Lincoln, Massachusetts. He has worked both in public relations and as a reporter and national TV news producer. His 2023 title *The Fireballer* was named Best Baseball Fiction Book by *Twin Bill* literary magazine and Best Baseball Book of the Year by *Spitball Magazine.* Stevens is a three-time Colorado Book Award finalist and the 2015 winner for *Trapline*, which also earned the Colorado Authors League Award for Best Genre Fiction. His *Antler Dust* was a *Denver Post* bestseller in 2007 and 2009.

Stevens has published short stories in *Ellery Queen Mystery Magazine, Mystery Tribune,* and *Denver Noir.* A two-time Rocky Mountain Fiction

Writers Writer of the Year, he hosts a regular podcast for RMFW and has served as president of the Rocky Mountain chapter for Mystery Writers of America. He also writes book reviews, which you can find at https://markhstevens.wordpress.com. The author currently lives in Mancos, Colorado.